-1 DEC ·   19.   08.

FE 08
          08.

JL

SLAVES
of the
SHINAR

SLAVES

of the

SHINAR

AN EPIC FANTASY OF THE ANCIENT WORLD

BY JUSTIN ALLEN

THE OVERLOOK PRESS
Woodstock & New York

This edition first published in the United States in 2007 by
The Overlook Press, Peter Mayer Publishers, Inc.
Woodstock & New York

WOODSTOCK:
One Overlook Drive
Woodstock, NY 12498
www.overlookpress.com
[for individual orders, bulk and special sales, contact our Woodstock office]

NEW YORK:
141 Wooster Street
New York, NY 10012

Cataloging-in-Publication Data is available from the Library of Congress

Book design and type formatting by Bernard Schleifer
Manufactured in the United States of America
ISBN-10 1-58567-916-X / ISBN-13 978-1-58567-916-4
10 9 8 7 6 5 4 3 2 1

For *You*

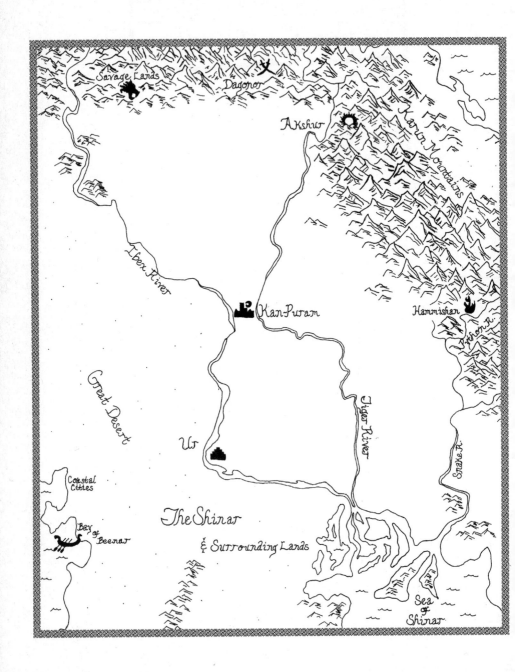

Book I
A CONVERGENCE

VIOLENT FLOODS HAVE EVER SHAPED THE LIVES OF THOSE POOR farmers and goatherds who make their homes along the banks of the Tiger and Ibex rivers. Each year, just as the summer heat finally breaks over the desert, a season of torrential rain begins in the Karun Mountains to the north and east of the Shinar. The hotter the summer, the heavier the rains. That is the way it has always been.

In the beginning, the mountains soak up the raindrops. After months of hot, dry days, wherin nothing can grow, the downpours are a blessing. Plants and animals drink deep. During a particularly wet year, a man might see the dandywillows grow and blossom in a single afternoon. But as with all of nature, what starts as a blessing quickly turns destructive.

The waters rise. Tiny streams swell to become raging rivers. Lakes fill until they can hold no more. Rivers overflow their banks, uproot trees and carry them like the clubs of savages, crushing the life from everything in their path. Even the soil, the earth mother herself, is washed away. Nothing can stand against the torrent.

When the mountains can no longer contain the fury, the water gushes through the Withered Hills and onto the valley.

Fields are swallowed. Herds are drowned. Homes are set adrift or else battered to nothingness by the unstoppable weight of the water and the continual pummeling of the debris carried in one colossal rush to the sea.

As often as not, the floods come without warning, leaving the people woefully unprepared. Children are swept away, only to be discovered weeks later, caught in the remains of a fence or washed against a rock. Their tiny, sun-browned bodies turned white and bloated. Mothers and fathers are drowned, leaving orphans to live or die as they are able. Entire families disappear, so that there is no trace of their ever having been. Sometimes whole villages are run under by the deluge—the land wiped clean by the god of storms.

Days and weeks pass. The waters recede. Eventually, the Tiger and Ibex form two distinct rivers once more, snug in their beds, and those left alive begin the long season of rebuilding.

It is not so difficult. The gods demand sacrifices but leave gifts. With each flood, the farmers are delivered a thick layer of new soil. Soil so rich and dense that they need only cast their seeds upon the ground and plants will spring up. The once ravaged floodplain is soon brimming with new life.

After a season of growth, barley and dates will be ready to harvest. Goats, grown fat from the lush grass, are mated or slaughtered. In due time, brewers, tanners, and weavers will ply their trades. The more violent the flood, the more abundant the surplus. That is the law of the land.

Finally, summer rolls around once more and the farmers, goatherds, and tradesman alike will go to the temples to make sacrifice. Some will offer food. Others give precious baubles or bits of metal. But whether they come bearing riches or hands clasped on empty air, all will pray: "Gods bless us."

Does this mean that they desire another crashing torrent? None can say.

The gods give and they take away. That is the way things are in the Shinar. That is the way it has always been.

CHAPTER 1

The Hunter

*U*RUK FLED ACROSS THE WASTES.

Desert extended over the entirety of the visible earth. Wave after slowly moving wave of glittering sand, devoid of life, marched on him from all sides. It flung itself into the air, mixed with wind and sky, and pelted him from every direction. It scorched in the sun and burned his feet. It was the grit in his mouth, ruining his food and muddying his water. He tore scraps from his clothes and tied them over his head and feet, but no matter how tightly he tied them, the sand got in.

He had been traveling east for a week straight. Of that he was certain. His sense of direction was perfect, and he had plenty of time to count, over and over, the passing of the days. He had come far. The weight of the water-sack hanging over his shoulder told him that he was beyond turning back. Three days beyond by his reckoning. And for those three agonizing days he had crested every ridge with a sense of hope. The city of Ur, and whatever treasure it held, was waiting for him somewhere ahead.

Though his sense of direction was perfect, his map reading seemed to be decidedly the opposite. Maps were worth more than gold in those days, and a good traders' map was protected with life and limb. Maps were the life's blood of the desert, showing canyons and streams, places for living and places for dying. Uruk had looked over a detailed chart of the land between the Bay of Beenar and Ur just before leaving the coastal cities, and it had seemed to him that he should reach Ur in no more than four days.

He'd measured off the distance on his thumbs. It was three thumb lengths between Ur and the coastal cities, and also three from the coastal cities to the Bay of Beenar. Not far. When he was still looting the treasuries of the Prince of Beenar, Uruk had traveled back and forth between the cities and the bay a half dozen times. If he hurried he could usually make the trip in two and a half days.

But there was no hurrying in the high desert. The faster Uruk walked, the more his feet slid in the sand. It took forever to climb one short dune, his feet slipping back nearly as fast as they pressed ahead. This was no place for human beings. Still, he ought to have traveled more than double the distance to Beenar.

It was a mindless sort of existence, out there on the sands. He found it difficult to focus on any one thought for more than a few moments. Bad habits cropped up with startling swiftness. For a while he'd been lifting his water-skin from his shoulder, feeling the weight of the liquid sloshing back and forth inside, and then dropping it back into place. He did this at least ten times an hour. Later, he'd found himself picking at his fingernails, peeling back the cuticles. As soon as he discovered these habits, Uruk set his mind to squashing them. He believed that a man ought to know exactly what he was doing, and why. Uncontrolled habits were the surest indication of a lazy mind, which a true hunter could not tolerate. Lately he'd been sucking on his front teeth. This had proved the most difficult habit to break. But conquer it, he would.

After a long climb, Uruk crested a medium-sized dune. There was still no sign of Ur—just sand as far as he could see. He coughed and rubbed his eyes. The wind was hitting him full in the face and his feet were starting to bleed. He needed rest and water. He glanced at the sun. It was almost noon. He let the water-skin fall at his feet and then sat down, turning his back to the wind. His knees were sore, his back throbbing from the strain of this seemingly endless trudge across the sand. But Uruk wasn't ready to give up.

He tore the rags off his feet and cast them aside. His blood was thick and sticky and oozed out of cracks in the skin around his toes. The desert was drying him, turning his body fluids to powder. He pulled the rags away from his mouth and tried to spit. Nothing. He tried to whistle, but no sound would come.

Uruk tore strips of cloth from the hemline of his tunic and bound them around his feet. A dust devil swirled over a dune to the west of him. He watched it build strength until whole mounds were lifted from the landscape. It moved toward him, gaining speed as it ran downhill, its cone towering into the sky. Then, just as it reached the base of the dune where he was sitting, it was hit by a crosswind and dissipated. Nothing could last in the waste.

His last water-skin was more than half-empty. He shouldn't drink. At his present rate, Uruk would be out of water by midnight. He stared at the water-skin, trying to will his thirst away. He couldn't. His hands shook as he took a long sip. The water was warm and tasted like baked leather. He felt it creep all the way down to his stomach. Unfortunately, it did little for his thirst. He was about to take another drink, but mastered himself just in time. He needed something else to think about. Anything. Uruk looked over the sand he had just crossed and saw that his tracks were already gone—filled in by the wind. He wondered how long it took for the wind to cover a body. A day—maybe two? Uruk groaned. His desire for life and his energy, both seemingly limitless until then, were seeping out of him along with his blood. He needed a short rest, he reasoned. At least until he stopped bleeding. Then he would go on. Just a short rest.

He was about to lay back on the sand when, without meaning to, Uruk put his hand on the hilt of his sword. The bronze was blistering hot. But instead of flinching away he grabbed onto the searing metal and squeezed. The burning helped to focus his mind. "Maybe this is the end of the world after all," he muttered. When he was a boy, the elders of Uruk's tribe believed that the plains that marked the northern edge of their territory also marked the beginning of the end of the world. They were wrong. Uruk had seen the plains turn to forest, and the forest turn to desert on one side and sea on the other. He didn't think the world had an end. Even the sea wasn't the end, just harder to walk. Uruk looked at his hand, still tingling from the heat of the metal cooked in the sun. 'The world may not have an end,' he thought, 'but it has a center.'

The jungle. The beautiful, soft, living jungle. Though it had been most of a lifetime, he could almost taste the lushness of it, see the uncountable shades of green, feel the pulse of overpowering life. He remembered digging his fingers into the soil and having a smell like birth come to his nose. In the jungle there were so many animals and plants that even his people had not named them all. In the jungle, where it rained every day, the idea of thirst was ridiculous.

Uruk wondered what Numa would say if she saw him, sitting alone in the desert. He tried to picture her next to him, a sword on her hip and a water-skin over her shoulder. 'No,' he thought, 'she doesn't belong here.' He closed his eyes and at once the image of her reaching out to him, her long fingers gently grasping his wrist, leapt into his mind.

* * *

"There isn't much to see in a person's palm," Numa said. Like all of Uruk's tribe, she was clothed only in a loincloth. She was muscular and beautiful. More so than the other girls. Her smooth, black skin gleamed with sweat.

Uruk inched closer to her. "Can't you see anything?" he asked. As he said it their shoulders touched. Uruk's stomach tightened. He was seventeen and nature was tugging at him mercilessly.

"I know some of the old women say they can see children or lovers in the lines, but I'm not sure I believe them. I know I can't." Numa stroked an old scar on his palm. Uruk had gotten it while helping a friend to skin a zebra. Usually, he didn't have much sensation around the scar, but Numa's touch was like the tickling of a feather. "I think you can tell more about a person from their scars," she said. "For instance, from this I'd guess you were careless."

Uruk closed his hand over her fingers. She smiled at him and pulled away. "But I have something we can use to tell your destiny," she said. She walked to the other side of her tiny hut and began searching through a pile of gourds.

Numa was the witch-woman of their tribe. Had been since the age of fifteen. According to the elders she could see through time and tell the future. Her hut was full of gourds and pots and masks. Only she knew what all was there and, more often than not, even she had a hard time finding anything. The ceremonial masks and drums she used during days of high prayer hung on the wall. Uruk recognized those. He'd also seen her use feathers, live grubs and, on one memorable occasion, cheetah urine. He hoped she was looking for some of the spiced yam she called 'spiritual food'. She had shared it with him many times, and though Uruk had never felt a bit closer to the gods, he liked the taste. Numa also had a pair of hunting spears leaning against the wall next to the door. In their tribe, you could be a priest or a cook, and you might take care of children, but everyone was a hunter.

"Are you looking for spiced yams?" Uruk asked.

"I thought you came to find out about your destiny."

"I did." She didn't have any more of the yams, Uruk was sure, otherwise she would have offered him some.

"Finally." Numa picked up a long, thin gourd, painted black. She set it down on her table.

Uruk had never seen this gourd before. He picked it up and shook it. Something rattled inside. He was about to pull out the stopper when Numa yanked it out of his hand.

"Stop that."

"Sorry," Uruk said.

"You have to concentrate."

"I know. I will."

"Good." Numa set the gourd back on the table. "First I should ask you what you see in your own stars."

Uruk turned her question over in his head for a good while before answering. "Great honor," he said at last.

She laughed. "And what else?" She looked deep into his eyes.

"I don't know."

Numa shook her head. "It's all there if you look." She pointed skyward. Uruk looked up, despite the fact that they were inside and it was the middle of the day.

"I meant that I see great honor and many noble hunts," he said, "but I don't know how I'm supposed to go about fulfilling my destiny."

"Destiny is." Numa picked up the gourd and handed it to him. "Don't shake it," she said. "Hold it steady."

Uruk held the gourd in both hands, cradling it against his stomach. While he waited, Numa took a mask from a hook on the wall and put it on. Uruk was surprised to see that she had chosen the mask that represented Mana herself. It was the face of a young woman, similar to Numa, though grotesquely oversized and with long hair that trailed down in back. The hair was made from the skin of an Okapi, cut into long strips. Okapi skin was said to give the wearer insight. The Goddess of the Hunt was a powerful mask indeed.

"I hate when you wear the masks," Uruk said.

Numa took the gourd from him and began rocking it back and forth in her arms. "Destiny is," she said. "Remember that. Once you know your destiny, you are bound to know it forever." Through the eyes of the mask, Uruk could see Numa squinting at him. "Sometimes, knowing your destiny is too much for a person to bear." She nodded for emphasis. "Are you sure you want to hear?"

"I do."

Numa pulled out the stopper and overturned the gourd on the table. A single dung beetle fell out and sat motionless. Uruk thought it looked very old, if not dead. And then suddenly, it scuttled right at him. Numa let it go until it was about to fall and then scooped it up and set it back in the center of the table. She studied it as it scurried from one end of the surface to the other, looking for an escape. Every time it looked as though it would fall, she scooped it up and plopped it back at its starting point. It was an arduous game for the beetle, and finally it refused to move.

"Strange," Numa said.

Uruk wanted to ask her what was strange, but thought better of it.

For a long time, they waited to see if it would make a last break toward freedom, but the insect appeared content to sit forever. It seemed to know the parameters of its captivity and realize the futility of struggle. Numa hissed at it, and even rapped her knuckles on the table, but it wouldn't move. Finally, she picked it up and flung it through the door of her hut.

She turned to Uruk and studied his face. "Tell me, Uruk, do you think you are destined for happiness?" She took off the mask.

Uruk said nothing. He hadn't learned to read the stars. He'd only guessed at honor. It'd seemed a safe guess. Something Numa would expect him to say.

She shook her head. "No, I'm not sure that's the right question," she mused.

"Is there a right question?" Uruk asked.

"There are many excellent questions. Sometimes it is the answers that are bad . . . or terrifying."

"Is my destiny really so bad?" Uruk asked.

Numa stared at him. "It's not the worst, I judge. But it's not the best." She took a deep breath. "I'll ask you once more, though Mana knows I shouldn't. . . . Are you sure you want to know?"

Uruk nodded. He was sure. When he came to her hut, he'd expected a pleasant afternoon with Numa, possibly eating some spiced yam and holding hands. Now, he wanted to know what terrors awaited him. If it was death, so be it. He was not afraid of anything that might happen to him.

"You'll find great honor, but no happiness," Numa said. "Yours will be a life of solitude."

Uruk shrugged. "I will never be lonely so long as I'm with the tribe." He smiled. "I'll never be lonely if I have you."

"That much is true," Numa said. She nervously ran her fingers through the long hair of her mask, now lying on the table.

"There's more," Uruk said. It wasn't a question.

Numa nodded. "According to Mana, you will be killed for a friend. Your best friend. Unfortunately, the friend will die, but that will make your struggle no less great. Your name will go down through time."

"And if I choose not to fight? Will my friend live?"

"Destiny is," Numa said. "I told you that from the beginning."

"But is there a chance that I might save my friend?"

"Destiny is."

He shouldn't have come. Numa was right, he would have been better off not knowing. From then on, he would always be wondering which friend he would have to see perish. Which friend would he fail to protect? In the years to come, he would flee from place to place, avoiding friends and companionship. Then a new thought struck him. He looked at Numa. Her lips trembled.

"You are my best friend," Uruk said.

Numa smiled. "I may be now, but destiny is unfulfilled."

"Is it you?" Uruk asked. "Just tell me that."

"I have my own destiny," Numa said. She moved closer to him. "I can't see everything. No one can. The only thing I can tell you is that you won't recognize your best friend until your destiny is fulfilled."

"When I'm dead," Uruk said. He groaned. "I don't understand."

"Destiny is. Expect nothing but what will be." She leaned into him, putting her arms around his neck. Her chest pressed against his. Uruk wrapped his arms around her waist and squeezed.

Uruk ground his teeth together. She'd been wrong. His destiny was much worse than she had foreseen. He was lonely. That much was true. But there was more than mere loneliness.

Over the years, Uruk's view of destiny had altered somewhat. He still believed in it—but surely it could be changed, was changed, by everything he did. Surely he made his destiny by his choices. That was the one thing he believed with all his heart. He had to. Without that belief, he could never have come so far. It was that hope on which he lived.

Uruk's father—he remembered him only as a large man, lying next to the fire with his feet resting on a pile of wood—had been killed by a lioness when Uruk was just a boy. Was that his father's destiny? And Numa, she had become the High Priestess while still very young. Was that her destiny?

To Uruk the answer was obvious. Destiny was always ahead. It was the result of your actions. His father was lazy and weak. He cared nothing for hunting and his skills were lax. So he had been killed. Numa was wise, studied stars and people, and spent many hours tracking beasts through the jungle, and so she had risen. Their destinies were a product of the choices they had made.

After the War of Three Tribes, Uruk had left his people forever. He demanded a new destiny, free of the suffering of those he loved. Since then he had learned the arts of the thief, the use of the sword and a half dozen languages. He had discovered the value of gold and the power of bronze. He had seen things that his people, living in huts and hunting with spears of sharpened wood, never could have dreamed possible.

Maybe one day he would go so far that the stars in the sky would forget him. Maybe he would reach beyond Mana, beyond destiny. Then he would stop and sleep in the same place for many years. But not yet.

Uruk put his hand on the hilt of his sword once more. The bronze was like fire on his palm, burning away the thoughts of Numa's touch. At times he needed that. The mind had to be cleansed if it was to be filled with new purpose.

Uruk stood and stretched his legs. He took another pull from his water-sack and started down the dune. His shadow stretched ahead of him. Numa would laugh at his constant striving, he knew. "Destiny is," she would say. He imagined her rolling her eyes at him, heard her call him stubborn. Uruk redoubled his effort.

Looking ahead of him, Uruk saw no path. He saw no final destination, nor anything waiting for him. He saw only sand and sky, and that was enough. Somewhere ahead of him was Ur, gateway to the Shinar, and the destiny he would make for himself.

CHAPTER 2

The Heart of Dagonor

*D*AGONOR WAS AWASH WITH ACTIVITY.

The sun had begun its final descent. Very soon, the valley would be swaddled in shadow. Everywhere one looked, slaves were busy. Around the forge, the smiths were cleaning and repairing tools. Serving girls swept the grounds and hung the day's wash. Cooks, having just served the evening meal, were scraping their pots. Niphilim guards watched them all, but offered neither threats nor encouragement. The slaves didn't need it. They had an incentive. The faster they put Dagonor in order, the more time they could spend in their barracks. More even than food, slaves loved to sleep.

Kadim watched them jealously. His troop wasn't going to the barracks. As soon as they finished eating, they were returning to the mine. After fourteen straight hours of carrying baskets, some loaded with nearly half a man's weight in rock, the chief guard had determined that they'd failed to meet the day's quota. If they were lucky, each man would have to carry just one more load to the crushers. Kadim hoped that would be enough. This would be their third late night in five days. His whole troop needed sleep.

His bowl empty, Kadim set it on the pile beside the cookhouse door. At least he didn't have to clean dishes, he thought. He went to the storehouse and selected a basket from among the stacks. By the time he got into line, the rest of his troop was already waiting. He took his place at the very back. Not that it made much difference. Once inside the mountain, in the deep darkness, you couldn't tell whether you were first, last, or all alone.

Their guard—the slaves called him Tonk, for reasons no one seemed able to comprehend—stood at the head of the line. The chief guard was with him. Like all Niphilim, men and women both, they were tall and blonde, with muscular limbs and pale skin turned rosy by the sun. The chief was older than Tonk, but not by much.

As soon as Kadim was in place, Tonk strolled down the line, counting the slaves. "All here," he said. "Shall I take them in?"

"Wait," the chief said. "Is that one in this group?" He pointed at a slave sitting in the shadows behind the cookhouse door. The man appeared to be asleep. Tonk affirmed once again that all of his slaves were accounted for.

The chief marched toward the man in question, drawing his whip from the hook on his belt. Kadim winced as the leather strap came down on the sleeping man's head.

"What are you doing?" the chief barked.

"Working," Ander mumbled. Kadim recognized him as soon as he looked up.

The chief struck him again. "Find a basket and get in line." He pointed at the spot right behind Kadim. Ander leapt to his feet and ran to the storehouse. The chief followed, whipping him whenever Ander so much as slowed to a fast trot.

Ander nodded to Kadim as he joined the line. Kadim didn't respond. Even the other slaves didn't like Ander. His skin was pale, like a Niphilim's, and his black hair grew in long, loose curls. He rarely spoke, and took every opportunity to avoid work. The guards thought he was stupid. Kadim didn't know what to think.

The chief searched for other malingerers he could press into service, but found none. At last, he waved them away.

Tonk led them through Dagonor, passing both the temple and forge, and onto the open field beyond. A pair of heads was mounted on spears in front of the temple. They were all that remained of two slaves caught trying to escape. One was female, Kadim knew, though he could no longer say which.

Across the field was an earthen ramp, carved into the side of Dagon's Mountain, leading to the open jaws of the mine. In years past, Kadim had enjoyed staring off the edge of the ramp. Normally the Withered Hills were gray, though dotted with stands of brush. But once in a great while, at sunset, when the last light of day reflected off the sky, they glowed pink. Kadim was born in a small city on the edge of these same hills, far to the east. Akshur, its people called it. If only he could get free of the Niphilim, the hills would lead him all the way home.

"It is not so far away," Ander whispered in his ear.

Kadim ignored him. In a moment, Tonk would cross the threshold of the mine, and another guard would be waiting just inside. Kadim didn't want to attract attention. One last load and he was done for the night.

But Ander didn't give up. "Do not lose hope," he said. "Maybe one day. . . ."

"Escape is death," Kadim hissed. It was a phrase every slave knew—the first words of the Niphilim language they were likely to learn.

"Maybe," Ander whispered. "But while you are here, what is life?"

Tonk led them deep into the mountain.

After first traversing the narrow tunnel from the surface, and passing a guard post marking the start of the main chamber—there were three guards, Kadim observed, one of them female—the going was fairly easy. Their path was lighted, every dozen strides or so, by a torch mounted atop a tall stake. They didn't do much to hold off the ever-present darkness, but that wasn't really their purpose. The torches were there to mark the path. So long as you followed from one point of light to another, you couldn't get lost.

There was only one major obstacle in the cavern. Slaves and guards alike called it simply 'the hill.' It was a subterranean mound, stretching from one side of the cavern to the other, larger than any of the hills outside and littered with boulders. The path wound up it in a series of tight switch-backs. Fortunately, there were additional torches to offset the difficulty, or more slaves might have been injured. As it was, they snaked their way over the top in just over a quarter-hour.

Once they'd crested the hill, the path became easier again. It raced straight down the opposite side without so much as a bend. Best of all, they were closing in on their destination.

Ahead, Kadim could just make out a pair of guards slumped against a rock wall. Ensconced over their heads was a trio of torches. To one side of the guards stood a ladder, the lower rungs fully illuminated, and on the other was a door. The ladder was new.

Tonk called for them to stop.

While he chatted with the other guards, Kadim stared at the door. It was constructed of wood, though banded by strips of iron for strength. Newly captured slaves were locked behind it until the Niphilim were sure they wouldn't run away. Years had passed, but Kadim still remembered his time in the cell. The beatings. The rapes. If anything, those memories felt more real than his childhood. Even the faces of his parents had grown hazy, driven out by darkness and torment.

"Up," Tonk said to them at last, and pointed at the ladder.

The climb wasn't difficult. The ladder was more or less uniform and Kadim climbed smoothly and easily. It was just one more load after all. Then sleep.

As soon as he reached the top, a guard grabbed Kadim by the arm and propelled him into a tunnel. This was the dig site. A team of slaves with hammers stood waiting to bring down a sheet of stone. "Spread out," the guard spat.

They did, and the guard gave the signal to begin. Kadim crawled on hands and knees to the feet of one of the hammering slaves. He was a big man, called Enoch. Kadim had worked with him for years, and liked him. Already he was chipping rocks out of the wall. Kadim scooped them up as fast as he could.

The bottom of his basket was covered in no time. If this kept up, he'd have the whole thing filled in half an hour—three-quarters at the most. Pebbles ground into his shins as he worked, but he barely noticed. Just so long as the rocks kept coming.

And then suddenly, and for no reason he could see, they stopped. Kadim looked up. Enoch's hammer was still crashing against the wall, hard as ever, but the stone wouldn't break. Slaves were having the same problem all down the line.

Kadim was about to point out a crack in the wall, just to the right of where Enoch was working, when something exploded behind him. His shoulder and neck were on fire. He put his hands over his head, rolling into a ball for protection.

"You're crowding him!" the guard screamed. His whip struck Kadim's forearms, drawing blood.

When at last the beating was over, Kadim crawled back from the wall. He wanted to give Enoch plenty of room to work. Unfortunately, it didn't seem to help. Still no rocks fell. Kadim braced himself, expecting to feel the lash again. But the guard had already moved on.

While Kadim cowered, Ander took control. Instead of waiting for Enoch to pound rocks out of the hardest part of the wall, Ander led him to a spot nearer the ladder. If the guard had seen him, Ander would likely have been whipped unconscious. Kadim was amazed that any slave was willing to take such risk.

A few solid hits on the spot Ander suggested and stones the size of fists were raining to the ground. Ander casually began scooping them up. Kadim, seeing that there would easily be enough for two, slid in beside him.

"Work fast," Ander whispered. "Fast as you have ever worked."

Kadim did.

The instant his basket was full, Ander leapt to his feet. "Done," he shouted.

The guard looked over at him, obviously surprised.

"We are done," Ander said again.

"We?"

"Kadim and me." Ander pointed and the guard glared. "Can we take our baskets back to the crushers?"

Kadim scrambled to his feet as the guard approached. His heart was beating so hard he thought he might pass out. Work all through the tunnel ground to a halt as the other slaves turned to see what would happen.

"You're fast," the guard said, looking in their baskets.

"Can we go?" Ander asked.

The guard stared. For a moment, Kadim thought he'd kill Ander. But instead he shrugged. "Fine. Get off my dig. . . . Both of you."

Carrying a basket down a ladder was difficult, but by no means impossible. The hardest part was getting started. Kadim quickly developed a rhythm of leaning in and shifting his free hand to the lower rung as he bent his knees. The climb went fast.

When they reached the bottom, Ander waved to Tonk. "Our baskets are full," he said. Tonk shrugged indifferently and they started back over the hill. The guards sitting beside him never even looked up.

Kadim walked as fast as he was able. His father used to take their whole family swimming in the Tiger River. Kadim had loved it. He liked to dive down, deep as he could go, until his ears and lungs felt like they'd burst. Then, when he started up, and could see the sun glimmering on the surface, he'd almost panic. The air looked so far away. Kadim felt like that now, like he couldn't get out of the mine fast enough. His feet struggled to keep up the pace he set.

They were just over the hill and starting down the opposite side when

Ander called for him to stop. "At the next torch," he wheezed. "I need to switch shoulders."

Kadim didn't want to stop. They'd be into the switchbacks in a few moments, and then onto level ground. If it were up to him, they'd go all the way to the surface in one fast march. But he understood Ander's need. Carrying a basket too long on one side could lead to back spasms. Let it get bad enough and you might not be able to work. That was as good as a death sentence.

As soon as he reached the next torch, Kadim set his load on the ground. Ander, who'd fallen behind him slightly, did the same. Both stood silently for a moment, rubbing their lower backs. Kadim was breathing hard. Strangely, Ander wasn't.

"Let me show you something," Ander said. He reached up the sleeve of his tunic. "I got it from one of the smiths."

It was the smallest hammer Kadim had ever seen. The head was only as long as his index finger, and about twice as big around. "What is it?" he asked.

"Smiths use them to repair the tips of swords, where the iron would be broken by a larger tool." Ander grinned.

"The guards are going to kill you," Kadim said.

"They do not know I have it." Ander put the hammer back up his sleeve.

Kadim bent to pick up his basket again, but Ander stopped him.

"Did you know that they are not even watching us?" he asked.

"Of course they are. We are always watched." Kadim looked around, half-expecting to see a pale face crowned by golden hair.

Ander shook his head. "Watch this." He pulled up the stake and waved it back and forth. The torch crackled and threatened to go out, then blazed up more powerfully than ever. Shocked, Kadim stepped back. But no one came.

"See?" Ander said. He flung the torch down between two boulders where it began to gutter in the dust.

When they reached the next torch, Ander pulled it down as well. At the third, he not only uprooted the stake, but also flung it off the path like a spear. Still nothing happened. "They will never know," Ander assured Kadim.

"I can see that," Kadim said, though he didn't really believe Ander's minor acts of sabotage would go unpunished. "But do no more. The other slaves will already have a hard time finding the way out . . . and Old Tonk."

Ander scoffed. "Tonk can be stung by spiders and eaten by rats for all I care."

They walked the rest of the way in silence.

The same three Niphilim still guarded the tunnel to the surface. Ander nodded to each, explaining that their baskets were full. But the female guard stopped them anyway. Like most Niphilim women, she kept her hair cropped short and spiky. It was a style made popular by the captain herself.

"Let me see your basket," she said to Kadim. He set it in front of her and she prodded it with her foot. Many Niphilim didn't care to touch the slaves or their tools. "Full," she muttered. "Yours?" Ander nodded and she waved them away.

With a last look at the red light playing off the cavern walls, Kadim stepped past the torches and into the tunnel. Ander was right behind him.

Kadim's eyes were open, but they may as well have been closed. The rest of the mine was dark, often with no more than a distant pinpoint of fire to offset an otherwise continuous sheet of black, but this was another world.

He blinked rapidly. Pure dark, like pure light, was shocking to the eyes. It seemed almost to itch, as though the darkness were pinching him somehow. The feeling quickly passed, but for those few moments, Kadim couldn't hear or taste or smell. He just missed light. All light.

The tunnel itself was narrow, barely wide enough for two men to walk abreast. In years past, Kadim had repeatedly run into the walls. No longer. He knew there were a total of twenty-two paces between the main chamber, behind him, and the first turn. And when he reached that turn, he knew to step on his left foot. Counting steps and putting the same foot on the same spot every time—that's how he did it. That's how they all did it. He couldn't remember the last time he'd hit a wall.

They came around the last bend in the passage and Kadim saw a halfcircle of open sky. Usually he was blinded by it. Not this time. The sun was down and it was a dark night. There were even a few stars.

He was nearing the end of the passage when a guard stepped out of the shadows, motioning him forward. Kadim lifted his basket off his shoulder. The guard at the mouth always looked in the baskets. Kadim didn't know why. He didn't even know if there was a reason.

Kadim set his basket at the guard's feet and stepped aside. As he did, Ander strode forward.

The guard was surprised. His hand jerked to the handle of his whip. "Why were you following him so close?" he asked.

Ander looked confused. "Close?"

The guard glared at him suspiciously, then began his examination of Kadim's basket. "What have you got?" he asked. Normally, these checks were minor. The guard looked to see that the basket was full and sent them on. Not this time. He dug both hands into Kadim's basket. Rocks spilled out and skittered across the floor. Kadim sighed. He knew he'd have to pick up every pebble.

Both of the guard's hands were buried to the wrist when suddenly, Ander dropped his basket. The guard turned just in time to see a tiny hammer whistling toward him, landing against the side of his head with a loud thump. Ander struck again and again. The sound was sickeningly dull. In a matter of seconds, both Ander's hand and the guard's face were bloody. Finally, the guard collapsed.

Not yet satisfied, Ander reared back and struck him one last time. It must have been quite a blow, because his hammer shattered, the handle splintering and the head spinning away. The guard was dead.

Ander mumbled something, but Kadim didn't recognize the words. He thought it was because Ander was out of breath. But no. The real reason was that Ander was speaking in the common tongue of the Shinar, a language Kadim hadn't heard, at least not in full voice, in years.

"It's over," Ander said again. "We're free."

"Escape is death," Kadim replied without thinking.

"You can go home."

"To Akshur?"

Ander nodded.

"Home," Kadim croaked. It was the first word of his native tongue that he'd openly spoken since. . . . He wasn't sure how long it had been. He licked his lips, noticing for the first time in hours how dry his mouth was. "Let's go."

They stumbled out of the mine. At the bottom of the ramp, beyond the field, Dagonor huddled in its narrow valley. A few twists of smoke rose from the corner of the temple. Nothing else moved. The slaves were already locked in their barracks—a single guard sitting in front of the door. Even the Niphilim were bedded down for the night.

Ander grabbed Kadim's arm, dragging him over the edge of the ramp and into forbidden ground. They hid behind a boulder, not five strides from the mouth of the mine. It was all so easy.

"Run east 'til you reach the Tiger River," Ander said. "Follow it south. . . . Sooner or later you'll recognize where you are."

"Where are you going?"

"I'll go due south. Once I reach the plains I'll turn east." Ander clasped Kadim's hand in his. "Maybe we'll meet again at the river. Or in Akshur." And then, without another word, he was up and loping down the side of the mountain.

Kadim watched as Ander bounded over rocks and brush, fast as his feet could carry him. He should get going too, he knew. So, turning his back to the camp, barracks, temple and forge, Kadim ran. A full moon, unusually bright, was just rising over the eastern hills. The night wouldn't be dark for much longer.

Simha took a sword from the pile in front of her fireplace and sighted down the blade. It wasn't sharpened yet, but the edge was on it and the tip was well honed. Unfortunately, it was also heavy—much heavier than her own weapon. The smiths, for all their progress, still hadn't perfected the process. She struck the blade against the floor and held it up to the light, looking for breaks or blemishes. Finding none, she smiled.

She put the sword back with its mates and sat down. Maybe there was a problem with the skimming process, she mused. When they'd conquered the Kenanites, the people who built the forge, portions of their technique had been lost. She clucked her tongue. They should have been more careful. The swords the slaves made were good, but the Kenanite swords had been better. Hers was a masterpiece.

Simha leaned over her table. She had a map of the whole area, drawn on hide, showing where her army was practicing troop movements. They'd better practice night movements as well as day, she thought. Bel was a good lieutenant, but tended only to drill soldiers on what was absolutely necessary. Simha was sure that the troops would be ready, but she'd send a reminder to Bel all the same.

Spread out next to the map of Dagonor was one of the savage lands. Simha tapped it with her index finger. She'd rather not be looking at that map.

There was a knock at her door, followed by her second in command—a pinch-faced man with slender shoulders and graying hair—poking his head inside. He was only a fair fighter, but an expert tactician. "Captain," he greeted her. Simha waved at him to enter.

She watched as Kishar walked across the room and around the table. He was favoring one leg. Probably another blister, Simha guessed. Kishar's eyes were drawn toward the maps. She could almost see his mind working, devising strategies both for attack and defense.

"What is it?" she asked.

"Word from Ezidha. She's trapped the last major pack of savages near the chalk downs. She thinks she'll have them herded up by the day after tomorrow."

"I see."

"She also lost five men."

"To be expected."

"Captain, trying to use the savages in battle will handicap our soldiers. They're no more than a sort of terrible, undisciplined line of shock troops." Kishar shook his head. "If we aren't careful, they could destroy all of our plans."

As a matter of fact, Simha agreed. But that made very little difference in the matter. "Antha-Kane says we are to gather and use them. Need I say more?"

Kishar blanched. The mere mention of Antha-Kane did that to most Niphilim. And the few who weren't scared of the High Priest—Simha included herself in those who were—couldn't be trusted. "If you want to explain your objections to His Holiness. . . ." She gestured at the door to Antha-Kane's chambers. "I'm sure he'd listen."

"No need," Kishar muttered. "Antha-Kane is always right."

"He says the savages will strike terror into the hearts of the enemy."

Kishar nodded. Simha could tell he wanted to change the subject.

"We've also had word from Bel," he said. "Our troops will be ready. She's drilling them in night movements even as we speak, and plans to begin the special formations we'll use for herding the savages tomorrow."

Excellent news. "Send word to her that we march in five days," Simha said. "Just as soon as Ezidha returns."

As she spoke, there came another knock at the door. Simha waved at Kishar to open it. He did, and Lagassar, another of her lieutenants, stepped inside.

She looked very much like Simha herself. They had the same build and features, though Lagassar was a shade taller. She was also one of the best fighters Simha had ever met. She'd have made an excellent captain someday, except that she lacked the essential spark of intelligence and creativity that Kishar possessed.

"Two slaves have fled," Lagassar said.

"Escaped? How?"

"They killed the guard at the mouth of the mine." Lagassar ran her fingers through her hair. Nervous, Simha guessed. No one liked to give bad news to the captain.

"How long ago?"

"Maybe an hour. . . ."

"Obviously no one saw them running away," Simha said. "Why weren't there more guards?"

"Most had already retired to their barracks. Apparently, the slaves also doused six or seven torches inside the mine."

Simha nodded. Privately she applauded the escaped slaves for their bravery. They'd seen an opening and slipped right through. Most slaves quivered at the thought of so much as passing water without permission. She couldn't let them go, of course, but she respected them—as much as she could respect a black-head.

Slowly, Simha crossed the room and picked up her sword. She strapped it across her back so that the grip seemed almost to peer over her right shoulder. "Where did they go?" she asked.

"Tracks heading east have been—"

"They're headed for the Tiger." She pointed at Lagassar. "Send a message to Bel—tell her we march in ten days." Then she looked at Kishar. "How's your leg?" she asked.

"Fine."

"Good. Then let's run these black-heads to the ground."

Kadim was being pursued. He was sure of it. For the last half-hour he'd been hearing voices. Not words exactly. Just the faint hum of chatter, carried on the wind. It sounded like they were just over the last hill, closing on him out of the very footprints he left behind.

He'd been running for five straight hours. His body was on fire. The muscles between his ribs ached. His heels were bruised from pounding over hard earth and rocks. He jumped a stand of nettles, careful to land on the balls of his feet, and kept going.

Many times he'd considered hiding, climbing under one of the larger bushes, curling into a ball and waiting till his pursuers passed him by. Twice he'd looked for a likely spot. But the moon was too full. His tracks were too obvious. He knew they'd find and kill him, and there'd be nothing he could do to prevent it. Kadim had no weapons, hadn't eaten since sundown, an unknown number of hours before, and was weak. He couldn't bargain or beg for mercy. They weren't sent to carry him back. This was a hunt. His head was the trophy.

Kadim cursed the day he'd signed on with the traders. He should have been a farmer, like his father. But no, he wanted to go to Kan-Puram. How naïve he'd been. His parents never even knew the caravan had been attacked and Kadim taken prisoner.

A large hill stood just ahead of him, cutting across his path. It was unavoidable.

He was only a few steps up it when he heard someone shout, "There he is—on the plateau." Kadim flinched. The feminine pitch of the voice quickened his heart.

Near the top of the slope, Kadim faltered. He had a pain in his side unlike any he'd ever felt. It was as if someone had thrust a shard of wood into his back. He could taste his breath now, feel it getting wetter, hotter and more acrid.

"Faster," the same voice called. "We've almost got him."

Kadim spurred himself onward, ignoring the stitch in his side.

"He's heading across it now." They were right behind him. He'd gained no ground at all.

For the first time, Kadim knew he wouldn't get away. He was out of energy. The night air cooled the sweat in his armpits and crotch, but offered no comfort. He tried to regain his stride, but couldn't. The only hope he had left was to get to the other side of the plateau and roll himself down. That would buy him a few minutes at least.

Kadim was still a few yards from the edge when he saw the river, like a long silver snake, rolling lazily out of the northern mountains. Something deep within him leapt at the sight.

He was only a half-dozen strides away, and already preparing to fling himself over, when his big toe caught a clump of dry grass and he went down. As he fell, Kadim noticed the way the moonlight rippled off the surface of the water. Then he was lying in the grass and the river was gone. His nose began to bleed.

A brown leather boot, laced almost to the knee, stepped into his line of vision. It was the woman. He could tell by the size of the foot.

Kadim heard a sword being drawn from a wooden scabbard, but didn't look up. The point touched the grass in front of his eyes. It was at once the most delicate and beautiful blade he'd ever seen. Very slowly, it lifted out of sight.

A moth flew out of the grass, flitted nervously on gray wings turning to rust at the tips, and disappeared over the edge of the plateau, headed for the river. Kadim watched it go, reveling in its freedom.

Then something heavy touched the back of his neck. Kadim was surprised. He'd expected it to feel hot—like a bee sting. But it wasn't. It was cold.

CHAPTER 3

The Ziggurat of Kallah

BLACK EYES STARED FROM BETWEEN THE LEAVES.

An oak stood near the southwestern wall of the four-tiered Ziggurat of Kallah. The leaves were yellow and the bark was peeling off—death seemed only moments away, but the old tree wouldn't give up.

It was out of place in the baked clay flats between the Tiger and Ibex rivers. Even holm and mastick trees wouldn't grow there, and they were desert bred. The oak needed rain, cool winds and deep, rich soil to flourish. It wouldn't get any of them. Still, the spark of life, though buried deep, was strong in it. On the lowest branches, shaded by the dead leaves above, a few green buds were just beginning to open.

Two priests strode up the path to the ziggurat. The first, the shorter one, had a bundle of willow limbs on his back and an axe in his hand. He was dirty and streaked with sap. His jerkin was torn in a dozen places.

The priest behind him had no bundle. He was tall and clean, with long white robes and new sandals. At his side was a little girl, just five or six years old. She had a robe as well, but instead of wearing it she had it hugged to her chest. One sleeve dragged in the dirt between her legs, drawing a long snake of dust in her wake.

"The moon will rise soon," the taller priest observed, looking past the ziggurat to the white light amassing on the horizon. He patted the girl on the head. "It will be a beautiful night."

"Are we going to eat soon?" the little girl asked.

"As soon we get to the temple, precious. It isn't far." He pointed. "You see it there, just in front of the moon?"

"Of course I do."

"Of course you do." He glanced down at the sleeve dragging in the dust. If she wanted to drag her robes, he didn't care. "There will be roast pig and barley bread," he said. "The cooks are even making honey candy.

You like candy don't you?" The girl smiled. "Of course you like honey candy. Every little girl likes candy."

"Is Kallah really going to be there?"

The tall priest nodded. "Tell me, what would you do if you saw the goddess? Did your mother teach you?"

"I'd say, 'I come from the faithful of Ur because we believe that the goddess is good—and that we are only alive because she protects us. I love my parents and the priests, and all faithful people everywhere. May the wicked be sent to eternal suffering at the hands of the creator.'"

"That deserves an extra piece of honey candy," the priest said, and smoothed her hair. "You'll always remember that won't you?"

The girl giggled.

"We're almost there," the other priest grunted. "Get them to open the doors."

The Ziggurat of Kallah was unique amongst the temples of the southern Shinar. Instead of a stairway leading up the face, as was typical of such structures, it had a pair of tall doors. And above the doors, standing on the roof of the first tier, were two colossal statues of the goddess, torches flaming in her hands.

The tall priest reached into the front of his robes, pulling out a reed flute. As they walked he blew a single, clear note.

"They didn't hear," the shorter priest said. "Blow it again."

He did. This time the doors swung open and a woman stepped out. She was naked but for a loincloth and sandals, and her skin shone red in the torchlight. As she stepped over the threshold, her hair was caught by a sudden gust of wind and whipped away from her body. She waved them forward.

"Hello precious," she said, bending over and putting her hands on the girl's shoulders. "Don't you want to put on your robe?"

"You aren't wearing one," the little girl replied.

The shorter priest chuckled. "I'm going in," he said, gesturing at the limbs on his back. "Have to add these to the pile."

The priestess waved him away and turned back to the girl. "We aren't the same," she said. Her voice was low and smooth. "You're supposed to wear your robe."

"But I don't want to."

"The goddess wants you to wear your robe. Will you do it for her?"

She squeezed the girl's shoulders as though they were old friends. "You can take it off again later."

The little girl clumsily pulled her robe on over her head. It was too long and one sleeve was filthy. The priestess inspected the dirty sleeve with a frown. "We'll discuss this tomorrow," she said, glaring at the tall priest.

He nodded, took the girl's hand, and together they walked into the temple.

The priestess was about to follow them when something caught her eye. She glanced at the old oak. Something about it wasn't right. The moon had risen, but darkness still hung like a foul liquid between the branches. Was there something there? She squinted, trying to make out a shape. Something moving? "We should cut it down," she muttered to herself. Then she turned and strode back into the temple.

Behind her, the tall wooden doors swung shut.

Uruk dropped from his hiding place in the oak.

He'd been climbing in amongst the branches for the last three nights, watching the temple. His eyes tracked every movement over its face, noting a nest of robins on the third level, watching as bats coursed around the torches, hunting for insects.

From his satchel Uruk took a handful of clay and a small water-skin. He kneaded the clay until it was soft and then started working in the water. When the clay was wet all through, he rubbed it over his face and hair. There was a good chance that someone inside would see him, and Uruk wanted to disguise his features as well as he could. He had close-set eyes and a broad mouth, but knew from long experience that most people would see the disguise, rather than the face beneath. In years past he'd worn a mask. No longer. While storming the libraries of Timbuktu he'd learned that a mask could shift or twist, blinding the wearer. That lesson had nearly killed him. Later he'd discovered that a thick layer of paint or mud hid the features just as well.

When his face was covered, Uruk stripped off his tunic and folded it into his satchel. His muscles bulged as he twisted and turned, applying a thin layer of clay to those parts of his upper body he could reach. When he'd run out of clay he tightened his belt, making sure his sword was secure. A steady diet of barley and roast pork had served him well. After

only a few days in Ur, he'd gained back all the weight he lost while crossing the desert. He felt strong and prepared.

Other than the food, which Uruk had stolen at will from the cook-
houses of the rich landholders south of town, Ur had been a dismal failure. The whole city ran on barter, which was bad for a thief. How was
Uruk supposed to carry away six bags of barley or a barrel of beer? Where
would he take them? He couldn't steal whores or slaves. He needed mov-
able wealth, the kinds of things he could hide in his satchel. After just two
days he'd been ready to move on—to Harap or the Indus valley. Then
he'd heard about the Maidenhead of Kallah. By all reports, *that* was a
prize worth stealing.

Uruk took a last look at the temple, noting the position of each guard.
A pair of sentries paced the roof of the first tier, making the circuit once
every hour—he'd watched each night as they climbed through the open
doorway between the statues—and another sat on the roof of the fourth. But
mostly the temple relied on sheer walls and stout doors for its protection.

He was ready. His plan was to scale the building and enter by the door
in the second tier. A guard would have to be incapacitated, but he didn't
think that would pose much of a problem. The difficult part would be
finding the jewel. He hung his satchel from a high branch so that it
wouldn't be found.

Uruk moved through the darkness like a panther, the light from the
torches catching only the glimmer of his eyes as he covered the distance
to the wall. He pressed himself into the shadows at the base and listened.
No alarm or sign of pursuit. He caught a hint of motion from the darkness and crouched down, his broad chest pressed against his knees, his
breath whistling to a stop.

A dirty yellow dog ran past him. It was all but starved. Even at night,
and in the shadow of the temple, its ribs were clearly visible. Uruk
watched as it slunk toward the oak and began sniffing for garbage beneath
the tree. He was glad that his satchel was hung too high for the dog to
reach. It almost certainly would have tried to eat the leather.

Uruk pressed his chest against the wall, reached as high as he could
and began searching for a handhold. His palms, toughened by swords and
spears, slid deftly across the surface until he found a usable indent. After
a few quick pulls to make sure it was solid, he worked his toes into the
crevice between a pair of sandstone blocks and slowly began to climb.

It was an arduous process, requiring total concentration. Halfway up, his forearms started to shake from the effort. His calves cramped. He wasn't in danger of falling yet, but he had to be careful. Tired muscles were unpredictable. The most important thing was to keep his mind focused on his hands and feet. Uruk didn't look up or think about reaching the top, and he didn't think about what he needed to do to find the jewel. Just the next handhold. And the next.

With only a few feet left to climb, Uruk made a foolish turn and his sword clattered between his hip and the wall. He cursed himself and hung still. His fingers quaked. Even he couldn't cling to the side of a wall forever.

But no one came to investigate the noise, so he pressed on.

At last, his fingers slid over the top edge of the wall. Now he just had to wait for the sentry to pass him by.

It took a long time, but at last he heard the scrape of sandals. His arms tensed for a final pull. This next part came down to luck. If the guard turned, or heard him scramble over the top of the wall, the adventure could become bloody. Uruk hoped it wouldn't.

He came up just to the right of the statues, but that fact didn't interest him at present. As soon as his feet touched, Uruk was running.

The guard paused, sensing the danger behind him, but it was too late. Uruk's arms encircled his throat.

His spear clattered at his feet as he struggled to break Uruk's hold. The effort proved futile. In a moment, the man was unconscious.

The sentry was black, like Uruk, though not nearly as large or dark-skinned. Most of the guards at the temple were black. Uruk didn't know why, nor did he care. He grabbed the guard by both wrists, slid him to the edge and began lowering him down the wall. Uruk didn't want the body discovered until he was safe inside. When he couldn't reach any farther, Uruk let go. He grimaced as the sentry landed in a heap.

'I hope he isn't hurt too badly,' Uruk thought as he raced back toward the statues.

They were identical, with large breasts, pregnant bellies and over-sized eyes. Uruk slipped into the shadows behind the closest one and took a deep breath. It was the first he'd taken since leaving the oak.

Beyond the goddess's legs, twinkling on the horizon, was the city of Ur. From that distance it seemed to burn. Red light blazed out of a thou-

sand points, from torches and lanterns in brothels and inns to the pale
glow of candles, shining through the doors of farmers' huts. Though it
held nothing for thieves, it was a fine town. A good place to raise a family.
A man with vision—or a large enough stake—could buy a small tavern or
become a broker, trading barley from the north for sugar from the southeast. Uruk smiled, imagining himself an innkeeper. It was a pleasant
notion. Maybe someday, when he was too old to swing a sword, he could
settle in just such a town. 'As soon as I outrun destiny,' he thought.

For Uruk, riches meant peace and solitude. They meant that he could
live without preying on the poor, or stealing from farmers. Uruk would
never steal tools, weapons or food—not from poor people, anyway. Those
things were the stuff of life. Gold was not. No man ever died from the loss
of a ring or crown.

Having caught his breath, Uruk crept from the shadows and sprinted
to the doorway. It was dark, and a strange smell, similar to roasting pig,
emanated from inside. The smell didn't make him hungry, however. It
was too dirty. Too sour.

He'd only gone a few strides down the passage when he came upon
another guard, slumped against the wall sound asleep. Uruk glided up to
the man on the balls of his feet, drawing his sword from its scabbard.
Slowly, so that it made no sound, he pushed the man's spear until it was
just out of reach. Then he grabbed the sleeping man around the throat
and squeezed.

The guard's eyes popped open. He reached for his spear.

"Sit quiet," Uruk whispered. He lifted the tip of his sword until it was
right in front of the guard's eye. "Make even the tiniest sound and I will
slit your throat." He tapped the point of his sword on the guard's cheek
for emphasis.

The guard nodded slowly.

"Where is the Maidenhead of Kallah?" Uruk asked, releasing his grip
on the man's throat.

"My duty—" the guard croaked.

"Your duty is to scream or fight." Uruk frowned. "I should spread
your whimpering guts on your shirt." He pressed the tip of his blade into
the guard's skin, just hard enough to draw blood. "Now speak up, dog,
where is the jewel?"

The guard cringed. "The High Priestess is wearing it for the sacrifice."

"Where?"

He glanced down the passage, further into the temple. "But you must not—" Before he could say another word, Uruk struck him between the eyes with the pommel of his sword.

Uruk left the guard where he lay senseless and strode deeper into the ziggurat.

Storerooms opened from either side of the passage. Inside, Uruk found barley and salted meat by the barrel. He wondered if one of them had gone bad. That would explain the strange stench. There were also bolts of unused cloth and racks of torches. But nothing to interest a thief.

Uruk kept his sword drawn as he moved from room to room. At any time he might happen onto a guard post or a priest's cell. He'd known about the sentries outside. Here he had to rely on skill and chance. So far, luck was with him.

The passage finally emptied onto a large, open chamber, at the center of which was an immense octagonal hole. Uruk had never seen anything like it. The sides of the octagon were as long as three men laid out head to toe. Support pillars stood at every corner, each as thick as Uruk's shoulders were broad. Orange light, spilling up through the hole in the floor, illuminated the ceiling and made the sandstone glitter like diamonds.

Uruk crept to the edge and peered down, careful to stay in the shadows.

At the center of the floor below was a heap of willow limbs. The shorter priest's pile, Uruk guessed. Around the limbs were a handful of priests, kneeling in prayer. They wore simple jerkins and breeches. Uruk watched as they bowed their heads, muttering chants and invocations.

Uruk had never lowered his head to god or man. Mana cared nothing for prayers. She was god of the hunt. She loved bravery and valor. Human or animal, it made no difference. She did not ask for offerings. She demanded action.

As Uruk watched, the priests stood and backed away from the pile of limbs. It was a curious sort of rite, and Uruk very much wanted to see more. But he also knew that he ought to be searching the rest of the ziggurat. This was his time—the thieves' time. While the rest of the temple was busy, he could ransack storerooms and cells. Stealing the Maidenhead seemed a less certain proposition, but who knew what other treasures might be secreted within those walls?

Uruk started around the octagonal balcony. He'd decided to go through the doorway furthest from the front of the temple. That was as good a place to start as any, he reasoned.

"Can I have another candy?"

Uruk was nearly to the door when he heard the little girl's voice. He recognized it from earlier.

"Not now, treasure," the taller priest said. "It's time for you to see the goddess."

Uruk hastened back to the balcony. He suspected some sort of chicanery, but on the off-chance that a goddess was about to show herself, he wanted to be there to see.

The girl and her caretaker were just making their way through a pair of double doors that led back toward the front of the temple. The girl carried a torch. It wasn't large, but it must have been heavy for her because she gripped it with both hands. As they walked, the little girl waved the torch back and forth, drawing circles with the flame. One of her sleeves, Uruk saw, was still covered in dust.

The double doors swung open again and two more priests stepped into the room. There were at least a dozen now, and they all stayed well away from the pile of limbs at the center of the chamber. One of the newly arrived priests carried a clay pitcher, the other a jar. More important than the priests, however, was the glint of metal Uruk saw as the doors swung closed. 'Spear tips,' he guessed. 'Four or five of them.'

He was contemplating his next move, and wondering whether it might not be best just to abandon the hunt for the night when, from directly below where Uruk was hiding, the High Priestess strode into the chamber. She still wore nothing apart from a loincloth—in all the times he'd spotted her while watching the temple, Uruk had only once seen her in robes—though now, round her neck hung a chunk of red carnelion the size of Uruk's thumb, polished and tied with a piece of leather cord. The Maidenhead of Kallah. It swayed between her breasts as she walked.

Uruk gaped. It was even bigger and more beautiful than the stories had led him to believe.

The priests carrying the pitcher and jar hastened over to her. "Pour," she said.

The man with the pitcher turned to his comrade and began to pour what appeared to be water into the jar. As it filled up, Uruk saw that the jar also contained something black and powdery. It looked like ash.

When the jar was full, the priestess waved to the little girl. "Come here precious," she said. The girl stumbled forward and the High Priestess handed her the jar of ash and water. "Go ahead," she commanded. "Drink."

The little girl handed her torch to the tall priest, so that she could grip the jar in both hands, and took a sip. "It's bad," she whined, wiping her mouth on her sleeve and handing the jar back to the priestess.

"Do you still want to take off that old robe?" the priestess asked.

With a nod, the girl did just that, dragging it over her head and casting it aside. Uruk liked this girl. She was bold. Feisty. If they'd chosen her to be their next witch-woman, they had chosen well. There was even something about her, the cock of her head maybe, that reminded him of Numa as a little girl.

The priestess laughed. "Better?" She waited for the little girl to smile and nod. Then she pointed at a pair of men waiting to one side. "Bind her," she commanded.

They grabbed the girl, tying her hands and feet with loops of cord that they'd hidden inside their jerkins. It alarmed Uruk, but the little girl didn't scream or cry out. She stood still, letting them work. Apparently she'd expected this.

"That's a good girl," the priestess cooed.

When they were done, the priests carried her to the pile of limbs and gently laid her on top. The tall priest with the long robe was already there, waiting.

"You remember what to say when you meet the goddess?" he asked, one hand resting on the girl's belly. She nodded. "That's wonderful." He leaned down and lit the pyre.

Flames glinted off the jewel around the High Priestess's neck.

Sword in hand, Uruk leapt from the balcony. He was like a hawk, diving from the heavens onto a rabbit, wings stretched and talons slicing at the air. As he landed, he drove his elbows down on a priest's shoulders, snapping the man's collarbone.

Uruk dashed at the High Priestess, standing between him and the little girl, the jar of ash and water still gripped in her fist. When he'd entered the temple that night, he'd done so hoping to avoid confrontation. No longer. Moving this woman out of his way would be a pleasure.

With a swing of his sword, Uruk cleft her jar in two, sending wet ash and tiny splinters of bone skittering across the floor.

The priestess howled in what sounded like equal parts outrage and agony, and flung herself at Uruk. Their naked bodies slapped together as she reached for his eyes. Uruk glanced at the pyre as he shoved her away. Smoke billowed off it now, rising through the hole in the ceiling and filling the second story of the ziggurat. The flames were growing as well. They had just begun to lick at the girl's skin. Her screams echoed off the stone walls.

Uruk had only seconds. He swung his free hand at the priestess, catching her in the jaw. As she fell back, Uruk caught the carnelian and yanked it free, breaking the cord with one sweep of his hand and jamming it down the front of his breeches. The jewel was warm from the woman's chest.

Meanwhile, guards had entered the room and were fast approaching. The first ran right at Uruk, spear lowered to kill. Uruk turned the point aside with a wave of his sword and then struck the man in the chest. Ribs snapped audibly beneath his fist and the guard went down. The others paused as Uruk turned his sword toward them.

Just then, the little girl let out another piercing scream. It sounded like she was calling for her mother, though Uruk couldn't be sure.

Uruk knew he'd never reach her in time. Even if he somehow got her away from the fire, she'd be horribly burned, and likely to die. There was only one thing he could do, though it made him sick even to contemplate it. Still holding his sword defensively, Uruk reached down and took the spear from the guard at his feet. It was well balanced, with a point of hardened bronze. Uruk sighted down the shaft, and then, as though it were a javelin, threw it across the room and into the little girl.

The force of it knocked the girl off the fire, putting an end to her screams—though the reverberations still echoed in Uruk's ears.

"Kill him!" the tall priest shouted. "Before he defiles the temple further."

The guards inched closer. But they were in no hurry. At least for the time being, they were perfectly happy to have him trapped.

There may have been many opportunities for escape, but Uruk could see only one. Keeping both eyes on the guards, Uruk bent and, with one hand, picked the High Priestess up by an arm. He held her against his side, her belly resting on his hip. "Stay back," he warned, laying the tip of his sword against her throat, "or she dies."

No one stirred.

"I will kill her," Uruk reiterated. He must have sounded sincere, because this time both guards and priests backed away.

Uruk began to inch toward the double doors. Somewhere beyond, assuming the passage ran true, he should reach the face of the ziggurat. 'Let it run true,' he thought.

As he neared the doors, a pair of guards moved to head him off. For a moment, Uruk thought they'd try to kill him despite his threat to their mistress.

Uruk cut the tiniest gouge into the skin behind her ear. Blood ran down her jaw and trickled off her chin. "I have not killed yet," he said. "But I can."

The guards glanced nervously at each other, and then stepped aside.

Uruk slipped through the doorway and backed down the passage beyond.

He'd only gone a few steps when the High Priestess stirred. A pool of sweat had formed between her naked belly and Uruk's. It trickled into his breeches and glistened on her breasts. She was still mostly unconscious, but beginning to struggle. Uruk could feel her trying to roll over in his arms. The sweat made her slippery. He shifted his hand to her loincloth, hoping to get a better grip, but the material was already beginning to unravel.

Uruk squeezed her tighter and kept going. She groaned and moved her arms, lightly slapping his shins. 'If I drop her, they'll kill me,' Uruk thought. She started to slip out of his hands.

Finally, knowing that he was going to lose her anyway, Uruk slid his hand under her hip and flung her at the guards. Spearheads clattered together as they were moved out of the path of her body, but not all of the guards were quick enough. One bronze point pierced the High Priestess's thigh and she screamed in pain.

Uruk flew up the passageway.

For a few seconds, it seemed that no one would follow. Guards and priests alike were shocked by everything that had transpired. Uruk could hear them stumbling around at the end of the passage, dumb with horror and grief.

By the time they came after him, Uruk was nearing the end of the corridor.

He tore the crossbar out of its slides and pulled. Even with all his strength, the door barely moved. Uruk pulled again, this time groaning with the effort. Muscles and joints popped and shuttered under the strain, but the door opened a crack. One last heave and Uruk was able to squeeze through.

He raced to the oak, tearing his satchel from its branch at full speed. The Maidenhead of Kallah knocked around in the front of his breeches, but he didn't stop. He wouldn't stop until he reached Ur.

Uruk ran fast, but still he was pursued. The footsteps were barely audible over the sound of his breathing, but they were there.

Fortunately, he was almost to the city. Very soon he'd be able to lose his pursuers among the twists and turns of the streets and alleys. He crossed a footbridge over the Ibex River and marched uphill. A few more farms and he'd be free.

Uruk was halfway through a barley field, the new plants just beginning to bud, when he heard the footsteps again. His hunter. Closer than ever and moving fast. Faster than any man could run. Uruk glanced back at the river, then at Ur. At the speed they were coming, he'd never reach the city in time.

Better to face it, he decided. Whatever it was. He slid his sword from its scabbard. From the darkness on the other side of the footbridge he could hear the thing panting, its breath whistling through its teeth. Then Uruk saw its yellow eyes.

Among his people there were stories of demons that ruled the night, eyes blazing in the darkness. Uruk had never believed those tales, as with all things supernatural he was a skeptic, but he gripped his sword tighter all the same. His heart raced as he went to meet this demon, whatever form it might take. He was almost to the bridge when it trotted from the shadows.

It was a dog. In fact, it was the very same animal he'd seen in front of the ziggurat, starved near to death. Uruk laughed at himself as he walked across the footbridge. The dog glanced up at him for only a moment, then slumped toward the riverbank. It was so tired that it lay down to drink.

Uruk sat down beside the dog and dug his toes in the mud. It looked over at him momentarily, and then went back to lapping up the river water.

"Careful dog, you will make yourself sick," Uruk said.

The dog kept drinking.

Uruk took his tunic from his satchel, turned it inside out and dunked it in the water. He used it to wipe the clay off his chest, face and head. It felt good to be clean.

When the clay was all gone, Uruk rinsed out his tunic and slipped it on over his head. He sighed as the cold water ran down his back.

The dog was the color of the desert sands, with short hair and a long tail that curved up slightly toward its back. 'A handsome beast,' Uruk thought. Or it could be, if only it wasn't so skinny.

He took the remains of a pork shank from his satchel, tore off a chunk of meat for himself and held out the rest.

The dog growled.

Almost too fast to see, Uruk backhanded it—flipping it over and sending it sliding in the dirt. The dog came up furious.

It jumped toward him again, growling, and Uruk thumped it on the nose.

This time the dog yelped and leapt away. It hadn't expected Uruk to be so fast.

Uruk held the bone out to the dog again. "If you want it, take it. But I will have no threats." He grinned. "Especially not when I am the one with the meat."

The dog put its head down and inched forward. Its teeth and lips nipped at the air. Fear and hunger were at war within it. Finally, the dog dodged in, licked the meat, and dodged away. Hunger was winning.

Uruk put the bone on the ground next to his thigh. He could see that this dog had dealt with men before. In the Shinar, and even as far away as the coastal cities, dogs were most often raised for their meat. "I never eat hunters," Uruk assured it.

The dog inched toward him again, this time with its head held high. Its eyebrows twitched as it sniffed him. Gently, it bent and took the meat.

While the dog ate, Uruk pulled the Maidenhead from where it lay hidden in his breeches and held it up to the moon. The white light shining through the jewel made a strange shadow, slightly red, at his feet.

"Beautiful," he muttered. Then he scooped up a handful of mud and smeared it over the jewel, hiding the red glow beneath dark earth.

Beside him, the dog's teeth clicked on bone.

Uruk strode through the city, headed toward the marketplace. There weren't many people out, though a few old drunks still prowled the alleys and street corners. Uruk nodded to them as he passed. None nodded back. There were a few other black people in Ur, but even they paid him no mind. As always, Uruk walked alone.

He turned down a deserted alley, noticing as he did so that the dog was following him again. Uruk stopped and the dog ran to him. "I have no more meat," he said. "Not even for me." He walked on.

The dog pranced ahead of him.

Uruk stopped again. "Are you going to follow me forever?" he asked.

The dog turned and looked at him, tail wagging vigorously. He seemed to be waiting for Uruk to tell him where to go.

"Fine," Uruk said. "Follow as long as you like." Even as he said it, Uruk knew that he'd never again punish or discipline the dog. He'd never hit the dog.

And neither would anyone else.

CHAPTER 4

Beat the Brush

*F*ROM WHERE HE CROUCHED, ANDER COULD JUST SEE THE TORCHES of the Niphilim. They burned with warm yellow flame, illuminating the profiles of two soldiers and casting a flickering glow over the hut. And beyond the hut, standing like pillars of freedom, were the last of the Withered Hills, opening to the endless plains of the Shinar.

Ander sat in a thorn bush, behind a waist-high rock, thirty or forty paces from the soldiers. He must have been allergic to the flowers that grew on the bush because his eyes were puffy and sore. He rubbed them furiously with the back of his wrist, but that just made them burn worse. What he really needed was a drink of cold spring water, though he wasn't going to get it any time soon. His body itched all over, both from the thorns and from his own sweat, drying and turning to salt on his skin. He licked the places on his forearms where the thorns had drawn blood. That helped a little. But even as he tended to his wounds, Ander kept his eyes trained on the backs of the Niphilim, and was as silent as the starlight.

The soldiers weren't nearly so quiet. The larger and blonder of the two was ill. Every so often he blew his nose in his hand and wiped it on his hip. The other had hair that approached brown, and his uniform was torn over the knees and elbows. Even the leather wrappings on the handle of his sword were unraveling.

They watched the plains. Runaway slaves weren't their concern. They were looking for savages or thieves, or anyone else foolish enough to wander into those hills. That's why they stood with their backs to him, only occasionally turning to peer up at the mountains. Besides, not a single Niphilim in all the world would've admitted that a lone, black-haired man could be dangerous.

It was like a child's game of beat-the-brush, only played to the death. Ander remembered hiding, watching as the other children hunted for him in the bushes and tall reeds. It was a marvelous game to play along the edge of the creek, where the grass and trees grew wild. Those were good times. The other children didn't let him play very often, but when they did Ander relished every moment. His favorite places to hide were in dense thickets, or beneath old logs, where he could watch the beaters searching for him. Ander's guts would ache from choking down laughter as the dirty feet passed all around him. What was that impulse? That desire to burst out laughing? Even now he felt it—the rush of superiority, the joy of being beyond detection.

The Niphilim hadn't spotted him yet, but they were still dangerous. Ander had to get past them if he was going to make it to the plains. There was no other way. He'd contemplated going back, finding some way around them, but it was far too close to morning. Other soldiers would be up soon. Even one accidental meeting with a group of Niphilim would be too many.

He'd also considered climbing the nearest hill and going around the guard hut that way. But the moon was too bright—the soil too dry. The guards would be sure to see or hear him.

For more than an hour he'd slid, inch by inch, over twigs and stones, through grass and shrubs, finally making his way into these thorns. It was a good hiding place, no matter how uncomfortable, but he still had to get closer. He had to take a chance, go beyond what was safe. His only weapon was surprise, and he had to use it extremely well if he was to fight his way past the soldiers.

He angled toward the rear of the hut, keeping his head down, peeking up only to make sure he was on course. Thankfully, the guards still had their eyes on the plain.

Even twenty strides, slithering on your belly through sharp thorns and over dry grass, was a long way. Every movement had to be deliberate and exact. If he moved too fast, he could rattle the foliage. If he went the wrong way, he might go over a patch of dry twigs, or through an area devoid of cover. He had to keep his hands going all the time, feeling out the terrain, pushing sticks and pebbles out of his path, determining the potential noise of the grass.

Finally, and instinctively, he felt that he could go no farther. He was fifteen long strides from the hut, but ahead of him was a patch of dead dandy-willow, agonizingly dried in the sun.

Ander raised up, searching for another path, but there was none. He was as close as he'd get. He curled up on his side and quickly rubbed the blood back into his wrists and knees.

"Got to find an edge," he mouthed to himself. And he had to find it soon. A lot of time had elapsed since he began the slow trek through the brush. The moon was hanging on, but the Star-Queen was preparing her final descent to the horizon. Before long, the sun would rise.

As a boy, Ander had spent his nights tending his stepfather's flocks. He'd stayed awake by watching the heavens. To the old women of his village, the stars were foretellers of doom and ill fortune. Nothing good ever came from above. But to a boy sitting alone, with nothing more than the bleating of goats for company, the stars were much more. They were companions. And they weren't just self-important farmers—they were queens and heroes, lovers and demons. They were the finest thing an unloved boy could call his own.

As he sat, peering through the twisted strands of dandy-willow, Ander wondered when he'd stopped looking at the stars. He glanced at the Star-Queen again and frowned. The last time he remembered looking at her was the night he was captured. He'd seen her since, no doubt, but there was a difference between seeing and looking—treasuring her beauty and the excitement he'd once felt as she approached the borders of her ebony kingdom.

A lot can change in a night.

They were boys, though they thought of themselves as men. It was late summer and the moon was three-quarters full. They were camped at the edge of the Withered Hills, due south of a mountain the villagers called The Watcher. They'd had a long, disappointing day of fishing—they hadn't speared a thing—and the other three boys were cross.

Ander pushed his hat back and bent over the fire. The gravy was just beginning to bubble, and the clumps of goat fat at the center were melting. He had to be careful not to stir too fast. If he agitated it too much, the meal would stiffen before the fat melted completely. Ander added a few drops of water to thin the pot, just like his stepmother taught him. He knew what he was doing. He'd been cooking for his family for as long as he'd been walking and talking.

"You're letting the gravy stiffen," Darius said, scratching at the patches of beard on his cheeks. Ander remembered every word, every look. Darius's best friends, Zakir and Warad, sat to either side of him. All three were heavily built, with thick necks and deep-set eyes, just like all the men in the village. All but Ander.

Ander nodded, but continued to stir the gravy in long circles, scraping the edges of the pot.

"Not like that." Darius pulled the stirring stick out of Ander's hand and started whipping the gravy in a series of tight swirls. "You're no help at all." He pointed at a stump a dozen strides from the fire. "Go sit over there."

The other boys laughed.

Ander wiped his fingers on the front of his tunic as he walked away.

"Why'd you bring him anyway?" Zakir asked.

"My mother said I had to." Darius kept whipping the stick in the pot, his jaw grinding back and forth as the gravy grew ever thicker. "Father's hosting a feast to celebrate the slaughter. We had fifteen full-grown males this season."

"Fifteen?" Zakir whistled. A good season might yield twelve. A very good season. Fifteen was almost unheard of.

Ander frowned. He'd hoped that his stepfather would show him some appreciation for having protected the herd so well, but of course there hadn't been even so much as a thank-you.

"But why is he here?" Warad asked.

Ander pulled his hat down over his eyes and looked at the ground. He hated Zakir and Warad. Hated their muscles and their families and their friendships with Darius. But it was better that they didn't see the hate in his eyes.

"Isn't it obvious?" Darius muttered. "They don't want him around." He used a piece of leather to lift the pot off the fire, and then reached for the loaf of black bread they'd brought for the evening meal. He broke the loaf into three pieces, handing the smaller ones to Zakir and Warad. Ander watched as they dipped the bread into the gravy and brought it to their lips. If there was any left over, they might let him have it.

"Why didn't they just make him watch the goats?" Warad asked, still chewing.

"The goats are penned," Darius said. "He milked the herd just after sun-up. . . ."

"I don't understand," Zakir said. "I thought your mother liked him. She sure screams if you hurt him. Even if it's nothing but a scratch. And on accident, too."

"Mother's soft-hearted," Darius explained. "She doesn't like to see him cry. But like him?" He paused to think it over.

Ander bit a fingernail.

"No, I don't think so," Darius finished. "He's basically useless."

"Useless?" Ander couldn't hold back his anger. He rarely spoke up in those days. Over the years he'd learned never to talk back, never to disagree. No matter what was said, he smiled and nodded. Even if it was clearly wrong. But not this time. Not in front of Darius's friends. "If not for me, your father wouldn't have even half those goats," he yelled, pointing at Darius. Hot blood rushed up and down his spine. He wished he could stab his finger clear through his step-brother's chest. "Not even half," Ander repeated. "I'm the real shepherd. Me."

Ander knew Darius would beat him. He didn't care. At that moment, Ander was ready to fight—even though he knew it was hopeless.

But Darius didn't move. Other than a slight turn in Ander's direction, he just sat there, chewing his bread.

Zakir and Warad looked even more surprised than Ander felt.

No one spoke as Darius finished his meal. It took a long time. He chewed each bite at least a dozen times before swallowing. As he ate, he watched the fire burn down.

Ander shifted back and forth on his stump. Something was coming. He could see it in his stepbrother's eyes. Some of the people in their village thought that Darius was slow-witted, but Ander knew that wasn't true. Darius just considered every possible angle before acting. He was careful. Ruthless.

When Darius was down to a single, small piece of bread, he paused. A strange look came into his eyes. It wasn't a smile exactly, though Darius' lips curled up at the ends, and it wasn't a smirk. There was something unsettled about the look.

Darius leaned back and stared at the stars. Ander watched as his eyes shifted back and forth, finally resting on the North Star. Zakir and Warad looked at each other and shrugged.

"You . . ." Darius began. He glanced at the bread, and at the few drops of gravy still lying in the bottom of the pot. His lips curled even more forcefully into that strange half-smile.

At that moment, Ander was sure, absolutely sure, that Darius was going to give him the bread. Their eyes met and something like understanding, what Ander imagined brothers everywhere felt, passed between them. It wasn't admiration. Not exactly. And it had nothing to do with who was stronger, or more cunning, or handsome. It was pure.

They sat like that a moment longer, and then Darius frowned. Ander thought he understood the look on his stepbrother's face. They had something in common. For the first time ever. 'They don't want him around the feast either,' Ander realized. The thought hit him like a punch in the stomach. They'd both been banished from their father's table. One more forcefully than the other, but both equally gone.

"You . . ." Darius began again.

"C'mon," Zakir urged, "pound him."

Warad nodded. "Give him a beating he'll never forget."

And with that, the look was gone.

Darius smirked. "He thinks he's my stepbrother. Did you know that?" He chuckled. "In fact, he's no one's brother. Or son. Mother found him years ago, half-starved and lying amid some reeds beside the creek." He paused, looking directly into Ander's eyes. "Father wanted to put him out of his misery, but mother wouldn't allow it. Not because she cared, mind you. She just couldn't stand the thought of a boy-child being left to starve . . . or worse."

Then, as Ander watched, Darius used the last, tiniest piece of bread to soak up the few drops of gravy, and dropped it in the dust between his feet.

"Do you know why he keeps his hair so short?" Darius asked, grinding the bread into the dirt with his big toe. The others shook their heads. "Because it grows in curls and twists, like snakes. He doesn't want people to think he's different . . . as though it weren't obvious." He pointed. "Look at his skin. He's like a stick of beeswax. He even shines in the dark." They all laughed. "When he was little, he used to rub dust all over himself, hoping the other children would think he was new in the village and want to play with him." Zakir and Warad laughed harder than ever. Ander suspected that they remembered him, covered in dust, sitting by himself while the other kids played, though this was probably the first time they knew why. "Mother first started making him wear hats because she was tired of treating his sunburns." Even Darius was laughing now. "He even wears his stupid hat in the dark." He was laughing so hard that he almost couldn't get the words out. They laughed until they could hardly breathe. And even that didn't stop Darius. Though most of what he said was unintelligible, he never stopped talking. Every terrible moment in Ander's life came out that night. Every embarrassment. The feelings of loneliness and inadequacy. Everything. Ander had to relive it all.

Finally, though the stories had by no means come to an end, Ander could bear no more. He left the fire. Hugging his chest with both arms, he started toward the village. He knew he couldn't go back there—maybe not ever—but he couldn't stay here either. Ander couldn't stand to look at their faces any longer. Especially Darius.

When he'd gone far enough to be lost in the darkness, Ander sat down and pulled his arms into the sleeves of his tunic. Many a night he'd sat just like that, listening to the goats chew the grass. He could still hear the boys laughing, but he could stand that. People had laughed at him all his life. If only it hadn't been Darius.

"If we'd been alone," Ander mumbled to himself. "If Zakir and Warad weren't here, we could have been friends." He looked up and saw the Star-Queen, arms reaching out to embrace her domain. "He'd have given me that bread. I know he would have."

But part of Ander wasn't sure. He'd pondered that look in his stepbrother's eyes a hundred times a day for years. Things could have been different—that was all he knew for sure.

Ander couldn't remember what happened next. Somehow he must have dozed off. He remembered thinking that the sun was about to come up when suddenly he heard voices, female voices, from back near the campfire.

He rolled over. His arms were still pulled up inside his tunic, so he had to shuffle his way up onto his knees to see what was happening.

Three warriors, all of them tall and blonde, were standing over the prone figures of Darius and his friends. They had swords drawn, and appeared ready to slay the young men.

Ander screamed as loud as he could and ran toward the warriors, thrusting his arms back through the sleeves of his tunic along the way. He didn't know what he'd do when he got there, he just knew that he had to be fast. Darius was in danger.

The closest Niphilim turned to face him. Only at that moment did he fully realize that he was charging on women. Quick as wind, one of them stuck out a foot, catching Ander square in the groin. He went down hard.

Ander remembered hearing the other three boys screaming, but he didn't move. He couldn't. He just laid there, hands cupping his genitals. It was the worst pain he'd ever felt, and his life had been painful by most standards. He'd been whipped, beaten with sticks, and punched until his teeth felt loose. He'd even taken a few similar kicks from other kids, and on one memorable occasion, a goat. But all paled in comparison to this. That soldier knew exactly what she was doing.

Moments later, a strong hand took hold of the back of his tunic and lifted him up. Ander could barely stand. His genitalia felt about twenty times larger than normal, and he was rocked with waves of pain and nausea. It was as though a knife-blade, chilled at the bottom of a mountain stream, was being twisted in his guts.

The woman who'd picked him up screamed something directly into his ear. Even years later, when he could speak the Niphilim language, Ander wasn't sure what she'd said. He guessed it was something like, "Hold still. Escape is death," but there was no way to be sure.

When she was done, another woman grabbed him by the scruff of the neck and flung him toward where the other three boys were lying in the grass. Ander stumbled over Zakir's outstretched legs and fell, landing on his chest at Darius's side.

The first thing he noticed was that the grass was sticky. Something was on his face and hands, and though he couldn't feel it, he knew it was all down the front of his tunic.

Ander was afraid to open his eyes. His one hope was that the blood was Warad's—or even better, Zakir's—though he knew it wasn't. Zakir had moved as Ander stepped on his legs, and he was pretty sure he could hear Warad sniffling somewhere close by. Ander ground his teeth and clenched his fists. Darius was the only person he could always forgive. No matter how many times Darius beat him, or led the others in teasing him, Ander had always loved his stepbrother. Not Darius's father. Not his mother. At least not anymore. Ander squeezed his eyes together, feeling the tears well and run down his cheeks. That was the closest he'd ever come to real prayer.

He knew Darius was dead, but still he had to look. To know. Ander opened his eyes and lifted his head.

Darius's body lay in a growing pool of blood. It was wickedly twisted, as though frozen while shaking off ants. Ander craned his neck but still couldn't see a face. He knew it was taking a chance, a terrible chance, but he couldn't resist. He arched his back and lifted up even further.

Just as he got his first look at Darius's head, the flat of a sword slapped against his shoulders and he fell back to earth, biting his tongue.

Ander spat blood. There was a wound on his back, he was sure, but whether it was a cut or a growing bruise, he couldn't say. There was too much pain everywhere. And worse, there was that image.

Darius's head had been split open. One eye was missing and he had a half-dozen strands of golden hair still clenched in his fist. Coils of brain poked out of the crack in his skull, like stuffing erupting through the seams of a child's doll. Ander never had a doll, but Darius did—one he'd carried everywhere, until the leather cracked and the stitching rotted away. Darius's neck was cruelly twisted as well, no doubt it was broken, and his lips were curled into the same bizarre half-smile Ander had seen earlier.

It took two days to get to Dagonor. Two gruelling days. Ander was beaten four times during the trip. Half as often as the other boys, but enough to keep his spirits down and his strength low. And that was the point, Ander realized later. Keep them walking, but don't let them run.

Throughout the trip, the image of that grin, those lips, came back to him again and again. Not the twisted neck or the broken skull or the brains. Not even the fistful of blonde hair. Just those lips, which had once looked to him like brotherhood, friendship and decency—now the very image of pain and death.

* * *

"What time is Kamran relieving you?" the sick guard asked. He spat at his feet and then kicked dirt over the phlegm.

It was the first time that either of the Niphilim had talked. Ander had begun to wonder whether they could.

"He ought to be here now."

Ander imagined Kamran, humming to himself as he ambled down the path. When he neared the hut, he'd casually gaze off to the side, see an escaped slave huddled behind some dandy-willow and call to his fellow soldiers. Then Ander would be bound, hand and foot, beaten and taken back. All his years of plotting would come to nothing. And when he arrived in Dagonor, he'd be lucky to be killed.

"He's made a habit of being late," the sick one said. "You should see Lagassar about it."

The other warrior said nothing. Ander listened for a change in his breath, a moment of exhale, a sigh, anything that would have indicated agreement. But there was only silence. Smaller though he was, Ander judged him the more dangerous. He was keyed into the night, ready for anything. Not distracted by thoughts of sleep or hunger. He seemed to be declaring to the darkness that he could stand, eyes scanning the sloping reaches of grassland, forever. He was a colossus, quiet but vigilant on the edge of his territory.

Ander quaked with fear. He knew he had very little chance of getting past these men, but he had to try. Thinking of Darius's face, those gently smiling lips, spurred him on. If there was ever even the slightest feeling of brotherhood between he and Darius. . . .

"Are you going straight to the barracks when Kamran relieves you?"

Still the smaller one didn't speak. No matter. Ander knew this was his chance. He waited for the sick warrior to speak again, to say any inane thing. The taller, more foolish soldier, so proud of his golden hair, was bored and tired, and Ander planned to use that to his advantage.

"Maybe they've started breakfast."

As the words started out of his mouth, Ander shifted his weight. It wasn't much, but he managed to get his feet under him. He was crouched as low as he could go, but he was ready.

"Did you hear something?" the shorter soldier asked. He was on the balls of his feet, striding away from the hut. Both hands were cupped over his eyes as he scanned the darkness.

It was then that Ander realized exactly how quiet this night really was. If not for the crackling of the torches, there'd have been no sound at all. Even his heartbeat, the ringing in his ears, seemed enough to give him away.

"I don't hear anything," the sick one said, and blew his nose once more. The smaller soldier wasn't convinced. He reached toward the pommel of his sword, fingers lightly caressing the blue-black metal.

Ander picked up a stone. His knees were screaming to be stretched out. He had to move soon or his legs would go to sleep.

The sick warrior leaned against the hut. "If there were anything out there, we'd see it," he said. "Look at all that moonlight."

Before he could get the second sentence out, Ander was up and streaking through the darkness, the stone in his hand raised to strike. He flinched as his legs tore through the weeds, but never slowed. There was no turning back. Ander saw himself as a sort of wasp or stinging fly, swooping in on his victims. He was acting on pure impulse. A quiet warmth began to spread through him, standing his body hair on end and fighting rabidly against his gooseflesh.

The shorter warrior turned, his hand closing on the handle of his sword. Ander, still running, watched as he drew the length of iron from its scabbard. The metal was clean and dark and glittered in the light of the torch. The shabby appearance and worn out pommel had been a sham. This man was ready.

Ander was close, very close, but still wouldn't make it. The Niphilim warrior had his sword out, and was ready to swing. So Ander did the only thing he could think of. He increased his speed by launching himself into the air.

The gambit paid off. The stone in his outstretched hand slammed into the soldier's forehead with dazzling force, while the Niphilim blade glanced harmlessly off Ander's shoulder.

They rolled together in a jumble of legs and arms, with Ander landing on top. He untangled himself and reared back to strike another blow, but found that the man was already knocked senseless.

Then, out of the corner of his eye, Ander saw the other guard. He hadn't drawn his sword, but came on with hands outstretched. Ander tried to crawl away, but it was no use. The hands encircled his throat, lifting and then flinging him down on his back. He took a last gasp of air just as the hands closed over his neck once more.

Ander looked up and saw his own face mirrored in the guard's blue eyes. He saw his hair, twisted into the same snaky curls Darius had always teased him about. He saw the patches of beard on his cheeks and neck. And he saw his eyes, black and twinkling from beneath a dirt-stained brow.

The Niphilim's lips twisted with effort. He was trying to break Ander's neck. Ander felt his strength flow out of him as the enormous hands squeezed tighter.

'The stone,' Ander thought. The feeling was just starting to go out of his hands. Dark spots floated before his eyes. He could no longer be sure, but he thought the rock was still resting in his fingers. Ander clenched his fist and swung with everything he had left.

It didn't make a sound. Ander watched as the stone came up, kissed the mane of golden hair and broke. One piece remained in his hand. The other spun out of sight. For a moment, nothing happened. Then the pressure on his throat released and he gasped for air. For the first time in years, he found it sweet.

The Niphilim warrior rolled off Ander's chest, cradling his head in his hands. Blood flowed from the wound over his ear, dying his hair a beautiful crimson.

Ander struggled to his feet. His legs quaked and he swayed like a drunk, but he was able to stumble a few steps.

He almost fell over again, but then noticed the huge blond soldier, still dazed and wounded but far from dead. He was pawing at his shoulder, reaching for his sword.

Ander ran. He was dizzy and his throat was drier than ever, but he didn't let that stop him. He had to run and keep running if he was to get away. The Niphilim would come for him again he knew, in Ur or Harap. Wherever he ran. But for now he was free.

He'd warn the towns he came to. Maybe somewhere an army could be raised to stop them. Ander smiled as he imagined the invincible Niphilim army crushed and bleeding. Then he thought of that once proud, golden hair turned a bright, lively red.

"If we meet again," Ander muttered to himself between breaths, "his blood will stain more than his hair."

CHAPTER 5

Merchants' Row

*U*RUK AWOKE, SPRAWLED FACE-UP ON A ROOFTOP, SUNLIGHT FULL in his face and a mass of fur pressed against his side. The dog was already wide-awake and staring at him. Uruk licked his lips and reached into his satchel, searching for his water-skin.

'Time to get to the market,' he thought, taking a long drink. They'd wasted too much morning already. Uruk took the Maidenhead of Kallah out of his bag and held it up to the sun, turning it back and forth to make sure it was still completely covered with mud. "What do you think?" he asked, patting the dog on the head. "Will we find anything worth trading for?" The dog sniffed at the mud coated jewel. "No. Probably not," Uruk muttered. "We will have to move on. Tomorrow or the day after. Harap is supposed to be a very rich city."

Uruk tied the carnelian around the dog's neck, hiding the cord under as many short hairs as he could rough up. "You hold the treasure, Dog," he said. "I doubt anyone will suspect you."

The fur along the dog's shoulders stood out as they turned down the main thoroughfare, merging with the stream of bodies headed south.

"Merchants' Row," Uruk said, as much to himself as to the dog. Once it had been a prosperous street, dominated by large estates. But that was decades ago. Since then, the rich families had moved to the southern part of Ur, nearer the river. Their houses were still there, but they'd been converted to taverns and harlots' commons. Women hung from the second story windows, usually without a thread on, cursing at the men walking the streets below and spitting at the women. Anywhere else they'd have been beaten for their insolence, but Merchants' Row was their world, and they ruled it as they saw fit.

The taverns were still mostly empty, but that wouldn't last long. Many of the city-folk had nothing better to do than to spend their days drinking and pawing at whores. A fact that appeared just as true of the women of Ur as of the men, Uruk had been surprised to discover.

The locals stared at Uruk as he walked down the street, but wouldn't make eye contact. That was the strangest thing about Ur. The people were afraid. It wasn't his sword, or even the dog skulking along at his side. Lots of people went armed, and the street was overrun with goats and rats and stray dogs. Besides, they did the same to each other. A woman looked at the ground as she passed a trader from the Indus valley. The trader acted like he was searching in his purse. The fear ran deep.

The dog stayed close to Uruk as they walked, often rubbing against his legs. There was a bad smell in the air—Uruk had noticed it often enough before—growing stronger the farther they walked. The whole city reeked of despair.

At the edge of the marketplace was the largest building in Ur. The Mohenjo-daro—Hill of the Dead. It was round and over two stories tall, like an enormous bubble rising out of a mud bog. The doorway was coated in white ash. Instead of a door, a huge flat stone was rolled across the entry.

At night, men walked the streets, especially along Merchants' Row and the surrounding alleys, looking for the dying and the dead. These they took to the Mohenjo-daro. They laid the bodies of the dead in one vast room and the bodies of the barely living in another. During the day, families would come to the hill to tend sick relatives, and it wasn't totally unheard of for a person to be taken into the tomb, only to wander out alive a day or two later. Usually, however, the bodies taken into the vast rooms beneath the dome were there to stay.

Once a month, the Mohenjo-daro was stuffed with charcoal and the bodies inside were burned. Greasy blue smoke could be seen for miles, billowing out of small holes in the top of the enormous oven.

After three days, when the great stone was rolled back from the opening, only ash remained. Farmers collected it, spreading it on their fields to ensure the coming crop.

As they passed the entrance to the Mohenjo-daro, the dog paused. The smell was coming from inside. Uruk patted him on the neck. "We are there," he said.

Sprawled in front of the door to the Mohenjo-daro was the market. Stalls and tents were set up in a wide ring around an open square. At the center of the ring were the locals. Farmers mostly. They had raw flax, barley and beer, pigs and goats—both roasted and alive—breads, candies, and linens. Anything they could grow in the fertile soil along the banks of the Ibex River. Uruk didn't approach the farmers. It was the outer ring he was interested in.

The first stalls on either side of the Mohenjo-daro were reserved for dealers from the coastal cities and the Bay of Beenar. They usually dealt in hardwood and lime, both substances unavailable in the southern Shinar. Beyond them were the traders from Kan-Puram and other northern towns. Uruk pawed through a box of statuettes, most were graven images of the goddess Kallah, and then moved on. The traders from the north tended to be poor, and most often traded in worthless trinkets or dubious medicinal cures. 'If they had anything worth trading, they'd still be in Kan-Puram,' Uruk thought.

They headed for the southernmost sections of the market, where the foreign merchants had their wares. There were traders from as far away as the Indus valley and the mountains of Nubia. If they were to find anything interesting, it would be here.

Uruk wandered slowly past the tables, looking, as much as he was able, like any ordinary buyer. He joined a group of black traders for a while, studying a heap of papyrus leaves. Uruk had no idea why anyone would want papyrus leaves, but the one they called Modan was trading for a whole bushel of the stuff. Uruk moved on.

At one booth he leaned in to examine a silver ring inset with a large round piece of lapis surrounded by chips of carnelian. It was gaudy and ridiculous, utterly useless. The trader was an Aegyp, and the silver ring was the only metal he had. "I know a man from Timbuktu with rings like this on every finger," he said, as Uruk slipped the ring onto his pinky. "He was not only rich, but very intelligent. He worked in the library. I don't suppose you know what a library is, but. . . ." The merchant shrugged.

Uruk smiled. It would take a dozen such rings to equal the value of the Maidenhead of Kallah, not that he'd ever let this trader know he possessed such a treasure.

"What have you to trade?" the merchant asked.

"Nothing so great as this ring," Uruk replied.

"You have that marvelous sword. Is it from the Bay?" The trader licked his lips. "And your dog. He's nearly starved, but may have possibilities."

Uruk handed back the ring. "Not today," he said, and they walked on.

He hung back as they reached the tables of the traders from Harap and Bahrain. These were the most unusual merchants in Ur. Their tables were covered with strange tools, and trinkets they claimed to have magical properties. Uruk watched them conduct business for a long time, trying to decide which had the largest selection. For the most part, the pickings were meager. There was no end to the demon stones and feathered spirit catchers, but nothing of worth.

One of the tables was all but empty. Behind it, an old woman, not a tooth in her head, sat gumming a piece of hide and pulling it into cord. On her table was a single demon stone, painted blood red with specks of amber, and a pile of wood figurines. If she had anything to trade with Uruk, she was keeping it out of sight.

Uruk looked through the figurines, finally finding a jackal with a long tail. "Did you carve this?"

The old woman reached out a trembling hand. She smiled, and Uruk noticed that pieces of the hide she'd been chewing were stuck to her gums. "Whit one be it?"

Uruk laid the figure in her hand. She squinted at it for a moment and then shook her head.

"It is a jackal," Uruk said.

The dog leaned out to sniff the figurines. He couldn't quite reach them, so he raised up onto his hind legs and put his fore-paws on the edge of the table. When he came to the old woman's hand, still cupping the figure of the jackal, he licked it.

"It tickleth," she cackled, patting the dog's snout with her fingertips.

Uruk wished he had some metal to give the old woman. He wanted the figure, though he couldn't say why. Maybe he just wanted to do something for her in her old age. But he had nothing other than the jewel, and that was too much to give.

As he contemplated the figurine, a man with a long white beard stepped up behind them. "She's not as poor as she looks," he said. "Are you, mother?"

She cackled again, and gave the dog another pat on the snout.

The man shuffled around the table, placing a hand on his mother's shoulder. He had rings on every finger and long yellow nails. He was from Harap, Uruk guessed.

"You like the jackal?" he asked. "It is a very good figure."

"I have nothing to trade," Uruk said.

The merchant smiled and scratched his chin. His fingers twisted through the ends of his beard. "No," he said at last, shaking his head. "You have nothing to trade." He leaned closer, until their noses almost touched. "But your dog is very rich." One finger stretched toward the chunk of mud dangling from the dog's neck. "Very rich indeed."

Uruk frowned.

"Come," the merchant whispered. "We have much to discuss."

Uruk followed him to a small wagon, parked in an alleyway behind the stall. Uruk kept his hand on the handle of his sword. If the merchant intended to kill him and take the jewel, this was the place to do it. No one would see, unless they happened to be standing right in front of the old woman, and Uruk couldn't imagine that ten people had stopped all day. All the merchant needed to do was have his brothers or sons wait, ready to ambush whoever came down the alley. But there didn't seem to be anyone nearby.

The dog ran all around the wagon, sniffing at the wood sides and wheels. When he was done, he licked Uruk's palm. Uruk hoped that meant it was safe.

"I am Baluch." The merchant held his hand out to Uruk who stared at it. "I think you are the man the city speaks of. That I'd bet."

Uruk eyed him warily. "What man?"

"They say a vicious devil, the color of darkness, entered the Ziggurat of Kallah and relieved it of its treasure." Baluch grinned. "It's a brave man who'd stay in this city if his dog had that jewel. A brave man."

Uruk grunted. He preferred for people to speak their minds, assuming that they had something to say. They usually didn't. Instead of answering the merchant, he patted the dog's head and fingered the hilt of his sword.

"Yes, it's a bloody sword you have," Baluch said, wiping a trickle of sweat from the end of his nose. "But no man has reason to threaten me, tribesman. No man has reason. I'm an honest trader, if ever there was one." He gestured at the jewel. "You want to trade and I am leaving town. So we may profit each other."

This was getting to the point. Uruk untied the Maidenhead from around the dog's neck and handed it to Baluch. "What will you trade?" he asked.

Baluch carefully picked at the mud until the carnelian shone clean, then held it up to the sun, searching for any sign of impurity or blemish. When he was satisfied, he held it next to his ear and tapped on it. "I'll have trouble getting rid of it," he muttered. "That will lower the price. And it's not perfect." He combed his fingers through his beard. Finally, looking at Uruk's chest he said, "I'll give you a bolt of finest linen. It's a fair price. Any man would call that a fair price."

"A fool in the halls of the dead would call it a fair price. A beggar, drunk and dying of whores-disease in that mammoth oven would call it a fair price," Uruk growled, thrusting his thumb at the Mohenjo-daro. "You will have to do a damned sight better than that. And it had better be something useful. No bags of barley or graven idols. No barter."

Baluch smiled. "My friend, I can see that you are not interested in the honored way of bargaining, so I shall be brief. I have something in my cart that I will give you in trade for the jewel. Something useful, as you say."

Uruk eyed the cart suspiciously.

"I have many things to trade," Baluch said. "The question is—what do I have for you?" He stared into Uruk's eyes. "What kind of a man are you?"

"A hunter."

"No. . . . You are a thief. A hunter of trinkets and danger, maybe. Little else." He nodded. "You tempt the gods. You dare them to kill you. That's why you go after treasures such as the Maidenhead of Kallah." He motioned toward his wagon. "Yes, I have something for you. A magnificent treasure. Very costly. I will trade it to you for the jewel . . . and your sword."

Uruk laughed.

"You laugh, my friend," Baluch said. "But I offer you something from which you cannot walk away." He reached under the wagon, to a secret compartment between the wheels, and drew out a long bundle of dusty cloth.

Uruk watched as he untied the bundle. Was it possible? Could this man have something for which he would give up his sword? Whatever he had, it was long and thin. Uruk's guts were gripped with curiosity. Finally, from a long woolen sack, Baluch pulled a sword.

This weapon was unlike any Uruk had ever seen. It was longer than a man's arm, straight and slender. The metal of the handle was black, with long strips of hide sewn round it for a grip. From the way Baluch held the sword, Uruk judged the weapon to be heavy. But when Baluch handed it to him, he discovered that it was actually extraordinarily light—much lighter than his old, bronze sword. He skinned it from its scabbard and held it at arms' length. It was perfectly weighted and balanced. The blade was so thin that it seemed almost feminine. The handle was just large enough for his hand.

"Beautiful," Uruk said. "But the blade will splinter the first time it meets bone."

"Try it," Baluch said.

Uruk swung the sword in a long overhead arc, burying it in the side of the wagon. The blade sliced a full hands-width into the wood before it caught. Uruk wrenched the sword free and examined the edge. The polish was dulled, but there was no sign of chip or crack.

"Mana," he whispered. "What is it?"

"Iron," Baluch replied, smiling. "Once, many years ago, I traded with a northern people who'd learned its secrets." His fingers combed through his beard once more. "They'd learned to mine and forge the stuff. They made many beautiful things, including swords. This was one of their very best, no doubt meant for their chieftain."

"Where are these people? Who are they?" Uruk asked. He passed his old sword to the merchant, pausing for only a moment to imagine the blood it had known in his hand.

"They called themselves Kenanites," Baluch said. "I doubt that most people even remember they existed."

"What happened?" Uruk fastened the iron sword to his belt. Already he felt faster. Lighter. His hand tingled as he imagined drawing the sword in battle.

"They were killed," Baluch said. "A race of warriors, calling themselves the Niphilim, discovered the Kenanites and—" He clapped his hands loudly and then rubbed them together, as though he'd killed a mosquito and was trying to rid his hands of the carcass. "Most of their skills disappeared with them. A great loss." He shook his head. "I've heard rumors that the Niphilim forge iron as well, though I have seen no evidence."

"Why would you let it go?" Uruk asked. "There has never been such a weapon."

Baluch shrugged. "I'm no warrior. As a weapon it means nothing to me. I deal in unusual items. This one I have had for a long time. A long time." He pointed at Uruk. "I try to find the right owner for each of my treasures. For you, a sword."

Uruk smiled. The right man for the sword. That felt good. He motioned to the dog, who ran ahead of him toward the marketplace. "Thank you," Uruk said. "Our trade was good." He turned to leave as well, but Baluch grabbed his arm.

"Tell me," Baluch said, "where are you going?"

Uruk turned just in time to see the Maidenhead of Kallah disappear down the front of Baluch's tunic and get covered over by his beard. "I will stay in Ur for a day or two," Uruk said. "Then I will make my way southeast. Toward Harap."

"May I offer you some advice?"

"Advice?" Uruk raised an eyebrow.

"Do not worry, my friend, the advice is free, and you may always disregard it." Baluch pointed toward the marketplace. "This is a hard place, tribesman. It's time you moved on. Now. Tonight. They are looking for you. In your mind, this," he patted his chest, "this is just a jewel. But to them it is life. . . . You're not safe here."

"Then I will go to Harap."

Baluch shook his head. "Go to Kan-Puram. Thieves can become something in that city—even kings. There you can change your life. You can be whatever you wish." His eyebrows raised. "Even make your peace with the gods."

Uruk considered for a moment. If Kan-Puram were as great as Baluch described, it deserved a look. If it could make kings of thieves, maybe it could remake destinies. "I may take your advice," he said.

The dog was resting his head in Baluch's mother's lap as they stepped out of the alley. The old woman stroked his neck while the dog licked her hands. Every time his tongue passed between her fingers she cackled with joy.

"Dog," Uruk said. "It is time."

"Be wary," the old woman whispered. She pointed a gnarled finger at the Mohenjo-daro.

A long line of priests was winding into the marketplace. At the front was the tall priest Uruk had seen the night before, the very same one who had lit the pyre beneath the little girl. He had dark circles under his eyes, and instead of long robes he was dressed in the same brown jerkin the other priests wore. By the look on his face, Uruk guessed that he'd had a long night.

Behind the priests were a dozen guards, all carrying spears like the ones Uruk had seen in the ziggurat. The guards themselves were different though. Not one of them was black.

They tore through the market, kicking aside both the farmers and their goods. Not one of them resisted. The farmers tried to pull as much of their produce to safety as they could, and smiled as the priests cursed them for being slow. Uruk was disgusted.

When a large space had been cleared at the center of the market, a pair of women marched forward carrying a large wooden box. They set it upside down in the clearing and the tall priest climbed on top.

"The goddess is defiled!" he screamed.

The farmers, even those whose goods had been kicked over or thrown aside, crowded around him. The other priests, and the guards, mixed with the crowd, stopping next to the few groups of black men and fixing them with cold stares.

Uruk glanced at Baluch, who squinted warningly and shook his head.

One of the guards positioned himself in front of Baluch's table. Uruk was glad he'd thought to cover his face with clay the night before. The priests of Kallah might eventually decide to search every black man in Ur, but none could say for sure that they recognized him.

"The goddess is defiled!" the tall priest said again. "And the guilty party is among us." He said it with such gravity that even Uruk looked to see if the accused would dare show his face. It was lucky he did. The guards were hoping to see someone blanche, or lower his head.

"Let us recall. It's a short tale, passed from the lips of the goddess herself.

"Before there was sky or earth, before rains fell in the desert, and long before the Tiger or Ibex flowed into the sea, the goddess was alone in the darkness.

"Then there was another. Which of you can tell me who he was?"

A murmur went through the crowd. "The desert god," someone shouted.

The priest nodded. "That's right. It was the god of the deserts, and of the winds, and of the stone and the fire. He found our lady and he laid upon her. From her he created the heavens and the earth.

"But the earth was formless, and so on it he placed the waters, over it he placed the sun and in it he placed the seeds."

The farmers, and most of the merchants, nodded along with every point. This was a tale they'd heard before. One they liked.

"He put the fish in the waters, the birds in the air, the animals on the land and the cattle in the fields—all through the body of the goddess." The priest spread his arms, as if to embrace the entire assembly. "But how did he do these things?" He paused, listening as a dozen voices shouted together. "That's right. He thrust his spear into her, forcing her to act on the void." This last bit was met with howls and cries of anger.

The dog pressed against Uruk's side, bristling with fear.

"Then, sons and daughters, the dread lord forced humanity from the goddess. We were placed alone and naked among the beasts." The priest shook his fists at the crowd. "But that was when the goddess rose up and shook the dark god from her, never again to lay with him. She made herself a virgin once more. And when she was free, she became the protector of the people, showing us all manner of wisdom—fire, planting and reaping, forming and regeneration. Kallah alone stands between us and the dread god of creation, whose tremors shake the land, whose winds move the deserts and create the waves, who sends drought and flood and disease, wild animals to tear our flesh, old age and death to consume our bones."

A single tear rolled down the priest's cheek. "But last night, little ones, the goddess was raped again. . . ." He paused, letting the idea sink in.

"How can any of us face her now?" More tears ran down his cheeks. "We must find her sacred jewel, stolen by the defiler, and rain down terrible punishment on any man possessing her property." His voice had grown strident. "The Maidenhead of Kallah must be found."

Trickles of sweat ran from Uruk's underarms. The guard in front of Baluch's table lowered his spear, but Uruk didn't move. He crossed his arms over his chest and nodded at the guard, as though he hadn't noticed the spearhead aimed at his heart.

Two tables down, near the southern edge of the marketplace, a pair of black men stood together, listening to the sermon. They were two of the same group Uruk had shadowed earlier. One was Modan. At his feet was the bushel of papyrus leaves he'd been dickering over. Uruk couldn't remember the other man's name.

As he watched, a pair of guards closed on them. Modan saw them first. He put a hand on his friend's shoulder and whispered something. Even from a distance, Uruk could see that his palm was soaking wet.

When he was a child, Uruk was allowed to hunt over the forest floor and kill rodents. He remembered catching a mouse once. While it was still alive, Uruk had felt its tiny heart beating in its chest. He'd seen and smelled pure terror as the mouse's whiskers twitched and its eyes darted. Uruk saw the same terror in Modan's eyes. 'Don't run,' Uruk thought. 'Stand strong.'

But he didn't. With a last pat on his friend's shoulder, Modan turned and ran, headed toward the southernmost tip of the marketplace, where Merchants' Row reemerged from the sea of tables.

Shouts rang out. Knives flashed.

Modan knocked a woman out of his way as he ran between a pair of stalls, and might have gotten away if he hadn't looked back at the approaching mob.

Just as he glanced over his shoulder, a gang of children ran from behind the nearest house, chasing a lamb. The first in the group was a little boy. He had a stray lock of hair that stood straight up on the back of his head. His hands were outstretched. He was just about to grab the lamb by the rear legs. A few more steps and he'd have caught it. He never even noticed Modan, angling toward him out of the market.

Modan's knee struck the boy square on the jaw, and together they went rolling through the dust.

The crowd was almost upon them, and Modan, to his eternal credit, shoved the boy out of the way. A moment later he was swallowed in a storm of fists and feet.

Modan was unconscious, but not yet dead. He had dozens of cuts, many deep, and his face was swollen beyond recognition. Uruk guessed that he had a few broken bones, mostly ribs, but would live if given the chance.

"What are they going to do with him?" Uruk asked.

"Difficult to say." Baluch swept his mother's wood figurines into a box. All but the jackal, which he left on the table. "Only one thing is certain. Nothing can save him now." With that, Baluch and his mother started toward their wagon. "Go to Kan-Puram, tribesman," Baluch called over his shoulder.

Uruk picked the jackal up off the tabletop. "You forgot this."

"Keep it." Baluch helped his mother into the cart. "Go to Kan-Puram," he said again.

"I will." In fact, Uruk wanted to go to Kan-Puram that very instant, but couldn't. He had to see what would happen to Modan first.

It took a long time for the priests to decide his fate. Death was the only answer, but how? They argued over the virtues of hanging and gutting, but were unable to make a decision. Finally, the tall priest stepped back onto his box at the center of the market. "It has been decided," he said. He turned toward the Mohenjo-daro, gesturing with both hands. "We shall prepare it for firing."

An hour later, Modan was inside, along with a dozen cartloads of charcoal.

"The guilty revealed himself," the priest shouted. "The jewel has not yet been found, but it's only a matter of time." He sneered at Modan's friend, tied hand and foot, lying on the ground next to the box. That man's troubles were only just beginning.

The sun would soon set, and torches had flared up all through the city, especially in front of the taverns on Merchants' Row. But there were no customers, no farmers or merchants—not even the harlots were inside that evening. All stood in the crowd around the entrance to the Mohenjo-daro, waiting for the fire to pop and growl within.

At long last, the tall priest flung a torch through the opening, setting the blaze. He watched it burn for a moment, then five stout men shoved against the round stone, rolling it across the entrance to the tomb.

When only a few inches of the opening were still visible, a voice burst from the mound. It was a scream like few in Ur had ever heard. To Uruk, it sounded like a wildebeest being torn down by a lion.

The stone continued its slow roll. As it closed off the last inches, the voice, which sounded much closer now, as though Modan were crawling toward the door, called out, "Please, do not shut—" and was silenced. The door was closed.

From where he stood, at the edge of the crowd, Uruk watched the stone sink into its grooves, sealing the Mohenjo-daro. For a moment, the mob was silent. Then, like the rumble of a volcano, a noise began to swell in the bellies of the people, bubbling as it increased in strength, and erupted into the evening twilight. They cheered.

Uruk and the dog walked away. Behind them, a party was just beginning. They heard it grow in intensity as they made their way past the taverns on Merchants' Row.

When they reached the edge of the city, Uruk broke into a farmer's hut and plundered it. He tied water-skins to the dog's back and put as much food as he could carry into a makeshift pack on his own. It was the first time he'd stolen from the poor, but Uruk felt no remorse.

He didn't look back as he left the city of Ur, but the dog did. When they reached the footbridge over the Ibex River, the dog turned to stare at the blaze of lights. His ears were cocked, listening for danger. There was a strange smell on the air, sick and sour. Above the Mohenjo-daro, the first tendrils of blue smoke were giving way to puffs and billows of greasy black.

Uruk turned north, walking toward where the mighty river starts as a trickle in a mountain far away. The dog raced ahead.

CHAPTER 6

The Lioness and the Falcon

*T*HE ASSEMBLY STARTED JUST BEFORE NOON AND CONTINUED RIGHT through the hottest part of the day. The granary, wherein most of the men sat on sacks of wheat and barley or leaned on tool racks, was starting to smell. Even the barrels of sour-mash, fermenting in the corner, weren't pungent enough to fight off the stench of bodies. Twice the women had called them to eat, but the men just kept talking. They argued over every miniscule point. In the beginning, a few had even suggested that their town was in no danger, that the Niphilim were a peace-loving people and had always been good neighbors. Ander listened to everything the farmers and artisans said, but that only convinced him of one thing. Men can't be reasoned with, only told.

"Be quiet, old man."

Ander glanced around the room, but couldn't determine exactly where the voice came from. Not that it mattered. Any of two dozen young men might have said it. And at least that many would claim that they had.

Over the last hour, the assembly had devolved to a shouting match, with the old on one side and the young on the other. It was a contest of strength and vitality against experience and wisdom. But both sides were dead wrong. One way or another, Akshur intended to fight.

"You young fools don't understand anything about a real battle. Why, when the Marauders of Malag. . . ."

Ander was only half-listening. He had a new hat, woven from strands of dry grass, but it was a bit too large for his head. So, while the rest of the assembly argued on, he gently tugged at the strands around the brim, pulling them closer together. He wanted it snug enough to stay on in a strong wind at least. Ander needed the hat, and wore it everywhere, especially now that he'd cut his hair short. The years he'd spent in the mines had left his skin pale, unable to withstand the harsh sun of the Shinar. It was like being a child again. He half expected to see his stepmother lean out of a kitchen door and tell him to put the soup on.

In addition to the hat, Ander had a new tunic and a hunting knife. Eleven days in Akshur and he'd managed to collect nothing else. The townspeople had fed him and let him sleep in a tool shed next to their smokehouse, but they were poor and possessions were hard to come by. Traders didn't come to Akshur anymore.

As soon as this assembly was over, Ander was leaving for Kan-Puram. The Niphilim army would arrive the next morning, ready for battle. He'd tried to explain what would happen when they arrived, but the Akshurites wouldn't abandon their homes. They couldn't believe that the Niphilim would destroy their little town—that they'd be taken as slaves and their children killed. Ander had no intention of being there to see it happen.

"If we stand at the edge of the city, as defenders, we'll be able to keep formation," one old man said, squinting at the crowd from under a pair of prickly white eyebrows. He reminded Ander of a stinging nettle. "Besides, the Niphilim don't care about Akshur, they want Kan-Puram. They'll pass us by if we can hold them off for. . . ."

He was shouted down.

"Whether they want Kan-Puram or not, we'll be swept up and destroyed. We need to attack them on the hills. Force them back. If we wait, they'll form up and march on us. We'll have no retreat." It was Brohman who spoke, the loudest voice among the youth. He was short, heavily muscled, and had a big belly that hung over the front of his breeches. He reminded Ander of his stepfather. "Besides, it's the young who'll fight," he sneered. "Not you."

"What'll you do when you're routed?"

"We won't be. From the hills we can push them down into the river."

Brohman had more to say, but just as he opened his mouth an old man seated near the center of the hall raised a hand. "May I speak?"

Ander recognized him, though he'd never actually spoken to the man. He was one of the oldest citizens in Akshur, and far and away the most respected. Ander had heard more than once about how he'd led the town in its one great battle, when the Akshurites defeated the Marauders of Malag. His name was Rahmat, but to the people of Akshur he was known as the Falcon.

The Falcon stood up. He had a cane, but instead of leaning on it, he held it in front of him like a club. The room buzzed, as people wondered aloud what the Falcon might say. He rapped his cane on the floor, quieting the assembly. Ander looked into his cold gray eyes and shivered.

"Tell me what great weapons we can use to attack the Niphilim." The Falcon stared at Brohman until the younger man blushed. "Force them back?" He scoffed. "We're farmers and herdsmen. Pitchforks can't go to meet swords in open battle."

The elders of the town smiled, sure now that their arguments would prevail.

"And when their armies come, will they be scared to fight on the edge of our city?" the Falcon continued. "Will we take some great comfort in knowing that our houses and barns are behind us? Our families a mere stone's throw away? If we fight at the edge of town, it will be we who have our backs to the walls, with nowhere to run."

Ander was astonished at the Falcon's poise. The more he talked, the taller he seemed to stretch. His council was grave but true. When he told the elders that Akshur could not be defended by forming up at the foot of the town, Ander fully expected to hear the young men scream in victory, but the granary was quieter than ever.

"No, we'll make our stand on the hills and fall back to the town to regroup."

A gentle murmur rippled through the granary. Suddenly they had hope. The Falcon was going to guide them to victory, just as he had so many years before. The men closest to him reached out to pat him on the back, but the Falcon waved them off. His gray eyes gleamed with tears.

"And there, with our homes and farms, herds and families behind us," he said, "we'll fall. And our blood will soak the ground. We shall die like true sons of Akshur before our city is taken—and taken it will surely be." Tears ran down the Falcon's cheeks, but that only made him look more heroic.

A chill ran up Ander's spine and over his scalp. He knew he couldn't run.

Ander trudged up and down, trying to work the blood up from his feet. He'd stood through the better part of the night and his heels were sore. He considered sitting down and giving them a good hard rub, but decided against it. If he sat down now, he wasn't sure he'd get back up.

The eastern sky had faded to a light charcoal, dotted here and there by stars. No sun yet, but Ander expected it to rise any moment. It looked to be a nice morning. A touch of humidity, and just enough of a breeze to set the brim of his hat fluttering. If only the Niphilim weren't on the way.

Most of the men were still sound asleep, their gentle snores defiantly filling the pre-morning gloom. Ander envied them. He didn't dare rest, or even sit down. He couldn't chance it. Around midnight he'd dozed off for a few minutes and woke bathed in sweat. He'd been standing ever since. The mines of Dagonor were the one place he never wanted to see again—even in his dreams.

Ander wasn't the only one that couldn't sleep. Somewhere close by, one of the men was playing pipes. It was an old dirge, one Ander remembered from boyhood. He used to sit outside his stepmother's window, listening to her sing as she carted wool. The chorus had something to do with the moon's face reflecting off ripples in a pond. It was a sad song. Ander wished he could remember more.

He was humming along with the music, trying to remember what the song was called, when the pipes suddenly whistled to a stop.

"Look," one of the men said. "Something's out there."

A single speck of orange fire bobbed and twinkled in the valley below. At first it was alone, like a lonely firefly searching for a mate. Then other points of light began to break off it. Soon the specks were multiplying so rapidly that Ander could no longer tell which was the original.

"Torches," he said at last, as though in answer to a question no one dared ask.

The Niphilim were moving, probably crossing the river. There was a shallow spot right at the end of the valley—the only one for miles. Traders used to wade across with their wagons and slaves, bound for Akshur. Ander had crossed at the same spot after his flight from Dagonor.

"Look at them all," the man next to him said, sitting up in the tall grass.

He was young, probably no more than seventeen or eighteen, but already sporting a thick beard. Ander was sorry he didn't know the boy's name.

"It almost looks like—" The boy grabbed his spear and scrambled to his feet.

"What?" Ander squinted but could only see the torches.

"Nothing." He shook his head. "I guess it's nothing."

For the next quarter-hour they stood together, watching as the dots of fire marched up the valley. By that time, every man on the hill was awake. At least half were praying feverishly, offering up all manner of future sacrifice. Ander kept an eye on them, unsure whether he should join in. He decided not to. Ander believed in gods, he just wasn't sure what he had to say to them.

"I don't feel well," the boy at his side muttered. His hand was pressed to his chest. A sick look spread over his lips.

"Me neither," Ander confessed. He'd heard about battle fright. The Niphilim told stories about it to scare the younger soldiers. Some sweated. Others got gas. Most felt like they had to urinate, though their bladders were empty. Ander just felt cold.

"My heart's beating so fast. . . ." the boy gasped. "Can you hear it?"

Ander put a hand on his shoulder. "You're all right," he whispered. "Just take a deep breath."

The boy sucked in hard. "I don't think I can do it," he said. Ander looked at him, but didn't say a word. "There are other cities. I could take my wife and—" His mouth fell open as the first rays of sunlight streamed over the eastern mountains.

The valley was still cloaked in shadows, but no longer so dark that they couldn't make out the approaching army. There were at least three thousand Niphilim and an untold number of savages. The Akshurites were outnumbered sixty to one.

Ander glanced at the boy, half-expecting him to bolt.

"What are they?" the boy asked, nervously squeezing the shaft of his spear.

"Savages," Ander muttered. "Lillin. Beasts from west of the Withered Hills." Even from that distance he could see their hairy bodies. The tufts of fur on their chests and bellies. The dense thickets that ran down their spines, disappearing into the cracks between their buttocks. "The Niphilim have been trapping them for months."

Watching the savages fight their way up the hill, Ander couldn't help thinking of a boiling pot, the bubbles growing ever larger as they rise to the surface. "Be careful," he said. "They're strong. And the more human ones carry clubs."

"More human?"

"You'll see."

The boy bit his lip. Ander was starting to like him. He was scared, but wasn't letting his fear get the best of him. That's just about all that could be said of anyone.

"Do you hear that?" the boy asked.

Ander listened. "Drums," he said. The rhythm was eerily similar to a heartbeat. Not a nice sound. "They just keep adding wood to the fire."

"What?"

"Nothing."

"How many do you think there are?"

"Too many," Ander said. "Far too many."

The savages howled as they stampeded up the hill. They were close enough now for Ander to see the bony ridges over their eyes, and their hooked, claw-like fingers. Most were painfully thin. Probably malnourished, Ander guessed. He glanced at his own arm. The bones and veins in the back of his hand stood out like those of a man twice his age. Ander frowned. A couple more weeks in Akshur and he might have filled out.

Ander was still contemplating his arm when he noticed the boy inching backward. "Stay in the line," Ander said, putting a hand on the boy's shoulder and gently pushing him back into place. "It's the safest place."

The boy glared. He thought he was being called a coward, Ander guessed. And trying so hard to prove he was a man.

"Keep the tip of your spear chest high," Ander continued, ignoring the look on the boy's face. "No reason to aim for their necks." As he talked, Ander thought of all the times he'd watched the Niphilim running drills and sparing in the field at the base of the mountain. "Keep the shaft level. It's strongest that way."

"What'll I do if they break through?" the boy asked. "What if they get past us and attack from behind?"

Ander pulled the hunting knife from his belt and handed it to the boy. "Take this," he said. "If they do get past us, throw away your spear."

The boy nodded morosely. "Thanks," he whispered.

The first savage was nearing the top of the hill. She had long teats, hairy right to the edge of the nipple, and big powerful legs. How she'd managed to fight past the others, Ander couldn't imagine. She was panting, mouth open wide, and had a full set of sharp, yellow teeth. The only part of her that didn't strike fear into Ander was her eyes. Looking into them he saw only terror.

Ander winced as the rusty tines of a pitchfork stabbed into her belly, just above her left hip.

The savage screamed.

Ander shut his eyes, took a deep breath, and pulled his hat down tight. A little squirt of urine soaked into the front of his breeches.

The pot was about to boil over.

Ander ducked, but not low enough. The club got him behind the ear, knocking his hat off and sending him sprawling. Fortunately, he still had wits enough to curl into a ball and put his arms over his head. He ground his teeth, expecting any second to feel the club crush his bones.

They'd been overrun almost instantly. Their line was too thin and the savages ran right through, though not without a few punches and kicks for the men trying desperately to hold them back. One young female bit Ander's arm just above the wrist. Blood still oozed from the teeth marks.

The Akshurites had managed to kill a few, but not nearly enough. Ander stabbed at every inch of naked skin he saw. Most of the time he didn't hit a thing, though every so often he felt the tip of his spear graze something soft. Soon, Ander thought, there'll be a whole legion of savages with scratches he'd given them.

It was almost a surprise when he thrust his spear forward and felt it stick. He'd somehow managed to stab a short, heavily built male with no teeth and a bald scalp. And it was a killing wound, too. Ander's spear was stuck in the savage's chest, a little to the right of center, and about a hand's length above the navel. Ander pushed until the shaft of his spear passed between the beast's ribs.

As the spear sunk into his chest, puncturing a lung, the savage slumped to his knees. His mouth opened wide, but no sound came out. He looked like a fish after it had been drawn from a stream, its mouth working hopelessly.

Ander gave a sharp pull, expecting his spear to slide free. It didn't. The head was stuck tight. His heart skipped. He twisted as hard as he could, feeling it start to work loose. Another good jerk and he probably would have gotten it.

But before he got the chance, a large male, carrying a club as big around as a man's thigh, leapt in front of him. He had knots tied into the fur on his head and chest, growing larger as they descended through the patches on his belly and groin. Even his penis was tied up at the center of a big, hairy knot. With his first thrust, the savage splintered Ander's spear.

Ander held tight to the small piece of broken wood he had left, even swinging it defensively once as the monster stomped toward him.

The savage wasn't impressed. He swung his club with both hands, aiming at Ander's neck. It came at him with such ferocity that Ander felt certain his head was about to be sent flying. Astonishingly, he only lost his hat. He heard the club woosh by, felt it nick the top of his skull, and it was all over.

Lying on his side, arms wrapped protectively over his head, Ander couldn't see what happened next. He waited, still expecting to have the life mashed out of him, along with a fair amount of blood and brains. But the fatal blow never landed. Finally, he put his arms down and looked up.

The Falcon was standing over him, a frown etched over his face. He had a bronze sword in one hand and wore a heavy leather vest. In the morning light his hair looked a rich golden brown. He grabbed Ander's hand and hauled him to his feet.

"What happened?" Ander began, looking around for the savage with all the knots. A half-dozen old men were fighting just a few strides away, holding back the savages as best they could. Brohman was with them, wildly swinging a pair of clubs, both of which were coated in blood and hair.

"Get back!" the Falcon shouted, waving at Akshur with the point of his sword. "Warn them."

Ander glanced at the little town, lying snug at the edge of the basin, the eastern mountains towering over it like giants. A torch was burning at one corner of the granary, as though to show the way back home. All the other buildings were dark.

The first wave of savages was nearing the town, headed straight for the smokehouse. 'Probably smell the meat,' Ander thought. He saw what looked like a handful of women and older children, maybe twenty in all, lined up to meet them. None of the men had managed to get back to form the second line of defense. None ever would.

"Warn who?" Ander asked.

The Falcon scowled. "Everyone." He pushed Ander away. "Hurry. The Niphilim are coming over the hill."

At least three dozen bodies were spread across the ridge—savages and men alike. Ander found it hard to think that he'd been standing there, talking to a boy whose name he still didn't know, less than a half-hour before.

The first line of golden heads was just rising over the carnage.

Ander took one last look at the Falcon, now bracing to meet them, and ran.

Kishar pushed open the granary door and stepped inside.

Simha sat on a milking stool behind a makeshift table. It was nothing more than an old door laid across a pair of barrels, but it would suffice. She was eating her dinner and looking at maps.

"Captain," Kishar said as he crossed the room. "The savages are under control and the last of the prisoners have been bound."

"Are the soldiers being fed?" Simha asked without looking up.

"Yes, Captain. . . . And they're enjoying the extra rations."

"Good." She picked up a piece of white cheese and began absent-mindedly squeezing it between her fingers. Her maps were covered in crumbs. "We march in ten days," she said. "After Bel arrives with the other savages." She popped the cheese into her mouth. "Make sure Lagassar knows," she said, still chewing. "And tell Ezidha to arrange for a garrison."

"Ten days?" Kishar had expected to start in two—three at the outside.

"What happened today?" Simha asked. There were deep creases in her forehead. Her hair stuck out like a lion's mane. "The savages were supposed to stop when they reached the top of the hill and allow the main force to come through."

"The savages may not be intelligent enough for such a complicated maneuver."

"They managed it in drills, didn't they?" Simha asked. Kishar didn't respond. "Well didn't they?"

"Things are different in the heat of battle," Kisher said. "They got a bit overzealous."

"Maybe."

"It's a good thing we had this battle. As a test. Now we know what the savages are capable of."

Simha frowned. "They're capable of nothing. I want every tenth man at the front of the lines issued a whip. When we march on Kan-Puram, I want them to beat the savages into a frenzy. After they've been driven mad with pain and fear we'll send them at the enemy lines. Then we'll see what they can do." She slammed a fist down on the table. "No more trickery. Straight battle."

Kishar was stunned. "But Kan-Puram is many times larger. . . ." He shook his head. "The black-heads will slaughter them."

"Yes," Simha nodded. "They will."

Ander stumbled down a long, rocky ravine, through a thick stand of dandy-willow and across a stream. His breeches were soaked to the crotch but he didn't care.

A dirty piece of canvas lay across his head, tied with a few strips of cloth he'd torn from the sleeves of his tunic. It wasn't a hat, but it kept the sun off his face. Ander had discovered the canvas crumpled up beneath a shelf at the back of an old lean-to, about two hours south of Akshur. Beside the lean-to were a small, dilapidated corral and some milking stalls. The men of Akshur must have brought their goats there in the spring, just after they'd dropped their kids. Ander thought about staying in the lean-to for a while, sleeping through the hottest part of the day, but decided against it. The Niphilim would be organizing patrols soon, and the old camps would be one of the first places they'd look for stragglers. Not that it would do them any good. So far as Ander could tell, he was the only one who'd gotten away.

As he walked, he imagined the Niphilim organizing their new slaves into troops. About half, men mostly, would be marched back to Dagonor, carrying sacks of flour and meal from the granary. The women would be kept in Akshur to serve the soldiers. Their children would be killed outright, though a few might be kept around as an ongoing threat. Rapes and beatings would be commonplace that first night. Ander had always judged the Niphilim women to be the more vicious. It took some of them quite a while to build up to serious abuse—but when they did, the result was incredible.

The town itself would remain mostly intact, though only as a kind of husk. The furniture in the little houses would be broken up and the wood used to burn the bodies. Tools would be broken to pieces or hauled back to Dagonor. Clothes would be soaked in resin to make torches.

Everything the people had ever cared about would be destroyed, befouled or stolen.

Ander was crossing over the same stream again, still headed toward the Tiger River, when he thought of the savages. He knew they were emaciated, but they still had to be eating something. They were too strong to be going without food completely.

By the shape of their teeth, and the fact that their eyes were so close set, Ander guessed that the savages were more or less strict carnivores. All the old tales agreed. The Lillin were often described slinking to the edge of a camp, waiting for the fires to burn out so that they could grab the babies and small children of the wandering herdsman.

'The Niphilim will give them the bodies,' Ander thought. He imagined the savages dancing over the corpses as they tore through flesh and snapped bone. For some reason, the body he kept envisioning was the Falcon's. In his mind, Ander could see the beasts tearing off the old man's head and flinging it into the air. The white hair standing out straight as the head flips end over end, then falls into the waiting jaws of an enormous beast, knots tied into the fur over its head and chest.

Ander swatted some thistles out of his path with the short chunk of spear he had left. He needed to get to Kan-Puram.

Book II
ON THE FIELDS
OF KAN-PURAM

BEFORE A SINGLE MAN OR WOMAN HAD EVER MADE THE LONG TREK over the eastern mountains, or crossed the desert from the west, or followed the twisting shoreline of the southern sea, the Shinar was home to the gods. Ten thousand there were, occupying hills and fields, streams and marshes. Lonesome by nature, the gods lived for forty millenniums in blissful isolation. And They were content.

It was Marduk, the far-seeing, who broke this peace. He saw that the other gods paid him no mind, being mired in the contemplation of their own magnificence, and He waxed wroth. So Marduk called forth humanity, directing that a temple should be built in his honor. And the people came. At his insistence, a priesthood was formed, from whence He could direct his followers in all manner of daily life. Offerings were made. Songs and poems written in obeisance of Him.

Seeing this, the other gods became jealous. They too demanded followers, offerings, and songs. So, They called to all the peoples of the earth, demanding that temples be constructed of wood, and brick, and stone. Kallah was honored with the great Ziggurat at Ur. For Moloch a palace, constructed amongst the lofty peaks of the Karun Mountains—from whence he could look down over all the other temples and smile.

But there was one place, midway between the Withered Hills and the southern sea, a place where the Tiger and Ibex rivers meandered closest together, a strip of land blessed with unrivaled fecundity, which all the gods claimed as their own.

Temples grew there like blades in a field of grass. Villages gathered round to support them, each constructed in a style meant to pay homage to the patron god or goddess. Conflicts naturally arose. Feuds became commonplace. As the citizenry grew ever more numerous, the domains of these temples began to abut, one against another. Over time, they interwove so completely that what had once been a hundred tiny villages became instead a single mass of struggling humanity.

The gods could not decide in whose honor this new 'city' had been built, and so they too fought. Chaos reigned.

To this megalopolis, formed unlike any other on the earth, the god Marduk gave a name. He called it 'Kan-Puram,' which means both 'home to all' and 'home to none.' And upon this, at least, all the gods could agree—for never had a name been so well chosen.

CHAPTER 1

The Snail's Horn

OF ALL THE QUARTERS OF KAN-PURAM THEY'D EXPLORED, THIS was the most monotonously dreary. Mud bricks and desiccated wood—everything they saw was built from one of those two materials. Walking the streets, one couldn't help feeling a kind of threat, or challenge, seeping from the crumbling walls. It was as if the whole neighborhood was whispering, 'stay away.'

Uruk paused at the corner, not sure which way to turn. They had two choices, three if you counted the way they'd come, but neither looked particularly promising.

Pictures, most no larger than a handprint, had been painted on the walls of the surrounding houses. Nearly all were faded or peeling from the heat, but one was easily identifiable. A naked woman on all fours. Under it was an arrow pointing north.

"What do you think?" Uruk asked.

The dog looked up at him, panting, but made no move in either direction.

Just then, someone yelled from across the street. "Trade? You want to trade?" At first, Uruk didn't know who was shouting. A pair of adolescent boys was watching them, arms crossed over their chests, but neither looked inclined to speak. Then Uruk noticed an old woman hurrying across the road, not even trying to avoid the urine pooled at the center. "Trade?" she bellowed again, as though terrified that Uruk might somehow get away. A goat stumbled along behind her, tied to a short piece of rope. The hairs on its muzzle were as white as bone.

When she was close enough for Uruk to smell her, the old woman grabbed the goat by one of its horns and gave it a shake. "Young and healthy," she said. "And fat as a merchant. I've been feeding him barley since he was a kid. Never a drop of clay or sawdust in his life." She lifted one of the goat's hind legs and patted its scrotum. "Ready to service a

whole herd, make you a rich man. Do more for you than this mangy cur."
She glanced at the dog. There was hunger in that look.

The dog had filled out as they moved north. Muskrats and rabbits
were plentiful along the Ibex River, and between the two of them, Uruk
and the dog nearly always had fresh meat. The dog had proved himself a
skilled hunter. He lacked patience, but was otherwise a natural killer.
Uruk began training him almost at once, and was amazed at how quickly
he'd learned. His strength had come back with nearly equal speed. Uruk
could barely feel the dog's ribs anymore, let alone see them. When he ran
his hand over the dog's back, all he felt were muscles.

"This way," Uruk said, turning and walking away from the old
woman. He'd decided to follow the arrow. Neither Uruk nor the dog had
any interest in the kind of woman depicted in that crude painting, but the
men they were looking for almost always did.

"Wait. You don't have to trade the dog," the old woman pleaded,
chasing after them. "I could give you the goat for a—"

"I do not want your goat," Uruk said.

"Maybe a fine cart or. . . ." The old woman squinted up at him. "A
woman?" She smiled, thinking she'd figured Uruk out. Her gums were
gray. "My son and his wife will be along any time. She's—"

"No." Uruk walked faster.

"My son's wife is better than any whore you'll find down there," she
called after them. "Better than all the whores in the dust."

Uruk patted the dog on the neck. "Stay close," he said.

Every step took them deeper into the poorest neighborhood in Kan-
Puram. Locals called it 'the dust,' and not without reason. Gangs of dirty
children ran the streets, stealing whatever the beggars couldn't get for free.
Excrement, covered in flies and crawling with rats, was piled outside windows and in the entrances to alleys. Whole families lived under rickety
staircases or camped out in doorways. The houses weren't much better.
They were dark and stiflingly hot. Bricks crumbled right out of the walls.
Why the people didn't just leave the city behind, Uruk couldn't figure. No
place in the world was as bad as this—not even the inside of a grave.

Uruk had come to the dust searching for thieves. Over the last few
days he'd heard rumors about a series of daring robberies, all inflicted on
a pair of rich families with compounds at the center of the city. Word had
it that these families, locked in an age-old feud of unknown origin, were

hiring thieves of unusual cunning to take revenge on each other, and that their agents had all the information as to how and where the burglaries were to be performed. But if anyone knew how to get hired for such a job, they wouldn't tell Uruk.

It was early afternoon and the temperature was still rising. He and the dog had been wandering the streets since just after sun-up, and the dog needed water. Unless they found something soon, they'd have to find shade and wait until the heat broke.

They made a few more random turns, fighting off petty traders at every corner. Uruk kept his eyes open for any and all criminal activity, but saw nothing of particular interest. Nothing professional. He was just about to call a halt when they happened on a small tavern.

It was just three walls and a canvas roof, with a saw-horse table set up at the back, but it was full of hard-looking men. They were drinking out of jars and watching traffic pass in the street. Whenever a woman happened by, even if she was old or obviously pregnant, the men hooted and shouted, made kissing noises and grabbed at themselves.

Four men sat in front of the tavern around an overturned box. They were playing a game of some kind. Tiles were stacked in six even piles, one in front of each player. The two remaining stacks were pushed to the side.

Uruk was halfway across the street, heading for the men around the box, when someone grabbed his wrist.

He spun around, and was surprised to see a woman. She was a fortune-teller, Uruk recognized. And like all fortune-tellers in Kan-Puram, she wore a veil over her eyes and a thin, nearly transparent, sleeveless robe. Around one arm, just above her elbow, she wore a copper band.

"Let go of me," Uruk said to her.

She did. "You've got terrible clouds over you," she said, whispering so only Uruk could hear. "The gods haven't been kind."

Uruk glanced at the tavern. An old man was slumped against the far wall, a long string of drool running from his lower lip. A naked little boy sat on the ground beside him, scratching miserably. Ringworm bloomed over the boy's chest. "Have the gods been good to anyone?" Uruk asked.

The fortune-teller frowned. "Their lives are terrible," she agreed. "But they have friends and families at least. Look." She pointed at a woman strolling down the street, nursing a baby and leading a toddler by the hand. "What do you have?"

Uruk walked away.

"I can answer all kinds of questions," the fortune-teller said, running to keep up.

"Any question?" Uruk asked.

A lock of black hair fell out of her veil. She brushed it aside. Her hands were clean, Uruk noticed. Cleaner than he'd have thought possible for someone in the dust.

"I want to know about thieves," he said. The men in front of the tavern were watching them, Uruk observed. Their game had ground almost to a halt.

The fortune-teller pursed her lips. "Why do you want to know about them?"

Uruk didn't answer.

"You have bad omens about you," she said. "But they can be changed."

Uruk had no intention of discussing destiny, omens, or fate with anyone, much less a fake fortune-teller from the dust. "I want to know about thieves," he reiterated, glancing at the men in the tavern again. "Should I ask them?"

"They don't know anything. They're here to forget, not teach."

"Then where should I look? Where are the thieves?"

She held out her hand. "I can tell you as much as anyone, but my time costs."

Uruk had a few small pieces of silver. He'd stolen them—and as many pieces of copper—his first day in the city, from a merchant headed south with a wagon full of grain. The copper was already spent. The silver soon would be. He took his purse out of his satchel and fished through it.

While he searched, the dog sniffed the fortune-teller's toes. She was wearing sandals, Uruk saw. He couldn't remember having seen another pair in the dust. Not one.

Uruk put a tiny piece of silver, not much larger than a kernel of barley, into the fortune-teller's palm.

"This will buy you more than enough information," she said, slipping the silver into a pocket in her robe. "The professional thieves are that way." She pointed west, toward the edge of the city. "I couldn't tell you who they are, or where to find them—even if I did know—but I will say that they aren't in the dust. There's no profit here."

"What do you know about the burglaries?"

"Which burglaries?"

"The ones from last week—you must have heard about them."

"Last week?" She laughed. "The last year. Last century. As long as there have been rich people and thieves in Kan-Puram, there have been burglaries. Right now there are probably a hundred merchants looking for a thief to steal some trinket or other, and a thousand thieves hoping to get hired."

Uruk shook his head. This was a lot to take in. Suddenly, the whole city seemed to him a new and amazing place. Depressing, but amazing.

"In Kan-Puram we say that revenge profits a rich man once, but a thief twice," she explained. "It goes on forever."

"Why do the town elders not stop it?"

"There are no town elders. There are priests, dozens of them, but they can't do much. The rich provide for themselves and the poor suffer." She shrugged. "That's the way it's always been."

The fortune-teller was still talking when, seemingly out of nowhere, something slammed against the backs of Uruk's legs. He'd been so focused on his conversation, and on the fact that he was finally getting someone to tell him about the situation in Kan-Puram, that he hadn't even noticed a woman pushing a wheelbarrow full of rotten wood down the alley behind him.

"Watch where you're going," the fortune-teller hissed at her. "You just struck my customer." Uruk was so astonished, first at having been struck, and then at the fortune-teller's response, that he didn't even think to speak up.

The wood-monger sneered. "Step aside, you great black beast," she bellowed, knocking the wheelbarrow against Uruk's knee again. A half-dozen sticks fell off the front and the woman cursed. "Now look what you did."

The dog growled, the fur rising on his neck and shoulders. Uruk pulled him aside.

"Control your bitch," the wood-monger said, "or my son will butcher it up quick." She licked her lips.

"Ignore her," the fortune-teller said, taking Uruk by the hand. She pointed at the tavern. "I probably shouldn't tell you this, but there are rooms in the back. Once in a while, thieves hide out in them. I don't know if there are any there now, but you could check."

Uruk listened to what she had to say, but his attention was still partly on the wood-monger. She'd picked up her dropped sticks, and was rearranging her load so that nothing more would fall out. The dog watched her every move. When she came too close, he nipped the air at her ankles.

"Curse your hide," she croaked. She glared at Uruk. "If it bites me, you'll pay." She shook a fist in his face. It was dirty from handling the wood, but the nails looked healthy and even. And she had very few scars. She wasn't as old as she looked.

The fortune-teller squeezed Uruk's hand. "If you go to a tavern called the Bronze Cauldron," she continued, "ask for a man named Sharik. It's only three streets down."

She'd only just mentioned the Bronze Cauldron when Uruk felt a tug at his shoulder. There was a hand in his satchel. Someone was robbing him. It took every ounce of control he could muster not to lash backward. But he managed. This was what he'd been waiting for. This was why he had come to the dust.

He felt the hand snake past the bundle of cord and the dagger, searching for his purse. It was hard not to jump as it dug ever deeper, even brushing against his left buttock. And then, just as suddenly as it had appeared, the hand was gone. No doubt his purse was gone with it, Uruk thought.

The fortune-teller grinned. "What else can I tell you?" she asked.

It wasn't her, Uruk felt certain. Both of her hands had been visible the entire time.

"Is there a leader among the thieves?" he asked. But Uruk didn't listen to her answer. He was watching the wood-monger out of the corner of his eye. She was still pawing at her wheelbarrow. And the dog was guarding her very closely. She couldn't have gotten close enough.

The pickpocket must have come up behind him, Uruk reasoned. He looked over his shoulder. There was the usual flow of traffic, but nothing close.

". . . so the thieves don't need leadership," the fortune-teller was saying. As she rattled on, the wood-monger finished loading her wheelbarrow and wandered off toward the tavern. Uruk watched her push between a pair of young girls, neither more than twelve years old. "Out of the way, sluts," she growled. There was something on her upper arm, Uruk noticed, rubbing against the inside of her sleeve. He bet it was a copper band.

"No more questions," he said to the fortune-teller, cutting her off midsentence.

"None?"

Uruk thanked her for her time and the fortune-teller smiled. He watched her amble past the men sitting around the box. Their game had resumed, but still they kept glancing in his direction. Big smiles spread over their faces. They were laughing at him.

When the fortune-teller was gone, Uruk took a small piece of leather out of the bottom of his satchel and held it out to the dog, who sniffed it over with interest. "Got the scent?" he whispered. Uruk had soaked his purse in a mixture of melioc resin and goat urine the night before. He'd soaked the little square of leather in the same stuff.

The dog started away, nose to the ground. He led Uruk south, only pausing for a moment as they reached an intersection. Uruk wasn't concerned about him losing the scent. If he'd used pure goat urine, the dog might have gotten confused. But mixed with melioc? No chance.

Uruk stayed close as the dog trotted around a corner and into an alley, nimbly leaping over the filth heaped at the entrance. 'To hunt is to worship,' he remembered. It was something Numa used to say. 'The greatest prayers are in the steps of the chase.'

The alley was narrow, barely wider than Uruk was tall, and twisted around a series of crumbling walls. Remnants of an earlier slum, Uruk guessed, pieces of an earlier dust. The people who lived in the surrounding houses had flung their waste out the windows, letting it pile up forever as a lure to the rats. It was almost as though they wanted the vermin, and the disease that accompanied such creatures. Uruk was beginning to think that the residents of the dust were bent on their own destruction.

The dog was still following the scent when Uruk heard a voice coming from just ahead. It sounded female.

"Far enough, Dog," Uruk whispered, scratching him behind the ears.

The dog licked his palm and started down the alley again. Once the hunt was on, it was hard to pull him back.

"Stay," Uruk said, pointing at a shady spot next to the collapsed rear wall of a house. The dog sat down reluctantly. He didn't like Uruk to get too far away.

Uruk smoothed the fur on the top of his head. "I will be right here," he whispered. Then he carefully picked his way to the end of the wall and peered around.

A pregnant woman stood a few dozen paces down the alley. She was wearing a filthy canvas tunic and breeches, just like any lower class person in Kan-Puram. Her arms were crossed over her belly and she was humming a light, airy tune. She had Uruk's purse clutched in one hand.

Moments later, a second woman emerged from around a corner further up the alley. It was the wood-monger, still pushing her wheelbarrow. And right behind her was the fortune-teller.

"How much did he have?" the wood-monger asked.

The pregnant woman handed her the purse. "Just a few pieces of silver."

"It's all here?" The wood-monger opened the purse and looked inside. Then she handed it to the fortune-teller, who glanced in the bag, shrugged, and handed it back. "It had better be," the wood-monger sneered.

Thieves were notorious for their suspicious natures, and for being outraged if they thought they'd been robbed—even if they'd lost nothing more valuable than a few grains of sand. Uruk was unusual in that respect. He stole the silver, and the silver was, in due time, stolen from him. That was life. Everything is eaten in its turn. You can prolong the end, but never fight it off completely. The only real question was how you were eaten, and by what.

"Fine." The wood-monger thrust the purse into her pocket, scowling all the while. "That was a poor take, barely worth the effort." The fortune-teller hung her head. "I can see why you chose him, I might have done the same, but it was a poor take. Terribly poor." She scratched the back of her head, thinking over what they should do next.

"We have time enough for one or two more hits. Then we had better get back to the Snail's Horn," the pregnant woman said.

The wood-monger nodded. "First, I think we should change roles. Strip them off."

All three women began pulling off their clothes. "Should I take off the hump?" the pregnant woman asked. She pulled her tunic off over her head, revealing that she wasn't pregnant at all. A leather contraption was lashed to her belly, fastening just under her breasts. She also had a copper band around her arm, Uruk noted, the same as the other two women.

"No, keep it on," the wood-monger said. "It's too hard to get placed." When all three were naked, the women traded clothes. The wood-monger put on the fortune-teller's robe and veil. The pregnant woman became the wood-monger, though still pregnant, and the fortune-teller became an ordinary woman.

The wood-monger—now fortune-teller—looked the other two women over. They must have been too clean, because she picked up a handful of dirt and rubbed it on their faces and hands. "Good," she said at last.

Uruk waited until they were out of sight before waving at the dog to follow.

They trailed the thieves all the way to the center of Kan-Puram.

Just after sundown, the wood-monger ditched her wheelbarrow in an alley. Since then they had stopped to wash, change clothes—discarding both hump and veil—and trade a piece of copper for some kind of meat on a stick. Uruk's stomach growled as he watched them eat.

When they were finished, the women crossed over a canal marking the edge of the old city and started north. The canals had been dug centuries before, as a defensive border. Since then, the city had engulfed them in every direction.

The thieves were moving faster now. No doubt closing in on the Snail's Horn, and getting excited. Between the three of them they'd managed to collect a fair pile of metal, most of it from merchants and traders new to Kan-Puram, though Uruk had seen them pick the pocket of an old woman as well. She'd just traded a suckling pig for a few flecks of copper and a couple of duck eggs. A poor trade even before she'd lost the copper, Uruk judged. He hoped she wasn't desperate.

Uruk caught a glimpse of the thieves as they made their way around a corner. They were laughing about something. A moment later, Uruk heard a door swing open, followed by the sounds of voices—lots of voices. He sprinted to catch up, but by the time he rounded the corner all three women were gone.

The dog wasn't fooled though. He walked directly to a heavy wooden door and sniffed at the latch. It didn't look like anything special, no different from any other on that street. But Uruk guessed that every thief in Kan-Puram would recognize that door. On the wall above it was a wooden snail. It was a little larger than the Maidenhead of Kallah, and had been painted red to match the rest of the building. Most people would walk right past it, never even suspecting.

Uruk was still looking at the snail when a man leaned out of a second-story window overhead. He was dressed in fine wool, with a silk collar and cuffs, but he was a slave. A silver band had been fixed round his neck as a symbol of his bondage. While Uruk watched, the slave fit a torch, dripping with melioc sap, into a copper sconce beside the window. The burning sap helped to keep mosquitoes away. Torches like it burned in the windows and doorways of every major estate in Kan-Puram. When he'd finished, the slave glanced down at Uruk, smirked, and then disappeared back inside.

Uruk opened the door.

The Snail's Horn was a tavern. It had a long counter against one wall and a series of dark alcoves set into the opposite. Uruk blinked hard as he walked between the tables. The room was intensely dim, and filled with smoke from the torches ensconced over the bar. Holes had been cut through the back wall to let it out, but much of the smoke still hung.

Uruk sat at a small table against the far wall, and the dog lay down at his feet. The women they'd followed were nowhere to be seen.

A group of men was sitting around a table in the corner, passing tiles back and forth. It looked like they were playing the same game Uruk had seen in the dust. The dealer was an older man, gray sprinkled generously through his hair. He glanced over at Uruk as he handed tiles to the other players.

Uruk's eyes were growing accustomed to the darkness, but he still couldn't see what was happening in the alcoves. He could just make out the shapes of people, but he couldn't say whether they were men or women, or what they might be doing. A young woman leaned out of the closest alcove, stared at him for a moment, and then settled back. She had a copper band on her upper arm.

The bartender was glaring at him as well, so Uruk motioned for a drink. He had no metal to pay for it, but would address that problem when the time came.

Just as the bartender handed Uruk a tall cup of what appeared to be mud drowning in urine, the door opened and a pair of prostitutes stepped inside. A few of the men hooted, but nothing like Uruk had seen in the dust.

"Who controls the women?" Uruk asked. He lifted his cup and choked down a few swallows of the bitter liquid inside. Uruk hated beer.

He'd first encountered it in the palace of the Prince of Beenar. The Prince brewed it himself, using grain he'd imported from Ur. The beer in Kan-Puram was thicker and more powerful, but Uruk wasn't sure that was something to brag about. When he'd had enough to be polite, he shoved his cup away. Even the smell was wretched.

"A former patron," the bartender replied. "He sends them around once a fortnight. Regulars don't drink as much when they're here, but I can't run them off."

Uruk nodded toward the nearest alcove. "Who are they?"

The bartender frowned. "You're looking for action, is that it? Want to move up and play with your betters?"

"Careful," Uruk said. "I may have betters in this world, but you are not one of them." The dog must have picked up on the tone of Uruk's voice, because he let out a low growl. "Dog thinks none too highly of you either."

"If you want trouble, go elsewhere." The bartender's eyes shifted nervously. "Patrons here are jealous of a new face. You have to have a permit to trade in the Horn, if you see what I mean."

"And where do I get this permit?" Uruk asked.

But the bartender wouldn't answer. He shook his head and walked back behind the counter.

Uruk crossed his arms and waited. He suspected the chance for a permit would come to him. He didn't have to wait long.

A woman strode across the room, headed right for him. She was short and heavy, her skin pocked and greasy. She wasn't wearing a copper band, Uruk noticed, but she did have a silver bracelet. He didn't know whether that was meaningful or not. She passed the tables grouped in the center of the room without a glance.

The dog lurched to his feet as she approached. "Easy," Uruk whispered, patting him on the haunches. The dog was particularly uneasy around women, Uruk had noticed.

"Don't like the beer?" the woman asked.

"Take it," Uruk offered.

"Thanks." She took a long sip, then wiped her mouth with her forearm. "Haven't seen you in here before. You some kind of thief?"

Uruk hesitated. This was obviously a set-up. As such, it might be better to keep a low profile. After all, the bartender seemed to think he was in danger, and he'd have been around long enough to know. On the other hand, this might be the best chance he'd ever have to make a name for himself. Uruk glanced around the room quickly. Many of the other customers were watching, he noted. Subtlety had never been his strong-point.

"Possibly," he said at last.

"Well are you?"

"I could be."

"Can you get in and out of a place without raising an alarm?"

"Sometimes." Uruk smiled. "But I can always get in and out."

The dog leaned in and sniffed the woman over, starting at her toes and moving quickly up to her crotch. "Hey." She tried to push him away. Uruk thought about calling the dog back, but decided against it. Eventually, the dog got bored and sat back down.

"Do you take him with you?" the woman grumbled, smoothing the front of her breeches.

"If he wants to go."

She pouted. "I'll let you know if I hear of something."

The woman turned to leave but Uruk grabbed her wrist. "Hold on," he said. A hush fell over the room.

"I told you I'd let you know."

Uruk let go of her. "I have a question or two," he said, leaning back in his chair.

She looked at him, hands on her hips. "What?"

"Who is that man?" Uruk's eyes flickered toward the nearest alcove.

"That's no man," she said. "It's the Princess."

"Is she the head thief?"

"No. She just runs some small-time pickpockets."

"Who usually roughs up newcomers?"

The woman frowned. "I don't know what you're talking about. I'm looking for a thief, just like I told you."

That wasn't what she'd said, Uruk remembered. She'd asked him if he was a thief, nothing more. "Why not ask the Princess, or one of hers?" he asked.

"She's small time. I'm looking for a big strong man."

Uruk nodded. "You can go," he said.

The woman's eyes narrowed. She was just about to say something, Uruk was sure. Something angry. But instead, she turned on her heel and strutted away. Uruk watched her stomp all the way across the tavern and out the door.

The bartender reappeared at Uruk's elbow. "All right stranger," he stammered. "Time for you to go." He glanced nervously at the door. "No charge this round, but you've got to get out before there's trouble."

"Bring me a cup of water," Uruk said. "And make sure there is nothing floating in it."

The bartender went pale. For the first time, Uruk noticed the red veins spread like a web over his nose and cheeks.

"A cup of water," Uruk said again. He watched as the bartender walked back across the tavern and started wiping off a cup.

Talk picked up around the tables after that. In the corner, the dealer handed a pair of knucklebones to one of the players. No one looked at Uruk or the dog. Even the eyes in the alcove were turned to other things. All the same, Uruk felt as though a silence had descended over his table. It reminded him of something his grandmother used to say. 'When it feels quiet at a campfire full of talkers, the talk is about you.'

The dog curled up on the floor again. Uruk reached down and rubbed the back of his neck. "Stay alert, Dog," he whispered.

Just as his water arrived, the door to the tavern slammed open and a man with a mustache and thick, meaty arms and legs swaggered in. A long knife stuck out of his belt. He surveyed the room quickly, finally stopping on Uruk.

Uruk set the cup of water on the floor for the dog.

The thief covered the distance to their table in a handful of strides. "You and me have business outside," he grumbled, clutching the hilt of his knife. He handled it like a butcher, fingers wrapped over the edge of the sheath as well as the handle.

"Step back," Uruk said, not even looking the man in the face. The dog growled, ready to tear into the thief at a word. There'd already been far too much hunting without a proper kill for the dog's taste.

The thief put both hands down on the table and leaned forward. He had a silver bracelet around one wrist. "I said," spittle dotted Uruk's forehead, "I think we have business—*outside*."

In a flash, Uruk grabbed hold of the man's wrists and pulled. The thief, who'd been resting his weight on his hands, crashed face first into the tabletop.

Then, just as fast, Uruk kicked the man's feet out from under him and rolled him onto the floor. He landed on his shoulder and let out a sharp groan.

Uruk stood up and casually made his way toward the exit. The dog followed right behind him.

Still slumped on the floor, the thief put a finger to his lips. He was bleeding. It had all happened so fast that he wasn't even really angry—yet. It was only after he looked around the room and saw the older men chuckling over their cups that he really got mad. "Where is he?" he bellowed. Then he saw Uruk, just slipping through the door.

"Well, are you going after him, Melesh?" the bartender asked.

Uruk waited outside. He was astonished at how long it took. No doubt the oaf was even stupider than he appeared.

Finally, the door slammed open and Melesh charged out. He was running, expecting to have to catch a fleeing man. Uruk's fist landed flush with his cheek and, once again, Melesh crashed to the ground.

This time, it took him no more than a second to assess the situation. He rolled to his knees, reaching for his knife with both hands. Uruk kicked him in the chest and Melesh went over backwards, his knife skittering away.

"I'll kill you," Melesh wheezed, still struggling to sit up.

"Dog," Uruk said.

The dog leapt on Melesh, shoving him right back down. His teeth clenched over and over on the thief's leg, drawing blood every time. "Kallah's teats!" Melesh howled, as the dog moved up and started on his hands and arms.

Uruk calmly strode over and picked up Melesh's knife.

The door to the Snail's Horn swung open and the patrons filed out, forming a ring around the combatants. A few cheered for Melesh—one or two cheered for the dog—and the rest just cheered. This was not a new occurrence. Men killed each other in the street nearly every night. But no matter how often it happened, the people of Kan-Puram, and especially the Snail's Horn, were pleased to watch.

"That is enough, Dog," Uruk said at last.

The dog reluctantly backed away, blood dripping from his teeth. Melesh was on his elbows and knees, curled up to protect his most vulnerable parts. Uruk couldn't help thinking of the image of the naked woman he'd seen painted on the wall in the dust.

Uruk grabbed Melesh by the hair and yanked his head back. "Is this yours?" he asked, holding the knife in front of Melesh's face.

Truth be told, Uruk had no intention of killing Melesh. If he'd wanted to kill him, he would have just thrust his sword through the thief's guts as he barged out of the tavern. Uruk wanted to make sure the crowd would remember him. He wanted his permit, as the bartender had called it.

"I am Uruk, the hunter," he said. "This is your knife?" He twisted it back and forth so that the blade shone in the torchlight. "Answer me."

Melesh nodded. His lips were trembling.

Uruk shoved Melesh back onto all fours, tossed the knife over his shoulder, and started back toward the Snail's Horn.

He was almost to the door when a man stepped into his path. "You're quite a fighter," he said. It was the dealer from the game in the corner. His gray hairs shone like silver in the starlight. He pointed at the beaten thief, just rising from the ground, blood dripping off the ends of his fingers and from a half-dozen deep wounds in his legs. "You and your dog didn't have much trouble with Melesh."

"You want a fight, too?" Uruk asked.

"No." The older man crossed his arms. "I'm sure you're as much as you appear."

The dog growled and Uruk reached for his sword. "Somehow, we do not feel entirely safe," he said.

"No need to draw that magnificent blade. I'm the one you've been looking for. I am Jared." He smiled, clearly expecting his name to be recognized. But Uruk was still new to the city. Though he'd learned a lot, he'd never heard the name Jared.

"I am the King of Thieves," Jared continued.

Uruk nodded, remembering what Baluch had told him about thieves becoming kings. He just hadn't realized that it was an official position.

"Tell me Uruk, where do you come from? You're obviously new to Kan-Puram."

Uruk frowned. "Have you ever seen a jungle?" he asked.

Jared shook his head. "No. But I know what one is."

"Mine was far to the south, somewhere. I am not sure I could even find it again."

"Well, you've made yourself welcome here." Jared smiled warmly. "You beat Melesh soundly enough." Saying his name must have reminded

Jared that the injured thief needed attention. "Make sure Melesh gets help," he said. "Take him to my house." Uruk didn't know who Jared was talking to, but he had little doubt the order would be followed.

The Snail's Horn was strangely quiet as they made their way back to Uruk's table and sat down. The rest of the patrons filed in behind them.

"Nikal." Jared motioned to the bartender, who was wiping a cup with a dirty piece of wool. "We'll have a few drinks, then Uruk here will run an errand for me." He winked.

Nikal quickly poured two cups of beer and brought them to the table.

"Tell me," Jared said. "How did you find us?"

"I followed three pickpockets from the dust. They stole my purse, but I considered it a decent trade."

"Pickpockets in the dust? Were they wearing anything unusual?"

Uruk nodded. "All three wore copper bands." He pointed at his own arm, just above the elbow.

"The Princess." Jared frowned. "The slums are supposed to be off-limits to thieves. We leave them for the children to pick over. Remember that."

"I never steal from poor people," Uruk said. He glanced at the alcove, but it was empty. Apparently even the Princess had gone out to see the fight.

"Good enough." Jared leaned toward Uruk. "There's a knife. It's a lot like the one you took from Melesh, but encrusted with precious stones. You can get it for me tomorrow." He whispered so that the rest of the room wouldn't hear.

Uruk squinted at Jared. He didn't want to offend the King of Thieves, but thought it was best to come to an understanding now. "I work for myself," he said. "I will not wear a bracelet." Jared leaned back in his seat. "I can profit better by waiting to hear the needs of some rich man."

"I don't think you understand, Uruk," Jared said, grinning. He picked up his beer, took a long draught, and motioned to Nikal for another. "I am a very rich man."

CHAPTER 2

Fire of the Faithful

ANDER LEANED AGAINST THE TEMPLE WALL, WATCHING THE LATE
evening traffic stroll by. There wasn't much to see. A handful of dirty men
rushing home for supper. A pair of slaves hauling a wheelbarrow load of
kitchen garbage into the alley next to their master's house. Some naked
children sitting in an upstairs window, kicking their legs and spitting into
the street below.

A sliver of moon hung over the buildings at the eastern end of the
street. 'Bad fishing,' Ander thought. His stepfather would never fish until
the moon was at least half full. Fish like to dance in the moonlight, he
used to say. The brighter the moon, the harder they dance. Some morn-
ings, he claimed, the fish were so tired he could just pluck them off the
bottom with his spear. There must have been something to it. Ander
remembered days when his stepfather would come home before noon, his
basket already brimming with shabbout, catfish and carp. Ander always
had to clean them, but he didn't mind. It was easy work, and if he did a
good job he'd get one of the fish.

Ander remembered his stepmother, coating the fish with honey and
flour and roasting them over the fire. The smell was like a deep breath of
summer.

He was still thinking about fish when the front door of the house
across the street opened and a young woman shuffled out, buckets swinging from either fist.

They must have been heavy because she was barely out the door
before setting them down to rest. Ander watched her wipe the perspiration off her forehead with the back of her wrist, leaving a dirty gray
smudge. Sweat had soaked through her tunic, forming dark ovals under
her arms and beneath each breast.

Ander nodded to her. "Nice evening," he said.

The woman reluctantly nodded back.

"Bad fishing though." Ander smiled.

She stared at him an instant longer, a puzzled look on her face, then dashed down the street. The buckets banged against the backs of her legs with every step.

It was his hood, Ander thought. His hood and cloak. People had been staring at him from the moment he put them on. Women pulled their children close and rushed away. Men sneered.

Ander began wearing the hood soon after arriving in Kan-Puram. He'd been searching for a hat to replace the one he'd lost, but was having no luck. The only hats he could find were either already on someone's head, or in the back of a basket-weaver's shop, and Ander had nothing to trade. Another afternoon was coming on, and the sun was boiling hot, when he happened onto a brown wool blanket hanging on a clothesline next to an open window. The slave-girl set to watch the drying clothes was asleep, so Ander took it. Using the blade of a broken kitchen knife, which he'd found rusting away in a rubbish pile, Ander cut some long threads from one corner of the blanket. Like most slaves, Ander was proficient at mending his clothes with minimal tools. In no time, he'd sewed one end of the blanket closed, forming a rough hood. Then he added a pair of ties so that he could cinch it round his neck. It looked bizarre—even Ander had to admit that—and was terribly hot, but it kept the sun off his hands, face, and the tops of his feet. Plus, unlike a hat, the cloak wouldn't come off until he took it off—something he hadn't done yet.

Ander was still staring after the woman with the buckets when a hand gripped his shoulder. Without thinking, he spun around, knocking the hand away and reaching for his dagger—a prize he'd discovered just that morning. The blade was unusually thin, with a hooked tip and a large hand guard. From the moment he saw it, Ander knew he had to have it.

"Easy," Isin said, backing away. "It's only me."

Ander had one fist knotted in Isin's jerkin, just below his throat. Slowly, reluctantly, he let go. "I've been waiting a long time," he complained.

"They had a lot of questions." Isin smoothed out the wrinkles left by Ander's fingers. He was a middle-aged man, a high-ranking priest from the local temple of Kallah, with deep lines in his forehead and around his eyes. Nestled against his chest was a small clay amulet fastened to a long chain. It had been carved into the likeness of his goddess—a pregnant woman with enormous breasts and thighs.

"What questions?" Ander asked.

"About you mostly." Isin shrugged. "They were afraid you might be. . . ."

"Not quite right?" This wasn't the first time they'd heard it.

"I vouched for you," Isin assured him. "I told them you weren't feeling well."

"Which is why I'm so pale." It was an excuse Ander had used himself, many times. Never with much success.

Isin nodded. "Now we have to hurry," he said, glancing at the moon. "It's getting late." He turned west, heading toward the center of the city.

"How many men did they promise?" As usual, Ander had no idea where Isin was leading. It made very little difference. They went from temple to temple, trying to enlist men to serve in the army. Isin did most of the talking while Ander stood in the shadows. Eventually, Isin would ask him to tell his story, which Ander did, always pausing to focus on the most brutal incidents. He'd told about the Falcon's death so often that he almost believed he'd seen it with his own eyes. Every so often, one of the temple officials would stop him to ask a question. Ander always tried his best to answer, no matter how inane or irrelevant the question might be. Then, when he was done, they'd send him outside and discuss the whole matter again. Ander knew it was so they could talk about him, but also suspected that they thought him too stupid to follow the line of their arguments. It didn't bother him much. He'd had the same experience all his life, and actually preferred to be outside anyway. Ander always felt a bit claustrophobic inside those enormous brick and stone buildings. He just couldn't imagine how they could stand up under so much weight.

"No men," Isin said. "No fighting men anyway." They made their way along a narrow street, running parallel to one of the canals.

"None?" Ander asked.

Isin shook his head. "They promised to organize a group of porters to bring food and water to the troops—"

"Waste of time," Ander grunted.

"Not entirely. We'll need porters, and the Creator is a powerful—"

"Where now?" Ander cut Isin off before he could start on another round of religious nonsense. During their short time together, Ander had heard more than enough pseudo-magical gibberish to last the rest of his life.

"We're meeting Doran," Isin said. He pointed at a small foot-bridge, all but engulfed by the shadows of a three-story house. "He's waiting for us."

Doran was the other leader of Isin's temple. He was younger than Isin and in better shape, though his hair was already streaked with gray. It gave him an air of authority. He was also the more secular of the two, known for taking his ministry to the streets while Isin huddled in his sanctum, pondering the arcana of the godly soul.

While Ander and Isin had been visiting temples and recruiting troops, Doran was collecting armaments and supplies. Thus far he'd been extraordinarily successful. Half the coppersmiths in the city were busy churning out maces and two-handed pikes.

Ander first met Doran during his third night in Kan-Puram. He'd been trying to get into the larger estates, hoping to tell his story to the rich merchants, but seldom saw anyone more important than a house slave. Finally, disappointed and hungry, he'd wandered to the edge of the dust. There he stumbled onto the temple of Kallah. At first, he mistook it for a warehouse. All he could see from the street was a flat, featureless wall and a handful of small windows. Ander was about to pass by when he noticed a pair of men standing in front of the door, dressed in match-ing jerkins and breeches. They were offering blessings to the poor. No food or clean water—just blessings. Ander recognized them as priests right away.

On the off chance that they'd listen, Ander told the priests all about the Niphilim, his escape from the mines and the fall of Akshur. The younger of the two wanted to send him away, but Doran believed Ander's story. He even invited Ander into their temple, gave him some stew and a crust of bread, and introduced him to Isin. They hadn't rested since.

"Why?" Ander asked at last. "Why are we going to met Doran?" He was getting tired of recruiting a dozen men here and a hundred there. The idea that they'd spent the last few hours working to enlist a few porters was particularly galling.

"Doran's arranged a meeting with one of the priests of Moloch."

"Another of these little cults?"

Isin laughed. "It's the richest temple in Kan-Puram."

"Why didn't we go there first?" Ander asked, annoyed.

"Their High Priest is an old man named Kilimon. He was an adventurer in his youth, some say a thief. But as he aged, Kilimon turned against his old ways. He's against violence of any kind. We doubted he'd support us in any way, so Doran has been trying to build support for us by other means."

"What other means?"

"He's been meeting with the priest next in line to Kilimon. Shamash is more forward-looking than his master. More easily reasoned with."

"Has it worked?"

"Not terribly well." Isin shrugged. "Shamash wants to meet you. If he believes your story, he'll take us to his temple."

"And if not, Kan-Puram dies," Ander said.

Isin nodded.

Kilimon sat upon his stool in the hall of prayer, eyes closed, trying to meditate. He wasn't having much luck. One of his legs was asleep and his back was sore. He shifted in his seat, but couldn't get comfortable.

For the last two weeks he'd been pondering the relationship between the mind and the body. It seemed clear that one was the self and the other was not. But what did that say about the gods? Did they have bodies? And if so, were their bodies like those of a human—subject to damage, age and corruption? Kilimon wasn't sure. Strangely, the hundreds, maybe thousands of stories he'd heard and memorized contradicted each other on this point. It was a difficult problem—one that needed solving.

Unfortunately, Kilimon was having a hard time focusing his mind. As soon as a thought entered, it slipped away, like water through a pot of sand. Worse, some of the stories Kilimon used to know were no longer there, and the harder he tried to hang onto them, the more they seemed to want to wriggle away.

Kilimon let out a long, slow breath, feeling the air rush over the whiskers around his mouth. 'Need to calm down,' he thought. 'Calm down and get comfortable.' In more then ten years of meditating on this same spot, Kilimon had only leaned against the wall a handful of times, but for some reason it seemed just the thing to do. He sighed as he leaned back and stretched his legs out in front of him.

The nuns were just finishing their prayers. Most nights, Kilimon barely noticed them. But with his mind so distracted, he couldn't help listening as they moved through the room, snuffing out ornamental candles and refilling jars of incense. He even felt one of them tip-toe past him and blow out the candles on the altar. They always turned away from him as they lifted their veils, though Kilimon hadn't been tempted to look for years. He wondered if they did it to protect their modesty or his.

When the candles were all extinguished, the nuns began to file out. They were headed for their quarters and a short night's rest. Kilimon listened to the creak of the door and the swish of their robes. They'd be up again before sunrise, ready to start the day's work. The nuns did most everything on the temple grounds, from cooking and cleaning to counseling widows and young mothers and making repairs. One of their most important jobs was to provide medical care for the recently baptized. They even maintained the gardens. How they managed to get it all done, Kilimon couldn't imagine. Over the years he'd come to believe that women were the stronger sex. Often he'd wished he had half their energy.

The door shut a final time and, for a moment at least, the hall of prayer was still. Kilimon smiled, thinking he'd finally be able to descend into his mind, when something grazed the top of his head.

Kilimon opened his eyes and looked around. Torches were mounted in ornamental sconces at each corner of the room. They'd go out on their own eventually, but not until long after Kilimon had retired to bed. Flitting over the torch in the southeast corner, just to the left of the door, was a bat.

It was one of the tiny species that made homes on the under sides of bridges. At night, the streets around the canals were rife with them.

Kilimon watched as the bat flapped from wall to wall, searching for an exit. Finally, after thoroughly exploring the entire room, it hooked its feet into a crack in one of the roof supports and relaxed.

After grooming its face and ears, the bat wrapped a wing over its head and hung motionless. 'A natural ascetic,' Kilimon thought, not without a twinge of jealousy. Tomorrow, one of the nuns would have to catch it and put it outside, but for now the bat was welcome to join his meditation.

Kilimon had just begun to settle his mind again when someone knocked at the door. 'Peculiar,' he thought. He wasn't expecting visitors at this late hour. His habit was to spend an hour in quiet meditation before retiring to bed, and everyone living in the temple compound knew it. Still, the bat had already disturbed him, and so he wasn't sorry to see Shamash lean his head through the door.

"Master?" Shamash asked.

"Come in." Kilimon stood up to greet him.

Shamash strode into the hall. He was a tall man, narrow through the shoulders and face, and had the energy and ambition of a teenager. When Kilimon was gone, Shamash would become High Father, a fact that Kilimon usually found extraordinarily comforting. The other priests joked, saying Shamash wouldn't stop there, that he'd want to be god next, but Kilimon liked him. Shamash was overly fond of drink—his breath routinely smelled of beer—and much too willing to spend the temple's gold on his own comforts, but he was popular with the faithful and active throughout the city. Kilimon had often said that Shamash could fill both coffers and pews without help from god or man.

"Welcome." Kilimon held a hand out to Shamash, who took it, kissing both knuckles and palm. His beard prickled on Kilimon's skin.

"I'm sorry to have disturbed your meditations, Master," Shamash said.

"Nonsense. In fact, you weren't the first."

Shamash blinked. "I don't. . . ." he stammered. "Is there someone . . . ?"

"Look." Kilimon pointed at the bat. "It came in just before you did." He paused, hoping it would spread its wings. But the bat just hung there. "We owe a lot to the bat," Kilimon continued. "It keeps the insects off us throughout the year. You know, I've been thinking of taking one as a pet. It could eat the mosquitoes that buzz around my room. Maybe I should get one of the nuns to take this one upstairs."

"I'm sorry, Master," Shamash said. "But I've come on an urgent matter."

"Have you? I thought you'd long since given up on my poor council."

"Master, there are terrible things happening in the outside world." Shamash gestured at the door, as though the whole city were waiting in the garden. But that wasn't what attracted Kilimon's attention. As Shamash raised his arm, the neck of his robe fell open to reveal a pendant as big around as a man's fist. Even in the dim torchlight it was radiant. A sun of burnished gold overlaid by a silver crescent moon. And at the center, a single green jewel. If it was an emerald, as he guessed it must be, it was the largest Kilimon had ever seen. The value of such a pendant was almost beyond imagining.

Kilimon was shocked. Shamash had always spent freely, but nothing like this. How had he even gotten such a jewel? Kilimon was embarrassed, both for the temple and for himself. If such things were happening here in the compound, under his very nose, what must the rest of Kan-Puram be like? "There are things happening within this temple that must be addressed first, I think."

Shamash lowered his arm and the pendant dropped out of sight. "The Niphilim have left the Withered Hills," he said. "They're in the Shinar, marching on Kan-Puram. They've crushed Akshur, enslaving men, women and children—"

"Who told you all of this?"

"Isin and Doran."

Kilimon's eyebrows raised. "And what does the temple of Kallah stand to gain from such a wild tale? Have you asked yourself that?"

"They introduced me to a man called Ander," Shamash continued, ignoring Kilimon's question. "He escaped both Dagonor and Akshur. His story is very powerful."

"Niphilim?" Kilimon scoffed. "They're nothing more than worshipers of dirt. Have you heard of their god?" He shook his head in derision. "They barely conquered the Kenanites. They don't have the numbers."

"They've captured the savages and are driving them at the city. You must see the wisdom in—"

"Wisdom? You would speak to me of wisdom?" Kilimon's embarrassment was quickly turning to anger. The worst part about all of this, he thought, was that Shamash seemed to have no idea how far from the path of righteousness he'd strayed. "Those who seek for wisdom bow to the gods . . . not the jeweler."

Shamash put a hand over his chest, clearly stung by Kilimon's comment. "Do the wise attack the man or his argument?" he asked.

Kilimon nearly cursed. In fact, he only avoided doing so by grinding his teeth.

"Isin and Doran are waiting outside. They brought Ander. I told them you'd listen to what they have to say." Shamash looked very pleased with himself. It wasn't often that someone reduced the High Father of the temple of Moloch to silence.

"Fine. Bring them in." Kilimon gestured for Shamash to fetch his companions, then went back to his stool and sat down. He was furious. More than he had been in a score of years. The pendant hidden beneath the folds of Shamash's garments was too much to be ignored. But his insolence—that was a personal blow to Kilimon's authority. Shamash had to be brought down, Kilimon reasoned. Both for his own sake, and for the future well-being of the temple.

Shamash went to the door and called to the men waiting outside.

As they stepped over the threshold, Isin and Doran both bowed.

"Thank you for seeing us, High Father," Doran said. He looked much as Kilimon remembered him, though maybe with a bit more gray in his hair.

"It is kind of you to receive us without notice," Isin echoed, bowing once more.

Ander neither bowed nor spoke. He stood to one side, wearing what looked to Kilimon like an old brown blanket tied under his chin with rags. His face was whiter than any Kilimon had ever seen. He couldn't help scowling as he stared at it. Ander scowled back.

"I see you feel free to bring a weapon into our hall of prayer." Kilimon pointed at the dagger hanging on Ander's hip. "You're obviously not among the faithful, but have you no respect?"

"I'm sorry if my knife offends you," Ander said. "But I won't take it off. I made an oath, to myself and to any god who'd listen. I won't go unarmed again until the Niphilim are destroyed."

"And you're the man to bring them down, no doubt."

"I've been their victim and their slave. Now I'll be their destroyer. Or die trying."

"Master," Shamash interjected. "This is Ander, the man I told you about. He escaped Dagonor and fought in the battle of Akshur. He wants to tell you about the Niphilim."

"Well then, young man," Kilimon said. "Tell us your tale."

Ander did just that. He told of his boyhood at the edge of the mountains north of Akshur, and of his capture—carefully describing Darius's body in full detail. He told of his years in the mine, and of his escape plan and how he'd put it into action, though he said nothing about using Kadim as a decoy. At first, Isin tried to interrupt—this was clearly not going the way he and Doran had envisioned—but Ander just kept talking. Finally, he described the battle of Akshur, the death of the Falcon and the ransacking of the town. When he was done, he crossed his arms and stood silent.

Kilimon waited for Isin or Doran to speak, but for some reason neither seemed particularly inclined. It was as though Ander had stolen the sun from their crops, as the old saying goes. "Is that all?" Kilimon asked at last. It came out in a harsher tone than he'd intended.

"It is not," Ander replied. "The Niphilim are marching. Their plan is to sweep over the entirety of the Shinar, killing or enslaving every man, woman and child in their path. Unless they're stopped here, in Kan-Puram, they will succeed."

Kilimon folded his hands in his lap.

"Master, it's as serious as it sounds," Shamash said. "The city is preparing for war. The rich have curtailed all feuds. Most of the other temples have already begun to assemble their faithful. Every able man is practicing in the northern fields." He pointed at Isin and Doran. "They've come to tell you about preparations that are already—"

"No," Kilimon said. "I do not wish to hear of preparations for war. Not yet." Shamash opened his mouth to argue, but Kilimon waved at him to be silent. "I wish to ask a few questions." The other men waited as he sat thinking. Finally, looking at the priests of Kallah, he began, "How do you know that what he says is true?"

"We sent a pair of young priests to make sure," Doran said. "The Niphilim are coming—slowly, but inexorably."

While Doran spoke, Kilimon kept an eye on Ander. If possible, his face went even whiter. Kilimon suspected that this was the first he'd heard of Doran's little scouting mission. "How many of your supporters will take the field?" Kilimon asked.

"About two thousand," Isin replied.

"And how many, all told? From all the temples and cults?"

"Maybe eight thousand."

"Eight thousand, eight hundred," Ander said.

"That doesn't sound like every available man to me," Kilimon said. He looked at Shamash, who scowled. "But maybe there are others? People without faith who'll fight at your side?"

"A few," Isin acknowledged. "The rich families have promised to send servants. Perhaps there could be a thousand more."

"And this is still Kan-Puram, if my mind does not escape me, so every man is armed. Knives, clubs, that sort of thing. Right?"

Doran nodded. "But better weapons are still needed. Spears and pikes, mostly, but also maces. Daggers will be useless."

"That is a great number," Kilimon said. "An overwhelming army. Far larger than the Niphilim could possibly muster. I think that will be sufficient to defend the city, should the Niphilim even come. They're fools, but not wholly foolish. I doubt they will."

Ander spoke up. "They'll come, both men and women, and they'll kill like you've never imagined killing before. They're bred to it, like lions. All the fighting men of Kan-Puram will be needed to stand against them, or all will be destroyed. The vultures and crows will grow wickedly fat."

"Please, Master," Shamash said. "You must listen. I told you that the savages—"

Kilimon rose from his chair. "Faith," he said. "You had it once. Powerful, awe-inspiring faith. What happened?"

"I still have faith," Shamash protested.

"Then use it. Remember the gift of Moloch."

Shamash looked at his feet.

"Take off your sandals. Show these men," Kilimon commanded. "Show them the gift."

Very slowly, Shamash did as he was told. He untied both sandals and kicked them off. When both feet were bare, he held each up in turn so that Ander, Doran and Isin could see the soles.

Isin winced. Doran took a deep breath. Only Ander seemed unfazed. Kilimon guessed that he'd seen such things before, possibly worse.

The soles of Shamash's feet were covered, heel to toe, in thick pink scars. The surface was more like that of a fried egg than healthy flesh.

"Show them the rest," Kilimon said. "Lift your robes."

Shamash grimaced, but obeyed. Just below his knees were more of the strange scars, still tender looking though they were obviously decades old.

"Now tell them the nature of your scars."

"They are from the holy fires of Moloch," Shamash whispered, staring at Kilimon as though hoping the other three men would somehow disappear. "They are the marks of my baptism . . . of my membership in the community of god."

Kilimon nodded. His eyes lit up with excitement. "Tell them about the blessing of the god. They must know."

Shamash's eyes lit up now as well. But the light that was in them was horribly different. Shamash was visibly filled with wrath. He boiled with anger and shame. It was as though the fire that had once burned his flesh had taken residence in the pupils of his eyes. Kilimon shuddered to see it. Finally, lips trembling, Shamash said, "All those who are touched by the god's holy fire are under His protection. For the fire burns two ways, and none may stand against Moloch."

"Exactly. So you see," Kilimon said, "we are quite safe." He looked at Doran and Isin. "Untouchable in fact. None of our people will go to war. We shall rely on faith, and on the vengeance of Moloch, as He would have us do. You have our prayers, but never our bodies. Never our souls."

"Master," Shamash sputtered, rage now wholly present in his voice, "this is madness. The Niphilim will swallow us like a storm. Did you not hear Ander's story? Did you not listen?"

Kilimon shook his head. "So little faith." He walked over to Shamash, gently laying a hand on his arm. "Even that little bat has more faith than you. Here, watch." Kilimon stumped across the room and began knocking on the wall with his knuckles. The bat didn't even look to see what was happening. "It's not afraid because it knows I can't reach it. The bat has faith."

"Master," Shamash pleaded. But Kilimon wasn't listening. He'd already turned to the other men, still waiting quietly.

"I do have a council to give, if you'd hear it," he said, "for I'm not insensitive to the plight of the other peoples of Kan-Puram."

"We listen gratefully, Your Holiness," Isin said, though clearly disappointed.

"Isin, take this man, Ander, to Ur." Kilimon made a vague gesture toward the south. "Exhort the High Priestess of the Ziggurat to send reinforcements. Ander's story is not without its influence. Doran can lead in your abscense. In the meantime, Shamash will trade away all of his fancy robes and fine jewelry, and take as much metal as can be taken, and more, from our coffers." He turned to Doran. "You may use our wealth to buy your spears and . . . things."

Shamash crossed his arms and stared at the floor.

"You will also have our prayers," Kilimon continued.

"I'll go to Ur, if Isin will go with me," Ander said. Isin looked at Doran, who nodded. "I only hope we return before the Niphilim have finished off the city—your people included." As he spoke, Ander picked up one of Shamash's sandals. He wrapped the strings around the leather sole, took careful aim and threw it.

Kilimon gasped as the sandal sailed across the room, striking the wall just to the right of where the bat was hanging. Ander grinned as the bat went flitting about, banging into walls and scraping its wings against the ceiling.

"Why?" Kilimon asked. "That bat never harmed you."

"You may think your god can protect you," Ander said. "But against the Niphilim, no one is out of reach."

CHAPTER 3

Bone's Luck

IKAL, FOUNDER AND PROPRIETOR OF THE SNAIL'S HORN, STOOD behind his counter, slopping the dregs from a long line of dirty cups. He tossed the undrunk beer into one barrel, then refilled the cups from another. There was also a third, smaller barrel filled with water, and a pile of old dishrags, cut from the remains of some tunics he'd found lying in the alley out back—but Nikal rarely touched either, and only for cleaning up at the end of the night. He also had a half-full jar of pickled dates— just in case Jared asked for them—a straw broom, and a cleaver as long as a man's forearm. No one in the Snail's Horn went unarmed. Not even the bartender.

Behind him, one of the prostitutes was singing. She didn't have much of a voice, but she was loud and lively and encouraged those around her to sing at the chorus, which they did at the top of their lungs. Nikal smiled as they sang 'The Tiger and the Ibex,' even humming along as he refilled the cups lined up on the counter. When he had twelve full ones, he'd take five to Jared's table and seven to the boys standing against the wall. Jared's table was first, of course. Always first. Nikal knew which side of the goat was the fattest.

He was having a good night. There wasn't an empty table in the place, the thieves were in high spirits, and he could barely keep up with the constant demand for beer. A few of the younger thieves complained about the slow service, saying he ought to hire some help, but Nikal didn't listen. The Snail's Horn was his to run and his alone.

Nikal arranged the cups on his tray and started across the room, side-stepping a pair of outstretched legs. The woman straddling the legs winked at him as he passed, and then went back to her business. Nikal winked back. She was young and pretty, with big brown eyes and a crooked smile. Just the sort of girl he liked to have in the Horn. If she winked at him again, he might even give her a free cup—something he rarely did.

These were high times for the Horn, but they wouldn't last. Even though they were laughing and chattering away like children now, the party was rapidly coming to an end, and Nikal knew it. He'd seen the soldiers marching in the street. The city was preparing for a long siege. Most of the rich merchants had already put aside their petty feuds. That was the real reason the hired thieves were all sitting around drinking—there were no scores to settle, no contracts to fulfill. Thus far, the war had increased Nikal's business two or three fold, but how long would that last? He wondered. Thieves weren't known for their ability to conserve. When their small fortunes ran out, what would they do? And what if the Niphilim invaded the city? Nikal hoped the thieves would find a way to band together and survive. He knew Jared would try to lead them, but would they follow? Even Nikal wasn't sure, and he believed Jared could do almost anything.

As usual, Jared was hosting a game of Bones' Luck at the back table. There were other games going, but his was the biggest. No bet too large, as Jared liked to say. Nikal hurried back and forth to his table at least twice an hour, always with a full round of drinks. Those who were winning bought, and those who were losing cursed. But for every loser there was a winner, and as the metal moved around the table, Nikal made sure a decent percentage of it lined his pockets.

They were between hands, so Nikal set his tray on the table and quickly distributed cups to the players, serving Jared last. The other players met him with grumbles and stares. Apparently Jared had just raked the table, and was even then stacking the metal from his take into neat piles.

"Luck's with me tonight," Jared said. Nikal gathered up the empty cups. "How many times have I bought?"

"Five," the bartender replied.

Jared whistled. "That is lucky." He scratched his chin. "I think I'll try to beat my personal record." He picked a couple of pieces of copper off his pile of winnings and flipped them onto Nikal's tray. "That makes six. Just five more to go. An easy handful."

"Seven," Nikal corrected him.

"What?"

"You once bought thirteen rounds. Your lucky number."

Jared laughed. "Then I'd better get down to work. The night's half over." The other players groaned.

There was only one woman at the table, an old prostitute by the name of Samsara. As usual, she was naked from the waist up. Once she'd been pretty, but time and gravity had taken their toll. She pulled a tiny sliver of copper out of a pocket in her skirts and tapped it on the table with disgust. No matter what, Nikal thought, she wouldn't be getting a free cup.

"Everyone in for the next hand?" Jared asked.

"Just deal, gods damn you," Sneaker hissed. He was a short, wiry thief with beady eyes and long front teeth, lending him a more than passing resemblance to an alley rat.

Jared mixed and dealt the tiles. He was quick and smooth. In no time, six neat stacks sat in front of him.

"Give me the bones," Sneaker growled. "It's my turn to roll."

"It's Samsara's roll," Jared said, handing her the bones. "She's down to her last bet, if I guess right." Samsara nodded. "You know the custom. She'll have to go out and do some earning if she doesn't make something off this hand."

Sneaker grimaced. His stack of copper was growing short as well.

Samsara kissed both knucklebones for luck, and then tossed them onto the table.

"Three," Jared said. He distributed the stacks of tiles accordingly, pushing the third to Samsara, the fourth to the man on her right and so on. There was one stack no one claimed. Jared shoved it aside, out of play.

From where he stood, Nikal could just see over Sneaker's shoulder. He had a fairly strong hand. Probably a winner. There were ten picture suits, and three tiles in each suit, which could be paired or melded for score. Each player pushed two tiles to the center of the table, eliminating them from play, then turned the remaining three face up. Sneaker had three jewel tiles—a pearl, a lapis and a carnelian.

In other versions of the game, the players bet only after seeing their hands, or after discarding. There were even versions where the highest hand took all. But not here. The only hand these players had to beat was the dealer's—Jared's—which should have made it easier to win, but rarely did.

Jared beat three of the four hands easily, with a gold and two precious stones. He paid Sneaker, the only winner, and pulled in his take.

Samsara stood up. "Nothing more up my sleeves," she said, glancing down at her bare chest and naked arms. The other players laughed. "Guess I'm out."

"Back to the dirty work?" Sneaker jeered. "Try not to spread yourself too thin."

"Good advice," Samsara said. "And when you're my age you have to be careful who you spread for." She reached for her cup. "I shouldn't worry too much, though. The way you're losing, I won't be seeing *you* again tonight, will I Sneaker?"

The men on either side of Sneaker howled with laughter. Jared smiled, picked up his cup and took a long drink. Sneaker flushed, took a tiny piece of copper off the pile he had left, and pushed it forward. "Deal," he spat.

Nikal turned and headed back to the counter, still chuckling. He had to dodge the same pair of legs, but this time the girl straddling them paid no attention to him, losing her chance at a free beer, though Nikal didn't suppose she much cared. He was just about to slip behind the counter again when he noticed Uruk, sitting at a table near the far wall watching Jared's game. The dog sat on the floor beside him, same as always. They looked bored. There were two other chairs at their table, both vacant. For whatever reason, the other thieves left Uruk and the dog alone. Nikal didn't know if they did it out of respect or fear. It didn't matter much, he decided. The result was the same.

"Water?" he shouted at Uruk.

Uruk nodded and held up two fingers. "In clean cups."

"I'd rather you drink the beer and take the cups I give you," Nikal grumbled. He set his tray down and quickly set about replacing the empty cups with full ones.

The table at the center of the room began singing 'The Tiger and the Ibex' again. For some reason, they'd skipped to the last verse. It was Nikal's favorite part of the song. His father used to sing it as he carried water to his fields.

"*And both rolled together to the sea, to the sea,*" Nikal sang along. "*Both rolled together to the sea.*"

Shamash avoided eye contact as he slipped past the tables and chairs, headed for the counter. He'd been standing outside for the last few minutes, staring at the tiny wood snail and trying to build up enough courage to open the door. It was the music that finally did it. Any group that'd sing 'The Tiger and the Ibex' couldn't be entirely bad, he'd told himself as he stepped over the threshold.

He was dressed in a simple tunic and breeches, both wool, and had a small leather purse over his shoulder, which he clutched with both hands. Shamash had come to the tavern expecting to find desperate men, one step removed from the dust. But the Snail's Horn was nothing like that. These men and women were mostly well-dressed. A few were ragged, but others looked positively wealthy. There was more silk in that room than Shamash had seen in one place in his life. Whatever else they might be, these thieves weren't afraid of luxury. Shamash couldn't help but admire them for it.

He waited at the counter until the bartender returned, carrying a tray loaded with empty cups. "Is the beer any good?" he asked.

Nikal glanced over at him, frowned, and then dropped a few small pieces of copper into a box in the corner. Watching him, Shamash wasn't sure whether the bartender would answer his question or have him beaten and thrown in the street.

"The best," Nikal grunted at last. He picked up an old rag, dipped it in a barrel of water and began scrubbing one of the cups.

"How much will this buy?" Shamash set a small piece of copper on the counter.

Nikal weighed it in his palm. "It's a good night and I'm feeling generous," he said. "Two cups."

Shamash nodded. The bartender was giving him a good deal and he knew it. That piece of copper would have been worth barely more than a cup in most places. He picked up the beer Nikal set in front of him—not in the cup he'd been scrubbing, Shamash noticed—and took a sip. It was good. Not the best. Not even the best in Kan-Puram, but good. Shamash drained the rest of the cup in one swallow.

Nikal cleaned a second cup and then filled both with water. Shamash watched him with interest. Given the choice, very few people in Kan-Puram drank water. Nobody over twelve years of age. Nikal carried the cups to a table near the back wall, setting one in front of the largest black man Shamash had ever seen, and the other on the floor in front of a sand-colored dog. Shamash didn't much like the idea of having a dog in the tavern. It seemed so filthy.

Now that he'd had a beer, Shamash felt more at ease. He'd expected to be watched from the moment he came through the door, but no one appeared to have noticed him. He glanced around the room, trying to take it all in. A whore, sitting on a man's lap just a few strides from the counter, caught his eye and winked. Shamash looked away.

"What are they playing?" he asked. Nikal was refilling another round of cups and lining them up on the counter.

"Who?"

Shamash pointed at the game in the corner. He'd noticed the black man watching and wondered what the attraction could be. Nothing about that table seemed particularly interesting or unusual, at least not to a newcomer.

"Bone's Luck," Nikal muttered.

"High stakes?"

"A rich man's game." Nikal set another full cup in front of Shamash. "A thieves' game."

"I never met a thief," Shamash said.

"You probably just didn't know it." Nikal squinted at him. "I'd not stick my nose into their game if I were you."

"No," Shamash agreed. "I guess you wouldn't."

He waited until Nikal started toward the large group at the center of the room with his tray full, then pushed away from the counter. Shamash wanted to see what was happening at that back table. He considered sitting down in one of the empty chairs by Uruk, but decided against it. Instead, he moved to a spot a few strides from Jared's party, where he could watch without being intrusive.

Jared had two large piles of metal lying in front of him, mostly copper and silver, and more in a bag at his elbow. He was just dealing the tiles for another round. Shamash looked for any sleight of hand, but could detect nothing. Of course, these men could probably cheat, drink, and pray at the same time, he thought. And he hadn't come here to get rich anyway.

Shamash watched a few rounds and quickly assessed the situation. The dealer was slowly bleeding the players dry. He was the only one who could last long enough to finally win all the metal, and was already well on his way to doing just that. The other three were holding onto dim hopes. Each had a small pile of metal, but that wouldn't last much longer. Unless they stopped playing now, they'd go home with empty pockets.

There was an empty seat at the end of the table, just to the right of the dealer. Shamash drank the last of his beer and sat down. "Mind if I play?" he asked.

When the newcomer sat down at Jared's table, Uruk was surprised. From the moment Shamash came through the door, Uruk knew he didn't belong there. His purse was draped casually over one shoulder, like a rich woman going to market, and he was unarmed. The Snail's Horn was generally considered safe and sacred by the thieves, but such a flagrant disregard for your own personal safety was shocking. This man had clearly come to the tavern for a reason—but gambling? That was hard to imagine. And even if he were a gambler, why would he choose Jared's table? Uruk couldn't believe it was simply because there was an empty chair.

The dog followed Uruk to a spot just behind the players' chairs. Jared glanced up at them but didn't say a word. He was counting out copper pieces and paying the winners from the last round. Shamash was still waiting for his chance to play.

"You've got metal?" Jared asked him.

Shamash pulled a tiny sliver of gold from his purse. "I have this," he said.

It wasn't much larger than a speck of dust, but still impressive. Everyone else was playing with copper.

"That'll do." Jared mixed and dealt the tiles, then handed the knucklebones to Shamash. "Good luck," he said.

Shamash gave a flick of his wrist and the bones rattled across the tabletop. It was a surprisingly effeminate gesture. Uruk wasn't impressed.

"Four," Jared said. He pushed a stack of tiles to each player. The leftover stack he shoved to the side, out of play.

Shamash turned the tiles over one at a time, studying each for a few seconds before moving on to the next. When he flipped over the fourth tile he smiled. "Automatic," he said.

"Show me," Jared said.

Shamash turned over his tiles. Three of the five had trees painted on them, the symbol for wood. "Builder's jackpot," he said. The other players stared.

Jared searched through his pile of winnings until he came up with two pieces of silver and a large chunk of copper, which he slid across the table. "Fair?" he asked.

Shamash nodded. "Plenty."

Uruk watched the rest of the hand play out, though he didn't really understand what was happening. Sneaker finished with two clays and a pearl, and lost, while one of the other men turned over a gold, the third clay and a bronze, and won. Uruk had never gambled. At least not like this. Many times he'd set wagers on contests of skill or athleticism. But on a simple game of luck? Never. He couldn't see the honor in it.

Shamash bet his gold piece again and won.

"Lucky night," Jared said, passing him a small stack of copper.

"So far." Shamash pushed everything forward. The piece of gold, both pieces of silver, and all the copper. "Let's see if it holds."

"Hey, Jared," Sneaker said, peering over the lip of his cup. "Mix the tiles well. We could use a decent deal on this end."

But Sneaker didn't win that hand either, though the players on either side of him did. It was a strange deal, much like the hand Nikal had witnessed earlier. Every hand was a good one. It was as if during the mixing, the high count had floated to the top, like cream from milk, and each of the players was getting to take a sip. Sneaker had two silvers and a jade. That was a good hand, worth the price of his bet, and would have won in either of the two previous deals. The thieves sitting to his left and right each had at least one precious stone and one metal. Shamash had a silver, a gold and a clay. All four players looked smugly at each other while they waited for Jared to turn over his tiles.

Jared slowly discarded two tiles from his hand and turned over the other three. He had a bronze, a pearl and a lapis.

"I can't believe your luck," Sneaker grumbled, as Jared swept away his little mound of copper. "That was my best hand tonight."

"Mine too," Jared said.

Shamash crossed his arms as Jared swept away his winnings, picking up the little speck of gold last. "No luck when it counts?" Jared asked him.

"We'll see." Shamash opened his purse and peered inside.

"Cleaned out already?" Jared asked. "I give loans on occasion, but something tells me I'd never see you again."

"I have one more bet," Shamash said.

"Then let's see it."

Shamash reached into his bag once more. He made a show of rummaging around. "Actually, I guess I haven't got any more metal," he said.

"Then you can't play," Sneaker said. "We don't let you bet hopes and dreams. Show us your metal or move on."

"I don't have any more metal," Shamash repeated. "But I think this might do as a bet." He reached into the neck of his tunic and drew out a small leather bag. After fumbling with the ties, Shamash worked the top open and peeked inside. "I think you might like this."

He looked at each of the thieves in turn, even glancing over his shoulder at Uruk. Then he turned the bag over and dropped a perfect green jewel onto the table. It was as big around as a woman's thumbnail and shone with an uncanny inner light.

"My last bet of the evening," Shamash said. He shook out the little bag, showing that there was nothing more inside. "Let's hope it's lucky."

Jared picked up the stone and examined it. He licked his lips as he held it up to the light. "I figure this is worth at least twenty times its weight in gold," he said.

Shamash leaned back in his chair. "If you say so."

Jared looked at the metal he had piled in front of him. "All I have here represents no more than three, maybe four times that stone's weight. . . . And that's figuring generously."

"Three times is fair," Shamash said. "Deal."

Jared smiled. He moved slowly and deliberately, mixing the tiles for at least twice as long as usual. "You want to stir them too?" he asked.

"No thanks." Shamash crossed his arms.

When the tiles were thoroughly muddled, Jared began arranging them into stacks.

Uruk watched for any sign of cheating, but saw nothing unusual. He wasn't surprised. The King of Thieves considered himself far above the level of petty scams and trickery. No way he'd cheat at his own table.

Jared had just finished stacking the tiles when he noticed that none of the other players had placed bets. "Are you in or are you out?" he asked.

The thieves stared at each other, not saying a word. Finally Sneaker spoke up. "That's the biggest bet I ever saw," he stammered. "I'm not going to try my luck against it. The gods don't smile on a man who plays out of his level."

"You could be right," Jared said. He picked up the knucklebones, and was just about to hand them to Shamash when Nikal suddenly arrived with another tray of beer.

"Lucky I caught you between hands," Nikal said. He set his tray down in the center of the table and began handing cups to the players. When he reached Shamash, he stopped. The color ran from his face. Uruk had never seen the old bartender so angry, not even on his first night in the Horn. "I'm sorry, Jared," Nikal said. "I told him not to bother you, but I guess he didn't listen. I'll throw him out if you want."

"That's all right, Nikal," Jared said. He handed the bones to Shamash. "This man and I have a very special bet going."

The bartender looked at the table, where Shamash's jewel lay glittering, and gasped. Shamash grinned, still shaking the bones in his fist.

"I'm sorry." Nikal set a cup in front of Shamash. "I had no idea."

Shamash picked up the cup and took a drink. "You do have good beer," he said. "Not the best, but good." He glared at Nikal until the tavern-keeper blanched and shuffled away. Finally, Shamash tossed the bones.

"Six," Jared said. He paused a moment before sweeping up the bones, letting everyone at the table come to the same count. Then he shoved the last stack of tiles to Shamash and took the first stack for himself. The other four he pushed aside.

Shamash had just begun turning over his tiles when a hush fell over the Snail's Horn. Uruk looked over his shoulder and saw Nikal, whispering something to the party gathered around the table at the center of the room. Moments later, people began to pile in behind him, pushing and craning their necks to see the jewel. The dog crawled under the table and sat down. He didn't look pleased.

Jared waited until Shamash had thoroughly studied his whole hand before even glancing at his own tiles. When he finally did look, Jared flipped each over one by one, his hands moving so fast that Uruk wondered whether he actually knew what was painted on the tiles. When he'd finished, Jared calmly crossed his hands. "Whenever you're ready," he said.

Shamash looked at his tiles again. He had two wood, a clay, a pearl, and a copper. It seemed to Uruk rather a poor hand. Of course, Uruk reminded himself, he'd won the first round with just three wood. And he still had no idea what Jared had drawn.

Finally, Shamash laid the copper and the clay face down and shoved them to the center of the table. Uruk badly wanted to ask one of the other spectators whether that was a good decision, but didn't dare. Not while the hand was still being played.

Without looking at them again, Jared shoved two of his tiles into the center of the table as well. All that was left to do was to show the hands and determine a winner—but neither man moved.

After what seemed eons, Sneaker banged his fist down on the table. "Turn them over for your gods' sakes," he hissed. "What's done is done."

Shamash took a deep breath and began flipping his tiles onto the table. "Two wood and a pearl," he said.

Jared stared at the pictures a moment, brows knit together, then quickly turned his hand over as well. As he set the third tile down, the whole tavern roared. Jared had the other two coppers and a gold. All metal. Somehow, Jared had won.

"The tiles came out against you," Jared said as he pocketed the jewel.

"Seems so," Shamash replied. They had to shout to be heard over the continued cheering of the crowd. "But I came here for more than just a roll of the bones." Everyone, Uruk included, leaned in to hear what the stranger would say. They needn't have bothered. He spoke loud enough for the whole tavern to hear, and then some. "I came to announce a bounty."

The instant he said the word 'bounty,' all cheers fell dead. The hired thieves jostled their way past the prostitutes and petty criminals. A few even tried to shove Uruk aside as they inched toward the table. But Uruk refused to be moved.

"It's an open contract, payable to the fastest man," Shamash continued. "The price will be roughly three times that of the jewel you just won."

The murmur that ran through the Snail's Horn was like a shout. Even Jared seemed surprised. "What kind of job is this?" he asked.

"Murder."

Uruk glanced down at the dog, still huddled under the edge of the table. A prize that large could change a life, he thought. Of course, he'd stolen a jewel that big once before, and had traded it for a sword. This time he'd try for something bigger. Maybe Mana was finally offering him a way out of his destiny. A man might be anything with a treasure like that, Uruk told himself. He might even become a hunter once more.

"Go on," Jared said. "We're all listening."

"I have all the details," Shamash said. "Including how and where it can be done."

"Start with a name."

"You can call me. . . ." Shamash paused to think. "Lacrimose."

"And the man you're after?"

"He's the High Father of the temple of Moloch." Shamash paused, apparently expecting a response, but nobody said a word. These were not religious people. "His name is Kilimon."

"Why?" Jared asked.

"I need the job done within three days." For the first time, Shamash turned so that he could address the whole tavern directly. "It's extremely important—to the whole city."

"Again," Jared said. "Why?"

"You know about the armies preparing in the fields north of the city?"

"Of course."

"The man I want killed stands between those armies and victory."

Jared stared at him a moment, the muscles in his jaw visibly clenched. "All right," he said at last. "Tell us how it's to be done."

CHAPTER 4

For One Righteous Man

*U*RUK SLID ACROSS THE TOP OF THE PERIMETER WALL AND DROPPED into the shadows beyond. The wall wasn't much taller than a man with his arms stretched overhead, and had been constructed from rough-hewn sandstone blocks. It must have been intended as a symbolic divider between the house of god and the outside world, because it certainly wasn't an effective barrier. Even with the dog cradled in one arm, breathing in his face, Uruk scaled the wall with ease.

They landed in a hackberry bramble, not far from the rear entrance to the main temple. Ahead of them stretched an immense courtyard, complete with trees, flowers and the occasional strip of open grass. There were also vegetable patches, where nuns raised everything from yams and squash to potatoes, barley and millet. The greater portion of the produce was burned as sacrifice, but a good deal was consumed as well. Each week, a few baskets of grain and vegetables, whatever the temple couldn't use, were flung into the street for the poor. Most of the food was rotten, moldy or stale, but it still didn't sit out long. There was always someone happy to take it home.

On the other side of the gardens, standing fully six stories high, until it seemed to hold up the clouds, was the tower.

Uruk couldn't see the first floor at all. There were too many trees between him and the building. But beginning on the second floor, and continuing all the way to the top, were row upon row of large open windows, each crowned by a single torch. Laundry hung from the fourth and fifth floors, drying in the hot night air. Uruk counted half-a-dozen pairs of breeches and at least fifteen tunics scattered among the blankets and robes.

As they approached the tower, Uruk got his first whiff of melioc resin. It had a sour smell, like figs left in the sun too long. The wealthy of Kan-Puram burned it to keep insects away, but Uruk didn't think it worked. The stench grew more pungent with every step and still the garden was rife with mosquitoes. Uruk swatted them, though he knew it was futile. For every one he killed, at least a hundred more were waiting, filling the air with their high-pitched whine.

They were nearing the eastern end of the courtyard before Uruk finally got a clear view of the tower's bottom floor. He paused, marveling at the wall of featureless gray stone. There were no doors or windows to mar the surface, which shone like still water, reflecting the cedar and olive trees clustered in that part of the garden. Uruk could just make out his own reflection as he crouched amid the branches.

Thus far they'd seen not a single guard, but that didn't mean they wouldn't. According to Lacrimose, there were sentries on the tower roof, and guards manning various points inside—more than two dozen in all—but they only made irregular circuits of the gardens, and that was primarily to chase neighborhood children out of the vegetables. Uruk wasn't particularly concerned about the sentries on the roof. From that height they couldn't possibly see what was happening in the compound. It was simply too dark. All the same, he preferred to scout a target for at least a week before launching an attack. Even then, burglary was a dangerous business.

Unfortunately, Lacrimose was desperate for speed and Uruk couldn't wait. By tomorrow night, this whole compound would be crowded with murderers, stabbing and strangling each other in their rush to get at the prize. It was this night or none for Uruk. He'd take no part in the free-for-all Lacrimose had proposed.

They dashed across the stretch of paving stones that circled the courtyard, and into the shadow of the tower. Uruk considered searching for a door, but was certain that any he found would be watched. He decided to go in through one of the windows.

"Hear anything?" he whispered. The dog looked up at him, but otherwise didn't respond. Uruk lifted the dog as high as he could, so that his nose was only an arm's length from the base of the closest window. The dog was exceedingly wary of people he didn't know. If he smelled or heard anyone inside, Uruk thought he'd growl. But the dog just lay in his hands.

After setting him back on the ground, Uruk ran his palms along the smooth stone wall, searching for a crack or ledge. But he could find nothing useable. The masonry of the tower was unlike anything Uruk had ever seen. The blocks were fitted so exactly that there was barely a line between them. Not even a spider could have scaled that wall, let alone a man. Uruk took a step back and looked up. The window wasn't as high as he'd originally judged. He thought he might be able to jump to it.

Uruk took the bundle of cord from his satchel and tied one end around the dog's chest, between his front and rear legs. The dog eyed the cord suspiciously, but didn't move or try to get away. The other end Uruk tied to the back of his belt, right next to his sword.

"Sit here, Dog." He pointed at the base of the wall. "And do not move until I say."

Uruk leapt as high as he could, but only managed to reach the window with the ends of his middle fingers. Worse, the slick wall let out a screech as he slid down it, landing at the bottom with a jarring thud. Fortunately, no one was close enough to hear.

After shaking out his legs, Uruk stepped back and looked at the window ledge again. He'd try one more time. Then he'd have to think of something else. This was making far too much noise.

Uruk took a couple more steps back, wanting to get a running start. It worked. He let out a grunt as his chest slammed against the wall, but was still able to latch on with one hand and drag himself up.

The window opened onto a balcony, running for a dozen paces across the side of the tower. There was just one door leading off it, and that was closed tight. Uruk put his ear to the wood, but could hear nothing over the crackle of burning melioc coming from the torches overhead.

Uruk dragged the dog up to the balcony and untied the cord. Relieved, the dog shook out his coat, then went to the door and stuck his nose into the crack along the base. The fur on his neck bristled.

"People?" Uruk mouthed. He dropped to his hands and knees and put his nose to the crack. Nothing stood out over the stink of the melioc, though that didn't mean the room beyond was empty. The dog's senses were on a level far above his own, Uruk knew. He had no doubt that there was someone behind that door.

But he wasn't ready to turn back yet. After repositioning his sword to the side of his belt, where he could draw it quickly should the need arise, Uruk raised the latch.

Luckily, the hinges made no noise as the door swung open, because the room was full of sleeping women. There were a dozen of them, doubled up on six pallets, all sleeping soundly. Uruk watched them for a moment, not daring to move or even breathe, before stepping into the room and silently shutting the door. The dog took no such pains. He casually trotted between the outstretched legs and arms, headed toward the open corridor on the opposite side of the chamber.

All but one of the nuns was naked, without even sheets to cover their bodies. The woman in the corner nearest the door was wearing a linen shift, but had somehow managed to pull it all the way up to her armpits, where it was twisted and drenched in sweat. They were all perspiring heavily. Tiny rivulets streaked their bodies and soaked the heavy cushions beneath them. Uruk couldn't see why they didn't just leave the door open. He'd only been in the room for a few seconds and already his brow and underarms were streaming.

As he made his way between the pallets, Uruk couldn't help staring at the women. Their mouths hung open, some snored, and none too few drooled in their sleep—the one wearing the shift had a trail of curly black hair that reached all the way to her navel—but they were all beautiful. They were young and strong. Muscles thrust against the skin in their shoulders and thighs. Every one of them had dirt under her nails, and most had dark smudges on their faces, legs or arms. They worked hard, and had the bodies to prove it. None had her luminous skin or full lips, but still they reminded Uruk of Numa. It'd been a long time since he'd seen such women.

The corridor widened as they made their way into the heart of the tower, but the heat persisted. Near what must have been the structure's center, they came upon a spiral staircase. The steps leading downward, toward ground level, flickered with an orange light. Guards, Uruk reasoned. He was glad he'd decided to come in through the window. By contrast, the steps leading upward were dark. According to Lacrimose, the High Father's apartments were at the very top of the tower. Uruk began to climb.

They were closing in on the fourth floor when the dog suddenly growled and leapt ahead. Uruk tried to grab him, but missed in the dark. Fortunately, he hadn't gone far. In fact, Uruk very nearly tripped over him on the next landing. And he wasn't alone. Uruk's toes brushed what felt like a man's arm.

In a flash, Uruk whipped his sword from its scabbard. But the arm never stirred. It never even twitched.

Carefully, Uruk bent and ran his hand over the man's chest, finding the coarse tunic of a low-level priest. He lifted the garments and reached underneath. The man's skin was hot, and coated by a thin sheen of sweat, but he had no heartbeat. Uruk searched for a wound, but could find none. No blood either. He pawed his way up to the man's neck. It was broken.

Uruk dashed up the remaining stairs. Another thief was ahead of him, maybe already in the High Father's quarters. Any further hesitation and this whole mission would come to nothing.

The stairs ended at a heavy wooden door. Uruk fumbled in the darkness, finally locating the latch. But the door was barred from inside.

The time for stealth was over. Uruk reared back and kicked. The wood around the hinges splintered and the door fell inward.

Beyond was a long hallway, windows running down one side and doors down the other. A priest lay face down at the center, blood pooling all around him. An elderly man bent over the body, his white robe and beard splotched with red.

"Where?" Uruk demanded.

The old priest looked up, clearly in a state of shock. "She has him," he mumbled. One gnarled finger stretched toward the farthest door. "In the High Father's cell."

Uruk bounded past him and flung open the door.

Standing over a pallet in the corner, fingers just inches from Kilimon's neck, was a thief. She was dressed in brown silk, both tunic and breeches, and from her belt hung a bronze sword. It was eerily similar to the one Uruk had given the trader in Ur. Around her upper arm was a copper band.

Kilimon sat up in bed. He stared at the intruders, obviously stunned at having his sanctum invaded by base thieves. But if he was scared, Uruk could see no sign of it.

"This is my kill, Uruk," the woman said. "You're too late."

"I can still collect. I just have to kill you first." Without taking his eyes off her, Uruk kicked the door closed and wedged a chair under the latch. Both were stout—the chair especially. Only the most ardent of guards would be coming through that door.

"Kill me?" The thief's voice lilted in disbelief. "You couldn't even kill Melesh."

"I might have."

"Then why is he still alive?"

"I am not a killer." And just like that, Uruk's whole purpose for being there fell away. Things had been happening so fast. He'd never paused to

131 / *Slaves of the Shinar*

wonder whether he'd be able to fulfill this contract. Now he knew. From the moment he'd entered that room, Uruk's every thought had been turned to preventing a murder. If he succeeded, could he then stand over this old man and, using his sword for the very first time, end a life? And for what? A jewel? No. Uruk had hunted and he had killed, but he was no murderer. The difference was slight, but enough for him to hold onto.

"I thought as much," the woman said. "Get out of here. Let me do my work."

Uruk shook his head.

She glowered at him. For a moment, Uruk thought she might try to break the old priest's neck anyway. But she didn't. Instead she backed away from the bed. "This is my one best chance," she said, drawing her sword. "Either he dies tonight, or I do."

"Who are you?" Uruk asked.

But the before she could answer, the temple guards arrived. They pounded at the door, demanding to be let in. One called for it to be broken down.

"Maybe none of us gets out of here alive," the woman sneered.

She was right. Something had to be done. Uruk pointed at Kilimon. "Tell the guards to calm down."

Kilimon did. He explained that he was alive, unharmed and in no danger. That was not entirely true, of course, but the old priest seemed to think it was. In fact, he said it as though it were an absolute certainty. As a result, the pounding at the door decreased. It didn't stop completely, but that would have been too much to hope for. At the very least, the guards would never break through knocking as they now were—a fact that encouraged Uruk somewhat.

He'd just begun to wonder if there might not also be some way of turning the woman thief away without bloodshed, when he noticed the dog inching toward her blind side. "No, Dog," Uruk called. But it was already too late.

The dog attacked.

The thief saw him coming out of the corner of her eye, and likely would have killed him if Uruk hadn't leapt in first, striking at her with the tip of his sword. She was much too fast to be caught by such a clumsy blow, but killing her wasn't Uruk's intent. He just wanted to attract her attention. In order to deflect his blade, the woman had to ignore the dog. It was a choice she'd all too soon come to regret.

The dog's teeth sunk into her thigh. It must have hurt, but she didn't even flinch. She kicked him away, but the dog came right back. His jaws snapped, mangling her silk breeches and tearing the pale flesh beneath. Amazingly, the woman barely seemed to notice. She had her hands full with Uruk, who hacked at her again and again, as fast as he could. Somehow, she deflected every thrust.

If not for the dog, the battle might have gone on like that a long while, with neither side gaining a clear advantage. But all of a sudden, after having sunk his teeth into her leg no fewer than a dozen times, the dog struck something tender. She didn't cry or call out, but she winced. Uruk saw it. The dog had a grip on some bit of flesh this thief simply couldn't ignore.

Incensed, she launched a counterattack, swinging at Uruk's head with every bit of strength she could muster. Their swords slammed together, and for the first time the woman let out a scream.

It wasn't pain, Uruk guessed. Nor was it the vibrations that ran up her arm. This was a scream of dismay. Somehow, as their swords met, her blade broke. The point splintered off, spinning across the room. Another shard buried itself in Kilimon's bed, sending up a puff of feather stuffing. Any farther and it might have gone through the High Father himself.

She was left with a handle, connected to no more than a finger's-length of jagged bronze, but she refused to give up. The thief hurled what was left of her sword at Uruk. He ducked it easily enough, but by the time he'd righted himself, the woman had grabbed the dog by snout and tail and lifted him off the floor. The dog wriggled like a fish, but couldn't manage to break free. Her grip was too tight.

"Not another step," she warned, holding the dog in front of her like a shield.

"Let him go." Uruk said. He stepped toward her. "No one needs to die here—" He was about to say that he'd gladly help her escape if only she'd just put the dog down, but never got the chance. The instant he moved, she turned and flung the dog with all her might.

Uruk watched in horror as he let out one final bark, his feet scrambling wildly in mid-air, and slipped through the window.

"Dog?" Uruk called. "Dog?!" But there was no answer.

Enraged, Uruk leapt onto the thief, ramming his sword into her guts, then yanking it free and sinking it to the hilt in her chest. Even as she collapsed to the floor, the cold sneer never left her lips.

Kilimon screamed. He tumbled from his pallet, racing on hands and knees to the dead thief's side. "What have you done?" He bent over the woman's body, his hands pressed to her wounds.

"He is gone," Uruk said, gazing out the window. It was difficult to believe. Over the last few weeks, he had begun to think of the dog as more than a mere companion. Uruk had fully expected that they would be together until one or the other died. He just hadn't imagined the end coming so quickly.

"It was only a dog," Kilimon said. "Just a beast."

Uruk winced, but otherwise didn't respond.

The pounding at the door intensified. Even the chair Uruk had used to wedge it closed was shuddering from the weight of the blows.

"Listen," Uruk said, pulling Kilimon away from the body. "You are a dead man. Understand? People like me will never stop coming." He gestured at the still-bleeding thief with the point of his sword. "We are only the first."

"Will you kill me now?" Kilimon asked.

"No. But your guards will come through that door soon—and they will certainly kill me." Kilimon started to say something, but Uruk waved him off. "You will not be able to stop them."

"Well then, you'd better get out of here," said a voice from behind him. Uruk spun around, fearing an attack, and was amazed to see Jared's face at the window. "You going to stand there gawping, or give an old thief a hand?"

Uruk reached out, expecting to grab onto one of Jared's arms. Instead, Jared pressed something furry into his hand. Uruk could hardly breathe as he lifted the dog through the window by the scruff of his neck.

"You met the Princess, I see," Jared said, as he crawled into the room. "Always planned to kill her myself one day, but. . . ."

Uruk looked up from petting the dog. "We are in your debt," he said. He was so choked with joy he could barely get the words out. "How did you do it?"

"I reached the window just as you came in," Jared explained. "Been waiting for one of you to finish the other off. Figured I'd step in and take the prize once the High Priest was dead. Doesn't look like you're going to kill the old man, though."

Uruk shook his head.

"Can't say as I blame you."

Just then, something large crashed against the cell door, causing the whole tower to shudder. A few more such blasts and the door would be torn clean out of its frame.

"Battering ram," Jared said. "Knew they'd get to it sooner or later." He turned to Kilimon. "Now then, what should we do with you?"

"Leave me here and pray for forgiveness."

Jared laughed. "We should. We really should. Unfortunately, we can't. Uruk was right. Stay here and you're all but dead. You ought to thank Moloch for sending you such a powerful protector."

"You are not going to kill him either?" Uruk asked. The battering ram slammed into the door again. The chair was splintering under the pressure.

"Not me," Jared said. "I'm King of Thieves. Not cowards who stab old men in the night. But if we leave him here, someone else will—and I can't have that. Most thieves couldn't handle so much wealth."

"Then what will you do with me?" Kilimon asked.

Jared considered a moment. "You'll have to come with us," he said. "We'll collect the reward based on your disappearance. That's all Lacrimose really wants."

"What if I refuse?"

Jared laughed again. "You can choose to make this hard, but either way you're coming. I hate to be the one to tell you, Holiness, but your days as High Father are over."

Kilimon frowned. "I understand. I won't resist."

"Good." Jared picked up the dog by the scruff of his neck and threw him over his shoulder. "Can't get out through there." He nodded at the door. "We'll have to go my way. You bring the old man. Or do I have to carry him as well?"

Uruk lifted Kilimon and slung him over his shoulder like a sack of meal. "Don't squirm," he warned. "It will do no good, and might cause me to lose my grip."

"I won't."

A slender length of rope hung from the roof. Uruk followed Jared down it. The going was slow. Kilimon never so much as shivered, but the extra weight was still difficult for Uruk to handle.

They'd just passed the fourth floor, and the windows with the laundry hung out to dry, when Uruk heard Kilimon's door finally give way.

Jared didn't wait another second. Without warning, he pushed away from the building and dropped. Uruk was amazed. Somehow, Jared hit the ground at a dead run. A moment later he was gone, lost to the trees and bushes of the garden

Uruk slithered further down the rope before he, too, dropped. Even then, the paving stones jarred him so badly he nearly collapsed. The old priest squealed in his ear.

Jared was waiting for them in the shadow of an old oak, the only one in the whole compound. "Guards," he said, pointing at the southwestern corner of the tower. "And there are sure to be others we haven't spotted yet."

"So we fight our way out," Uruk said. "Or die in the attempt."

"Of course not. We just disappear."

"How?"

Jared grinned. "Follow me."

They ran to the center of the garden, gliding from shadow to shadow, tree to tree. The dog ran in front, his nose to the ground. Uruk followed at the rear, Kilimon still slumped over one shoulder.

At last Jared stopped. "There it is." He pointed at a large, open well. It was ringed by stones and easily wide enough for a full-grown man to fall into.

"You want us to climb down a well?" Uruk asked.

"It's not a well. Not a real one, anyway. The estates in this part of the city all draw water from the canals. Can't be drunk, of course, but it'll feed a plant better than anything in the world. Go ahead, I'll follow."

A tingle of danger crept up Uruk's spine as he neared the ring of stones. If Jared wanted to be rid of both he and Kilimon, without getting any blood on his own hands, this was certainly the way to do it. Uruk would throw the old man down the well and then jump in after him. If the fall didn't kill them outright, the icy water at the bottom certainly would. Still, it seemed the only way. More guards were piling into the compound all the time. Soon there'd be enough to sweep the gardens.

Uruk watched as Kilimon dropped into the darkness, then leapt in after him.

The fall wasn't nearly as long as he'd feared, and the resevoir was more than deep enough to cushion their landing. They had to tread water, but that was better than breaking a leg on the bottom.

"Are you all right?" Uruk asked.

"I'll live," Kilimon wheezed.

"Good." Uruk grabbed him by the sleeve and hauled him out of the way. No sooner were they in the clear than Jared came shooting through the darkness, the dog clutched to his chest. They landed just an arm's length from where Uruk and Kilimon had been swimming. Both came up sputtering.

"Now what?" Uruk asked.

Jared looked around. What he hoped to see, Uruk couldn't guess. Other than the hole through which they'd just leapt, there was no sign of light anywhere.

"Just trying to get my bearings," Jared assured them. Finally, he swam into the darkness. "This way."

They swam for what felt like leagues, though without light it was nearly impossible to say how far they'd actually come. Kilimon kept up surprisingly well, which was fortunate. Uruk was starting to tire, and he already had to help the dog, who wasn't much of a swimmer as it turned out. By the end, Uruk was forced to pull him along by the scruff of his neck.

"Just keep swimming," Jared urged. But he was tiring as well. Uruk could hear it in his voice. "All these underground channels are connected. . . . We just have to keep going. Sooner or later we're sure to find an opening."

A short time later they saw a light. They paddled toward it, eventually swimming beneath a stone arch and into the grand canal. The cold glow of the crescent moon seemed harsh after so much darkness.

Jared swam to the opposite shore and crawled out. Kilimon was right behind him. Uruk came last, pushing the dog up before scrambling out himself.

When he was finally on dry ground, Uruk lay back and sighed. Powerful though they were, his arms were wrung out.

"Let's go to my house," Jared suggested. "We'll have a drink and a hot bath. Don't worry, it's not too far."

They stumbled toward a row of houses.

"You saved Dog," Uruk said to Jared, as they turned down a lane flanked on either side by palatial estates. "The bounty is yours."

"We'll split it." Jared slapped him on the back. "You can pay your debt some other time." He laughed. "Who knows? Maybe you'll save my life one day."

CHAPTER 5

I See War—Blood and Iron

*R*IPPLES ON THE SURFACE OF THE TIGER RIVER SHONE LIKE GOLDEN hair as the morning sun rose over the desert. A muskrat floated through a gently swirling eddy, nibbling what remained of a ground worm. Egrets waded through the shallows, studying the newly hatched fry, clinging to the undersides of small rocks and dashing here and there among the weeds. All along the river, animals were working hard to scrape up the day's provender. They didn't have much time left. By noon it would be too hot to do anything but cower in the shade and wait for sundown.

A Niphilim company, better than a dozen strong, tromped across the muddy western bank to the river's edge. They had dark circles under their eyes from a virtually sleepless fortnight.

"How far to their pickets?" Simha asked. She scooped up some water in the palm of her hand and lifted it to her mouth.

"We're not sure." Kishar took a drinking-skin from his pack, filled it and then dumped it over his head. He sputtered as the water ran down his chest and back. "Far as we can determine, they don't have pickets."

Simha yawned. She took a small loaf of bread wrapped in a piece of oil-skin from the top of her pack. Bits of dried leather had collected on the loaf, which she hastily brushed off. Not that it helped much. At that moment, it was difficult to imagine anything as disgusting as that dark bread. They'd survived on such rations for nearly a week. It was nutritious, required no cooking, and large quantities could be carried with very little effort. One or two loaves and a bit of butter or grease was enough to feed a full-grown soldier for an entire day. But Simha couldn't help imagining a nice roast, or a fish, or even a fistful of goat cheese—anything to break up the monotony. She sat down in the mud and watched the sun as it climbed the eastern sky. "It'll be a hot day for fighting," she muttered. She tore her loaf in two and offered half to Kishar. He slumped down next to her but waved the bread away. "How long until the rest of the army catches us?"

"We're at least two hours ahead," Kishar said. "Maybe three."

"How many are there, according to our most recent figures?"

"Black-heads? They outnumber us slightly."

"Including the savages?"

Kishar nodded.

Simha ran her fingers through her hair. It had been a long time since she'd washed, and her scalp was crusted with sand and dust. A few tiny blemishes were beginning to appear along her hairline. She felt infected. Everyone out there must have. Simha rubbed her eyes and blew her nose, squeezing a fistful of black grit from her nostrils before washing her hands in the river. "The march is beginning to wear," she said. "Even on me."

Kishar's response was to lay his head on his knees and close his eyes.

On the other side of the river, a family of crested wood ducks waddled across a rotten log, searching for grubs. So far, they didn't seem to be having much luck. Simha considered tossing them the remains of her bread. But just then, and for no discernible reason, the smallest duckling—it was little more than a puff of yellow fuzz—slipped into the river and was swept away. Its mother never even noticed.

Simha looked at the other soldiers lined up along the riverbank and saw, as though for the first time, that her tiny band was barely functioning. They were dirty and half-starved. A handful chatted, or ate what was left of their provisions, but most just stared at the water, struggling to keep their eyes open. A few didn't even manage that. Lagassar was slumped against an old stump, snoring quietly. A long string of saliva ran down her chin. Simha wondered how the main army fared. It might be better to let them rest before going into battle, she thought. She needed troops who could fight.

After plunging her head into the river and taking a long drink, Simha stood up and brushed the mud off her breeches. There'd be no rest for her, not until the war was over. She was a soldier. Hers wasn't a life of beauty or comfort. There was no pleasure in sleeping on rocks, with only your sword for a pillow—no happiness in seeing your friends butchered. The dirt and sweat on Simha's leathers had hardened in recent days, chafing her skin and forming blisters on her inner thighs and underarms, but she could take it.

"Kishar," she said.

Reluctantly, Kishar opened his eyes. "Captain?"

"Have the army stop here for one hour," Simha said. "One." Her brows arched menacingly. "Make sure every soldier drinks their fill, strips off their battle togs and bathes. Every single one of them. And I want sores and blisters attended to."

Kishar stared. "Rest, Captain? This close to Kan-Puram?"

"It's not a reward," Simha said. She waved at the soldiers around her. "These are the very best our army has to offer, and most of them are barely able to stand up straight."

"But Captain, by then it'll be past—"

Simha cut him off. "Bel, Lagassar, come with me." Both women jumped to their feet. Lagassar tightened her belt. She'd lost weight during the march. "We're going to find their pickets." Simha turned and tromped back through the mud. "The rest of you bathe and sleep. We'll join you again before the battle. And Kishar, make sure that Kamran waters the savages. Tell him the order comes from me. But I don't want them getting anywhere near the river. Understand?"

Kishar nodded. "We'll follow exactly one hour after the army arrives. Not a moment later."

"I know you will," Simha said. "Because if you don't, I'll have your head placed on a spear and hauled back to Dagonor by a naked savage."

Kishar flushed. The captain wasn't known for idle threats.

Uruk yawned and sat up. The sun was barely risen and he was sweating already, had been all night. He rubbed his eyes, yawned a second time, and climbed off his pallet. The dog was stretched out beside him, still sound asleep. "In no time you are the laziest of beasts," Uruk muttered.

The dog opened his eyes just long enough to turn over, then settled back into his cushion. He wasn't ready to get up yet.

Uruk ambled to the window and peered out. His room was on the third floor of an inn, not far from Jared's house. He'd chosen it for the view. From up there he could see the whole eastern half of Kan-Puram. Thousands upon thousands of flat roofs, crowding against each other like wildebeests on the savanna. If he leaned out and craned his neck, Uruk could even see the tower of Moloch, hanging over the city like a watchful god, swallowing whole blocks with its enormous shadow.

In the alley below, an old man and woman were struggling to pull a loaded cart. A pair of goats was tethered to the back. They were muzzled to prevent them from chewing on their ropes.

Farther down, near where the alley emptied into the street, a caravan of slaves was marching, each with a large box strapped to his back. The family strolling at the center of the caravan was clothed all in expensive silks. One of the women wore a headdress of dark wood inlaid with silver and lapis. The men wore earrings.

Uruk stretched. In the last three days he'd done nothing more strenuous than walk to the Snail's Horn, watch a few hands of Bone's Luck, and walk back. But still his legs were stiff and his back sore. In his joints he felt a lethargy he'd never known. More than anything he wanted to crawl back onto his pallet and close his eyes. He almost did. At this rate, he'd be as fat as a merchant in no time.

"Get up, Dog," he said, kicking the dog's cushion. "Jared will be expecting us."

Instead of the ragged wool of earlier days, Uruk slipped on a tunic of fine blue silk. It was much lighter than his old tunic, and felt oily against his skin. He buckled his sword around his waist and slung his satchel over his shoulder. "First we eat," he said. "Then we go see what the world can offer."

In his purse, Uruk had a few small pieces of copper and a pair of semi-precious stones, all on loan from Jared. The bounty for Kilimon still had to be collected. Jared hoped to receive payment by the end of the week, though he could be no more specific as to when. In the meantime, Uruk intended to buy a house and servants. Or maybe a tavern. Or a herd of goats. He patted the dog on the rump. They were on the verge of a whole new life. No more burglaries. No long walks across endless deserts. No killing. He would pass into comfortable obscurity, lost in a city of thousands. Henceforth, Uruk would live a life of blissful peace. Contemplating the possibilities made him giddy.

They went downstairs to the kitchen. The cook, Tumac, was standing at the counter, slicing what was left of a jar of dates. The dog pranced right up to him and pressed his nose against the cook's thigh. They'd made friends the day Uruk moved in, and the dog took advantage of every opportunity to beg a chunk of roast mutton or pork belly. No matter the time, the kitchen was always well stocked with beer, spicy foods and heavy cream, all sold at a good profit to the innkeeper. Uruk couldn't abide the rich food, but had found that his metal would get him plain meat and clean water as well.

"What do you have to eat this morning?" he asked.

Tumac flipped a piece of date to the dog. "Master Uruk," he said. "You're up late. There isn't much left, I'm afraid. A bit of salted meat and a few dried figs are about all I have in the larders."

"We will have the meat, the figs, and some of those dates," Uruk said.

Tumac took a platter from the rack by the door and set it on the counter. "I wish I had something better," he said.

"Where is all the food?" Uruk asked.

"The innkeeper, Master Hamm, took it." Tumac reached into a cupboard for the figs. The meat was in a sack, hanging from a hook on the back of the door. "He left before dawn, along with every trader in the house." Tumac pointed at the kitchen door with the tip of his knife. "Doesn't look like they'll be back. Not today anyhow."

"Are they going to the war?" Uruk asked.

Tumac laughed. "To war?" He scraped the sliced dates onto the platter, then started on the meat. "No. They're going to Ur, or maybe the coastal cities. How should I know?" He flipped a piece of fat to the dog, who caught it out of the air.

"Are all the rich men fleeing?" Uruk asked.

"Seems so."

"What about the poor?"

"According to Master Hamm, the dust is still crawling with them. He also said that if they could just force the beggars to fight, Kan-Puram would win easily." Tumac shrugged. "I don't know about that."

"I saw some old people from my window," Uruk said, thinking of the couple with the wagon. "I think they were leaving the city, but they were far from rich."

Tumac nodded. "I saw them. Don't know where they'll go. They looked like followers of Baal to me. If so, the High Priestess in Ur won't let them stay there." He shrugged. "And what about you Master? Will you be going to the northern fields or heading south?"

"Neither," Uruk said. "I have been south. Ur is not a good place."

"I'd leave town if I could." Tumac handed the platter to Uruk. He'd done the best he could, but still nothing looked particularly appetizing.

"Then you do not think Kan-Puram will win the war?" Uruk ate a piece of sliced date and a strip of meat. Neither was fresh, which explained why the innkeeper had left them behind. "I heard that with the followers of Moloch joining, Kan-Puram will outnumber the Niphilim by three to one."

"Maybe." The cook shrugged. "But who knows what might happen?"

"Either way," Uruk said, "it means nothing to me. This is not my city. These are not my people." He picked one of the figs off the platter and set the rest on the floor for the dog. "This is not my fight."

"You've made no friends here?"

Uruk thought of Jared, crawling through the window with the dog in tow. He liked Jared, respected him even, but they weren't true friends. Not yet, anyway. Uruk had no real friends. Mana didn't allow him any. "No, I have no friends," he said. "And I am not the kind of friend that a man would want in a war anyway."

Tumac looked surprised. "I'm sure I know less than nothing, but you look like you can handle a sword to me. You wear one well enough." He smiled. "You have no trouble filling out a tunic, that's for sure."

Uruk laughed. "I am fit. That is not the reason I do not fight."

"No doubt. I'm sure there are many reasons."

The dog had just finished gulping down his share of the food, and was licking the platter. Uruk took another bite of fig and tossed the rest to the dog. He wasn't in the mood to eat.

"Aren't you even going to watch the battle?" Tumac asked.

"Watch?" The idea had never crossed his mind. When Uruk's people fought in the War of Three Tribes, there'd been no spectators. Everyone who could hold a spear did.

"I'm taking my daughter—soon as you've finished your breakfast. By then, the rest of the rich people should be out of the streets."

"I fought in a war once," Uruk said. "Years ago."

"Did you? Was it in the Shinar?"

"No. Do you know what a jungle looks like?"

Tumac nodded. "Trees. Like in the groves north of the city. I took my wife there for a picnic once and—"

"A jungle is nothing like that." Uruk shook his head. "I am not sure I can explain it to you. I may have traveled too far." He looked around, as though something in the kitchen might help him to describe his home. "Imagine a place where it rains every day. You cannot see five strides ahead because the trees are so thick."

"No, Master," Tumac admitted. "I sure haven't heard of anything like that."

"We were fighting against two tribes of farmers. Normally our tribes got along well. We provided them with meat, and they provided us with. . . ." There was no word for 'yams' in the common tongue of the Shinar, and Uruk could think of nothing similar. "They gave us something like figs, only much larger. A kind of plant that grew under the soil."

Tumac frowned. "Underground? In a cave?"

"It does not matter." Uruk didn't want to go too far off the point. "In order to grow these plants, the farmers needed lots of open land. But that meant they had to cut down trees, which endangered our hunting grounds. We tried to convince them to plant around the trees, but they said they could not . . . or would not. After a few years, the movements of the animals began to change. We pleaded with the farmers to stop, but. . . ."

"Did you win?" Tumac asked.

"It is difficult to say." Uruk stroked the dog's ears. "They stopped cutting down the trees, I think. If that is winning, then we won."

"Did you kill anyone?"

"We're all here," Uruk said.

Numa stared across the open field at the waiting tribes of farmers. It was early afternoon and the sunlight glinted off her bare shoulders. "Smell that?" she asked.

Uruk took a deep breath. "Wild flowers."

"And grass . . . wilting in the heat."

"I think we're ready," Uruk whispered. "But you have to give the—"

"I know." Numa sounded sad. Across the field, the farmers raised their spears. They were ready. It was time for battle. Numa opened her mouth to give the order. But before she got a single word out, a wasp buzzed past her nose. She watched, seemingly transfixed as it flew in a straight line for about twenty paces, and then suddenly, as though it had struck an invisible wall, turned and raced away.

"Are you all right?" Uruk asked. Numa smiled. He wondered if the wasp's strange flight had been some kind of portent.

Finally, still staring into Uruk's eyes, Numa said, "Go." And then again, in a much louder voice, "Rush them."

A cheer went up from their side of the field as the hunters bounded forward. They were excited for the war to finally begin. Over the last few nights, Numa had been retelling the old tales, about the wars of their grandparents' time, when people were still valiant and brave. Children loved those stories. Uruk remembered hearing them when he was a boy and dreaming of a time when he too could be bold and daring. When Numa told the stories, she always emphasized the needs of the tribe, and how wars were fought to fill those needs. She explained that the men and women of the old days had to be ever-vigilant, or the other peoples of the great jungle would play tricks on them, stealing meat and pelts, or burning their huts with children still inside. The young men, Uruk included, knew what had to be done. The farmers were trying to steal the food from their children's mouths. They were trying to take the land itself, driving the larger game onto the grasslands and leaving the hunters with nothing but a few sparse groves, barely enough to sustain a few birds. Some called it an attack on Mana, an attempt by the gods of the farmers to drive the wild spirit out of the world. Uruk's people couldn't allow so terrible a thing to happen. 'Killing those who deserve to die,' they called it. And Uruk thought the same. This was just a new kind of hunt, they told themselves. Mana would be made happy by the kills they'd bring her.

Years later, Uruk realized that this wasn't true. Wars were not hunts. A true hunter loved and respected his prey, even as he stalked it through the trees. And the animal may fear the hunter, but it never hated. No, war was very different. On that day, as he ran across the field, spear lowered, Uruk hadn't just wanted the farmers to die. He'd wanted to hear them scream. War was killing. Neither more nor less. Whether that made it wrong, he couldn't say. If he ever came before Mana, he'd ask her. Until then, he'd make no judgments.

From the very beginning, Numa was in the lead. She was quick, somehow managing to slash deep into the farmer's lines. In no time, Uruk lost sight of her. Every time he tried to catch up, another farmer stepped into his way. He traded blows with each that came along, but it was difficult to know whether he'd done any real damage. Once or twice, he managed to strike at one with the side of his spear, but never felt the tip cut anything more substantial than some leather clothing, which tore free and hung round the shaft of his spear throughout the rest of the battle.

Uruk moved sideways down the lines, searching for a way through. But very few holes opened up. It was like looking for a shallow place to cross a river after you'd already stepped into the stream.

He'd just decided to back up and start again when he heard Numa scream. Later, he'd think about how amazing that was. How he recognized her voice over all the others. But at the time he was too scared to notice.

"Numa!" Uruk called. He tore through the center of the fighting, swinging his spear back and forth to clear a path. But she was nowhere to be found.

The goddess must have been watching over him that day because Uruk forgot

145 / Slaves of the Shinar

all about the war. His only thought was of Numa. They'd always been good friends, but over the last few months they'd grown closer. Numa let him spend the night in her hut. Uruk brought her herbs and rare insects. The whole tribe talked about what a nice pairing they'd make. Even Uruk's mother was in favor of it.

Finally, after searching for what seemed like hours, he saw her. Numa was lying, propped up on one elbow, near the eastern edge of the meadow. And she was wounded. Even from a distance, Uruk could see the blood. "Numa," he called to her again. His stomach felt like it was full of cold water.

Tears glistened on her cheeks. Blood spurted from a nasty cut in her side. She still had her spear clutched in one trembling fist, though none of the farmers appeared particularly inclined to attack.

"I'm coming!" Uruk screamed.

He waded through the fighting without thought of injury. Uruk had never run so fast. Spears thrust at him from left and right, but he turned them aside. There was a man standing between him and Numa, but Uruk bowled him over with a lowered shoulder. He never knew whether that man was from his tribe or one of the others. It made no difference. Even a lion couldn't have kept him from Numa's side.

Uruk flung away his spear and scooped her up mid-stride. He'd never forget the feel of her life's blood running down his chest and over his thighs.

Many of Uruk's best friends died as he raced away. He might have saved a few of them if he'd stayed and fought, but he couldn't stop running. Uruk had to save Numa. By the end of the battle, nineteen of his people had been carried from the field. Most died. The few that lived were never entirely the same.

For three days and nights, Uruk cared for Numa, feeding her and bathing her wounds. She was unconscious for most of that time, and delirious the rest. Often she woke up cursing his very name, but Uruk never lost hope. He carried water from the river, trying to bring down her fever, and held her head when she was sick. While she slept, Uruk prayed, offering up his soul to whichever god would save his friend.

Finally, at the end of the three days, her fever broke. She opened her eyes and whispered something, but Uruk couldn't hear what it was.

"Rest now," he told her. He took off his loincloth and used it to wipe the sweat from her face and neck. His mother had given him a white orchid, the traditional betrothal gift for men of their tribe, but Uruk wanted to wait until Numa was whole before he gave it to her.

She motioned for him to bend down. "Uruk," she croaked. Her lips tickled *his ear as she talked. "You're the strongest of us." She coughed, still holding his ear against her mouth. The down on her upper lip was bathed in sweat. "But," she paused to catch her breath, "destiny is."*

"I'm still alive," Uruk said. He cupped her cheek. "And only you think I'm worth anything. The rest of the tribe—"

"Our destinies are not linked," Numa said. "I'm sorry." She stroked his chin. "Remember, destiny is a gift from Mana. It can make you great, bring you honor. But only if you accept it." She groaned. "Live your life."

Uruk laid a hand on her chest. It was boiling hot. He felt her forehead. The fever had returned. He was about to run to the river for more water, but she sat up and grabbed his hand. Sweat ran off her beautiful, ebony skin. Uruk checked her bandages. Her wound was beginning to ooze again.

"What can I do?" Uruk asked. He knew there were herbs in Numa's hut that could help bring down her fever, but Uruk didn't know which they were. Tears welled in his eyes, but he fought them back.

She shook her head. Her jaw was clenched tight.

Uruk pulled her into his arms. "I'm here," he said. "I'll never leave you." Her head lolled against his shoulder.

Numa sucked air, but it didn't seem to do her any good. With every gasp she grew weaker, her breath fainter. "You'll be fine," Uruk whispered. "And I will give you my mother's orchid."

He wept as she died.

Tumac stared at him. "You did, didn't you?" he asked. "You killed someone."

"I am not sure." Uruk shrugged. "Gods hide many things from the eyes of men."

"They do that." Tumac picked the platter up off the floor and laid it on the counter. "Don't guess I'll clean up after all," he said. He took off his apron and laid it on the platter. "If it's all right with you, I'm going to look for my daughter."

"Why did you stay so long?" Uruk asked.

"I don't know." Tumac shrugged. "It's my job."

Uruk took a piece of copper from his purse and handed it to Tumac. It was well in excess of what the food was worth, but Uruk didn't care. He liked this fat old cook.

Tumac looked at the copper for a moment, then shoved it in his pocket. "Thank you," he said. He shuffled to the door, and was just about to push it open, but stopped. "You know, it's funny—by tomorrow all the gold in the world might not buy me a cup of beer. A slave can't very well spend a fortune." Tumac smiled. "But let's hope otherwise."

Uruk stared at the door as it swung closed behind him. "Mana," he cursed. He should have known. Unless Jared collected their bounty that very day, there may not be anything left to collect. Uruk's stomach turned. His dreams of a sedentary life were tied to that bounty. If he was ever to get free of destiny, ever to own a place of his own, he needed that gold.

"I guess we should go to see this battle after all," he said to the dog. "They are not much for watching, if memory serves, but. . . ."

Uruk searched through the cabinets until he found a pair of small water-skins, which he filled from the barrel in the corner. The dog found a dead mouse next to the refuse bucket, but Uruk took it away before he could eat it.

There was a door that led directly from the kitchen to a back alley, but Uruk decided to leave the inn by the main entrance. He was surprised to find so many beggars in the street. It was unusual to see poor people in that section of the city. Innkeepers usually chased them off.

Uruk was trying to decide whether he ought to bar the door, and if so how, when a pair of women crossed the street toward him, followed by a troop of dirty children. "Is it deserted?" one of them asked. Her teeth were worn to nubs from eating cheap grain.

"We were the last," Uruk replied.

"Hurry," she hissed, pushing past him. "Get inside before someone else takes it." The women rushed the children through the door, swatting each on the back of the head as they passed. Uruk couldn't help feeling bad for the children. He hoped that a few days at the inn would improve their lot.

When they were all safe inside, the woman who'd spoken turned back. "Don't suppose you're looking to trade?" she asked, motioning at the dog.

"No," Uruk said.

"No?" She pulled up her tunic to reveal a pair of long thin breasts. Her nipples were red and swollen. Uruk guessed that most, if not all of the children that she'd led into the house had nursed at them at one time or another. A few probably still did.

Without a word, Uruk and the dog turned and started down the street, headed for the main north-south thoroughfare.

"Sure?" the woman called after them. "My sister and I would love to have you—and you can have a share of the meat." Her voice trailed away as they rounded a corner.

The northernmost neighborhoods of Kan-Puram bordered on barley and millet farms. It had been a nice area once, before the Niphilim came to the Shinar. There were still folks who remembered those days, but not many. The neighborhood had changed. The inns and shops that had once catered to the traders from Akshur, and villages north, were all gone. No trader had gone that way in years. It was too dangerous. Too much chance of having your cargo stolen and your workers pressed into slavery. As a result, the old northern quarter had withered and died, only to be reborn as a massive harlots' common and tavern district. Over the last few hours, it had died again.

A steady stream of onlookers was making its way toward the battlefield. Children cried. Old men kibitzed while their wives chatted. Uruk and the dog stayed as close to the buildings as they could, sometimes scraping brick as they passed the slower traffic. As usual, the crowd made the dog nervous. One young girl skipped too close and narrowly avoided a bite.

They were closing in on the northern edge of the city when Uruk first noticed a little boy with a wiry shock of black hair. His lips were twisted in rage. "I want to go home," he screamed.

His mother gave him a good hard yank and the boy nearly fell to his knees. "We're going to watch your father," she hissed.

"I don't want to."

Uruk agreed with the boy. It would be better if he didn't see the war. No child should see his father die—or worse, kill.

"I don't care!" He stomped his feet. "I don't care!"

He screamed until his mother could stand no more. She grabbed the boy by the chin and shook. "Be quiet or I'll give you good reason to cry. Understand? Now move."

Uruk laughed. He couldn't help it. Even after all those years of travel —through jungle, forest, grasslands and desert—some things had never changed.

"I hate you," the boy whimpered. His mother set her jaw and gave another sharp tug at his arm.

They were just passing the last few buildings when the mother suddenly stopped. This time the boy didn't say a word. They stood side by side, mother and son, holding hands and looking at an almost endless expanse of black.

The farms were gone. They'd been burned to the ground, until not even stubble remained. The golden lawn of midsummer grain, dotted by barns and hog pens, had been replaced by an armed camp swarming with soldiers, and a huge expanse of ash.

"What is it, Mama?" the boy asked. "What happened to the farms?"

"They're gone."

"Forever?"

"I don't know."

Uruk watched as she led the boy into the throng of nervous spectators. A few had staked out space for a picnic. One rich woman had a whole troop of slaves, pouring her drinks and feeding her morsels of roast meat and honey candy. Uruk wondered if Tumac and his daughter were somewhere in the crowd.

"Do not worry, Dog," Uruk said. "We will not go out there." He looked at the buildings on either side of the road. Both were three stories high and had large open windows overlooking the field. "I think we can find a perch."

For no particular reason, Uruk decided to head east. The first two buildings already had people in them, but the third was empty. Uruk guessed that it had been a harlots' common, with a tavern and kitchen on the ground floor and 'sleeping' chambers on the second and third.

'The owner left in a hurry,' Uruk thought. The door was wide open, though partially blocked by broken furniture and assorted refuse. The ground floor wasn't much better. It looked like a dust devil had struck, overturning tables and chairs and leaving a thick layer of grime on walls and floor. The beer was gone, Uruk noticed. He was endlessly amazed at what people valued.

In the kitchen, the dog found a few strips of salt-pork and a sack of meal. He also sniffed out a sack of rotten figs. A puddle of sticky black liquid had formed under the sack. It was just beginning to grow a fine layer of light green mold.

Uruk searched through the wreckage until he found a large clay bowl. It was chipped, and the maroon glaze was peeling off in a dozen places, but it would hold water. He wiped the dust off on the front of his breeches as they climbed to the third floor.

They passed a number of small cells—not one of which had a door—before finding a room that must have been reserved for the master of the house. It was large enough not only for a full-size pallet, but also a pair of chairs. Most importantly, it had a large window from which they could see the entire northern field.

Uruk filled the bowl with water and set it in the corner for the dog, then slid the chairs over next to the window. The dog jumped into one of them and looked out.

Until that moment, Uruk thought he'd seen war. He was wrong.

What they'd seen from the end of the north-south thoroughfare was only a small fraction of the overall force. The armies of Kan-Puram stretched across the entire northern border of the city. It was awe-inspiring. Uruk had seen herds of almost every grazing animal that lived. He'd seen antelope and water buffalo so thick that even a snake would have trouble slithering through. But nothing he'd ever seen could prepare him for the sheer magnitude of what was being assembled in the field below. The only thing he could think of to compare it with were the enormous termite mounds that dotted the grasslands north of the jungle where he was born. These men were indistinguishable one from another, and wholly dispensable. If one man fell, a thousand more were ready to take his place. Like insects.

Battle lines were already forming in the distance. The men were pressed so tight that it was almost impossible to see them as separate creatures. Uruk estimated that as many as ten thousand men were already in place. Another five thousand were preparing to join them. It made his skin crawl.

Not fifty yards from where Uruk and the dog sat, a large tent had been pitched. More than a dozen banners dangled from its poles, each bearing the mark of some family or sect. One was emblazoned with a six-pointed star. Another showed a large green eye engulfed in a bright yellow flame. The only banner Uruk recognized at all was the one bearing the symbol of the followers of Kallah, and that was only because the pregnant woman upon it bore such an uncanny resemblance to the statue he'd hidden behind on the ziggurat in Ur. For some reason, the flaming eye appealed to Uruk most.

He was still staring at the banners, trying to figure out which belonged to the tower of Moloch, when someone shouted up at him. "You! In the window!"

Uruk leaned out and saw a young soldier. He had a mace slung over one shoulder and a patchy layer of dark fuzz on his cheeks. Judging by his thickly muscled shoulders and neck, Uruk guessed that the boy was a farmer or shepherd, and so used to carrying heavy water barrels from the river. A pile of leather armor lay at his feet. So far, he'd only managed to strap on the pieces that covered his shins and groin. "Come down," he called, waving up at Uruk. "Come down and fight."

"No." Uruk shook his head. "I am not from here. I follow none of your gods."

"You'll be happy to live in Kan-Puram when we win, though," the young man grumbled. He laid down his mace and began strapping the armor to his chest and arms.

"Will you win?" Uruk asked.

"They say we will."

"Who says?"

He pointed at the tent. "But they sound too sure, if you see what I mean."

Uruk did. Numa used to talk about upcoming hunts with such assurance that the other hunters couldn't help but believe with her. Sometimes though, she was just a bit too sure, too excited.

"How long until your war begins?" Uruk asked.

"They say the Niphilim will be here before noon." He had most of his armor on now. It made him look strong and sleek, though vaguely simian. The armor must have been hot, because sweat was dripping down his face. He flexed his muscles and patted his chest, making sure everything was solid. Then he bent down and picked up his mace.

"Just a moment," Uruk called.

The young soldier stared up at him.

Uruk wasn't sure what he wanted to say. It seemed like there ought to be words that could help the boy to stand firm, but there weren't. Words paled next to what he was going to face. Uruk wanted to tell him to be strong, and to keep his eyes open. To stay close to the other soldiers. He wanted to tell him to watch out for his friends. But he couldn't. Nothing Uruk said mattered. Uruk wasn't going to fight.

Finally, unable to think of anything, Uruk thrust out his fist. It was a sign of strength among his people, but men everywhere seemed to understand it.

The boy responded by sticking his own fist out, and holding it there until Uruk waved him away. His hand looked tiny compared to Uruk's.

"The Niphilim are late," Uruk muttered. He propped his feet up on the windowsill. His knees were stiff and his back was sore. In all his life he'd never spent so much time sitting in a chair.

Morning had passed, along with a fair amount of afternoon, but the only things they'd seen moving on the northern edge of the field were a dust cloud, and the ever-increasing heat waves. The dog leaned out the window for a moment, sniffed the air, and then ducked back inside. He looked at Uruk as though he'd been slapped in the face.

"Be glad you are in the shade," Uruk told him.

He wondered how the men in the lines were doing. Heat like this could be painful, especially if you didn't have enough to drink. Porters carried water to the men, but it couldn't have been enough. Uruk doubted that the men at the front had drunk more than a mouthful since early morning. It made his throat hurt to think about it.

Uruk was thinking back to his trip across the desert, and wondering how much longer he could have lived without water, when the Niphilim finally arrived. The dog noticed them first. The hairs on his neck bristled.

"What is it?" Uruk asked him. He leaned out the window, squinting against the glare, and gasped. What he had taken for a line of heat waves, was in fact the Niphilim army. It was at once the most beautiful and horrible thing he'd ever seen.

The dog growled. Uruk wondered if he smelled something. If so, it was too light an odor for him to pick up. Or maybe it was a sound? He listened as hard as he could.

"Drums," Uruk said at last. He patted the dog on the head. Uruk hadn't heard such deep drums for many years. Among his people, the deep drums were pounded only for the most solemn occasions. When Numa had been laid out on her funeral pyre, Uruk had beat just such a drum, slowly and through many tears.

These drums weren't for celebration or mourning though. They kept time. As the drums beat, the army moved. That's how they maintained such straight lines. Uruk marveled at it.

The dog jumped off his chair and slunk across the room, tail between his legs.

"Is it the drums?" Uruk asked. After everything they'd seen together, it was hard to believe that the dog would cower at something so benign.

Uruk listened harder. It took upwards of a half-hour, but at last he caught a hint of what he guessed the dog must be hearing. It was a high snapping noise, almost too quiet for Uruk to hear. As it came closer, the dog got more anxious yet. He even stuck his head under one of the pallet cushions, though that didn't appear to help much. Without meaning to, the dog let a few drops of urine squirt onto his hind feet.

The whips scared him that bad.

The Niphilim army came to a halt better than a hundred paces from the lines of Kan-Puram. The savages were much closer.

Shamash rose onto the balls of his feet, trying to see over the heads of his men. He'd never seen a savage before. Old women still told stories about the wild men sneaking into houses and stealing naughty children, but none had been seen this far south in generations. Shamash had expected giants, with extra limbs and long sharp teeth. The reality was disappointing. Only a few had clubs, and most weren't much bigger than a full-grown woman. There were one or two monsters, great hulks of muscle and fur, but they were the exception. For the most part, the savages looked exactly like what they were, scared and pathetic. It was hard to imagine them tearing a man's head from his shoulders, or feasting on the bodies of the dead.

Shamash drew his sword. Most priests, regardless of their temple, had decided to stay out of combat. Not Shamash. He couldn't imagine sending his devotees to do something he wouldn't do himself. 'It'd be a sin,' he'd told every priest that'd listen. Few cared. Maybe it was his guilt over Kilimon's disappearance, but Shamash felt he had to be here. Even his own temple had begged him to reconsider. There was still no clear successor, should the worst happen, and Kilimon's body had yet to be found. But Shamash would not listen. His mind was made up.

Time passed, but the savages showed no desire to engage in violence of any kind. Shamash thrust the tip of his sword into the dust at his feet. It had cost him a full set of new robes—not as nice as those Kilimon made him trade, but very fine all the same—and a necklace of Aegyp pearls, but the value of the blade felt surprisingly unimportant at the moment. Shamash was hot, his throat was dry, and his palms were wet and slick. He passed the sword back and forth between his hands, wiping the perspiration off on the front of his tunic. "What are they waiting for?" he muttered. "The hand of god?"

"The longer they wait, the more nervous the savages become," the man standing at his left answered. He had big, full features. His nose thrust out like a bird's beak, a finch or sparrow. "If the Niphilim wait long enough, they're likely to go into a frenzy."

"Should we do something?"

"Wait."

"That's all?"

"I'm afraid so."

After they'd stood a while longer, the man pointed at Shamash's sword. "Not to be disrespectful, Your Holiness, but do you know how to use that?"

"I should hope so." It was just a matter of swinging it back and forth, Shamash figured. How hard could it really be?

"I hope so too."

"What's your name?" Shamash asked.

"Nader."

"You seem to know quite a lot, Nader. What else can you tell me?"

Nader thought a moment. "Just remember," he said, "don't strike too soon. In fact, don't swing 'til you absolutely have to. And make sure you don't hit the man in front of you." He smiled. "Or the one standing beside you."

"Not until I must," Shamash agreed.

Nader peered over the heads of the men lined up ahead of them. "I think they're about ready," he said. He lifted his mace to his shoulder. It wasn't much longer than a man's femur. The copper ball at the end wasn't much thicker than the shaft. "Here they come."

The savages tore across the ash-covered field, filling the air with their howls. The largest and fastest of them trampled the rest. Suddenly, they no longer seemed pitiful or weak. These were all monsters.

Shamash closed his eyes. He couldn't bear to look at the half-human faces twisted in hate.

The army shuddered as the first savages crashed into the lines.

CHAPTER 6

The Last Hours of the First Men

Shamash wiped his eyes with the back of his hand. It didn't help. If anything, the burning increased. Tears coursed down his cheeks and chin, but they were little comfort. He plucked at his lashes, trying to work the grit out, but only succeeded in further irritating his already swollen and bloodshot eyes. It took every ounce of concentration he could muster just to keep them open the tiniest crack. Finally, unable to bear it a moment longer, he ducked behind the broad shoulders of the man in front of him and hid his face in the crook of his elbow.

It was the dust. The entire Shinar was rife with it. Even in the temple, where nuns waged a constant war on the ever-creeping grime, dust was a fact of life. It could be forced back for a day, maybe two, but eventually the desert had its way. From dust, the people of Kan-Puram had molded a city, and to dust it would return—a fact with which the denizens of the slums were already all too familiar.

War aggravated the situation. The ash from the burning of the farms was lighter than the dry soil beneath. A single kick was enough to send up a puff as thick and black as barley smut. In their maddened rush, the savages had given birth to a cloud more than ten stories tall, and dense enough to cloak even the tower of Moloch. From where he stood, Shamash could make out not so much as a single golden hair on the Niphilim side of the field. The savages were little more than inhuman shadows, locked in combat with somewhat more familiar forms. It was as though a sheet of sackcloth had descended over the field, enveloping everything in darkness.

As his vision cleared, Shamash noticed that Nader was still up on the balls of his feet, peering over the heads and shoulders of the other men. Tears streamed from his eyes and a crust of ash ringed his mouth. Seeing him, Shamash couldn't help licking his own lips—a mistake he wouldn't make twice.

"What's happening?" he shouted.

"A few more of our men are down." Nader paused to let out a long shuddering cough. "At this rate, the savages will break our pikes within the hour. If that happens we'll lose our spears." He wiped his mouth on his sleeve. "I can see no way to stop it."

"The savages seem to be fighting harder all the time."

"Do you hear the whips?"

Shamash listened. It was difficult to know what he heard. The battle was so noisy—so utterly deafening—that it was almost impossible to pick out any one sound. "Maybe I do," he said. "Is it fast or—"

Before he could get another word out, the whole center of the lines lurched backward. It was as though the men ahead of him had been struck with an enormous hammer. Screams and shouts filled the air.

"They're breaking through." Nader pointed at a knot of savages. They looked nearly human, but fought like animals. One long-limbed female—she carried the sharp end of a broken pike, gleaned no doubt from one of the bodies—wounded three men before a spear caught her in the neck. Blood splattered over the lines three men deep.

"This is horrible," Shamash screamed. As a priest, he'd seen a lot of pain. A lot of death. He'd seen women perish in childbirth, babies suffering from the pox. Shamash had even given the final blessing to a man killed in a street fight. But none of those compared to the sights and sounds of battle.

"It'll only get worse," Nader replied.

"How?"

"It just will."

Another shock, even more intense than the first, blasted through the lines. A few of the men were knocked down. Shamash would have gone sprawling as well, but Nader caught him.

"We have to force them back," Nader said.

"What should I do?"

Nader pointed at the man in front of him. "Push with everything you've got."

"Push? What for?"

"With any luck it'll start the whole army moving forward. Doesn't take much to begin a counterattack, just one or two brave men."

Reluctantly, Shamash did as he was told.

At first, nothing happened. A bit more jostling perhaps, but little else. He pushed harder, until the man he was shoving let out a pained grunt, and still nothing. It was like trying to punch a hole through stone with nothing but your fingers for tools. Then, just as he was about to give up, Shamash felt the whole column slip forward. It was only a tiny shift, not enough for him to take a step or even change his footing, but it was a start.

"I think it's working," he shouted.

"Push!"

Shamash felt the next jolt almost immediately. Before long he was taking actual strides. The counterattack had begun.

It reminded him of an avalanche he'd seen once, years before. A delegation of priests was on pilgrimage to the temple at Hammishan, and Kilimon had chosen Shamash to accompany them. He was only a novice at the time, barely fifteen years old. They'd hiked for the better part of a week, the last two days in high mountain canyons. It was the morning of their last day, and Shamash was gathering wood to cook the porridge when he happened to see a rock tumbling down the opposite side of the gorge. Halfway to the bottom it struck a shelf of larger stones. Instantly, the whole mountain was tearing itself to pieces. Shamash remembered standing there, arms loaded with sticks, marveling at the absurd power. Whole trees were torn up. Boulders the size of houses split in two.

Looking back on it, Shamash had no doubt that the avalanche had been the work of gods, demonstrating the limitlessness of their powers. They had imbued a single stone with force enough to destroy an entire mountain. Shamash wondered if he were being used similarly. Maybe Moloch was using him to push His followers into the teeth of battle. If so, Shamash reflected, they could not be defeated. This war would be won, and would serve forever as proof of His majesty. It was a thought Shamash would momentarily come to repent.

He was still pushing—head down—when the air around him was suddenly swept away. It felt as though the sun had ceased to shine. He gasped. Without thinking, Shamash had pushed his way directly into the heart of the dust cloud.

"What now?" He looked for Nader, but couldn't see him anywhere. The urge to vomit was almost overwhelming. He fell back a few steps and tried to wipe the ash out of his eyes. Other soldiers did likewise. If anyone were still pushing, Shamash couldn't tell. Already their counterattack had fallen apart.

In his confusion, Shamash stumbled over a dead savage. He squinted, but still couldn't make out whether it was male or female. "Where should I go?" he screamed. He didn't expect an answer.

"Get back." Nader's voice pierced the cloud. "Back to the lines."

Shamash blinked and ran, praying that he was going the right direction. At least he hadn't come upon any living savages, he thought. He thanked Moloch for that.

His eyes were so blurred, the ash on his face so thick, that he didn't even notice it when he finally lurched into open air. Shamash ran until he came to the javelin throwers, stationed better than a dozen strides behind the main army. At least he hoped that's who they were. His vision was so obstructed he could only guess.

Shamash collapsed to his knees, overcome by a coughing fit. He tried to bring the hem of his tunic up to clean his eyes, but couldn't. The armor strapped to his groin was too tight, and his tunic was tucked underneath it. He might have used his sleeve, except that it was filthy.

"Here." Nader stood over him, face turned black with dust. He pulled a small square of clean cloth from the back of his breeches. "Wipe your mouth."

"Thanks." Shamash cleaned his face as best he could.

"Burning the fields was a mistake," Nader said. His voice was hoarse. "I told Doran, but he wouldn't listen."

Shamash felt guilty handing the cloth back to Nader. That bit of wool would never be clean again. But if Nader noticed, he didn't let on. He took the cloth, blew his nose on it, and then flung it down.

The rest of the troops were beginning to reappear. Most looked no better for their experience inside the cloud. "Did we accomplish anything?" Shamash asked.

Nader shrugged. "Killed a few."

As they spoke, the battle lines began reforming. A handful of men were out of place—spears and pikes behind maces—but most were still alive, and that was the main thing.

Nader dragged Shamash to his feet. "We have to get back," he said. Behind them, Nader's square of dust-blackened cloth lay in the ash where he'd dropped it.

The men did their best to close the gaps in the lines, but they were too late. A lone savage sprang toward one of the holes. Pike-men moved to cut it off, but the beast shoved them aside like children.

It was a monster, far more animal than man, with an enormous, misshapen head and thick tufts of fur on its neck and chest. Its nails, long and sharp as lion's claws, had chunks of what looked like skin dangling off them. Whether it was the flesh of a man or a savage, Shamash couldn't say.

Surprising no one more than himself, Shamash sprinted toward the gap, trying to cut the beast off. 'Don't swing until you have to,' he told himself, remembering Nader's advice.

The savage picked up speed as it neared the rear of the lines, but didn't seem to have noticed the human with the sword angling toward it.

A little thrill went through Shamash's heart. He'd been High Priest of Moloch for less than three days, and now he'd be a hero as well— greater even than Kilimon. After paying off Jared and donating everything else to the war, he'd still turn a profit. It would be in honor rather than metal, but so far as Shamash was concerned, the adoration of your fellow man was worth fifty of any trinket or bit of finery.

When he was only a few strides away, close enough to imagine the feel of the monster's breath on his face, Shamash closed his eyes and, using both hands, swung his sword in a long arc.

His stomach dropped as he felt the flat of his blade slap against something firm and glance harmlessly off. Instantly, all thoughts of heroism were extinguished. Living through this battle would be miracle enough.

Shamash still had his eyes squeezed shut as the savage's fingers encircled his throat, lifting him into the air. The stench coming off the beast was unlike anything he'd encountered. Once, Shamash's father had made him bury a dead goat, but that didn't even come close. He felt the bile rise into his already parched and aching throat, but swallowed it back. With the beast's fist around his neck, Shamash couldn't have vomited even if he'd wanted to.

It seemed longer, but in fact Shamash's feet only dangled for a second or two before the savage tossed him aside. Fortunately, it was his buttocks that struck first, though he did roll a number of times before finally coming to rest on his back.

"Are you hurt?" Nader asked.

"Moloch," Shamash cursed. "I hurt all over." He didn't like to use the god's name in vain, but thought the events of the last few seconds called for an exception.

"It's gone," Nader assured him. "The savage. . . . It ran off."

"Where?"

Nader grabbed Shamash by the wrists and helped him to his feet. "I guess he wasn't as interested in killing you as in getting away." He pointed at the city. The savage was racing toward a group of spectators assembled near the end of the main north-south thoroughfare. Unlike the soldiers, the spectators quickly moved apart, allowing it a wide path to run through.

"Don't close your eyes again, Holiness," Nader said. He pressed Shamash's sword into his hand. Then he led him back to his place in the lines.

The savages were attacking. Spear- and pike-men were dying faster than they had all afternoon. Shamash wondered if he'd been knocked unconscious without realizing it.

"What happened?" he asked. "A moment ago we were winning."

"That's why you have to keep your eyes open."

Shamash flushed. In battle, a lot could change in a few seconds. He was just beginning to realize that. If the wrong man fell at the wrong time, a hole could be opened in a critical spot and the line of defenders broken. Likewise, if the right savage was killed, or the defenders pushed with enough intensity, they could force back a whole wave of the beasts.

"This didn't happen because of me, did it?" he asked.

Nader ignored the question. He was gazing straight up, as though searching for birds. "Did you see something?" he asked.

Shamash searched the skies but saw nothing unusual. Blazing sun, a few puffs of white cloud—not much else. "Like what?" he asked.

"A javelin. I'm sure I saw one."

"So?"

"It's too soon."

Shamash looked at the monsters breaking through their lines. "Maybe not."

"We have to counterattack again," Nader said.

"Right." Shamash crouched, preparing to push. This time he'd be ready for the dust and chaos.

But Nader waved him away. "Not you."

"I'm fine. Just a bump on the head."

"Look." Nader glanced skyward again. This time, Shamash saw the javelin, too. "Find a man called Barley. He has an axe. You'll know him when you see him."

"But—"

"Tell him it's too soon."

"Where should I—"

"Go. Now."

Shamash turned and ran. It took him only a moment to reach the javelin throwers, but in that time the counterattack was launched. It seemed to go easier this time. Shamash wished he were with them.

"Barley!" he called. But no one answered.

Most of the javelin throwers had only just begun to untie their bundles, though a few were already sighting down the long shafts, ready to let fly at a moment's notice.

"Barley!" Shamash called again.

"Over here." He had an axe slung over one shoulder and three full bundles of javelins at his feet. But Shamash hardly noticed his weapons. Barley was gruesome. A long pink scar ran over his scalp, which was bald as an egg, and through one yellow, partially deflated eye.

"What do you want?" he asked.

Shamash was about to speak up when one of the other men, not five strides from where he was standing, flung a javelin over the army and into the dust cloud beyond.

"I said no one throws!" Barley yelled. His face flushed until it was the same color as his scar. "Next man I see with a javelin in his hand deals with me." He waited until they'd dropped their weapons, then turned back to Shamash. "Sorry about that."

"Nader sent me to make sure the javelins weren't wasted." As he spoke, Shamash realized that, far from being a hero, or even the leader of this army, he'd been reduced to a common messenger. Wars do change things.

Barley grinned. "Tell him thanks, but I've got everything under control."

"What about the others?" Shamash pointed down the lines, toward where the other armies of Kan-Puram were stationed. From what he could determine, they were throwing their javelins as fast as they could pick them up.

"What would you like me to do about them?" Barley asked.

"I. . . ." Shamash began, then stopped. "Nothing."

"Looks like your counterattack is almost over," Barley said. "The savages must be just about finished."

"How can you tell?" If anything, the dust appeared denser than ever.

Barley pointed at a soldier. He was dragging two other men away from the battle by their wrists. Shamash couldn't tell if they were alive or dead.

"So?" he asked.

"'Til now, the savages have killed any man that tried to drag a body away, let alone two. It's a good sign."

"If you say so."

"I'll take what I can get," Barley said.

"They did poorly," Uruk muttered to himself. "Unless they learned something that will help against the Niphilim, we may have to leave."

He watched as the last few javelins soared into the enormous column of dust. Uruk couldn't see where they were going, and doubted the soldiers could either. "Waste," he spat. They'd be lucky if one of every ten shafts struck a target.

While Uruk grouched, the dog went to his bowl and drank what little was left inside.

"I think we ought to continue north," Uruk said. "No use going back to Ur, anyway. I doubt the Niphilim will be satisfied with Kan-Puram."

Food never crossed his mind.

"We'll let the dust settle," Simha said. "The longer we wait, the more it'll mix with the savages' blood. With any luck, we won't have to suffer through it the way they did."

Her lieutenants nodded faithfully. All but Kishar, who frowned.

"There's to be a slight change of plans," she continued. "I'll take the center. Kishar, you can help Bel on the left."

Kishar started to protest, but Simha waved him off. "At this point, fatigue is our most powerful enemy. If any of you feels incapable of handling your post, say so. I'll have Kamran take your place." She waited until all four shook their heads. "Good. Now get into position. The drums will begin on my signal."

CHAPTER 7

Once More, with the Marks of Kane

SHAMASH CROUCHED OVER THE BODY OF A DEAD SOLDIER. HE WAS barely full-grown, though tall, and his hair needed cutting. A pike was clutched defiantly to his chest.

"Take the weapons from their hands," Shamash yelled. "Or I can't give the blessing." He twisted the pike out of the dead boy's fingers and cast it aside. There were men whose job it was to find and redistribute usable weapons to the troops newly repositioned on the front lines, but Shamash didn't care. If someone wanted that pike, he could come and find it.

"I'm sorry, High Father."

"That's all right," Shamash muttered, never even looking up. With his thumb, he closed the young soldier's eyes. "Just be more careful next time."

"I will. It's just. . . . He was a friend of mine. His mother asked me to watch out for him. I couldn't stand to. . . ."

Shamash turned. A boy, fifteen or sixteen at the oldest, stood behind him. His eyes were swollen and pink. A first beard had just begun to sprout on his chin. He sniffled, trying to fight back tears.

"What's your name?" Shamash asked him.

"Lamech."

"Will you do me a favor, Lamech?"

"Anything, High Father." He wiped the tears out of his eyes. Shamash pretended not to notice.

"Do you know Nader?"

Lamech nodded.

"Find him for me. Fast as you can."

"Right away." Lamech turned and ran. Shamash went back to his work.

Bodies were still being hauled from the battlefield. Piles of the dead and dying lay scattered through the ash. Shamash closed the eyes on as many corpses as he was able, saying a short blessing over each, but could make no dent in the work still to be done. He had to go faster. The idea of a mass blessing was odious, but he was left with no other choice.

He was about to bless a third pile when he noticed Barley striding toward him. His good eye was fixed on Shamash. The other goggled blankly, seeing nothing.

"I hear you're looking for Nader," Barley said.

"Do you know where he is?"

Barley pointed at one of the larger heaps of bodies.

"Dead?"

"Afraid so."

Shamash started toward the pile, but Barley grabbed his arm. "If you don't mind my saying, High Father, you've got more important business."

"Let me go." Shamash tried to pull free, but Barley held him fast. "How dare you?" A whole litany of curses sprang to mind, some intensely vile. He was about to let fly when a soldier stumbled past, a wounded man cradled in his arms. Blood dribbled from a puncture in the injured man's guts. He wouldn't live another hour.

"I have to give the blessings," Shamash said. "I'm the only one who can."

"Where'd you get that sword?" Barley asked.

"I traded for it."

"Why? Because you're such a masterful warrior?"

At first, Shamash refused to answer, but Barley seemed poised to wait all day. "I wanted to help," he replied at last.

"You've got a terrible job," Barley said. "At a time like this it's hard to know which is more important, caring for the living or the dead." He clucked his tongue. "Both need it, that's for sure. But the living can *feel* it."

Shamash grimaced. It'd been years since anyone other than Kilimon had advised him on matters related to the care of his followers. Even then he could barely stand it. But Shamash didn't say a word. Despite his scars and simple upbringing, Barley was right.

"My every instinct has proved wrong," Shamash said through clenched teeth. "I had to fight to get us into this war, do things I'm not proud of." He glanced at the bodies lined up at their feet. "I'm not sure it was worth it."

"There are times when men have to do horrible things," Barley said. "You know that."

"But was I right? If we lose, it'll have been for nothing. These were good men."

"You're wiser than I am, but I can't see what winning's got to do with it." Barley shrugged. "Seems to me, happiness and comfort make no difference either. What I mean is, something could be right while being terrible. Maybe as terrible as this war."

Shamash glanced at the soldiers, still standing in their ordered lines, waiting for the fight to begin anew. And the dying. They were scared. Had to be. But Shamash didn't have a clue as to how he could help them. He had no battle experience. Even as a boy he'd avoided rough play. His only talents were talking and arguing. Kilimon once said that no problem was ever so serious that Shamash didn't solve it by giving a sermon.

"I'll speak to the men," Shamash said at last. He started back toward the lines.

"Glad to hear it." Barley tromped along behind him.

They'd just passed the other javelin throwers when Shamash paused. "Did you know Nader?" he asked.

Barley nodded.

"What sort of man was he?"

"A roughneck. Used to guard trading caravans bound for Akshur and the villages of the Withered Hills. That was years ago. Before the Niphilim."

"Did he have family?"

"I don't know, High Father. You want me to find out?"

"No." Shamash turned and stalked back to his place in the ranks.

The dust had mostly settled. A few puffs still hung over the battlefield, but nothing significant. Drums began to rumble just as he reached his spot. They sounded like the thunder that precedes a summer storm.

The Niphilim began to move. They'd be across the field and over the bodies of the savages in no time. A few of the beasts were still moving, Shamash saw. But the Niphilim would soon put an end to that. Crushing them beneath the heels of their boots if nothing else.

Shamash took a deep breath. He hadn't been so nervous in years.

"My brothers," he cried. His voice felt huskier than usual, no doubt as a result of breathing so much dust. "The enemy is on the march."

Dozens of soot covered faces turned toward him. Their eyes shone like pieces of coral on a black sand beach. "The Niphilim are terrible, and they're strong. But so too are we." Shamash saw a few nods, but not enough. "Like the lions of our beloved Shinar, let us grab them by their throats and squeeze the life out. For today, we need not worry about gold . . . or glory . . . or even gods. Our friends and families ask but one thing. We have but one mission." Shamash drew his sword from its scabbard and pointed it at the advancing Niphilim army. "To win!" This was so much like giving a sermon in the temple that a shiver ran up his spine. "To win!" he screamed again. "To win!"

The armies lurched into each other and the real battle began.

Simha grimaced. She loathed these first moments. The tastes and smells, the first sounds. It was always the same—a screeching, tearing noise, like a file run over a piece of hot iron. No matter how many times she heard it, Simha always cringed. Even worse were the howls of the wounded. Over the years she'd seen thousands of soldiers go down screaming. Their cries cut clean through to her soul.

The Niphilim army was divided into three more or less equal parts. The tallest men were at the front. They were meant to hack at the enemy's weapons, especially the pikes and spears. It was hard duty. Most would be killed. A pike was a brutal weapon, capable of incredible piercing force. Simha had seen soldiers run through three and four times before finally slumping to the earth. Worse, because of their reach, pikes were often capable of disabling or killing a soldier before she got close enough to use her sword. The sooner the enemy pikes were destroyed the better.

The second ranks consisted primarily of women. They were the most vicious and bloodthirsty troops in her army. Most had been trained, at least in part, by Simha herself. They were faster than the men, more durable, and had the vision and instincts necessary to expose an opponent's weaknesses. Thus far, they hadn't engaged the black-heads, and wouldn't until Simha gave the signal. That was the best thing about the women. They followed orders. During their free time they could be difficult—displaying shocking cruelty to the men, each other, and especially to the slaves. But when the war started, Simha could count on each and every one of them to dedicate herself to killing. She could ask nothing more from a soldier.

Finally, bringing up the rear was the balance of the men. Simha liked the soldiers at the rear to be physically powerful, capable of pushing her army into and through the enemy. The Niphilim had never failed to break a line.

As the fighting intensified, most of the drummers cast their instruments aside, took up their swords and raced to join their comrades. As drummers they were no longer needed. The long march had finally reached its conclusion. From here on, the troops knew what to do. A few drums were still playing along the western end, but they would quit before long. Like all Niphilim, they'd be anxious to get into battle. Eventually, there'd only be one drummer left—standing beside Simha herself—and even he'd join the battle once his task was complete. Among the Niphilim, everyone fights. That was Simha's most basic rule. It was what brought them together as a people. They were all soldiers, taking the same risks and sharing in the same rewards. The only exception was Antha-Kane, and Simha couldn't do anything about him, even if she'd wanted to. In fact, as far as she was concerned, he could stay in his temple, meditating in the darkness, until Dagon himself walked the earth.

Simha glanced at the sun. Nearly four hours of daylight left. Plenty of time.

"I'm going to lead the women in the second ranks," she said to her drummer. "As soon as the black-heads counterattack, switch to a hard fast cadence. Play it for thirty beats. Then you may join the others."

"Yes, Captain," he said. "I just hope the black-heads last that long."

The line of defenders was already beginning to thin. Uruk was no expert in warfare, but that seemed a bad sign to him. The army of Kan-Puram had only one advantage, as he reckoned it, sheer weight of numbers. If they stayed together, and kept their lines tight, the Niphilim couldn't get past.

"They might last until sundown," Uruk muttered to the dog. He could almost feel their fortune slipping away.

Shamash gave the man in front of him a friendly pat on the shoulder. "Stay strong," he said. "Head up. Eyes open."

The war was going better than anyone could have imagined. Even after a full hour of heavy fighting, the Niphilim hadn't forced them back more than a dozen strides. Sadly, the spear- and pike-men were mostly gone. It had taken the better part of the hour, but eventually the Niphilim swords had gotten through.

"Stiffen up." Shamash was just repeating things he'd heard Nader say, but it made him feel good to do it. The men around him needed to believe that someone was in control. "We don't want to be shoved any farther."

Shamash had visions of his followers breaking through the Niphilim army. Cutting it down like a scythe through grass. He imagined himself at the head of a victory parade, women and children screaming. It was time to counterattack. He could feel it.

There was very little dust this time. The blood and dead bodies were holding down the ash. Nothing would prevent his men slicing through the Niphilim ranks. Their women were still waiting to get into battle. No longer. The followers of Moloch would bring the fighting to them. After all, how tough could a bunch of women be? Shamash smiled as he pressed his shoulder into the back of the man ahead of him. "Now," he hollered. "Push. Run."

Only a handful of men could hear what he said, but that didn't matter. The shoving built in strength and momentum, just as it had against the savages. In no time, they'd recovered every step of the ground they'd lost. Shamash imagined Nader smiling down at him. "Victory," he whispered to himself. "Victory."

The beat of the lone drum was like the patter of rain on a wood roof. Audible, but just barely.

The black-heads fanned out as they forced their way into Simha's troops, just as she knew they would. They fought like dogs. Maces struck again and again, snapping bone and tearing muscle. Simha smiled.

Around her, the women trembled with excitement. Kishar, Lagassar, and the other lieutenants had done their job. The enemy was spread apart. Simha watched as the black-heads overran the last of her front lines. They were so sure of victory. She couldn't help respecting their valor. Unfortunately, courage wouldn't be enough to save them.

Simha thrust her sword overhead, so that the soldiers around her could see it. The iron blade was so dark that it almost seemed to suck the light from the sun.

The Niphilim charged.

Shamash's sword was broken, cut in two by one of the superior blades of the Niphilim. The piece he had left wasn't much longer than a kitchen knife, but he still gripped the hilt with both hands.

Without knowing it, he'd rushed his men to their deaths. The Niphilim fell upon them like owls onto field mice. Those caught at the front were lost. The men at the back—those who'd been stationed directly in front of Shamash—desperately tried to retreat. But the Niphilim wouldn't allow it. Every step meant another blond warrior moving in to attack.

One Niphilim woman—blood dripping from her hair—came right through the center of their lines, howling as she sliced armor, flesh and bone. Shamash shrank back, hoping she wouldn't notice him. But it was too late.

She raced toward him, shoulders lowered, eyes fixed on his chest. Shamash stumbled, nearly tripping over his own feet. He held out what was left of his sword, but the woman never even broke stride.

"Now," Barley shouted. He picked up a javelin and sighted down the shaft. "Throw them at the women in the center." Barley had thrown javelins since he was a boy, hunting wild grouse and rabbits around the groves north of his father's farm. He'd had a good eye once. If he still had even a fraction of that skill, he could help Shamash and the other warriors trapped at the center of the battle. If not, they were dead.

Barley watched as his first bolt sliced through the Niphilim woman's foot, pinning it to the ground. "Moloch," he cursed. He'd been aiming for her chest. Still, Shamash managed to stumble away, and that was the main thing. The High Father was of little use in a fight, but the men rallied around him.

Shafts plummeted into the center of the Niphilim ranks. Barley flung his as quickly as he could, not even looking to see whether he'd hit his target before reaching for another. The men around him did the same.

It must have worked, because the Niphilim scattered. For a moment, they were more like fleeing ants than soldiers. Barley grinned as he picked up another javelin, took aim and threw. It felt good to see them run. Too bad it couldn't last.

"Damn," Barley cursed as he picked up his last javelin. Three bundles. Forty-two shafts. It had seemed like an enormous number while he was lugging them across the field. Truthfully, Barley couldn't have carried a single stick more. But that fact offered little comfort now.

The Niphilim were already coming together, preparing to renew their attack.

Barley nervously chewed his lower lip as he searched for a target. He knew he should aim at the place where the enemy was grouped tightest. But as he scanned the field, he noticed a woman. She had short, spiky hair, and was shouting orders. Blood streamed down her face and chest. Her blade dripped gore.

The woman turned toward him and Barley shuddered. He'd never seen a harder gaze. Even from that distance she seemed to know his every weakness, to track his every movement. It was like looking into the eyes of a lioness.

Without another thought, Barley stepped forward and let fly. He watched as the javelin spun through the air. But so did his target. At the last moment, she stepped aside and the bolt stuck harmlessly into the ash at her feet. It came close, but close didn't count.

She chopped the javelin in half and dove back into the battle. Blood sprayed all around her.

Barley picked up his axe. He'd seen a war axe once, many years before. Like most such weapons, it had a double-edged blade and the handle was thin and round. Barley's was nothing like that. It was just a normal axe, designed for splitting logs and chopping down trees. It had the heaviest head Barley could find, but was otherwise utterly unremarkable. Barley bounced it in his hands, feeling the weight.

"Let's get in there!" he shouted.

After hours of heavy fighting, with little movement in either direction, the lines tore apart surprisingly fast.

Shamash was up on the balls of his feet, peering over the crowd, praying for a miracle, when the men ahead of him were suddenly shoved apart. Instantly, Niphilim women were racing through the cleft. It happened so quickly that Shamash couldn't even get out of the way.

The first blade caught him under the right arm. It sliced between two ribs, cutting skin and muscle but stopping just short of serious injury. Shamash opened his mouth to scream, but couldn't get enough breath. It hurt so badly.

Shamash ran from the pain, hoping to escape the danger as well. If a small cut hurt like this, he didn't want to risk worse. Where he went wasn't important. Anywhere would be fine, so long as he got away from all the fighting and cutting.

The second blade hit him as he ran. It struck him behind the ear, peeling back his scalp. To Shamash it felt as though a bucket of water had been poured over his head. It didn't so much hurt as confuse and annoy him.

Ahead of him was a pack of men, all racing toward the city. They were like him, with brown skin and black hair. But there were also women— taller than the men, blonde and pale. Blue-black swords were clutched in their fists.

Unlike the first two, Shamash saw the last blade cut into him. It went in just above his knee, sliced through an expanse of flesh as long as his hand, and reappeared at the top of his thigh. Shamash dropped what remained of his sword, using both hands to squeeze the gash closed.

Blood fell all around him. It was everywhere. Shamash wondered who else was hurt. All that blood couldn't be from him, could it? Heat flooded out of his wounds. Pure, gods-awful heat. Like the sun, or Moloch's fires. He hadn't felt heat like that since he was baptized. The soles of his feet tingled as he remembered it.

Shamash fell face first into the mud. It was then that he noticed the legs. They were huge and powerful, standing between him and the enemy. It was those legs that had saved him, Shamash decided. Somehow he'd crawled in behind them and was safe. He could sleep. That's all he wanted anyway.

"Smells awful," he muttered, as his face sunk in the mud. "Just awful."

"Get His Holiness to safety," Barley howled.

But nobody came.

Shamash lay at his heels, half-sunk in the mud. The wound in his leg was terrible. From the right angle you could see bone. But Barley was even more concerned about the cut on the back of Shamash's head. If necessary, a leg could be amputated. Heads had to stay on.

Barley swung his axe with both hands, trying to keep the Niphilim at a safe distance. He wasn't sure how much longer he could hold them off. They might rush him at any moment. He could probably kill one, maybe two, but they'd get him. Worse, they'd get Shamash. Barley couldn't allow that.

"Anyone!" he called. "Help!"

Finally, a pair of men ran from what was left of the ranks, lifted Shamash like a sack of meat and carried him away. Barley stayed where he was, protecting their backs.

When he was sure they were safe, Barley began shuffling backward. He'd only gone about five strides when a woman burst through the crowd of Niphilim warriors, headed right at him. Barley recognized her instantly. She was the one Niphilim he didn't want to meet. Ever. Anywhere. He swung his axe at her with everything he had, but she sidestepped it easily. "Moloch," Barley hissed.

She thrust out her sword, trying to cut the head from his axe, but Barley pulled it back just in time. For an instant, the woman looked startled. It didn't last.

Until that moment, Barley would have said that women had no place in warfare. No longer. He swung at her time and again, but never landed a single blow. She was too fast. Too skilled.

He had to do something bold, that much was obvious. But Barley could only come up with one ridiculous, crazy, stupid idea. Unfortunately, he didn't have time to formulate anything better.

Barley swung his axe, just as he had so many times, and then let it go. He didn't see it glance off the woman's leg and go careening into the crowd of blond warriors beyond. Even as he threw it, Barley was sprinting for cover. Unfortunately, he wasn't a fast runner. 'Slow enough to see the grass growing ahead of him,' his father used to say. Barley could almost feel the breath of that terrible white woman on the back of his neck. And then, beyond hope, he reached the line of defenders and plunged in.

Amazingly, he was alive.

Simha watched him go. A knot was already forming in her right thigh. She was going to have a massive bruise. For an instant, just after the axe struck her, she'd even wondered if her leg could be broken. Not that it would have mattered. Nothing short of death would stop her.

"This war is over," Uruk muttered.

He stood up from his chair, picked up his satchel and started toward the door. The dog scampered toward the door. He was glad to be moving on, Uruk guessed. The smell of blood grew stronger with every passing moment. Even with his weak human senses, the stink was overpowering. They were in danger. Great danger.

Uruk leaned out the window, taking a final look at the spectators amassed at the edge of the field. They were hoping for one last sight of a loved one, he supposed. Most would be disappointed. Uruk couldn't blame them for trying, though.

"Time to go, Dog," he said.

CHAPTER 8

Stolen Defeat

*U*RUK WAS HALFWAY DOWN THE FIRST FLIGHT OF STAIRS WHEN HE heard a most surprising noise emanating from outside the house. It sounded like cheering.

The dog, already on the second floor, looked up.

"Do you hear that?" Uruk asked him. "Sounds like. . . ." He shook his head. "I know fortunes can change rapidly, but. . . ." It was impossible to imagine the Niphilim being routed, or even forced back. Wasn't it? He'd expected shouts or curses, even screams. But cheers?

Uruk raced back to his spot at the window. The dog followed.

Just as he'd feared, the Niphilim army was still marching toward the city. If anything, they appeared to have gained momentum. Instead of moving in fits and starts, as they had for the last quarter hour, the combatants from both armies were streaming across the field. Unless something unexpected occurred, they'd be in Kan-Puram within the hour. Uruk wondered how long they'd fight after reaching the streets. Could be years, he surmised. Resisters could hide in the spiders-web of slums and back-alleys forever. Not that it would do them much good. Killing a few Niphilim here and there wouldn't bring back their home. Kan-Puram, at least as they knew it, was already gone.

Uruk leaned out the window. He wanted to know who was cheering and why.

It was the spectators—the very same group that had been sitting quietly at the edge of the city since early morning. Only now they were on their feet, yelling at the top of their lungs. Stranger yet, their focus was directed back toward the city itself. Why?

As Uruk watched, the front of the crowd split apart, creating a wide passage. They reminded him of the spectators at a parade. He'd seen one just a few months before. The Prince of Beenar took his entire retinue, including five wives and dozens of children, from his palace to the temple compound at the edge of the bay. People lined up all along the route, hoping to catch a glimpse of the great man. Uruk remembered the strange way his wives had of waving to the crowd. Eyes unfocused, staring at the cheering masses as though they were all parts of a single animal.

Uruk was still reflecting on that moment, and wondering what it could mean, when the first thief shoved his way out of the cloying horde and onto the open field.

He was tall and gangly, with long black hair tied into a loose knot atop his head. A silver bracelet hung round his wrist, very similar to the one Melesh had worn on Uruk's first visit to the Snail's Horn.

Uruk was amazed at how many thieves there were. Five hundred at least, and he didn't recognize a tenth of them. Each carried a bronze short sword and wore a long-sleeved tunic, though many didn't appear to fit properly. A few hung all the way to the wearer's shins, looking more like a rich woman's gown than a warrior's togs. Uruk couldn't imagine the thieves looking less like soldiers—but they were going to war all the same. And judging by the way they flourished their swords at the spectators, they were excited to do so.

Jared was the last to emerge. He had two short swords, one in each hand, and silver gauntlets around either wrist. Once again, the spectators roared in approval.

After a quick nod to the crowd, Jared thrust both swords at the battle and the thieves sprinted away. The cheers were deafening. Jared was about to follow his brethren, but paused a moment to look at the buildings that bordered the northern fields, and at the people perched in the upper windows. Uruk felt certain that Jared had spotted him, though he couldn't be sure. And then, with a grin so large Uruk could have counted his teeth, Jared raced into battle.

Uruk looked at the dog. He thought about the surprise he'd felt as Jared handed the dog up and through that window. The way the dog had licked his hand, and he had petted the dog's head. No other moment in his adult life could compare to it for pure joy. None even came close. Uruk ground his teeth. "Dog," he said at last. "We are called to repay a debt." He hadn't wanted to get involved in this war, but could see no way around it. Mana had ever more tricks to play, it seemed. Uruk suddenly felt extraordinarily weary.

"We have to get down there," Uruk said. The dog licked his lips anxiously, then started down the hall. Uruk followed. They were going to fight in this war after all.

Jared leapt at the first Niphilim he saw. One blade hacked into the man's neck while the other cut deep into his chest. Blood flew, splattering everyone in the immediate area. But not Jared. He was already gone, elbowing his way into the approaching armies, swords whirling, enemies falling in his wake.

Uruk wouldn't have been surprised at Jared's skill. After seeing him drop from the side of the tower, nothing the King of Thieves did would seem impossible. The Niphilim, on the other hand, were shocked.

At a dead sprint, Jared sliced through a pair of Niphilim women—both at least a head taller than he was—and went for a third. Over the years, Jared had developed a kind of artistry to his movements. There was not a single wasted thrust. Every swipe and parry was controlled. Jared was faster than any man his age had a right to be. He flew like a dancing girl past enemies and allies alike. Niphilim dodged his short swords where they could, or used their longer blades to turn them aside, but Jared never faltered. He cut through the battle like a fish through a wave.

The other thieves struggled to keep pace, engaging the enemies he passed by in his mad rush, but most were quickly left behind.

When he'd reached the very heart of the battle, Jared saw that he could go no further. A wall of blond warriors blocked his path.

Jared smiled and attacked the closest one. He laughed as the Niphilim repeatedly struck at his swords, trying to break the weaker bronze blades. Thus far it hadn't worked. He doubted it ever would.

When he saw Uruk cut through the Princess's sword, during their battle in the Tower of Moloch, Jared had been impressed. Since that day he'd been trying to come up with a way to defeat such a weapon, though he could only obtain blades of bronze. Then, that very morning, while making his weekly rounds, he'd come across a pair of children pulling at either end of a length of twine. They broke it easily when it was long. But when they pulled on one of the shorter pieces, the twine held. And it continued to hold no matter how hard they tugged. If it worked for twine, Jared reasoned, maybe it would work for bronze. The rest of that day he'd spent gathering short swords and arming every available thief. He'd finished just in time.

After the thieves entered the war, the battle ceased moving toward the city. The Niphilim were no longer able to drive the defenders back. Everywhere they turned, a thief appeared, ready to lend aid to a soldier in need. The thieves were rested and ready to fight. Better yet, they knew how to kill. The Niphilim were far from defeated, but they were no longer on the march.

Simha strode through the rear of the battle, headed east. She hoped to find Bel somewhere amid the fighting. Thus far she'd had no luck.

A black-head rushed past her and, with a flick of the wrist, Simha slit his throat. He was one of the newcomers—those with the short swords and the silver bracelets. Simha spat in his face. Yet another surprise, she thought. Just like those accursed javelins. And equally welcome.

She trudged on, past tangles of fighting and through lakes of blood, but still could find no sign of Bel. Simha glanced over her shoulder, wondering if she'd somehow walked past her lieutenant without spotting her. Even Simha made mistakes. In the thickening darkness it was difficult to distinguish one soldier from another. Looking back over the way she'd come, Simha saw innumerable blonde women with short spiky hair, but none who moved like Bel. Unlike her other lieutenants, Bel was broad through the hips and had a substantial bosom. Her shape affected her every movement, and was obvious even at a distance.

Simha hastened toward a knot of blond soldiers. There were five of them—three women and two men. At the center of their circle stood a man—clearly a black-head, though his hair was generously sprinkled with gray. He was well-muscled, especially in the chest, and had a short sword in either hand. This man was obviously dangerous. Faster than any black-head she'd yet seen, and no doubt stronger as well. He also had a knack for exposing weakness in an opponent. Twice Simha saw him cut the sword-arms of her soldiers, causing them to drop back. But even if he was the greatest black-head warrior in the world, that was no excuse. Simha's troops were the best-trained fighters in creation. That a lone man could hold off five of them was an outrage.

She was about to put an end to this ridiculous standoff when one of her warriors tackled the black-head from behind. He somehow managed to throw the woman off, but during the resulting scuffle left himself open to attacks by the other Niphilim. They leapt on him en masse, swords raised to kill.

Simha moved on. The black-head was still standing, even under the weight of five bodies, and in spite of the fact that he was bleeding from at least a dozen minor wounds, but Simha was sure he'd come down eventually. And she had more pressing concerns.

Finally, after a good deal more searching, she found Kishar. He was behind the main battle, though still doing grave damage to the enemy flank. His limp, the same one Simha first noticed weeks before, back when they'd gone after the runaway slave, had returned. He also had a hand pressed to his side. Blood ran between his fingers.

Kishar spun around as Simha approached, leveling a blow at her face. Simha casually knocked his blade aside.

"It's too dark," she shouted. "We can't see."

Kishar nodded. "I didn't recognize you, Captain," he said.

Simha moved to his wounded side. She'd just gotten into position when a black-head ran toward her, swinging a mace. Simha cut him down mid-stride, then leapt aside as his body skidded past her in the mud. It was almost too easy.

Unfortunately, Kishar wasn't faring as well. Simha could hear him wheezing.

"Get back to the drums," she commanded. "Begin the withdrawal."

"Fall back?"

"Look around you," Simha said. The battlefield was in chaos. If the fighting continued, they could probably kill every black-head out there. Eventually. But the cost would be high. And Simha had to win not just the war, but also the conquest.

"We haven't lost," Simha continued, "but we can't press forward now. We have to pull back and wait for the sun." She pointed north, toward where the drums were lying on the field, obscured by darkness.

"On my way," Kishar said.

Simha guarded his back as he turned and headed north. Never in her lifetime, nor even in the lifetime of her mother, had the Niphilim failed to take a field of battle. That they were going to their nightly rest with the task only half finished galled her deep in her soul. Tomorrow, Simha vowed, they'd make the dark-heads scream until even the gods would hear, until Dagon himself would bow down in awe.

An hour passed and the Niphilim drums still beat frantically, though the field was more or less deserted. A handful of wounded men were still desperately trying to crawl back to camp. From the looks of it, most would never arrive. Both sides had set up picket lines, just in case the other decided to attack in the night. And of course there were bodies. Thousands and thousands of bodies.

"This is hopeless," Uruk said. He and the dog had been going back and forth over the battlefield, concentrating on the areas where they'd last seen Jared. But there were just too many bodies to check. Even within shouting distance of the city there were more corpses and blood than the dog could sniff through if they took all night. The King of Thieves had vanished.

The dog sniffed the body closest to him and sneezed. Jared's trail was dead, even to his keen nose.

"The moon will rise soon," Uruk said. "Until then, we can do nothing." He glanced toward Kan-Puram. A few enterprising tavern-keepers had hauled wagons loaded with barrels of cheap beer to the encampment. Long lines were already forming.

"Maybe someone else will know where to find him," Uruk muttered.

CHAPTER 9

And a Farmer Shall Lead Them

*T*HE COUNCIL TENT, WHERE THE PRIESTS AND LEADERS OF THE ARMY met to strategize and argue, glowed like a lightning bug on the edge of the city. Armed guards were stationed at all four corners and in front of the entrance flaps. Their job was to keep the ordinary soldiers away. The great and powerful didn't want the commoners to hear their plans. They didn't want to smell the common sweat.

Barley was in no hurry to get to the council. He was enjoying the night. Never in his life had the city been so dark and quiet. Not a single torch burned in the northern quarter. No noise came from the streets. It was as though the whole of Kan-Puram had moved into the fields and was huddled around the campfires for fellowship. It was beautiful.

As he made his way through the camp, past fires with cook-pots sunk in the coals, soldiers called out to him. Most he'd never met. Barley was embarrassed by his newfound fame. He was just an ugly old farmer after all. At rare intervals he waved, or called a quick "hello" over his shoulder, but mostly he just nodded and walked on.

A cricket chirped as Barley started across the narrow strip of open ground surrounding the council tent. The stars over the eastern horizon were magnificent, clear and sharp.

"Where are you going?" the guard in front of the tent flaps asked.

"I was invited here," Barley said.

"Who are you?"

"My name is Beril, but I've been called Barley since I was a boy playing in the fields." He frowned. "Back when there were fields with something more than dead men in them."

The guard stepped aside. "They're expecting you."

"Maybe you can help me," Barley whispered. "I don't know who I'm supposed to meet. I heard I was supposed to come by word of mouth, if you get my meaning."

"Can't help you." The guard shrugged. "Every night I memorize a list of names, and tonight yours is on it."

"Is it crowded?" Barley asked.

"Tent's full to the peak, and more arrive all the time. There're even a couple of thieves. Dirty, with shifty eyes." The guard squinted for emphasis.

"Well, if there was ever a day when thieves could go among decent folk, it's today," Barley said, and with that he slipped inside.

The tent was as full as the guard had claimed. No sooner had he parted the flaps than Barley found himself pressed against a woman's back. He was almost afraid to move. Nothing good ever came of a farmer touching a rich woman, no matter how innocently. He backed away as far as the tent wall would allow. Even then his stomach was only a few inches from her.

There was a lot of talk coming from the center of the tent, but Barley couldn't understand a word of it. He'd hoped to see someone he knew, but these people all looked to be far above his social level. Barley shifted his feet, trying to get comfortable. The woman in front of him turned around. Her nostrils flared. "Stand still," she growled.

Barley bowed his head. "Just trying to get a bit of space."

The woman stared through him. Around her neck was a collar of light-gray wood, inlaid with perfectly round bits of lapis.

"Pardon," Barley said. The woman sniffed.

Barley decided to squirm around the outer edge of the tent. It looked like there might be a few open spaces on the far side, if he could only get to them. He shuffled past at least a dozen more rich women, all in jeweled finery, begging the pardon of each. Finally, as he reached the far corner, he found a place. It was large enough for him to move his arms without having his elbows rub on the folks to either side. Barley still felt crowded in, but not as bad as before. "And I thought the rich folk had all left town," he muttered to himself. Barley took a deep breath and wrinkled his nose. The air was heavy with perfume.

He'd only been there a few seconds before a man with a short-cropped beard waved to him from the center of the tent.

Barley looked around. He could hardly believe that this man was waving at him. By the way he was dressed, in a simple leather jerkin, Barley guessed the man was a priest of Kallah. It was a sect with which Barley had never much dealt. But the man waved again, a big smile spread over his lips, and finally Barley waved back.

The man pushed his way through the crowd, took Barley's hand and drew him toward the center of the assembly. Barley was sorry to leave his spot in the corner. The scent of perfume increased with every step. Barley couldn't help wondering what he was being drawn into.

"I'm Doran," the priest shouted into his ear. "You have to be Barley."

Barley was amazed. He had heard that Doran, and to lesser extent his fellow priest Isin, had organized the defense of Kan-Puram. Isin had disappeared in recent days. Not Doran. He was the closest thing the armies of Kan-Puram had to a captain, a fact the other sects found particularly suspicious.

"Have we met?" Barley asked. "How do you know me?"

Doran laughed. "How many farmers with scars over their bald heads do you think we invited?" He squeezed Barley's hand. "As for how I know you," he said, "I don't. But your reputation was more than made on the battlefield today. I asked that you be invited here tonight."

Barley didn't like to talk about his scar, and he hated having others point it out to him. It had been a source of shame since childhood. But Doran didn't seem to mean any harm, and Barley would forgive a demon, as his father used to say.

"By reputation you're a pretty fair leader," Doran continued. "In battle. On the lines." He gestured disgustedly at the assembly. "How many of them look like they were in the fighting today?"

Most of the people in the tent were pudgy and weak, with clean faces and fingernails. Even the men wore expensive clothes, and no one—other than Barley himself, who had a cut on one shoulder—appeared to have been wounded. Plus, there was something easy and callous in their eyes. None of the relief, shame or exhaustion Barley had seen in the camp. "There's a pair of roughnecks in the corner," he said at last, pointing at two men, arms folded over their chests. One wore a silver bracelet. Barley guessed he was a thief. "And there are a few priests here I'd bet saw some fighting."

"One or two," Doran agreed. "But nothing like you. Word has it you held the center of the lines single-handed until Shamash could be taken to safety."

"Is he alive?"

"They took him to his temple. Last I heard he was raving about Kilimon, claiming he was guilty for the old priest's death." Doran put a hand on Barley's arm. "I'm sorry. The nuns think his wounds are turning septic."

"It's not true, you know. I didn't hold the lines alone," Barley said. "There were men—" But he wasn't able to finish. A woman's voice suddenly broke through the din so shrill and loud that the whole tent went quiet.

"Damn you for a mongrel, Qadesh," she shouted. "Did you not see the battle today? Were none of the priests of Marduk even present?"

Doran leaned toward Barley. "That's Nippur," he whispered. "Leader of the temple of Baal. She's a great supporter of the war."

Barley had never seen Nippur before, though hers was a face he wouldn't soon forget. Full lips, tangled black hair and a long pointed nose, but beautiful all the same.

"I only said that we must find a way to drive them back again tomorrow," Qadesh said. His robes swept the ground as he turned to address the assembly. "I see nothing foolish in that." His long beard shook as he talked.

Nippur rubbed her eyes. "I tire of explaining this to you, Qadesh." She spat out his name as though it were a particularly vile curse. "I didn't fight today, because we elected to keep women out of the ranks, come what may. But I saw what happened. I helped to carry the dead back from the front after the battle with the savages." She held out her hands as though they were still covered in blood. "We did not drive the Niphilim back. We stalled them, and by luck and blind trickery as much as valor. Our men fought bravely, and still they died. We have no hope of defeating the Niphilim tomorrow."

"Then shouldn't we offer terms of surrender?" another voice yelled from the crowd. Barley couldn't tell who it was.

This time Doran spoke up. "I know that a number of you met Ander. Do you remember what he said? I was there when he told the High Priests of Moloch, both Shamash and Kilimon, about the mines of Dagonor." He grimaced. "Thus far, everything he said has turned out true. If we surrender, the Niphilim will make us slaves. Those of us who aren't marched away to their mines and forges will be killed." He paused a moment, catching the eyes of as many priests as he could. "A few

184 / JUSTIN ALLEN

might be left as servants, but they'd be stripped of everything—including their gods."

"What happened to Ander?" Nippur asked. "Where is he?"

"He went to warn Ur," Doran said. There was something in the tone of his voice, and the way he glanced at the ground, that made Barley question this last statement. It looked to him as though Doran were hiding something.

"Ander probably fled," Qadesh said. "And it looks to me like we ought to follow. Maybe we should all go to Ur." Most of the richest men and women murmured in agreement. "If we can't hope to defeat the Niphilim, why should we stay?"

"Because if they take Kan-Puram," Nippur said, "Ur will be next. Their captain is a bloodthirsty woman, as some of you saw. She will stop at nothing. And when Ur falls, then where will you go?" She paused, letting visions of lost fortunes sink into their minds. "Are you willing to give up everything? What will your lives be, when all you had is gone?"

No sooner had Nippur finished than the crowd erupted into argument. It was just like when he first came into the tent. Barley couldn't make out a single word.

Finally, Doran called for silence. "Friends," he said, "instead of bickering, why don't we listen to what one of the heroes from the front has to say?" The talk died just enough for Doran to continue. "Let's hear from Barley, the man all of Kan-Puram is talking about."

The tent went ghostly quiet as Barley lumbered forward. His face blushed bright red, until his scar shone almost white. "I don't really have much to say," he began.

"Why do I want to listen to a farmer?" someone called from the back. There was a murmur of agreement from the crowd.

"I want to hear what he says, at least," Nippur said. "Where the wise have given us despair, maybe a farmer can give us hope." She held her hand out to Barley, inviting him to continue.

Barley cleared his throat. He looked around for a kind face. Doran and Nippur were nice enough, but they weren't his people. Even the thieves in the corner appeared to think he was nothing but a dirty farmer, with blood on his breeches and ash on his face.

"I guess you're right," he said at last, nodding to Nippur. "I don't guess we can defeat them, or drive them off, or anything else. Probably we'll all be killed or taken prisoner, or left wounded on the field until some animal comes to finish us off."

The last words had only just left his mouth, but already the assembly was threatening to split apart. Most called for a plan of retreat. Qadesh motioned for his underlings to prepare to leave.

Barley leaned in to Doran. "I wasn't quite finished," he said

Doran held up his hands. "Barley has more to say."

Now the eyes that looked at him were openly hostile. Barley felt like one of the grass beetles he'd liked to play with as a child, just before he smashed it under the heel of his sandal. "The least we can do is make the Niphilim sorry for taking our city," he began. "Thing is, those men out there—" He gestured toward the camp. "They know what's going to happen here tomorrow. Know it better than you do. And they aren't going to run. They're going to stay and fight it out. And they won't stay because you tell them to, or to give you great and rich folk a chance to get away." He cleared his throat again. "They're going to stay because this is their life, and their city, just as much as it's yours. And whether they live in outlying farms, or in the slums—or even if they live in secret dens like so many jackals—they have lives to defend." Barley nodded at the thieves, standing out of place against the far wall, and for a moment he felt a kinship with them. He'd never seen them before, but he knew how they felt being invited to such a gathering. "You great people think we live small lives," he continued. "And maybe we do. But they aren't small to us. We have wives and children we love, maybe more than you love your own, because they're all we've got. And some things are worth fighting for, even if you can't win." He spat on the ground at his feet. "No one will be made a bit happier by what happens here tomorrow, but a great many men will be made noble. They're already noble, by Moloch, and each and every one of you men should join them."

Likely none of the priests or rich men assembled in that tent had ever been openly criticized by a man of lower class. It was unthinkable. The only poor people they dealt with were slaves, and on the rare occasions when they had to deal with a free man below their station, they expected to be bowed to and worshiped. For the rich and powerful women it was even more of a shock. They were speechless. Nippur wept. Only the thieves made any noise at all, and they just stood laughing at the great men, struck silent with shame.

Finally, Doran spoke. "I for one am with Barley," he said. "I fought today, and I'll be proud to fight again tomorrow. My only hope is that I can lead the worshipers of Kallah with half the heart Barley will show in leading the followers of Moloch."

Barley could hardly believe what he'd just heard. "I can't lead," he mumbled. "Shamash was High Father. I'm just. . . ."

But Doran wasn't listening. He gave Barley a solid slap on the back. "From this point forward, he'll be replacing Shamash."

Nippur, her eyebrows lifted in surprise, gave Barley a slight bow. It was hardly more than a nod, but it made Barley blush once more. He couldn't help bowing back. For the first time in his life, he felt like a great man. A leader. And though he was sure he'd regret it later, he accepted their praise.

"I'll go to the battlefield tomorrow as well," Nippur said. "I'm not asked to fight, nor will I. But I'll lend support. And when it's my turn to die, I hope I'll be worthy."

"You're all fools, and so are your so-called soldiers." The words came from a rich woman standing near the tent flaps. Barley recognized her at once. She was the same woman he'd been pressed up against earlier. "I am leaving within the hour," she declared, "and I shall take my slaves with me." She turned, and was just about to stride out of the tent, when Qadesh spoke up.

"One moment," he called. His lips were twisted into a deep frown. Barley expected him to say that the followers of Marduk would be leaving as well, but he didn't. "If it is your will to leave, then do so," he warned. "But know this, you rich men and women who would turn and run." He pointed toward the city. "After you're gone, you may never return. You forfeit everything that you cannot take in a single haul. We who stay will not fight to protect your riches. Henceforth you'll be counted as traitors and cowards, and Kan-Puram will be forever turned against you."

The whole tent was deathly quiet. The rich woman at the center of the conflict stared at Qadesh. Her eyes blazed. Twice now, in less than an hour, the richest members of the council had been berated by those they considered beneath them.

"Qadesh is right," Doran said. "You make this choice once and for always."

The woman lifted her nose to Doran, a gesture of utter contempt, stepped between the tent-flaps and was gone.

So began the exodus. Most of the richest men and women left, calling those that stayed fools and worse. Barley hoped a few of them would return, but none did. The tent was quiet long after they were gone.

"They'll all take their slaves with them," Nippur sighed. "Our ranks will be that much thinner."

"They're only a handful," Doran said. "The war won't turn on so few." Suddenly he grinned. "And many of the slaves could be convinced to stay, hoping for freedom."

"We are still with you," one of the thieves interjected. "We'll fight for Kan-Puram to the last man."

Heads still hung. The council had already counted on the thieves joining the fight.

"But the followers of Moloch can't hold the middle," the thief continued. "They took the most casualties."

"Sneaker's right," the other thief said. The silver bracelet he wore glittered as he combed his fingers through his mustache. Barley also noted a wound—it looked something like a dog bite—on the back of his hand. "You've got the most men now." He pointed at Qadesh. "You'll have to hold the center as best you can."

"We shall do our best." Qadesh bowed. He had more to say, Barley saw, and would have continued if not for the sounds of a scuffle coming from right outside.

"What's all the commotion?" Nippur asked. But no one seemed to know.

"Someone look," Doran suggested, pointing toward the tent flaps.

Just then, they heard a man shout, "I mean to pass." He had an accent reminiscent of traders from the coastal cities, but there was something else in his voice as well, a sound very few of the men and women present had heard before.

"I can't let you enter. You're not invited." It was the guard. Barley recognized his voice from their earlier conversation. Apparently, someone was trying to force his way in. Barley began to wish that he still had his axe.

"Who's there?" Doran shouted, elbowing his way through the crowd. He was halfway across the tent when the flaps were suddenly torn aside and the guard came sailing in, plowing headfirst into one of Nippur's priests. Both men landed in a heap.

Barley rushed toward the tent flap, but he was too late. Someone was already stepping through.

Uruk strode into the tent, sword drawn. His breeches were encrusted with blood, as were the hem of his new tunic and the tops of his feet. "Who is in charge?" he asked.

No one spoke.

Uruk looked at the man standing at the center of the room. His face was marred by a particularly cruel scar, and he'd been rushing forward as Uruk entered. Both seemed like favorable signs. What's more, he was one of the very few people in the whole tent that didn't appear positively overcome with terror. He was cautious, but not afraid.

"Is it you?" Uruk asked.

The scar-faced man pointed at a priest in a leather jerkin. "He is."

Just then, the guard sat up. He quickly untangled himself from the priest, shook his head to clear it, yanked his knife from his belt and leapt to his feet.

"Don't," someone yelled. Uruk had just enough time to glance in the direction of the voice. He was surprised to see Melesh, the wounds from his battle with the dog still fresh on his hands and arms. Unfortunately, the guard didn't take his advice.

The guard slashed at him, but Uruk was too fast. Like a striking viper, he caught the man's wrist and gave it a hard jerk. The knife fell from his outstretched hand. Then Uruk punched him in the forehead and watched as he toppled over backward and lay still.

"Warned you," Melesh said. Beside him, Sneaker shook his head.

The priest already identified as leader of the assembly slowly approached Uruk, hands raised to show that he had no weapon. He stopped when he saw the dog slink into the tent. The dog's mouth and chest were dyed a deep crimson.

"Are the other guards still down?" Uruk asked him.

The dog growled, showing a full set of rosy teeth.

"What do you want here?" the priest asked.

"Not what," Uruk corrected him. "Who." He was just about to continue, but noticed movement out of the corner of his eye. Melesh and

Sneaker were backing toward the wall of the tent. Uruk guessed that one or the other of them had a knife secreted on his body, and was planning to cut his way through the canvas. It was a poor plan. If he wanted to, Uruk could probably kill them both before they even got the first cut made.

"Everyone stay where you are," Uruk commanded.

"What do you want, hunter?" Sneaker hissed. Melesh took another tiny step backward.

"Where is Jared?" he asked.

"Dead," Sneaker replied. "Killed."

"You saw him fall?"

Sneaker grimaced, but shook his head.

"Melesh? Did you see your King die?"

"Who is this Jared?" the man with the scar asked.

"Jared was King of the Thieves," Melesh explained. "And no, I didn't see him die. But I saw him fall."

Uruk frowned. The dog let out a low growl. Melesh was little more than an old enemy in the dog's mind—one they shouldn't have let get away.

"You lie," Uruk said. "We saw you, standing on the field while all the others rushed by."

Melesh muttered under his breath.

"Did anyone actually see Jared die?"

"I ran with him as far as I could," Sneaker said. "But he was cutting them down so fast, I lost sight of him." He held out his hands, as though to prove that he hadn't somehow palmed the King of Thieves.

"I see." Uruk considered for a moment. This was the third gathering he'd visited in the last hour, and far and away the least well-informed. So far as he could tell, no one knew what had become of Jared. It was time he tried something else.

"Where are you going?" the man with the scar asked, as Uruk backed toward the tent flaps.

Uruk thrust his sword at the battlefield. "No one saw Jared die," he said. "He may have been captured. I intend to find out."

CHAPTER 10

The Wounds of War

A LOW FLAME BURNED IN THE CAPTAIN'S TENT, PUTTING OUT MORE smoke than light. Two loaves of dark bread sat on an oilskin next to the fire. Each was at least a week old and hard as stone. They'd have to be soaked in water before anyone could choke them down. Simha decided she'd rather go hungry.

She tossed a couple of sticks on the fire and then moved her bedroll and pack to the far side of the tent. She needed light, but the heat was almost too much to bear.

Outside, the voices of the soldiers had died away, replaced by the low whistles and snores of deep sleep. A few guards manned the camp perimeter, but half of those would be asleep within the hour. Keeping them up would be pointless. The men of Kan-Puram had to be just as exhausted as the Niphilim. Probably more so. There'd be no attacks that night.

Simha sat on her bedroll and unlaced her boots. The sour reek of feet filled the tent. She tossed the boots to the fireside where they lay in a heap. The open flame would keep scorpions out.

She loosened her clothing and began applying salve to the numerous cuts on her belly and chest. The salve was made from a mixture of mastick resin and holm leaf. It burned and stank, but it stopped the bleeding, and the old women said it helped cuts to heal. Simha made sure there was always plenty in her tent, and that every soldier carried a jar in his pack.

Most of her wounds were small, but Simha also found a long gash running over her ribs and across her stomach. The blood dribbling from it was thick and sticky. She groaned as she rubbed the salve into her damaged flesh. Her ribs were sore. She tried to remember how she'd got the wound, but couldn't. It might have been any one of a dozen moments during the battle.

When she was done, Simha drew her hand out of her tunic and found it covered with blood. She cursed. The wound was still open. It would have to be cleaned and the salve reapplied. She spat in the dust between her feet and drew her tunic over her head.

The cut was deep and full of grit. That's why it wouldn't stop bleeding. Dust and sand prevented it from closing and drew the blood out, even through the resin. Simha ground her teeth as she ran a fingernail across the wound. She gasped as her nail caught in the tender skin. Tears came to her eyes and sweat ran from under her arms, but the sand was still there. She scratched at it again, faster, as though daring the wound to hurt her. She had to scrape her nails back and forth at least a dozen times before she got the sand out, each pass hurting more than the one before.

Simha smiled as she reapplied the salve. The burning was welcome this time. It meant health and strength. Besides, anything was better than scraping out that sand.

After her wound was properly filled, Simha washed her hands from the water-skin in the corner. It wasn't easy. Once mastick resin touched flesh it held tight, almost like a second skin. She had to scrub vigorously to get it off. A lot of water was wasted in the effort.

She sat back down on her bedroll, legs spread wide. More than anything, she wanted to lay down and sleep, but couldn't. The next day's battle still had to be planned. She shook her head and yawned. There were detailed charts in her pack, but she ignored them. She smoothed the dirt between her feet and began to scratch out a simple map with her finger, just as she had dozens of times before. She drew lines to represent both armies, and behind one of them put a long slash, representing the main road leading into Kan-Puram. The map was crude, but helped her to picture the length and depth of each army. As she ran her fingers through the lines, she imagined dozens of possible troop movements. Last, she drew a large circle to represent the city. What was inside the city made very little difference in her mind. It was hers to conquer. That was all she cared about.

Simha yawned again. She was tempted to just line the soldiers up and march them at the city. No strategy. No thought. Tell them to start where they left off the day before and kill every living thing they came across. Sometimes brute force could move mountains.

But that wasn't the answer this time. At the very least, she had to determine how best to distribute her soldiers. It might be wise to keep all the strongest women in one area, ready to bust through the enemy lines on her signal. The pikes and spears had to be gone, and without them the black-heads would be fighting close up. Simha pictured a wave of blonde women striding over a sea of dark hair, blood cascading off their swords and down their faces. It was a wonderful image.

Suddenly, she realized that her eyes were closed. Another second or two and she'd have been sound asleep.

Simha shook her head and slapped both cheeks. No rest, not yet. She pounded her thighs with her fists. The pain revived her somewhat. Simha hadn't slept more than two hours in a night since the army marched out of Dagonor, and she was close to the end of her reserves. Even she couldn't go without rest forever. She rubbed her eyes, discovering a slight tremor in her hands. It was a phenomenon she'd experienced before, always after a particularly hard fight. Simha squinted, slowed her breathing and stared at her fingers, willing each digit to come under control. Slowly, the quivering disappeared.

She was still staring at her hands as Kishar ducked through the open flaps and into her tent.

"You're late," Simha growled. She pointed an accusing finger at him. It was as still as death. Simha doubted that she looked very intimidating, sitting half-naked on a dirty bedroll, but discipline and consistency had to be upheld. "Do it again and you'll be explaining yourself to Antha-Kane."

"Ezidha and Lagassar just returned with the scouts," Kishar said. "They found no sign of Bel anywhere."

Simha felt her eyelid begin to quiver, but hoped Kishar wouldn't see. He might take it as a sign of weakness. Simha knew she would have.

She stood up and turned her back to him, as though thinking about what he'd said. "Where did they look?" she asked, gently massaging the offending eyelid.

"Everywhere. From one end of the battlefield to the other. They went forward 'til they were afraid they'd burn themselves on the enemy's cook-fires. Nothing." Kishar shuffled toward her, but stopped far short of touching. No one touched the captain without permission. "I'm afraid. . . ." He bit his lip. "Bel's dead, or at least unable to get back."

Simha crossed her arms. She'd never abandoned a lieutenant on the field. She wouldn't let Bel be the first. "I'll look for her myself," she said.

"We're all tired," Kishar said. "Even you can't possibly—"

"I decide what I do. No one else. I determine what every person in this army does, for that matter. And I say nothing is impossible." Simha turned as she spoke, daring him to contradict her.

Kishar lowered his head. It was better not to look the captain in the eye when she was frustrated. She tended to see it as a challenge. This was clearly one of those times.

So he stared at her chest. Kishar had forgotten how small her breasts were. He'd seen her without clothes hundreds of times, maybe thousands, but had seldom really looked. Simha had the chest of a girl barely entered into womanhood. She also had a particularly nasty scar running above her right nipple. Kishar wondered how she'd gotten it. He watched as a drop of blood trickled from the gash over her ribs and ran down her belly. That wound would turn to a magnificent scar one day. "At least tell me how you want the soldiers distributed tomorrow, and finish tending your wounds before you go," he said. "You're still bleeding."

Simha wiped the blood off with a shrug.

"You have cuts all over your back." Kishar pointed at a scratch running over her shoulder.

"Are any of them bad?"

"They could be, if you let them rot."

Simha wanted to go after Bel that very instant. Her natural inclination always ran toward action, quick and decisive. At the same time, she was no fool. In a matter of days, dozens of her soldiers would be suffering from gangrene. She could almost smell it, even now. Simha didn't intend to join them. She grabbed the jar of Mastick resin and went to work, twisting and feeling for the wounds she couldn't see.

Kishar noticed the map she'd scratched out on the ground. "Do you know your plan?" he asked.

Simha struggled to reach her shoulder blade. Resin was smeared across her back, most of it nowhere near a cut. "The battle will hardly have begun before it's over," she muttered. "We need only decide which of us will march into the city first."

Kishar nodded. "I've spoken to the soldiers. Most already know which patrols they'll be in." He smiled. "The occupation should go smoothly." He considered telling her that there was barely one full patrol of soldiers left unwounded. Most of those still alive looked something like Simha herself, with cuts and bruises covering their bodies. But he decided against it. Simha held her soldiers to the same standards she set for herself. March, fight and die. And if by some miracle you still live? Tend your wounds and then march, fight and die again. No weakness.

Simha strained to reach a scratch in the middle of her back.

"Let me help you," Kishar said.

She handed the jar of salve to Kishar and turned around. Her legs were spread slightly, as though preparing for battle, and her hands were on her hips. Simha hated to be helped by anyone. "Make sure it goes only in the cuts," she said. "I don't want to stick to my bedroll any more than is necessary."

Kishar began by wiping the blood, dirt and excess salve off her skin. She tensed at his touch. He was slow and methodical, taking more time than was necessary, staring at her back all the while.

It wasn't the muscles that most interested him, nor the wounds she'd acquired during the day's battle, though both were astonishing to behold. It was the scarring that ran like a net over her flesh. Many had been earned at the end of a whip. They were the same scars every Niphilim child would have by age twelve, though Simha had more than most. Mixed with those were the jagged marks of blades, and on her lower back there was even the unmistakable sign of an animal bite. Probably a dog. One particularly nasty scar ran out of the hair in her left underarm, clear across her back, and finally disappeared over her right hip. Simha wore her scars with honor.

When he was done wiping off the dirt and blood, Kishar put a light coat of resin over the wounds in her shoulders and lower back—the ones she'd already begun to fill. There were also a number of minor wounds that had been ignored, and a long thin cut that ran along her spine. Kishar tended to them all. Most had already scabbed over, so he just smeared a thin layer of salve over each and moved on.

"There's a lot of blood on your breeches," he said when he was done treating her back. "Do you have any wounds in your legs?"

Simha shrugged.

Kishar slid his hands over her thighs and calves, searching for cuts or tears. At first, he didn't find anything. The leather was covered with blood, some still wet, but none of it seemed to be hers. He was just about to tell her he was done when he noticed that her breeches had been sliced open on one side, right where her thigh met her haunches. Kishar got down on one knee and peered into the wound.

"How many of their men do you think you killed?" he asked as he untied the leather drawstrings over her hips.

"I doubt any Niphilim ever learned to count so high," Simha boasted. "Or that any ever will." Slowly, she drew her legs together.

Kishar gently slid his fingers along her waist, then began peeling the leather down off her haunches. Simha crossed her arms over her chest. He continued pulling her breeches away until her whole backside was laid bare and he could see the wound in the light. From where he knelt, he could also see the thick hairs curling between her legs.

"Looks like you were stabbed," he said.

"Just fill it."

Kishar pressed on the cut, trying to determine how much resin the wound would require. It was deep, and as he pushed into it, blood boiled out over his fingers.

"I said fill it," Simha said. "I've had worse than that in my chest and still strode into battle with my sword held high."

Kishar scooped a large measure of salve from the jar and began working it into the cut. He found that the first daub wasn't enough and went back for more. It had to hurt, he thought, as he pressed and worked on the wound, but Simha never moved. She never flinched or even made a sound.

When he'd finished, Kishar set the jar down next to the fire. But he continued rubbing the flesh around the wound. It was bruised and purple, but very smooth.

As Kishar rubbed, a tingling started in the arches of Simha's feet and worked its way up until it hung just under her belly. Every time his hand swept over her, the sensation intensified, becoming heavier and denser, moving lower in her groin until it threatened to cascade back down her legs. She took a deep breath and arched her back.

Kishar lightly patted the wound a final time, stood up and went to wash his hands. He found that he was suddenly thirsty. Even before his hands were totally clean, he had to take a good long pull on the bag. The water was warm, but that didn't matter to him.

Simha peeled her breeches the rest of the way off and threw them in the corner. She bit her lip as she touched the spot where Barley's axe had glanced off her leg. There was a mark the size of a fist, fiery red, just beginning to bruise. It didn't hurt yet, but it would. Terribly. She went to her pack and dug in it until she found a second pair of breeches. The leather was stiff. She had to stand there naked, stretching it between her fingers, before she could pull them on over her legs. Kishar watched her every movement.

It had been a long time since she'd felt desire for anything other than battle and conquest. Years at least. Simha was long since closed off to such feelings, or so she thought. As she pulled her breeches up over her hips, she struggled to shut off the sensations that raged inside her, just as she had the trembling in her hands. She squinted her eyes, lowered her breathing and concentrated, but those feelings would not be quieted so easily. She was suddenly very aware of the leather running tight between her thighs. Her chest colored deeply as she addressed Kishar once more.

"We'll spread the men out evenly, so that the first ranks appear the same as they did today." Simha drew a line in the air with her finger. "The black-heads will line up, waiting for us to fight just the same. But we'll keep the lion's share of our able-bodied women to one side, at the very edge of the battle." She made a fist. "That clump of soldiers will smash through the edge of their lines almost immediately, heading toward the main road into the city." She put a finger to her lips, thinking. "Tell them they're to kill every old man, woman and child gathered there. The black-heads will break ranks after that."

Kishar nodded. He took a last look at her chest as she slipped her old, blood stained tunic on over her head. It was torn in at least a dozen places. "What if the women aren't able to break through as quickly as you expect?" he asked.

"There's nothing to prevent it."

"There was nothing to prevent our taking the city today, yet here we sit."

Simha stared. "You forget yourself," she said. "Just because you tended my wounds, don't think you can lecture me."

"I only meant to remind you that there is an alternative." The people of Kan-Puram had on two occasions fought off what seemed like sure defeat—once with javelins, and the second time with a group of unexpected reserves. Kishar was afraid that, should they stem the attack a third time, the war would be lost.

"And what is this alternative?" Simha asked. She picked up her leather over-garments and began lacing them onto her chest and hips. They were shredded even worse than her tunic had been.

"We declare victory and then fall back to Akshur to let our soldiers rest and heal," Kishar said. "We've won the war, after all. We need only send word that we didn't have sufficient men to hold the city, and that we can return to occupy it as soon as the rest of the Niphilim are ready to make the final move from Dagonor."

"And you don't think Antha-Kane will discover that we fell back just before crushing both their army and their spirit?" Simha slung her sword over her shoulder, checking its placement by drawing it out of its scabbard in a single, quick motion.

"I only worry that we'll have to tell a story of defeat instead," Kishar mumbled.

"Defeat?" Simha wondered whether she could have heard right. The desire she'd been fighting against for the last few minutes, and which had been burning through her inner thighs, was suddenly gone. "There's no chance of defeat," she said. "I'm leading this army." She pulled her boots on and began lacing them up.

Kishar thought the chance of defeat was reasonably good, and that even if the war was won, as Simha promised, the city would not be easily occupied. They still had a long, bloody war left to fight, against guerilla tactics and a citizenry with nothing left to lose. And that was only after the battle had further weaned the Niphilim army of hundreds more good soldiers. He wished he could explain his thoughts to the captain, but knew he couldn't. Simha would have called his ideas blasphemy. Warrior's heads had been cut from their necks for much less.

"We'll take the city and then send for the rest of the Niphilim," Simha said. Her smile was so broad that Kishar could see her grinders.

"Of course your way is best," Kishar said. "I only thought you should be reminded of all possible alternatives." He dared not look her in the eyes.

"I'm going to find Bel," Simha said. "Make sure Ezidha and Lagassar know the plan before I return."

Kishar watched as she ducked between the tent flaps and disappeared. He was about to follow her when he noticed the uneaten loaves lying beside the fire. Not sleeping, and now not eating—the captain was close to being unfit. She was taking unreasonable chances and the army was forced to follow. Kishar feared the morning and the coming battle as he'd feared nothing in his memory. 'Maybe I should find a way to join the front ranks,' he thought, half-seriously. It would be far better to be killed fighting than to return to Dagonor in defeat.

CHAPTER 11

Fang and Claw

*U*RUK BARELY GLANCED AT THE CORPSES AS HE HEADED NORTH. He'd seen more than his share of gaping wounds and staring eyes already. Much more. If he came across a head of gray hair or a pair of silver gauntlets, he'd investigate. Otherwise, he intended to keep moving. His plan was to cut straight across the battlefield to the Niphilim camp. If Jared was a prisoner, Uruk wanted to know it.

As he walked, he kept his eyes trained on the ground at his feet. Dodging the mud wallows and blood pools that had grown up around the bodies wasn't easy. The moon had just begun to peek over the eastern horizon, and in the darkness one expanse of black earth looked much the same as another. Uruk wasn't squeamish about blood—he'd skinned enough animals to cover the Tower of Moloch twice over—but he didn't like the idea of trudging through it either. There was something fundamentally unclean about wading in another man's death.

Bodies became more numerous with every passing step, their stink more pungent. Soon he was passing heaps of them, legs and arms intertwined. The pools of congealing blood became deeper, thicker and harder to avoid. A few of the wounded may have even drowned in them. Of all the deaths he could imagine, that was easily one of the worst.

Uruk was making his way around one of the larger piles, going out of his way to give it an extra wide berth, when he saw a flicker of movement out of the corner of his eye. "Dog?" he called. "Is that you?" He reached for his sword.

A jackal popped its head up over a heap of corpses not ten strides away. A long strip of hairy skin was clenched in its teeth. Uruk could see only its head and neck, but knew it had to be standing on the dead. Jackals have long legs, but not that long.

He took a cautious step toward it. Normally Uruk wouldn't have bothered. But this was an abnormally large beast. He was concerned that it might have a mate hiding somewhere among the shadows. Maybe a whole pack.

The jackal watched him approach, eyes shining a sickly yellow. It seemed to be sizing him up, deciding whether he was in fact a danger. Uruk waved the point of his sword in front of its eyes, all but daring it to attack.

Finally the jackal got the message. It ducked back behind the pile of dead and was gone, leaving nothing but the sound of its footsteps squashing through the mud.

Uruk thrust his sword into its scabbard and continued on his way. He chose a path slightly east of the one he'd been following. If he could avoid happening upon that jackal a second time, he would.

He was nearing the portion of the field where the army had formed into lines, but there was still no sign of the dog anywhere. He'd run off just after they left the camp, probably chasing rats amid the bodies. At the time, Uruk hadn't thought much of it. During their long walk from Ur, the dog had often disappeared for hours at a stretch. He always showed up eventually, usually with a muskrat dangling from his teeth. Knowing that didn't make Uruk feel better about the dog's disappearance, though. From the moment they'd entered Kan-Puram, the dog had been at his side. Uruk had come to rely on his company. Plus, now there were jackals on the field. The dog was tough and mean, but against wild animals? Uruk picked up his pace.

He was three-quarters of the way across the field when he came upon an enormous wall of bodies, stretching for at least a quarter-league in either direction. It was all that remained of the original battle lines, complete with shattered weapons of every description and the corpses of savages, Niphilim and defenders alike.

They were piled four and five deep. Sometimes more. In places, the bodies reached as high as a man's hips. Uruk's mind raced, trying to calculate the number of dead required for such a barrier. Easier to guess the number of stars in the sky, he thought. He couldn't help remembering how he'd left his people in shame after a battle in which a mere dozen had been killed. Twelve. Of course, back then he never would have believed that something like this was possible.

Uruk looked east and west, but could see no easy way across. Going around would be simple enough, and would allow him to keep his feet free of the carnage, but it would also take time—a commodity of which he was running short. If he was going to scout the Niphilim camp while the soldiers were still asleep, he had to get across the field soon. The sun wouldn't stay hidden forever.

After a bit of deliberation, Uruk decided to follow the wall east. With any luck he'd find a gap. It didn't have to be much—just enough for him to squeeze through with his sword and satchel. That meant wading in blood, Uruk knew. If it meant crawling across bodies, Uruk would do that as well. But he sure hoped he wouldn't need to.

He walked a fair distance before finding a likely spot. Getting through wouldn't be easy. The gap Uruk had discovered was by no means clear—the bodies just weren't stacked so deep. Patches of dark earth peeked out from between arms and legs, heads and torsos. If he was careful, he ought to be able to glide from one to another, like leaping on stones across a river. Uruk rolled up his breeches. The night wind felt hot against his knees.

The first body he stepped over was that of a female savage. Her skull had been smashed in, leaving a hole as big as a man's fist. Uruk grimaced as his foot brushed her hair and sank into the muck next to her open mouth.

The mud was both sticky and slippery at the same time. In some places, it seemed to grab hold of Uruk's foot and pull him down. He had to rock back and forth, and heave with all his strength before it would come free. Other times, bubbles popped around his ankles, releasing a stench that brought tears to his eyes. It might have been worse, Uruk reminded himself. The mud might have been deeper. Or the holes might have had bodies submerged in them. At least he hadn't been forced to walk on the dead.

When he finally stepped free of the morass, Uruk let out a sigh. It was such a relief to stand on firm, dry earth.

Uruk took a half-empty water-skin from his satchel, rinsed his mouth, and then used what was left to wash his feet. After he'd squeezed out the last few drops, he tossed the empty skin onto the bodies. Water-skins were easy to come by, and he had another full one still in his satchel.

There were a few savages lying here and there on the field ahead of him, but nothing like what he'd just come through. If he did find Jared, and somehow managed to free him, Uruk thought he'd take him back to the city by way of the Tiger River. It was the long way round, but if Uruk had his way, he'd never cross that field again. Nor even go near it.

Unfortunately, destiny had other plans for him.

Uruk had gone no more than a dozen strides when he heard footsteps, coming on fast. He turned toward them and saw a woman, tall and lean, heading right at him. She had to have been there the whole time, but in his rush to clean the muck off his feet, Uruk hadn't noticed. Too late now. She'd reach him in seconds. Trying to run would be futile.

Simha was equally surprised to see him. She'd never seen a black man before, and hadn't expected to see one anytime soon, though she'd heard tales. Lots of them. Antha-Kane claimed to have trapped one once, years before. He always described the black-skinned men as small, with heavy features and long, sinewy limbs. This man was none of those things. He was enormous, as tall as any Niphilim man, but even bulkier through the chest. In fact, when she'd first spotted him, climbing out from among the corpses, Simha had mistaken him for one of her own soldiers. He had the look of power.

"Run away," she said. She flicked her fingers at him, as though swatting an insect. "Get back to your camp and I'll let you live to see morning."

The language she spoke was unlike anything Uruk had ever heard, though her threat came through loud and clear. She was dangerous. Uruk clenched both fists at his side, but otherwise didn't move.

Like most Niphilim, Simha had never bothered to learn the common language of the Shinar. Languages were not her strength. She was a master of iron, not of words. She tried again, slower and louder, pointing toward Kan-Puram. "Get away—or I'll cut you to pieces."

Uruk stood his ground.

"For the last time. . . ." Simha reached for her sword. "Be gone."

The instant she touched her weapon, Uruk whipped his sword from its scabbard and leveled it at her throat. She was still out of reach, but he figured he could come at her in two steps. Three if she tried to get away.

They both stared, each waiting for the other to make the first move.

"You needn't die here," Simha said at last.

Uruk shook his head. "Say something I can understand or be quiet." He turned his sword back and forth, as though he'd already run her through and was slowly twisting the blade in her guts.

"Where did you get that?" Simha asked. There was just enough moonlight for her to recognize the careful workmanship that had gone into the making of his weapon. The thin blade and circular hand guard—even the delicate leather wrappings on the handle. His sword was just like hers. Maybe a bit longer through the hilt, but otherwise an exact match. Simha was stunned. She held her weapon out so that he could see. "Where did you find it?" she asked. "I thought I was the only one with such a blade."

"They are the same," Uruk said, and shrugged. He understood what she was getting at, more or less, but didn't think it important. The idea that his sword could be one of a kind had never occurred to him. Rare? Certainly. But unique? Uruk had come too far to think that anything was truly unique. "I traded for it in Ur," he explained. "A merchant named Baluch told me it was made by a lost northern tribe."

Simha chewed her lip in annoyance. She hadn't understood a word he'd said.

Uruk tried again and again, in every one of the seven languages he knew. He even tried his native tongue, though he knew that was hopeless. Nothing seemed to break through. The woman just stared at him, her eyes utterly blank.

Finally he fell silent. Simha was glad. She was done talking. For years she'd believed that her weapon was without equal. That nothing so powerful could possibly have a mate. It was a point of pride. The thought of that other blade being passed from hand to black-headed hand made her feel dirty.

"Give it to me." She stepped toward him. Whether he gave the sword up willingly, or she had to kill him to take it, made very little difference to her mind. Either way, the weapon was leaving the battlefield with her.

Uruk backed away.

Simha came in low, slashing at his belly. She hoped to end the fight quickly and get back to searching for Bel.

But Uruk was faster than he looked. And he was tricky. Instead of dodging backward, the way any trained soldier would do, he knocked her blade aside and leapt straight at her. He was hoping to end the fight quickly as well.

His fist glanced off her jaw, driving her head back and causing dark spots to burst in front of her eyes. It was easily the hardest punch Simha had ever taken. One of her teeth was cracked, and she'd come close to tripping over her own feet. If his knuckles had landed flush, Simha doubted whether she'd have been able to maintain consciousness.

Only her reflexes kept her alive. She heard him grunt, felt his breath on her face. He was right in front of her. Almost touching. Too close to bring his weapon around quickly. Even with her eyes squeezed shut, Simha was able to leap aside, narrowly avoiding his blade as it whistled past her ear.

Her vision cleared as she backed away. The pain in her jaw was intense. She opened and closed her mouth a few times, making sure it wasn't broken.

Uruk didn't press his attack.

By all rights she should be dead, and Simha knew it. He should have cut her down when he had the advantage. But he'd made a mistake. He'd gone in for the kill too fast. At close quarters, a warrior can swing a sword across the thighs or knees much more quickly than he can bring it up and across the neck or face. Then, with his opponent crippled, he may kill at his leisure. Simha would make him pay for his ignorance.

She circled to his left, watching as he turned with her. He had a peculiar defensive stance, crouched and with his sword held at arm's length, as though fending off a wolf or bear. Simha watched the muscles in his sword-arm flex, keeping the tip trained on her neck. He gripped the handle too tightly, she saw. Another mistake. All in all, she was less than impressed with his skills. If not for their earlier tussle, she might have thought him an easy target, as bad a fighter as all the other black-heads. But he wasn't that. No. The look in his eyes spoke of long experience.

She attacked again, this time staying well out of reach, aiming blows at his arms and shoulders. Uruk easily fought them all off. Too easily. She was playing with him, he realized. Testing him. She was too far away for her attacks to be anything more. She'd decided that he was dangerous, and was taking no chances.

Suddenly, after a few seconds of banging swords together, she lunged and stabbed at his chest, leaving her flank wide open. Uruk knocked her thrust aside and was about to counterattack, but stopped. Something in her expression held him back. He didn't know how she'd have parried, but was sure she already something in mind. This woman was like a jungle cat, a lioness, playing with her prey before sinking her teeth into its neck. She was the ultimate predator, the mightiest hunter, and she knew it.

204 / J U S T I N   A L L E N

Once again, Uruk backed away.

Leaving her flank open had been planned, just as he'd guessed. Simha was ready to leap aside the moment he attacked. But he never did. For a moment she was confused. Any warrior, no matter how green, ought to have seen that opening. He should have gone for the kill. Then it struck her. That was his weakness. He lacked that instinct most fundamental to the Niphilim soul. Love of the kill. He didn't know the pleasure inherent in crushing an enemy.

From then on, she drove at him mercilessly. Her speed and agility were awe-inspiring. Uruk could do little more than stay out of her reach. Every time she hacked at him, he took another step back. And another.

Finally, Uruk could retreat no farther. He took a last step and his heel came down in mud. The wall of bodies was right behind him.

Simha saw his predicament and smiled. He was a dead man.

Her blade flew at him from every direction, landing nearly as often as he managed to turn it aside. In no time, Uruk was bleeding from wounds in both arms and one leg. He also had a cut in his sword-hand, which nearly caused him to lose his weapon, and another in his chest. None were serious, but Uruk saw in them a sign of what was to come. 'I am going to die,' he thought. Thus far he'd managed to block her killing blows, but how much longer could that last? Uruk was getting tired. One missed feint. One hard thrust. That's all it would take. The worst part of it was that she was killing him so easily. Uruk hadn't managed to cut her even one time. She was just too fast. He was honestly glad that the dog had run off. He felt certain that she would have killed him, too. That would have been too much to bear.

Uruk had all but resigned himself to his fate, when an idea sprang to his mind. It was something he remembered from childhood—an old story, about a hunter who found himself being tracked by a lion. Finally, seeing that he could never outrun the beast, the hunter gave up. He flung himself into the lion's jaws. And by so doing, he stabbed the lion in the throat and was saved. Numa called this the 'path of fang and claw.' It meant throwing your body directly into danger—giving yourself up, without reservation, to the teeth of destiny. In Uruk's case, that meant Simha's sword. He'd always laughed when Numa told that story, and he wasn't the only one. It was so old-fashioned. Even the title felt old—'Fang and Claw.' None of the young men could take it seriously. But now, fighting this white woman, it was that old-fashioned story that came to him. Uruk could see no other way. He crouched, ready to try. Truth be told, he didn't have much hope.

Simha saw him bend down, but thought nothing of it. She was tired. Her hands were numb from the clash of iron. The wound in her flank, the one Kishar had filled for her, throbbed. Her jaw was swollen. Worst of all was the knot in her thigh, where Barley's axe had struck her. The pain in that leg went clear to the bone. As far as Simha was concerned, this fight couldn't end soon enough. She swung time and again, and was getting closer. He was bleeding from no fewer than a dozen tiny wounds. But somehow, she hadn't been able to finish him off.

And then suddenly, his sword dropped, leaving his neck wide open. Simha almost couldn't believe it. At last she'd won.

Uruk saw her sword whistling toward him, but could do nothing about it. He was already on the path. The only thing he could do now was to spring forward, right into her chest. At least he might kill the woman who killed him, he thought.

Her sword crashed into the side of his head. Uruk was surprised. Judging by its trajectory, he'd have guessed that it would strike him in the neck. Instead of being decapitated, he supposed, she must have sheered off the top of his skull. His last thought, as his muscles went slack, was that he hoped someone would find his body before it slipped beneath the mud.

But Simha hadn't chopped off any part of his head. In fact, she hadn't cut him at all. Somehow this black man, who she wanted to kill with every ounce of her being, had ducked forward just enough so that only her fists, and the hand-guard on her sword, hit him. They landed with enough force to knock him unconscious, but he'd live.

Simha, much to her surprise, would not.

She howled as his sword bit into her. This was not the death she'd envisioned. There was too much pain. Not enough honor. Simha looked down and saw his blade thrusting from between her ribs. Only the tip had gone in, barely more than the width of a woman's hand, but that was enough. She spat. Blood ran from the tooth he had broken earlier. This wasn't right at all, she thought.

Simha grabbed his sword by the blade, cutting her palm as she wrenched it free.

Blood rushed from her in torrents, sapping the last of her strength. She took two shuffling steps, trying desperately to remain on her feet. It was hopeless. "Dagon forgive me," she groaned, and collapsed to her knees. She glanced at her killer, lying face down in the dust, just out of her reach. His back rose and fell peacefully.

With a last grimace, Simha fell forward. Her chin ploughed into the mud.

Uruk woke a few moments later. Blood ran down his right cheek and off his ear. It trickled down his neck. He couldn't remember how he'd come to be lying down next to a pile of dead bodies. As he lifted his head off the ash, Uruk couldn't help believing that he'd somehow died, and that this was the underworld.

He picked up his sword, wondering how it had gotten out of its scabbard. The tip was red with blood. Uruk tried to wipe it off on his breeches, but was overcome by nausea. Cradling his sword in his lap, he hunched over and vomited. Blood rushed to his head with every heave. He felt faint.

Uruk forced himself to stand and walk. He vaguely remembered searching for someone, but couldn't say who. For now, it was enough just to get away from the bodies. The tip of his sword dragged in the dust behind him.

"Dog!" he rasped. At some point, he'd noticed that he was alone, and decided that he must be looking for the dog. There was no answer so he tried again. Flashes of ghostly light burst in front of his eyes with every shout.

Finally, Uruk could go no farther. The lights seemed to be coming right at him. "Dog?" he whispered.

Another wave of nausea overcame him.

Uruk leaned over to vomit. He pushed on his forehead with the heel of his free hand, trying to counter the pressure building up in his skull. It didn't work. Blood rushed to his head again, and this time he couldn't force back the darkness. He stumbled and fell.

His sword landed at his side, sending up a small puff of ash.

Book III
ANDER RETURNS

*T*WO QUESTIONS REGARDING THE HISTORY OF THE WAR WITH THE Niphilim have ever troubled historians.

The first relates to Uruk. How did he survive? Having been gravely wounded in the head, and by no less powerful a combatant than the Niphilim commander herself, he was rendered unconscious upon the field of battle. Given the unhealthy conditions, the sheer number of scavenger animals that would subsequently descend upon the bodies of the dead, and the incredible heat of the climate, his later reappearance has long been viewed, and rightly so, as a sort of minor miracle.

Priests and people of faith have ever attributed his survival to the divine protection of gods. Which gods? That question has served as a subject for lively debate. It will surprise no one to read that the temple of Kallah tells a story of the goddess herself, standing watch over the prone hero. The followers of Marduk disagree, claiming that it was their own god's famous dragon that, having wrapped Uruk in its protective coils, saved his life. Priests of Moloch tell tales of a ring of heavenly fire, surrounding him, sealing him off from the dangers of the battlefield.

But the truth is more astonishing yet.

It was the dog who stood watch over the prostrate Uruk—both through the balance of the night, and even into the hottest part of the following day. During many long hours without food or drink, or even the barest hint of shade, the dog guarded the life of his companion and friend. Many times he was forced to fight off the carrion birds that had come from leagues around to feast upon the corpses. Likewise, the dog risked his own life by standing his ground against the cunning and wile of no less an opponent than a wild jackal. Indeed, without his steadfastness and courage, Uruk certainly would have perished on that field—a fact that, when viewed through the prism of the coming days and weeks, and the integral part Uruk was doomed to play in the ultimate outcome of the war, would have changed inexorably the entire history of the Shinar.

The second major question plaguing scholars has proved no less divisive, and maybe more so. That is: To what extent was Isin—leader and longtime spiritual stalwart of the temple of Kallah, unquestionably the man closest to and most often in contact with the usurper himself, having accompanied him on his many visits to temples both in Kan-Puram and eventually Ur—cognizant of, and in fact culpable for, Ander's planned and eventual domination of the armies of Kan-Puram?

The debate still rages.

To put it another way: How did Ander manage, in so short a time, to wrest control away from the rightful leaders? And how much of his plans did he confide to the priest, or priests, of the temple of Kallah? It goes without saying that the followers of that goddess deny any suggestion of complicity. As do the followers of Marduk, Baal, and Moloch, whenever their roles in the coup are mentioned.

But whether Isin was fully aware of Ander's plot, or merely an unwitting pawn, there can be little doubt as to the importance he played in its success, or of the damning consequences it was to have for all the peoples of the Shinar.

Lead Us Not into Temptation

*I*SIN WOKE WITH A CRAMP IN HIS LOWER LEG. HE REACHED FOR HIS toes, but the muscle wouldn't relax. "Kallah's teats," he cursed.

"Stand up," Ander suggested. "It'll help."

Isin jumped up and took a few limping steps. He walked in circles, stomping his own blankets into the dirt, trying not to disturb the other men, stretched out in the short grass for as far as he could see.

"Now bend over. Touch your toes."

He did. Mercifully, it worked. Over the last few days Isin had gotten a good deal more exercise than he was used to. Unlike Doran, who was constantly searching for reasons to take Kallah's ministry to the streets, Isin tended toward the monastic side of temple life. Exercise was neither something he liked, nor sought. Now he was paying the price. The muscles in his legs had begun to firm up, and his lungs no longer troubled him. But Isin wasn't sure the results were worth the effort. He'd woken with leg cramps each of the last three nights.

"Where did you learn about aches and pains?" he asked.

"In the mines," Ander replied. "Slaves are often hurt."

"Of course." Isin sat down on his bedroll and stretched his feet toward the fire. "Is it almost morning?"

"Not even midnight."

For the first time, Isin noticed the packs. There were at least a dozen of them, lying in the grass to either side of Ander. Those to his left were open—contents spilling from their tops. Isin watched as he picked up one of the unopened packs and began rifling through it. "Can't sleep?" he asked.

Ander shrugged. "I never can." From the satchel Ander took a joint of pork wrapped in oilcloth, which he set it on the pile at his feet. He'd collected a lot of food. Bread and meat for the most part, though there were figs and dates as well. "You might have noticed."

Isin had. Ander sat up night after night, staring into the fire. Truth be told, Isin couldn't say for sure that Ander had ever slept. Even in Ur, when they were guests of the High Priestess, Ander sat awake. Once, Isin woke to find him staring at the wall of their room, muttering in some foreign tongue. "Maybe you're too tired to sleep," he offered. "You know what they say, 'Rich men sleep lightly—working men not at all.'"

"I'm used to losing sleep," Ander said. "As a boy I spent my nights tending goats." He tossed aside the pack he'd been searching through and reached for another. "Then there was the mine. Day after day locked beneath the earth, darkness lost some of its power. And I spent nights plotting my escape. Sleep just got left behind."

"I see." Isin had little doubt that Ander believed every word he'd just uttered. Every excuse. In some sense, it may have even been true. But he'd also missed the point entirely. It wasn't just sleep. Ander rarely ate, never washed, and only talked when necessary. And he was getting worse. At the banquet in Ur, Ander sat slumped in his chair, staring at his food disgustedly. The other priests repeatedly tried to engage him in conversation, but Ander would do little more than grunt. Later, when they'd stated their case to the High Priestess, he gave a stirring account of the Niphilim threat, just as he had at the various temples in Kan-Puram, but then responded to questions with a single word or haughty glare. Isin had thought the mission a failure. He was shocked when, despite his companion's crude manners, the High Priestess elected to send an army. Ander had done something, Isin felt sure. But what?

"I'll be gone within the hour," Ander suddenly announced.

"Gone?"

"I'm taking a few of the men on ahead. We should be able to make the city in about four hours—if we run."

"If Kan-Puram were that close we'd see lights."

"Not if the torches were never lit."

Isin glanced at the northern horizon. For the first time the darkness seemed putrid. Deadly. He watched as Ander picked up the last pack and opened the top. Inside were a spare tunic and a pair of sandals. There was also a knife, some rope and a pair of gaming bones. Nothing edible. Ander tossed the pack aside. "Give me yours," he said.

"What are you looking for?"

"I know you still have some of the honey candy the High Priestess gave you. I'm going to give it to the men I take with me."

213 of the Shinar

"Fine." Isin was sorry to lose the candy, but wasn't willing to argue over it.

"I want to see if the war has begun," Ander said. "Your city may have already fallen."

"You don't believe we could have won?"

"Without the followers of Moloch? Never."

"And with them?"

Ander squinted at Isin. He was suspicious.

Isin stared into the fire. He knew of Shamash's plan for bringing the followers of Moloch into the war, as did Doran. But they'd agreed to keep it secret. If the city was ever to return to normal, that information had to be kept in strictest confidence. With luck, no one would ever find out that the new High Father of the temple of Moloch had hired his predecessor's killer. Ander certainly didn't need to know.

"I still don't think they'd win," Ander said at last.

"What if the Niphilim have taken the city? Then what will you do?"

Ander began placing the food he'd collected into his own pack. "Try to get back. Warn you." When all was tucked safely inside, he tied the pack closed and slung it over his shoulder.

"And what if you can't get back?" Isin asked.

"That means I'm dead. You'll have to take care of yourselves."

Isin imagined the men of Ur marching into the city, discovering only too late that the Niphilim were waiting. He shuddered. "Maybe you shouldn't go," he said.

"I have to."

"Why?"

Ander sighed. "Because when I close my eyes, I see only Niphilim faces. When I speak, I have to translate every word from the Niphilim language. I can't eat because the food is too good. My stomach doesn't know what to do with it." Ander drew his hood over his head, pulling it down until his face was obscured by shadow. "Until they're dead, my own existence will be an abomination to my eyes."

Isin sat as though struck dumb. Even when he spoke of his years in the mine, Ander was usually so cold, his voice lifeless. Not this time. Hearing him go on that way, Isin was even a bit afraid. Did Ander have boundaries—spiritual or moral—across which he would not go? Isin couldn't be sure. "We'll follow at daybreak," he said at last.

"Good." Ander got up and shook out his cloak. Bits of dry grass fell at his feet.

"Before you go," Isin said. "Answer me one question."

"Go on."

"How did you get the High Priestess to send this army?"

Ander grinned. "Do you remember her story? About how the black giant stole her precious jewel?"

"The Maidenhead of Kallah."

"I told her about a conversation I'd once overheard, between the Niphilim captain and one of her lieutenants. They were hiring black mercenaries to steal jewels and other religious paraphernalia. Treasures like your Maidenhead of Kallah."

"Is that true?" Isin peered into the shadows under Ander's hood, hoping to get a glimpse of his eyes.

"Of course."

"Do you think they have it then? Do you think they have the Maidenhead?"

"Yes. I'm sure they do."

"This way." Ander turned down a narrow alley. His men shuffled along behind him.

They were tired. The sun still hadn't risen, but they'd already twisted through the narrowest, darkest sections of Kan-Puram for better than two hours. Even Ander felt it—a weariness that hung on their legs and dragged down their heads. Every few steps one of the men yawned.

It was slow going. The alleys turned erratically, pushing them off course. Once, they'd followed a passage for nearly a quarter hour, only to have it fold back on itself, leaving them where they'd started. Thankfully, only Ander seemed to have noticed. Most of the time, the men kept their eyes trained on the road one step in front of their feet—and for good reason. Garbage, crumbling brick, animal waste, even human waste, was piled all around them. Rats squeaked out of unseen holes. Pictures were carved into walls, advertising every form of explicit activity. Even in Kan-Puram's nicer quarters, the back ways were little more than a dumping ground.

As they neared the center of the city, they began to see people for the first time. At first, the men wanted to talk with them. None of them had ever been to Kan-Puram before, and they were all curious about the people who lived there. But Ander wouldn't allow any interaction, apart from a quick glance. He was helped in this regard by the horrible conditions under which the vast majority of the people lived. Most of the denizens of the back-alleys were women and children, often naked and nearly always starving. One little girl waved to Ander as they marched by. Ringworm bloomed over her arms and across her belly. It was the worst case he'd ever seen. The last thing any of the men wanted to do was to stop and chat.

Fear and suspicion also helped to keep them separate. Not long after seeing the girl with the ringworm, they came upon a pair of elderly men divvying up a handful of millet. As soon as they saw Ander, the younger of the two moved over until he was sitting atop their horde, making sure to hide every last kernel. Ander nodded to them and hurried on. During his first visit to Kan-Puram, he hadn't seen so many poor people. Isin had explained that they were primarily confined to a few slums. Places like the dust. Ander doubted that there had ever been so many of them this close to the center of the city. It seemed to him an improvement. So far as he was concerned, the poor could keep these houses forever.

Ander led his men around another corner and stopped. At the opposite end of a long alley stood the tower of Moloch. He'd been making his way toward it, though by a circuitous route, from the moment they entered Kan-Puram.

"We're a bit east of where we should be," Ander muttered, still gazing up at the tower. The last time he saw it, torches had burned over every window, filling the night with the sweet scent of melioc. Now it stood gray and lifeless in the pre-morning light, like a column of ash or bone—hardly worth saving from the Niphilim.

"It sure is tall," one of the men remarked. He was the oldest member of their group. The other men called him Pops. Sunspots dotted his forehead and the backs of his hands. He pointed at the tower with his pitchfork. "But what are those black things?" He glanced at Ander. "Do you see them? Beyond the tower."

Ander squinted. "Vultures," he said.

"Can't be. There are better than two dozen in that one patch of sky."

"And probably ten times that many already on the ground," Ander said. "There must be thousands of bodies. Maybe tens of thousands."

None of the other men spoke. They stood, leaning on the handles of spears and pitchforks, staring at the tower. This wasn't their world. They were good men. Family men. Four of the five had farms, with livestock to tend and fields of ripening grain. Pops even had two grown sons. The man they called Tubs—for obvious reasons—worked in a tavern on Merchant's Row. Ander didn't know any of their real names. He didn't want to know them. He preferred to think of these men as a single unit. His leaders. The foundation on which he would build an army.

Ander had been formulating a plan for taking over the armies of Ur and Kan-Puram for better than a week. Since just after his audience with Kilimon. He'd realized that the Niphilim could only be defeated—truly defeated—by an organized, well-run army with a powerful leader. Nothing else would suffice. If he left the war in the hands of priests, the Niphilim might be pushed back, but they'd never be destroyed. The priests would discuss every possible action, form committees and hold councils, while the Niphilim prepared for war. Someone had to take control.

Still, Ander had to start small. It had taken him a long time to formulate a plan. He'd spent nights thinking over it, plotting dozens of different strategies. But what always stood in his way was the fact that the priests would never join him. And not because he was wrong, or because his ideas were faulty. The priests wouldn't join him because he was poor—a former slave—and had pale skin. Facts he could neither hide nor overcome.

Then, one evening, while he and Isin were sitting in a banquet at the Ziggurat, the solution had come to him. It was so simple. He'd been looking at the whole problem from the wrong angle. He didn't need to convince the priests. Priests don't fight. If he could only convince the army to follow him, the priests would have to fall in line or risk becoming irrelevant.

"Look at that," Pops said.

The sun had finally risen, bathing the top floors of the tower in the reddish light of morning. It was magnificent. But sunrise also meant they were running out of time.

"We have to get moving," Ander said. He pointed down an alley between two large houses. It wasn't much wider than a man's shoulders, and dark. From where they stood, it was impossible to tell whether it led to another alley, a wall or a thoroughfare. It was by far the most difficult path available.

"We're coming very near the center of Kan-Puram," Ander warned. "If the Niphilim have taken the city, they're probably in that tower."

The men looked nervously at each other. Stories of the Niphilim had been circulating for days. Most were outlandish fictions, full of blood drinking and gratuitous sexual torture, but Ander encouraged them all the same. These men were scared, and he thought they should be.

Ander pointed at Tubs. "You first."

"Me?" Tubs shook his head. He'd never been more than a day's walk from home. No doubt Kan-Puram seemed a terrible place.

"Go," Ander commanded. "Now."

Tubs looked at the other men, clearly hoping for support. Receiving none, he pointed his spear down the alley, took a deep breath, and started in.

"The rest of you fall in line," Ander said. "I'll guard the rear."

No doors opened onto the tiny alleyway, and there were no windows before the third story. It was as close to marching in a tunnel as anything Ander had experienced since fleeing Dagonor. He hated it.

They'd gone less than two hundred strides when the men ahead of him suddenly stopped. "What's wrong?" Ander asked.

"Rubbish," Tubs hissed. "A heap of bricks, blocking the path."

"So?" Ander spoke matter-of-factly, as though this was part of his plan.

Tubs grumbled something under his breath, but started up. The pile was little better than man-height, and very old. Tubs used his spear like a walking stick, poking at the bricks, searching for solid places to put his feet.

The rest of the men went over the pile easily, using the same footholds Tubs had already discovered. By the time Ander reached the top, the rest of the group was already safe on the other side.

At long last, they emerged from the alley onto a decent-sized road. To the south was a deserted blacksmith's shop, and what Ander guessed had once been a brothel. To the north, the temple of Moloch. There were no doors on this side, but it was an easy dash around to the main entrance.

"Follow me," Ander said. He led them to the temple at a dead sprint. Their path led across a bridge overlooking the grand canal, and past a

half-dozen small byways, but Ander ignored them all. He hastened round
the southern edge of the temple and up the steps. To his men it must have
seemed as if they were being led directly into the jaws of the enemy.

Of course, there were no Niphilim in the temple. No priests either.
Ander had counted on an empty room and thus far his luck was holding.
In reality, Ander had known that Kan-Puram was free of Niphilim for
hours—a fact he'd concealed from his men. If the Niphilim had taken the
city, there'd be guards watching over the southern gate or patrolling the
neighboring farmland. Likewise, whole troops would be assigned to herding up the poor for counting and processing—either to be sent to Dagonor
or killed outright. And, contrary to what he'd told his men, the Niphilim
would have moved into the alleys and side streets almost immediately.

Ander strode into the temple with a smile. During his previous tour
of Kan-Puram, he'd been in many houses of worship. He'd seen the temple of Kallah—where the walls were carved to depict the goddess through
all four ages of men. And he'd visited the temples of Marduk and Baal—
filled with multicolored tapestries and treasures of gold and silver, then
lighted from all sides until the room blazed like midday. The strangest
he'd seen was the temple devoted to the desert god, which some men
called the Creator. It was just one small chapel, kept by three priests—the
last of their sect. Ander wondered what would become of the building
once they were gone. Most likely it'd be torn down and the materials used
elsewhere. The problem was the building's shape. It was a cross, constructed so that one could only see the whole chapel by standing at the
very center, at the intersection, where an enormous six-pointed star had
been chiseled into the floor. Ander shook his head as he thought of it.
Utter folly. He'd also visited the homes of rich merchants, where concu-
bines sat in rooms filled with silk pillows, eating sweets. But of all the
things that Ander had seen in Kan-Puram, the temple of Moloch was easily the most awe-inspiring.

There were no carvings or tapestries. In fact, Ander doubted whether
there was anything in the whole temple worth stealing. That's why they
could leave the doors unlocked. The building itself was constructed, as
was the tower, from blocks of sandstone, meticulously carved and polished so that the walls were smooth to the touch. At the center of the
room, beneath a round skylight, stood a simple quartz altar. Tongues of
flame flickered out of grooves cut into its top. Shamash had called it the

'eternal light'. It was supposed to burn by faith alone, though Ander would have bet that every few hours someone came to feed the fire.

But it was the ceiling that most fascinated him. It had been painted a rich velvety black, with points of silver and gold to mark out stars. According to Shamash, the ceiling represented the sky as it would appear at midnight, one full day after the vernal equinox. On that day, the sun would rise until it shone straight through the hole in the ceiling, its light bouncing off the sandstone floor, revealing each star in full majesty.

Ander walked slowly through the room, wishing he could see it fully lit. On the far side, near where the ceiling and wall met, was the morning star, the jewel in the crown of the queen of heaven. It wasn't as beautiful here as in real life, but close. Very close.

When he was within reach of the altar, Ander turned around. He'd expected his men to be right behind him. Instead, they were standing to either side of the main doors, backs pressed against the wall.

This was the final test. Ander was no expert in religious matters, especially those dealing with Kallah, but he knew that if he could pull away even a tiny bit of the loyalty they felt for their goddess, the power of the priests would be broken.

Ander might have ordered them into the temple, he knew, but that would have made their whole trip into the city pointless. The men had to want to follow him. They had to believe that, though the path was hard and dangerous, it was well worth it. Fortune, power, and honor—those were the things men craved most. But there were other things as well, and Ander had thought of them all.

He dropped his pack at his side, sat down and leaned against the altar. The quartz was warm on his back.

His stepfather had taught him only one thing of value, but he'd learned it well. "Don't be an idiot," Ander remembered him saying. "You can't herd the goats if they won't let you." He'd pointed at a large female, glaring at them through the slats in the fence. "She's faster, stronger and more stubborn that you'll ever be."

"Then how do I do it?" Ander had asked.

"Herd no goats. But leave no goats behind. Understand?"

Ander nodded. He hadn't understood, of course. Hadn't understood at all. But he'd never admit it. For months after that, he'd done his work just as before, using a switch to move the goats from pen to pasture. Often as not, one of the rams would get separated from the herd and he'd have to go looking for it. By the time he got back, the other goats would have dispersed, and he had to begin all over again. It was horrible work.

Then, one day, as he was tending to the birthing mothers, he made a discovery. He'd just given a last handful of millet to a nursing goat, when the whole herd began to press around him. Ander still had a spoonful of grain in his pocket, but didn't dare give a kernel more away. His stepfather had given him explicit instructions as to the amount each new mother was to receive. He'd also made it perfectly clear that, should any of the others get even a single mouthful, Ander would pay for it with his hide.

But the goats weren't so easily dissuaded. Ander had to shove his hand in his pocket and walk as fast as he could to prevent them from nosing after the grain. He led them all the way to the pasture without stopping once. And best of all, there were no stragglers. The whole herd was accounted for. From that day forward, Ander always made sure to have at least one pocket full of grain.

Men were not so different. Ander had learned that while watching the Niphilim herd their slaves. If anything, men were easier. They wanted to do what they were told.

"How long are we going to stay in this evil place?" Tubs asked.

"Not long," Ander replied.

"Shouldn't we help with the fighting?"

"Five men won't turn the tide either way. Besides, what if the Niphilim are waiting right outside that door? Wouldn't you rather be in here?"

As he spoke, Ander began to unload his pack. First he took out a joint of pork, which he ate, licking the grease from his fingers. When he'd finished with that, he reached into his bag again, this time pulling out Isin's honey candy. He carefully opened the wrapping, making sure his men could see the golden sweets inside, then set the packet on the floor. Before long, all the food he'd collected lay scattered around him.

"You can eat too," Ander offered. "Whatever you brought."

But they hadn't brought much of anything, and Ander knew it. Nearly every man who'd marched with him from Ur was out of food. They were planning to replenish their supplies when they reached Kan-Puram.

"I don't have anything," Tubs said.

"Nothing?" Ander frowned, feigning surprise. "Not very good planning."

"We were hoping to trade for food when we reached the city."

"And if the city was overrun, what then? Starve?" Ander smiled. "Fortunately I brought enough for all." He gestured at the food around him. "Eat."

Tubs looked at the skylight. "I guess it'd be all right." He hesitated only once, with his fingers poised over a strip of salted meat. Ander picked it up and pressed it into his hand.

"Taste good?" he asked.

"Sure does." Tubs picked up a loaf of black bread and took a bite.

The other men stared. The battle going on inside them was etched over their faces.

"What about the rest of you?" Ander asked. "Not hungry?" He pointed at the ceiling. "It's just paint. Even the High Priest of this temple would tell you that."

"Looks powerful," Tubs muttered, his mouth full of bread.

"It certainly does," Ander agreed. "And beautiful." He picked up a loaf, broke it in two, and held the pieces out to the other four men. "But looks aren't everything."

Finally, another of them strode forward, smiling cautiously. Ander tossed him a piece of the bread.

Moments later they were all sitting by the altar, passing food packets back and forth, sharing and talking. All but Pops. He was going to need special attention.

Ander went to stand with him. "Tubs is nearly through his second loaf," he remarked, leaning against the wall. It felt cold after the warm altar. "You'll want to get your share."

"I can't," Pops whispered. "My eldest son hopes to become a priest one day." He shook his head. "If the High Priestess ever found out. . . ."

"She won't."

"How can you be sure?"

"Who's going to tell her? Them?" He pointed at the other men, all sitting within reach of the altar. "What would happen to them if they told?"

Pops grimaced.

"Do you really believe in magic and godly protection?" Ander asked.

"Of course."

"Are you afraid of Moloch?"

"I don't even believe in Moloch."

"Then why are you scared of His temple?"

Pops thought for a moment. "I just can't," he whispered.

"I understand." Ander picked up a small loaf—the larger ones were already gone—and tossed it to him. Pops looked at it for a moment, wondering if there were any good reasons not to eat it. Finally, he nibbled off a bit of crust. Ander smiled.

"Hey, Pops," Tubs called. His face was sticky with sugar and grease. "We saved some candy for you." He held up the packet, shaking it so that Pops could hear the remaining sweets rattle around inside.

Pops smiled nervously and shuffled toward the altar.

Doran stood in front of the council tent, staring at the line of soldiers in the distance. The sun had been up for better than four hours, but there was still no sign of the Niphilim. He scratched his head.

"Makes you wish you'd set up in one of the tall buildings, doesn't it?"

Doran turned toward the voice. He was surprised to see Barley rounding the corner of the tent, a mace clutched in one fist. "I bet you could see a long way from up there." Barley pointed to a three-story house with large open windows. "A long way."

Doran ducked into the tent. "What do you want?" he asked.

He sat down at a small table, carried in after the council the night before. There was an empty pitcher and three cups on top of it. Barley might have sat down as well, but there was only the one chair.

"How long do you plan on keeping the men in the field?" he asked.

"What else can we do?"

"Pull them back to the edge of town. They can take turns sitting in the shade, getting food and water." Barley ran his hand over his scalp. It was burned a dusky pink. "I don't think any of us can take another full day in that sun."

Doran drummed his fingers on the tabletop. "Fine," he said at last. "I'll send word. Anything else?"

Barley started to answer, but was interrupted by the sound of the tent flaps being shoved aside.

An old man stumbled in. His left leg had been amputated above the knee, but he still moved surprisingly well, using what looked like an old barge pole for a crutch. He even managed to carry an axe in his free hand.

223 / Slaves of the Shinar

"Barley," he said, setting the axe on the table. "I'm glad you're here."

"What do you want?" Doran asked. "This tent is for leaders from the temples and great houses."

"That's why I came." The old man patted the axe with his free hand. "A gift for the hero of yesterday's battle. I expected to have to send it to him through Your Holiness, but since he's already here. . . ."

Barley picked up the axe. It was his—the very one he'd thrown at the Niphilim woman the previous evening. "Where did this come from?" he asked.

The old man pointed toward the battlefield. "Took me most of the night to find it, dragging my old corpse around as I do."

Barley lifted the axe and set it on his shoulder. It felt good. "I didn't feel like myself without it."

"You have my thanks as well," Doran added. "But if that's all—"

"Actually, I have two more things to tell you, if I might." The old man smiled nervously. "You see, I have a son. Strong boy, fought in yesterday's battle and has the bandage to prove it." He gestured at his good knee, showing where the wound was located. "Lamech—that's my boy's name—he even helped to carry our new High Father back to the temple. A terrible business that." He shook his head morosely. "And he never did get back to the field."

"Who didn't?" Doran asked. "Shamash?"

"My boy. He was scared, Your Holiness. But he wants to come back. Will you have him?"

"Of course we will," Barley said. "Just tell him to find me."

"Lamech!"

A young man in full battle gear, sixteen at the oldest, pushed his way into the tent. A bandage, white as a winter cloud, was wrapped tightly around one knee.

"Barley himself says you can come back." The old man struck his son's shin with the end of his crutch. "What do you say to that?"

"Thank you, sir," Lamech whispered. He looked about ready to pass out.

"Glad to have you," Barley said. "In fact, I need you to do something for me." He glanced at Doran. "Go to the faithful of Moloch—they're on the far right—and tell them to pull back to the edge of the city. Tell them the order comes from me. Got it?"

Lamech nodded. "To the edge of the city," he repeated, and started backing out of the tent.

"Wait." Barley picked up his mace. "You might need this."

"No he won't." The old man laughed. "Show them Lamech."

The boy did as he was told, drawing his sword from the scabbard he wore, Niphilim fashion, across his back. The blade was blue-black.

"Where did you get that?" Doran asked him.

The old man grinned. "A man might find a good many things among the dead, if he's brave—or has a son he lives to protect."

Barley set his mace down on the table. "Since you're already armed," he said, "I guess you'd best get moving."

Father and son hugged. It was a loving embrace, broken off finally by the older man. "Don't worry, I'll say goodbye to your mother," he said. Then Lamech turned and strode out of the tent.

"You've something more for us?" Doran asked.

"Just one last thing," the old man said, still looking after his departed son. "Though it's hardly worth mentioning. . . ."

"Go on," Barley urged.

"Well, there're these men from Ur. What they want, I can't say. But they smell horrible, have dark circles under their eyes, and are carrying spears and pitchforks—an all-around ugly group." He frowned. "And their leader's the worst. A pale fiend, white as any Niphilim—whiter maybe—and he wears a hood. A real nasty character."

"Where are they?" Doran asked, suddenly very interested.

"With your troops, Holiness. Their leader keeps asking about the Niphilim camp. Whether we've sent scouts. How many casualties they suffered. He expects us to know all about them. Even sent one of his own men out to look. A big fat fellow with a spear."

"Do you know something about these men?" Barley asked Doran.

"I hope so." Doran started toward the tent flaps.

"So who are they?"

"Maybe our salvation." And with that, he disappeared outside.

Barley and the old man looked at each other.

"Our salvation?" the old man asked. "Those ruffians?"

Barley went to the tent flaps and pushed them apart. He was astonished to see Doran, racing across the field as fast as his legs would carry him.

CHAPTER 2

It Is Waking That Kills Us

SOMETHING SOFT LANDED ON URUK'S CHEEK. IT TICKLED HIS NOSE, lifting him out of a deep sleep. He tried to swat it away, but the thing got caught between his fingers. It weighed next to nothing.

Uruk opened his eyes.

A black feather, no larger than a child's index finger, clung to his hand. He spread his fingers and it blew away.

Sitting beside him was the dog—close enough for Uruk to have reached out and grabbed his tail if he'd so desired. Thus far, the dog hadn't noticed that he was awake and moving. The dog's attention was focused elsewhere.

A few strides beyond the dog lay a vulture, lifeless and bloody. Its neck had been snapped, and one wing appeared to have broken as well. Feathers, just like the one that had blown against Uruk's face, ringed the dog's mouth. They were black and gray, for the most part, but a few were bloody red. The dog also had a trickle of fresh blood running down his chin, not a drop of which was his.

He hadn't escaped his trials without injury, however. A wound the length and width of a knife blade stretched across his left flank. The dog had been attacked by a vulture, Uruk guessed. Not the dead one, but a much larger bird.

Uruk closed his eyes, glad that the dog was alive and healthy. And close by.

Over the last hour, a dream had been replaying itself through Uruk's subconscious mind. It was an old dream—one he'd had, albeit sporadically, for decades. There were minor variations that cropped up, reflecting changes in his life to that point, but it always began the same way.

Uruk flees.

Grass—every blade of it identical, colorless as dust—is waving in the breeze. There are no hills, no trees, nothing but an endless plain, darkness and stars. The only sound is the rhythmic hush of Uruk's own footsteps.

After having run for what must have been a full league, Uruk pauses to catch his breath. Nothing living would chase him so far, he reasons. Either it would have caught him already or been left behind. Even so, the feeling that his enemy is standing right behind him, close enough to stir the hairs on the back of his neck with its breath, remains.

Uruk wheels around, expecting to see a narrow swath of trampled grass cut through the endless plain. Instead, he discovers that he is standing at the edge of a stream. The shadows of fish glide among the rocks on the bottom.

Beyond the stream is a jungle choked with trees, vines and shrubs. Some look soft, with bark like silk and long flat leaves as smooth as a baby's skin. Others bristle with thorns. To anyone else, these trees might seem eerie. But not to Uruk. To him it looks like home.

Uruk steps into the stream and immediately jumps back. The water is intensely cold. He barely touched it, but his toes burn as though he'd thrust them into a furnace. The skin around them feels waxy and stiff.

He glances up and down, hoping some limbs might be hanging over the stream. Anything he might use to cross, even an old log or some stepping stones. But there is nothing.

"Is anybody there?" Uruk calls.

Even as the words leave his mouth, Uruk notices something moving through the brush. A vine as thick as his wrist quivers as though it's been shoved out of the way.

"Show yourself," he shouts. "I mean you no harm."

A woman strides out of the trees directly in front of him. Her skin is black, darker even than Uruk's, and so shiny that it reflects the stars. A long wooden spear, its tip hardened by fire, is clutched in one of her fists. She has nothing else—not even clothes. Uruk half-expects her to try concealing her more sensitive parts—with her hands if nothing else—but she appears to feel no shame.

When she reaches the stream, the woman kneels and drinks, dipping her mouth to the water like an animal. Her teeth, especially her canines, are horribly sharp.

She pays no attention to him, not even glancing in his direction as she laps up the icy water. So, Uruk decides he'll drink as well. He bends to take a handful of water from the stream, but again finds it too cold even to touch.

"Mana," he curses as he rubs the blood back into his fingers.

The woman looks up at him and smiles.

"It's too cold for me," Uruk says. "Is there another way across?"

She points at the sky with her spear.

Uruk looks up. He is astonished to find that the stars are moving. Not turning, as they do over the course of a night—nor revolving, as they do during the change of the seasons. They are gathering.

New constellations form. Others are torn apart. They whirl about, building momentum until, suddenly, the whole sky rushes together.

Anticipating a blast, Uruk shields his eyes. But instead of exploding, the stars meld, becoming larger, more powerful. The woman raises her spear again, calling to the newly formed sun as though it were a dog. And it comes.

Uruk trembles as the enormous fireball speeds from the sky. His dream of a calm, dark jungle turns into a nightmare. Tears run down his cheeks. More than anything, he longs to turn and run over the endless grass. He wishes he'd never stopped. But it's too late now. How can you turn and run into a lie when the truth is laid bare before you?

He watches as the fire plunges into her—elongating into a javelin of purest light and driving into her eyes. She is almost knocked off her feet by the power, and has to use her spear as a crutch to keep from falling.

When it's over, Uruk calls to her, "Do you need help?" Somehow, he can still make out her shape, though there are no stars left to see by.

The woman totters. Her eyes are still squeezed shut.

"Are you well?"

Still no answer. She doesn't even seem to have heard him.

Uruk picks up a pebble no larger than a child's finger and casts it in her direction. The stone plops harmlessly into the sand at her feet.

Instantly, the woman straightens up. Her lips part, and Uruk wonders if she is finally going to speak.

Then she opens her eyes.

Uruk screams as the power of a sun, newly born, lashes out at him.

The last things he sees are the woman's teeth, points glinting savagely, before all the world is extinguished in yellow fire.

Uruk put a hand over his face. Even with his eyes closed, the sun was far too bright. Pain unlike any he'd ever known pulsed across the top of his skull. He groaned.

At the sound of his voice, the dog leapt up. He barked and chased his tail. And when he'd had enough of that, he licked Uruk's face.

"Enough." Uruk stroked the dog's neck with a shaky hand. His voice was little more than a whisper. "Enough." He swallowed hard but his throat wouldn't clear. Not enough saliva.

"Chasing birds?" Uruk asked, picking the last few feathers from around the dog's lips. "You could not wait for me. . . ." He turned his head to see the elevation of the sun. Every movement was screaming agony. "Not for even an hour or two?"

The dog licked him on the end of the nose.

"Need a drink." Uruk reached for the water-skin in his satchel. One little swallow could do a lot, he knew. Maybe save his life.

He felt the bundle of cord first and hastily shoved it back into his bag. His head hurt so terribly that he didn't even pause to wonder how it had gotten out. Then his hand swept over the empty water-skin. His little finger slipped through a hole in the rawhide and his breath caught in his throat. The dog had chewed through it, Uruk saw, no doubt trying to get at the water inside. He felt around under the skin, fingernails scraping through what was left of the mud, and sighed.

Uruk had to get up and get moving. He had to find water. It wasn't easy, the pounding in his head was almost more than he could bear, but somehow he managed to sit up. Colossal swells of nausea streamed up from his stomach. His throat quivered, threatening to close altogether. It reminded Uruk of the first time he'd seen the ocean, and tried to drink the salt water. That was a bad memory, but nothing like what this was going to turn into.

He gulped air, trying to keep the bile from rising. It didn't work. Uruk hung his head between his knees and vomited. There wasn't much left in his stomach, but what little there was came out in a hot rush. It hurt so much that he had to squeeze his head between his hands to keep from passing out.

The dog sat at Uruk's side and watched. His elation had passed. Uruk was still in trouble and the dog knew it. Maybe as well as Uruk himself. In addition to the wound in his head, Uruk was dehydrated, and likely suffering from some form of heat fever. His skin was painfully dry, never a good sign. They needed to get to water right away.

"Have to try to stand," Uruk whispered. He rolled onto his hands and knees. Even that simple action left his head spinning. "I will need your help." He grabbed hold of the dog's shoulders. "Just stand still."

Thick streams of hot blood trickled from both nostrils as Uruk pushed to his feet. There was a point, just before he got his knees straight, when he wasn't entirely sure he'd make it. The dog was almost crushed to the ground under his weight.

When Uruk felt steady enough, he wiped his nose with the end of his tunic. No good rushing things, he told himself. Better to take a moment to get your bearings than to fall down. Climbing to his feet had been difficult enough once. He doubted he could do it a second time. If he fell, he might never get up again.

After a quick look at his surroundings, Uruk decided to head east. He'd skirt the edge of the battlefield and make for the city. Either that or aim directly for the Tiger River. The one thing he wouldn't do is try crossing through the dead again. Not with all those buzzards dancing around. There were ten thousand of them at least, and more flying in all the time. Uruk shuddered as he contemplated the damage they must be doing to the bodies of the fallen soldiers.

The dog started barking before he'd even gone a dozen steps.

Uruk turned to see what was wrong. At this point, he wanted nothing more than to get to the river and flop down in the cool water, but he trusted the dog too much to ignore him. It was lucky he did. The dog was sitting a few strides away, staring at Uruk's sword, still lying in the dust where he'd dropped it the night before.

The pain in his skull intensified as he bent to pick it up, but Uruk figured he deserved that. Leaving your weapon behind was one of the worst sins a hunter could commit. Without his weapon, a hunter quickly became prey. Worse yet, Uruk had come close to dying for that sword.

The tip of the blade was covered in dried blood and crusted over with ash. Normally, Uruk would have cleaned it, using dust or sand if necessary, but not now. He was too sick. The sword went into its scabbard dirty. "Thanks, Dog," Uruk muttered, wiping his nose with the back of his hand.

But the dog had already gone. He was better than fifty paces to the north, headed toward a stand of trees. "Shade," Uruk hissed. He glanced at the sun. It'd be well past noon before he reached the eastern edge of the lines. If he reached it at all. It seemed just as likely that he'd pass out and die. And even if he did reach the end of the lines, he'd still have a long walk ahead of him, whether he continued on to the river or cut back toward the city. Finding a shady spot and waiting for the heat of the day to pass could make all the difference.

The first hundred or so steps flashed by without difficulty. The next hundred were a chore. By the time Uruk got near the trees he felt like he was sleepwalking. He stared at his feet, willing himself forward. "Never would have made the river," he muttered to himself between lungs-full of air. "Never."

As soon as he reached the tall grass, Uruk dropped to his knees. His patella struck a rock, but he didn't care. His legs were mostly numb anyway, and the grass was soft and welcoming. More than anything, he wanted to bury his head in a pile of it and sleep.

The dog was lying belly-up in a pool of still water as Uruk crawled between the last blades of high grass. The water was muddy, and there was a ring of algae growing along the outer edge, but Uruk couldn't bother with that at the moment. He scooped up a handful and took a couple of sips. The water tasted greener than he liked, but it was wholesome, and the dog seemed to be doing well enough. He lifted another handful of water to his lips, and this time he drank it all.

When he'd had as much as he could stand, Uruk dipped his face into the puddle and wiped his nose and chin. Drops of blood floated to the surface and hung amid the dog hair. Now Uruk needed to sleep. He crawled to one of the little holm trees that grew around the edge of the pool and leaned against it. A twig poked into the back of his neck, but it was still better than lying in the sun.

He woke a half-hour later to find the dog standing in the pool, tromping up and down and splashing water and clay onto the surrounding grass.

"Get out of there," Uruk grumbled. "It is stirred up enough already." He grabbed the dog around the neck and pulled him out. Normally that would have been easy. Not this time. Uruk was weak and the dog didn't want to go.

When the pool was free, Uruk leaned down and stuck his head in the water. He came up sputtering, clay dripping off his hair.

"Nice," Uruk said. "A couple hours to soak and I think I could feel like myself again." He stuck his head back into the pool. The pain in his skull was still intense, but the water—or maybe it was the clay—seemed to help. He remembered the vast majority of his last battle now, though his survival remained a mystery.

This time, he kept his head down as long as he could. When he finally did come up, the dog was standing at the edge of the tall grass, staring at the battlefield.

"What are you looking at?" Uruk asked. "Is someone on the field? Are the soldiers marching?" It was about time, he thought. Uruk had never been a soldier—not a real one anyway—but it seemed to him that any sane man would much rather fight in the cool of early morning. He craned his neck to see over the tall grass. As he did, another wave of dizziness swept over him. Uruk felt better, but still wasn't completely fit.

Six Niphilim warriors, four of them women, were marching south across the field. They'd already reached the nearest bodies, savages mostly, and were rapidly approaching what had been the main lines. The male warriors at the center of the band carried a litter. Every so often, they paused to inspect a body.

"They are looking for someone," Uruk said.

The dog sat down, but didn't relax. He kept his eyes trained on the warriors.

They were stopping more frequently now. One of the women at the front of the formation used her sword to flip a corpse. She stared at it for a moment and then moved on. One of her comrades chased a vulture away from another body. Uruk smiled as she turned and vomited.

After that, three of the women separated themselves from the group and quickly began picking through the carnage. The litter carriers stayed well back, as did the other woman, who kept her sword at the ready the entire time. It almost looked like she was guarding the two men. Uruk couldn't understand that. They were in no danger. So far as he could tell, the soldiers of Kan-Puram were doing little more than stand in their lines on the other side of the field, waiting patiently.

It took another quarter-hour, and the inspection of hundreds more bodies, but at last they seemed to have found what they were looking for. One of the women put up her hand and the men with the litter trotted over, led by their guard. The two women conferred for a moment, then the one who'd found the body called out.

Instantly, the other two women dropped what they were doing. Judging by the way they moved, Uruk guessed that they were only too happy to escape the filth and gore they'd climbed into.

When their troop was reassembled, two of the women grasped the body by hand and foot and heaved it onto the litter. It must have been heavy. The man at the front nearly fell to his knees under the weight.

They bound the body into position, making sure it wouldn't flop off to either side, then picked up a sword and set it on the litter as well. From that distance, Uruk couldn't see the body or sword well enough to know what the Niphilim had discovered. It just looked like another half-eaten corpse to him. In fact, it had been so thoroughly pecked over by the vultures that, from a distance at least, Uruk couldn't even tell whether it was male or female. Still, the Niphilim had somehow managed to pick it out from amongst the thousands of bodies on the field. Maybe the clothes were distinct, Uruk mused. Or the sword. He thought back to his battle with the Niphilim woman. Could that be her? He wondered. If so, what had happened to her?

The women checked the bindings one last time, and then started north.

As they approached, the dog leaned forward. His muscles tensed, ready for a fight, but Uruk pulled him back. "Stay here," he whispered. "We have no reason to get involved." The dog twisted and wriggled as hard as he could, but Uruk held him fast. "They are just caring for their dead."

As they neared the grove, the Niphilim veered slightly east. That suited Uruk fine. He wasn't ready to fight anyone, let alone a trained Niphilim soldier. How he'd survived his last encounter, Uruk still couldn't remember. All he knew was that he'd been lucky to get away alive.

They'd nearly passed him by before Uruk noticed the man at the back of the litter. His stomach turned over. What he'd taken for streaks of blond, while the man was at a distance, was actually a generous sprinkling of gray. Uruk couldn't believe what he was seeing. Jared was carrying the rear of that litter, his fists tied to the handles to keep him from running away.

The dog twisted in his arms again, and this time Uruk let him go. Together they crawled out from under the trees, the dog leading the way. Uruk fully intended to attack the Niphilim. Sick or not, he wouldn't let Jared get away. Not this time.

But even as he hauled himself to his feet, another jolt of dizziness washed over him. The whole world rocked, as though floating on the open sea. Uruk stumbled, caught his toe on a rock and went sprawling.

By the time he felt strong enough to stand, Jared and the Niphilim were gone.

The dog kept after them, chasing the Niphilim until they'd passed all the way through the grove and into the grasslands beyond. Uruk could hear him barking, and hoped he would know enough to maintain a reasonable distance. But he couldn't go after him. He simply lacked the energy.

Finally, the dog came back.

By that time Uruk was sitting in the pool, eyes shut tight, taking deep breaths in an effort to clear his head. Blood streamed from his nose. His skin was ashen.

"I think we should head for the Tiger River," Uruk said. The dog plopped down at his side and licked his cheek. "We will catch them. No matter what."

CHAPTER 3

Qabalah

*T*HE NIPHILIM ARMY MARCHED DEEP INTO THE NIGHT, ONLY STOPPING once to refill their water-skins at the river. Kishar hoped to reach Akshur within four days, spend an hour or two replenishing their rations, and then make the turn towards Dagonor. It would require pushing his troops to the edge of human endurance, but it would be worth it in the long run. Should the black-heads decide to give chase, and he suspected they might, they would find a Niphilim army snugly settled into its home base. From Dagonor they could crush any force that ever came against them. Of that, Kishar was absolutely positive.

He called a halt at midnight, and the soldiers got busy forming camp. Latrines were dug within the hour, the captain's tent—Kishar's tent now, he reminded himself—set up even faster. Only one fire would be lit that night, but it would be a large one. Already the new slaves were adding wood and bundles of straw to the pile. Soon it would be high enough for the light to be seen for leagues around.

Kishar sat outside his tent. He had no desire to go in. Simha's body was in the tent at present, waiting to be added to the top of the pyre. He never would have admitted it, but Kishar found her presence unsettling. And not just the smell, either. Simha was a gruesome reminder of the battle they were leaving behind. Already some of the other Niphilim were beginning to grumble, suggesting that she would not have 'fallen-back' to Dagonor, as Kishar had suggested, but would have stayed to finish off the black-heads and occupy Kan-Puram. The sooner she was burned and gone, the better.

Kishar had started to doze when Lagassar came to tell him that the pyre was finished. "The slaves are all ready to set her litter on top," she said. "You just have to give the order."

"Consider it given," Kishar replied. "If possible, I'd like to have her body burned and gone by the end of the hour."

"Do you plan to say anything?"

"No."

Lagassar frowned. Speeches were uncommon at Niphilim funerals. Simha, for instance, had never said a word at any one of the thousands she had presided over. But still, Simha had been extremely popular, especially with the women. Kishar wondered if he should make an exception.

"What about her sword?" Lagassar asked.

"What about it?"

"Will it be buried along with her ashes?"

"No. I'll keep the sword, and pass it on to the next captian in turn."

Lagassar nodded, but she still didn't look happy.

"We can call it the Simha Sword," Kishar suggested. "In honor of her."

"I think that would be right," Lagassar said. "It will please our people."

"Announce it at the burning then."

"Me?"

"Simha was fond of you. I think she would be honored to have you speak on her behalf."

Lagassar grinned. It was the happiest Kishar had ever seen her. "It will be my honor," she said.

"My apologies," Isin said. He went to the empty spot on the far side of the fire and sat down. A cook-pot lay in the dust beside him, but there was nothing inside. If there'd been any supper that night, Isin had missed it.

"You're late," Ander grumbled. The men sitting to either side of him glared.

"Too much to do," Isin explained. Just walking across the encampment was a challenge. Prostitutes and beer merchants swarmed thick as mosquitoes after a summer rain. Isin didn't like them, but supposed they were necessary. They tended to wounds no priest could ever reach. Whole battalions would sleep through the night due in large part to their gentle ministrations. But for the deeper sorrows, and the grieving masses, they could do little. As he'd crossed the field, Isin discovered a whole army of mourners—widows, orphans, mothers who'd lost sons, fathers whose every hope had been stricken dead—all searching for a miracle. Unfortunately, Isin had none to offer. One young woman was convinced that she'd conceived on the night before the battle. Her only hope was that the goddess would send her a boy—one strong enough to replace the husband she'd lost. Isin knew that Kallah didn't grant such requests. But how could he deny this girl? How could anyone? "The war has destroyed so many," he sighed.

But Ander wasn't listening. "It might help if she were in a foul mood," he remarked to the other men. Isin knew that Ander had formulated a plan aimed at steering the council toward continued war with the Niphilim. It hinged on presenting the idea for a mass attack on Dagonor, and then getting those who were most likely to come out against such a move to unwittingly argue in its favor. The details were fuzzy at best, and Isin questioned the logistics, but Ander thought that it could be fleshed out with a bit of help. No doubt this was what they'd been discussing when Isin arrived.

"Nippur's always in a foul mood," one of the other men responded. "She's intolerable."

It was Qadesh, High Priest of Marduk. Isin couldn't imagine how he'd failed to recognize him before. Of all the temples in Kan-Puram, the temple of Marduk was the one he liked least. They were powerful among the tradesman, but poor neighbors. They believed themselves favorites of the gods, even calling their followers 'Sons of Heaven.' Worse, they refused to marry outside their community, and taught that charity should be offered to outsiders only after your own are fully served. It wasn't a philosophy that won many friends.

"And you're sure she'll disagree with you?" Ander asked.

Qadesh nodded. "She disagrees with everything I say, no matter how wise." He looked down his nose at Isin. "They all do."

Isin started to protest—if a follower of Marduk had ever said anything wise, he'd never heard it—but Ander cut him off.

"I don't place my trust in what's gone before," he said. "Nor in what's likely. That's no way to go into battle." He glared at Qadesh. "There should be no doubt. I want Nippur ready to fight."

"Leave that to me," the man sitting to Ander's right said. "She'll fly into a rage, I can promise you that." He licked his lips. "Kind of excited to see it, myself. Nothing stirs a man's blood better than a beautiful woman that's spitting mad." He laughed. "And a priestess, too."

Isin had to squint to make out the speaker's face. It was one of the thieves Ander had met soon after his return to Kan-Puram. Isin thought his name was Sneaker, or something equally unpleasant. He had all the attractiveness of a drowned rat, though with more teeth.

"Nothing obvious," Ander cautioned.

Sneaker shook his head. "I know just the thing."

"What about the black man?" Qadesh suggested. "He makes an impression."

"We can't find Uruk anywhere," Sneaker said. "Probably got himself killed chasing after Jared. Besides, what I have in mind is better anyway."

Ander agreed, though he didn't look overly confident.

"And then we get the Niphilim treasure," Sneaker continued. "That's what you promised. All of it."

"Everything but the weapons," Ander said. "And the Maidenhead of Kallah. That belongs to Isin and Doran."

Isin imagined the look on the High Priestess's face as he marched into the Ziggurat, her jewel dangling from his outstretched hand. It could go a long way toward mending the schism that had grown up between their temples. They might even convince her to stop sacrificing children.

"How'll we haul it all back?" Sneaker asked. "If there's as much gold as you claim, we won't be able to carry it."

"That's none of my concern," Ander said. "Once the Niphilim are dead you can build carts from their bones and sew sacks from their hides for all I care."

Sneaker laughed. "Sacks from their hides," he repeated, slapping his thighs. The sound of his laughter reminded Isin of the Titsi-birds that migrated through Kan-Puram every spring. They hunted the streets for mice and crickets, cackling maniacally over every kill. If the prey was too large, the other birds helped tear it to bits.

"It's getting late," Ander said. He pointed at the council tent. A few of the leaders had already arrived. More were coming. "And I still have to explain our plans to Isin."

"One question," Sneaker said. "How are you going to deal with the others?"

"We have to hope they'll join willingly. Convince them that they have more to lose by being left behind."

"That's not much of a plan," Sneaker said, climbing to his feet. "But I like a risk."

Qadesh stood up as well. "I shall be most persuasive," he assured them.

Ander waited until they were both out of earshot, then looked across the fire at Isin. "How are the men?" he asked.

"A few have run off," Isin said. "Tubs has organized a search party."

"How many did he take with him?"

"Eight. All volunteers."

"Did you tell them that we'd be marching again the day after tomorrow?"

"I told them. Most were none too happy to hear it, even when I reminded them that we had a chance to recover the Maidenhead of Kallah. Their religious fervor is draining away, I'm afraid."

Ander shrugged. "It'll come back." He nodded at the battlefield. "They won't spend much time slogging through that mess without a little righteous anger swelling their chests. Pops has them out there, doesn't he?"

Isin nodded. "Fifteen at a time. And if they come back with anything less than a Niphilim sword he sends them again. By morning, they should all be armed."

"Real warriors." There was no mistaking the pride in Ander's voice. "What else?"

"There've been some strange stories."

"Really? What about?"

"You, mostly."

"Good or bad?"

"Apparently, the men think you're a sorcerer. They say that's the real reason you wear a hood—to confuse demons." Isin shook his head. "The worst of it seems to be coming from the men you led through the city."

"What do they say?"

"That you took them through some kind of maze, with dark spells carved into the walls and giant rats—even savages."

"That's it?"

"The rest is ridiculous. Rooms as big as the sky. Stars shining in the middle of the day." As he spoke, Isin watched for any sign of recognition. But Ander just sat there, arms crossed, staring at the coals. "Can you imagine?"

"Nonsense," Ander agreed. "Do the other men believe these stories?"

"Some do."

"Are they afraid?"

Isin shook his head. "The opposite actually. Most wish they'd been with you. At least fifty men have volunteered to join in your next adventure."

"Fools," Ander muttered. But Isin thought he saw a smile curling the edges of Ander's lips. That wasn't so bad, he supposed. If Ander took pleasure in being some kind of semi-fictional hero, what harm could it cause?

"Do you know anything about a man called Barley?" Ander asked.

"Just more stories—stories almost as preposterous as yours."

"I want you to offer him something."

"What?"

Ander smiled. "Command over the army from Ur, or a part of it."

Isin was shocked. "Is this part of your plan? Because Doran will never agree."

"It's the most important part. And I'm counting on you to find a way past Doran's objections. You know him better than anyone. There must be something we can do."

"I don't know what."

"Well, think about it." Ander pushed back his hood and ran his fingers through his hair. "Do I look presentable?" he asked. "For the council I mean." He looked at his hands. "If only I had normal skin. The darker the better."

Isin looked him up and down. "You need a good wash," he admitted. "And for Kallah's teats, keep that blanket off your head."

"No hood," Ander agreed. He got up and began brushing the dust from his cloak.

"Why do you want me to offer our army to Barley?" Isin asked, climbing gingerly to his feet. He'd lost weight during their travels, but not nearly enough.

"I'll tell you everything on the way," Ander said. He started toward the city.

"Where are we going?" Isin asked.

"We'll need clean water if we're to wash."

"But the council—"

"Plenty of time," Ander said. "It's all been arranged."

As usual, water was easier to talk about than to locate. Not a drop had been brought to the field since before sundown. Plenty of casks and skins, even a whole wagonload of barrels, but no water. Beer was the order of the hour, and so beer was what the merchants brought. No wonder the army was rolling drunk. 'The Niphilim should attack now,' Ander thought. 'This city is defenseless.'

Finally, after an exhaustive search—during which Ander explained the entirety of the script he'd devised for the coming council, including Isin's part and how he was to play it—they came upon one of the makeshift brothels springing up all over the camp. Men were lined up outside, patiently waiting their turn, though not as many as Ander might have guessed. But what really set this tent apart was a young prostitute, fourteen at the oldest, kneeling over a shallow pan of water, washing the sweat from her neck and chest. Ander could see the shapes of writhing bodies through the open tent flaps, and hear the slickery sounds of coupling, but decided to ask the girl if they might buy some water anyway. Isin didn't want to, but Ander insisted. They were running short of time. If they were to wash—and both needed to in the worst way—it'd have to be now.

The girl thought their request peculiar, but was more or less happy to comply. She slipped into the tent, returning a moment later with a second pan.

Ander went first, beginning with his face. As he bent over the pan, he noticed that the girl who'd brought it was staring. There were men waiting to be serviced, but she never even glanced at them. Probably looking at his skin, Ander thought. Children did that. He mopped the excess water from his face with his sleeve and went to work on his hands.

When they were clean, Ander picked up the pan and poured some water into his mouth. He only wanted to rinse his teeth, but as soon as the first drop hit his lips the girl burst out laughing. It was the same kind of laugh Ander had heard every day of his youth. This whore was laughing at him.

Ander spat the water on the ground, then quickly ran a finger over his gums. The girl kept laughing, joined by a few of the men in line. Ander ignored them all. Without saying a word, he went to work scrubbing his neck and hair.

When he looked up again, the girl was gone. Inside the tent, a pair of long gangly legs spread painfully around a man's hips. It might not have been her, but Ander guessed that it probably was. Two older women had emerged in her place. They were washing up in the other pan. Neither got a drop on anything above her waist.

They washed quickly, using their skirts to dry off. And when they were done, instead of dumping the used water on the ground, one of them carried it back into the tent. A moment later she stuck her head out, motioning for the next man in line.

When it was his turn, Isin kne0lt in front of the pan. He was about to dip his fingers into the water, then stopped. "Can I get this refreshed?" he asked.

The woman standing in front of the tent flaps looked over.

"The water," Isin complained. "It's brown."

She glanced at the line of waiting men. None appeared likely to cause trouble, so she walked over. Her thin wool shift was dark with sweat.

"What's the problem?" she asked.

"It's dirty," Isin said.

The woman looked confused, as though Isin's comment was among the strangest she'd ever heard, then bent and picked up the pan.

Suddenly it all made sense. The girl's laughing. The water being taken back into the tent. Ander had to bite his bottom lip to keep from gagging.

The prostitute stared into the water for a moment before dumping it on the ground. "Too brown," she agreed. Then she ducked into the tent to refill the pan.

As soon as she was out of sight, Ander leaned toward Isin. "They're using the water over and over," he whispered. "You know that, right?"

But Isin had no time to answer. The prostitute was already coming out of the tent.

He peered into the water she set before him. It looked clean enough by starlight.

"Hurry up," Ander said. "Wash and let's go."

The prostitute nodded in agreement. "Wash," she urged. She pantomimed scrubbing her face and armpits.

Very slowly, Isin dipped both hands into the water. His nose wrinkled in disgust. He scrubbed his hands and forearms, then ran his fingers through his hair. A few drops trickled down his forehead. They were black with ash.

"Enough," Isin said, and handed the pan back to the woman.

Ander tossed her a few bits of copper. It was all the metal he'd taken from the men's packs that morning. She inspected the copper, then took the all but untouched water and ducked into the tent.

"I'm ready," Isin muttered.

"Good. Have you come up with anything for Doran yet?"

"I think I have something that will work," Isin said. "It's about the easiest thing there is. We just don't let him talk."

Ander nodded. "It's a good plan."

The council had been up and running for more than two hours. But what they'd accomplished, Ander couldn't begin to guess. Thus far, the whole meeting had been devoted to recounting, in excruciating detail, every moment of the last two days—including reports on the number of women porters and how much water they'd carried to the ranks. After that, each leader stepped forward and made a short speech, followed by rough estimates of the dead and wounded. Barley—Ander recognized him by description—had lost better than three-quarters of his men, far and away the heaviest casualties. According to Nippur, her temple was stuffed with injured soldiers, and even more were being tended in the taverns, inns and harlots' commons bordering the northern fields. She was vague as to who might be tending to these men, however. Ander suspected that most were either being looked after by family or no one.

"What are we to do with all these heroes—perish the thought—should they die?" Qadesh asked.

Isin glanced nervously at Ander, who nodded. This was part of the plan. First they would upset the sensibilities of the assembly, and then steer their passions in the direction Ander wanted to go. Assuming Sneaker and Melesh both played their parts correctly, the whole council would turn as smoothly as a miller's wheel. The best part of it was, they didn't even need the vast majority of the attendees to willingly go along. In fact, a certain amount of foot-dragging was both desirable and necessary. But Nippur had to be dealt with first. She was, by all accounts, the loudest voice in the council, and one of its most respected. As such, Ander had determined that she ought to be the focus around which all else turned. If they could convince Nippur to advocate a march on the Niphilim, Ander thought, the rest of the priests would be easy. The trick would be convincing her. For that they had decided to use a touch of misdirection.

"The dead will be looked after according to their sect. Same as always," Nippur replied. But even though she was answering his question, she wasn't looking at Qadesh. She was watching a young woman, one of her own novices, standing in the far corner with the thief, Melesh. He had waxed his mustache and was wearing a silk tunic, Ander noticed with some amusement. The silver bracelet around his wrist looked to have been polished as well.

Melesh had his hand on the young woman's shoulder, drawing her toward him. It was a bold tactic, certain to cause a fuss. Maybe too bold, Ander reflected, though it was too late to do anything about it now. The young priestess was resisting, but only half-heartedly. She pushed him away with the heels of her hands even as she leaned into him with her pelvis. If her smile was any indication, she didn't really mind the attention.

Nippur, on the other hand, was greatly alarmed.

"And how shall we tell the faithful of Baal from the faithful of Moloch?" Qadesh asked her. "Or Kallah? Or a hundred other sects?"

"There are ways," Nippur muttered.

"Maybe you can tell us what those are."

A murmur ran through the crowd. This was a serious issue for almost everyone. Not Ander. He couldn't tell one cult from another. Some wore hats. Others didn't. Some wore simple jerkins. Others dressed in elaborate robes. Many believed that the gods were men, and still more that they were women. But at heart they were all the same—substantively identical. Or so it seemed to him. Ander made a mental note to ask Isin what, if anything, made his temple different. He suspected the answer would have something to do with 'truth,' whatever that meant. Still, it might be interesting.

"The fact is, we can't distinguish between the bodies," Qadesh said. "We might be able to do something with the wounded, but those—" He gestured toward the battlefield. "Their mothers wouldn't recognize them."

"If the followers of Kallah aren't burned, they can never find grace," Isin interjected.

"Baal demands that her dead be buried," Nippur said. "It's the only way to. . . ." Her voice trailed off as she glanced once more at the corner. Things there had deteriorated. Her novice was trying desperately to pull away from Melesh, but he had a fist clamped round her arm. By the look on her face, Ander knew she thought their little game was over. She'd had her fun. Unfortunately, Melesh wasn't getting the message. The young priestess was on the edge of panic. And not without good reason, Ander thought. If this had been real, she'd be about to learn a painful lesson. Fortunately for her, it wasn't. Melesh was just playing his part. Of course, the girl didn't know that, and neither did her mistress. Ander wondered how much longer Nippur would allow this distasteful scene to continue. He didn't have long to wait.

Isin had just begun to explain how the cremation process allowed souls to enter the garden of heaven, when Nippur lashed out. "Get your gods-forsaken hands off her!" she shouted.

The tent was suddenly quiet. All eyes turned toward Melesh, who casually released the girl, giving her a pat on the backside as she ran to her mistress. Nippur glared, but Melesh was unperturbed.

"I'll tell you what you can do," he said. "Burn the bodies and bury the ashes."

"Shut your filthy mouth," Nippur hissed.

"I think he's right," Qadesh said, calmly combing his fingers through his beard.

"What?" Nippur's face was pale with rage.

"Burn the bodies and bury the ashes," Qadesh said. "I can think of no other way."

Nippur stared. Her eyes narrowed to mere slits.

"That would satisfy us," Isin spoke up. As the conflict escalated, he'd moved to the other side of the tent, right next to Doran. The idea was to make it seem as though the leaders of all the major temples, Isin and Doran included, were against Nippur in some way, and that she was surrounded. Judging by the look on her face, it appeared to be working.

"If that would satisfy you, Nippur," Isin continued.

Her lips moved, but no sound came out.

Ander smiled. The thieves had performed well. Nippur was livid. Seething. No doubt imagining ways to verbally emasculate half the men present. And she would, just as soon as the initial shock passed. Ander was counting on it.

"What about the Niphilim?" someone else shouted. Ander didn't see who.

"Let them bake in the sun," Melesh growled. "They deserve nothing better."

"No," Isin responded. "The field must be cleared."

"Who gives a damn about the dead?" Sneaker suddenly piped in from his position beside the tent flaps. "You can build carts from their bones and sew sacks from their hides for all I care." He glanced at Ander, but never cracked a smile. "I only want to know one thing. What are we going to do about Jared?"

"Not this again," Doran said. He looked at Isin and then shook his head. If Ander didn't know better, he'd have guessed that Doran was aware of their plans. Anyway, he was playing his part magnificently.

"When are we going after him?"

This time Barley spoke up. Ander couldn't have been happier. "Thousands have died and you want us to send the few men we have left after one old thief?"

"Uruk thinks he's alive," Sneaker protested. His outrage looked so authentic that Ander almost laughed.

"We can't continue this war for one man," Isin said. "The price is too high."

"What if it's not for one man?" Ander asked. This wasn't exactly the moment he'd been waiting for, but he doubted a better one would come.

Ander had learned a few things while a slave of the Niphilim. How to mine iron, how to survive on a few ounces of stew twice a day, and how to stay out of sight. But those were just the obvious things. He'd also learned how to stand out from the crowd, and when it was useful to do so. That bit of knowledge had culminated in his escape. Catching the chief guard's eye and getting placed at the end of that work line had been no accident. Ander saw an opening and leapt through. It was time to do it again.

"What are you saying?" Isin asked him. He held out his hands, trying to appear mystified—just as Ander had taught him.

"There may be as many as a hundred men marching with the Niphilim," Ander explained. "All prisoners. I read the signs myself."

"Even for a hundred," Barley said. "How can we possibly afford to march after the Niphilim?"

"What if it was your son?" Ander asked. "How could you afford not to?"

"Are you suggesting that we wage war on the Niphilim?" Isin shook his head in mock outrage. "Our city's safe. And we are not soldiers."

"No you're not," Ander agreed. "If you were soldiers—like the

Niphilim are soldiers—you'd never have let them get away. Not when you had a chance to win this war once and for all." He paused, letting the words sink in. "No. You'll wait until the Niphilim come back. And then even more will die. They'll bring the rest of their army next time. Every blond man and woman they can find will march right through your precious city, crushing temples and filling your canals with blood. You hurt them. That's something the Niphilim won't soon forget."

"What can we do?" Doran asked. Ander had expected Isin to ask the same question, or one like it. This was even better. More convincing.

"Chase them down," he replied. Ander reached into his cloak and drew his sword, its handle still bloody from lying in the field. More than a few of those present gasped as he sunk it into the earth at his feet. "Kill each and every one of them."

For a moment no one spoke. All eyes were fixed on that blade, rising from the ash as though composed of death itself.

"How do you know they'll come back?" Isin asked finally.

"War is in their blood. They'll replenish their forces and fight again."

"We beat them this time," Qadesh said.

"They'll return by year's end," Ander said. "Right after the floods. I'd stake my life on it."

"But we can't possibly march on Dagonor." Qadesh shook his head, feigning despair. "This is an outrage. The Niphilim are beaten. We've won."

Ander waited for someone to say something. For or against, it made little difference. If things had been going exactly right, Nippur would have already spoken up. But she hadn't said a word since the incident with Melesh. Maybe the thieves had pushed her too far after all.

"Let's clean up the bodies and go back to our lives," Qadesh continued. "And if the Niphilim attack again, in a year or two, then we'll fight. Just as we did yesterday."

His followers nodded in agreement. And they weren't the only ones. More than half the tent believed that they could go back to the way things were. Qadesh had come out with a ridiculous lie, and nearly everyone there believed it.

"No," Nippur said at last. Ander nearly sighed in relief. "Qadesh is wrong," she spat. "Wrong about everything. We can't risk their coming back. This is our chance to put an end to it, once and forever."

247 / Slaves of the Shinar

"She's right," Isin shouted. "Nippur's right."

"Then we march the day after tomorrow," Ander announced. "Everyone agreed?"

Of course, almost no one had agreed. Thus far, their army was a tiny amalgam of three or four hundred thieves, the followers of Baal and Marduk, and the men from Ur—none of whom had battle experience. All together they represented less than half the force needed even to consider such a mission. To get the rest of the army to follow, they'd need at least one more leader. Someone they all believed in and trusted. They needed a hero.

"Doran and I have a favor to ask," Isin said. "If Barley's willing, we'd ask that he leads half of the men from Ur. They are all followers of Kallah, but we think they will do well to be with him."

A murmur ran through the tent. Doran gaped. Barley wasn't a priest, but he was a representative of the temple of Moloch, no matter how unofficial. In all the history of Kan-Puram, no temple had ever willingly given its followers over to the direct command of another. It was unthinkable.

"It'd be in the best interest of all," Isin continued. "Barley can restore his ranks, and the men from Ur will benefit from being around soldiers who've proven, if anyone has, that they'll stand and fight. Plus, Barley will then be in position to lead the march north. Our hero can be our vanguard."

Ander held his breath. It all came down to this. Nippur's part in the farce had worked beautifully. Now it was up to Barley. If he agreed, the rest would fall into place. If not, the war was lost. The Niphilim would get away.

"Is this what you want?" Barley asked. "Doran? Is this what both of you want?"

"Doran will command the other half of the troops," Isin said. "This really is in everyone's interest."

Doran nodded, but didn't say a word. Ander suspected that, like Nippur earlier, he was in a kind of shock. No leader, regardless of how incompetent, likes surprises. When he'd finally processed all that had happened, Doran would be angry—possibly to the point of irrationality. It'd be up to Isin to show him that everything had worked out for the best. Ander hoped he could do it. If not, they may have to remove him from his post.

As he considered all the various consequences of what had just occurred, Ander noticed something about Barley. He had no one tending to him. No messengers or bodyguards. No assistants. There was no one to help him make up his mind—or take the blame if he was wrong. Every other leader had scores of underlings. A few had so many that Ander couldn't help wondering if they even fed themselves, or wiped their own backsides. But Barley was alone. Ander still didn't think the one-eyed farmer looked like much of a hero, but he couldn't help respecting him.

"I'll do it," Barley said at last. "I'll lead them."

Ander yanked his sword out of the ground, turned and began pushing his way through the tent.

"Wait," Isin called after him. "We're not finished. The—"

Ander paused. "I have no more time," he replied. "There are fifty men under my personal command, none of whom have proper weapons."

"So what do you plan to do?" Isin asked.

"Hundreds of good swords are lying out there, just waiting to be discovered."

"And what about the bodies?" Qadesh asked. "We still haven't decided what to do with them."

"I'll organize the women," Nippur said. "We'll care for the dead as best we can. There are far more important issues to discuss now."

"Good," Ander said. "We march the day after tomorrow." Then he shoved through the tent flaps and was gone.

They'd likely talk for many more hours, but Ander didn't want to hear another word. These people talked their way through everything. Cut them and they'd describe the flow of their blood—or discuss ways to prevent infection. Not one in twenty would just grab a cloth and stop the bleeding.

Ander had no time for such nonsense. He was already contemplating his next step. Barley had become a leader despite a poor upbringing. It shouldn't be impossible for him to do the same. With luck, he might even seize command of the whole army. He could see no openings yet, but one would present itself. Of that he had no doubt.

CHAPTER 4

We Are Watched

*I*T WASN'T YET NOON, BUT ALREADY URUK WAS BEGINNING TO THINK of stopping for a rest. He thought he saw a likely spot over by the river, and was heading toward it when he stumbled upon the remains of a Niphilim fire.

The mound of ash and soot was enormous, large enough to cremate a dozen bodies. But strangely, there was a remarkable dearth of charred flesh, or even the tiny bits of bone one normally found on such a pyre. He did spot one small vertebra, just poking out from amidst the ash, and what he guessed must have once been a wrist or foot bone. But nothing else. Remarkable as it seemed, the Niphilim had apparently constructed this enormous pyre to dispose of one body. There was no other explanation. It could not have possibly been used as a cook-fire. When it was burning its brightest, Uruk doubted whether anyone had been able to stand within ten paces of it. The heat must have been incredible.

Nearby, Uruk found the remains of some latrines, hastily dug and even more hastily covered over. The turned soil was dry, he noticed. This camp had been abandoned at least two days before.

The dog found another place where the Niphilim had buried something, and in no time had dug up the remains of a body. There were only a handful of bones, whatever was too large to be fully consumed by the fire, and a large quantiy of light-gray ash. The dog tried to carry off one of the leg bones, but Uruk took it away from him. He tossed it, along with the vertabra and the other bone he'd discovered earlier, into the hole and covered it up.

As he finished smoothing out the grave, Uruk called the dog and together they walked to the river. He was feeling sick again. Over the last few days the vast majority of his strength had returned, but he usually got one or two bouts of lightheadedness sometime around mid day.

The Niphilim were a long way ahead of him now. Two full days at least, and getting farther by the moment. Uruk hadn't given up on rescuing Jared, but knew he'd never catch up before they reached the Niphilim village. What he would do when he finally got there, he had no idea. If escaping from the Niphilim were easy, Jared would have done so by now. One thing Uruk did know was that the task would likely require his full strength and mental clarity. If that meant a slower walk north, then so be it.

The sun had just reached its zenith, and the army of Kan-Puram was taking its daily rest. They'd only been on the road a few hours, but already most of the men felt completely sweated out. After five days marching over hard gray soil, with nothing to eat but raw millet and dry goat meat, their energy had begun to fail.

Barley thrust his water-skin into the river. Bubbles squirted from the open neck and popped on the surface. The skin had only been a little more than a third empty, but Barley thought he'd top it off anyway. A man could drink a lot of water over the course of an afternoon in the Shinar.

He wasn't the only one spending his free time along the river. The bank was crowded for as far as Barley could see. Younger men waded in the shallows, splashed and threw rocks. Some of the older men were napping in the tall grass. The only ones who hadn't made the short trip to the river's edge were the men from Ur. They sat in the middle of the road playing Bones' Luck. Barley wasn't surprised. The instant the army stopped moving they went for their tiles. Not one in ten had so much as a speck of metal left—the prostitutes and beer merchants in Kan-Puram had pretty well fleeced them—but that didn't stop their gambling. Mostly they bet on chores, focusing especially on the least desirable and most humiliating tasks. Barley doubted that they'd dug a single latrine without a losing hand being involved somewhere.

When it was full, Barley lifted his water-skin from the river. The hide was soaked, but he tied it on his belt anyway. Wet breeches wouldn't kill him. Not having enough water might. He'd just finished looping the laces around his belt when he noticed a long spindly shadow stretched over the river beside him.

"How far away do you think they are?" Lamech stood over him, his face twisted into a deep frown. Thinking back on it, Barley couldn't remember ever having seen the boy happy. Not when his father brought him to the tent and introduced him to Doran. Not when Barley had offered him a job as runner for the army. Never.

"Who?" Barley asked. The scouts, Ander included, were expected back sometime that day, though none of the men were supposed to know it. Doran wanted Ander's movements to be kept secret.

"Them." Lamech pointed across the river, at the mountains rising from the eastern horizon like a line of jagged black teeth. A pair of empty water-skins dangled from his outstretched hand. Three more were clutched to his chest.

"The mountains? Farther than you'd guess," Barley said. "Full day's walk at least. Probably more." He pulled a piece of canvas out of his pocket and began wiping the sweat from his head and neck. His scar was tender to the touch—probably sunburned. Barley rinsed his rag in the river and carefully pressed it to his bad eye. The hike had left it parched and dusty. "Why? You planning to go?"

Lamech shrugged out of his pack and began refilling his empty skins. "I've been watching them," he answered. "We walk and walk, but the mountains just stand there—never moving, but never left behind either." He tied off one water-skin and reached for another. "It almost feels like they're tracking us."

"Must be thirsty."

Lamech looked up.

"You, I mean," Barley said. "What have you got—five skins? And every one empty."

"These belong to the men in my squad. Mine's still nearly full." Lamech gestured toward the water-skin tied to his pack. "See?"

"Why don't they fill their own skins?"

"They're playing a game."

"And you offered to help?"

Lamech nodded. "They asked if I would. I don't mind."

"Do they ever invite you to play?" Barley asked.

"No. But I don't really want to anyway."

"Why not?"

"They're. . . ." Lamech shook his head. "I don't know. They just don't seem like they'd want me playing."

"Have you asked?"

"They're so much older."

"So?" If there was one thing Barley knew about Lamech, it was that age didn't intimidate him in the slightest. Lamech had been following at

Barley's heels from the moment they met. He'd made such a pest of him-self in Kan-Puram that, when it came time to assign him a position in the marching column, Barley stuck him with a squad at the back. It didn't work. The moment they stopped, Lamech was there. It would have made Barley angry except that the boy was so pitifully eager to please.

"I don't think they like me," Lamech said.

"Nonsense."

"And I don't have any metal."

"Neither do they." Barley clapped him on the shoulder. "Why don't you run back and ask if you can't join them for a quick game?"

"Well. . . ." Lamech looked Barley in the eye. He didn't want to go. The expression on his face was as clear as the wind and strong enough to move Barley's hair—if he had any. "If you think I should."

"What's really bothering you?" Barley asked. "You miss the city?"

Lamech took a quick look around, making sure none of the other soldiers were listening. "I've never been outside Kan-Puram in my life," he whispered. "My mother took me to see the farms when I was little, but we never went so far that I couldn't see the buildings." He winced. "I guess . . . I never realized the world was so big."

Barley laughed. He knew exactly how Lamech felt. In all his life he'd never been more than a dozen leagues from home. He'd heard about mountains, of course, but this was the first time he'd actually seen one. He wasn't impressed. For Barley, there was nothing so beautiful as a strip of well-turned earth. He loved the way his farm sprouted anew every spring. Seeing the young crop, its tiny green buds just poking from the soil, was so full of promise that he couldn't help feeling reborn. "It sure is a lot of nothing out here, isn't it?" he said.

Lamech grinned.

"Don't know what I expected, but. . . ." Barley looked up at the cloud-less sky, his good eye blinking against the sun. "Sure is a lot of nothing."

"But it's not just the city," Lamech said. "I miss. . . ." He leaned toward Barley, his voice dropping to a whisper. "My mother cried when we left. And my old dad . . . I think I might have seen tears in his eyes, too." Lamech's forehead wrinkled so deeply that Barley could almost see the worries forming in his mind. "Who'll take care of them if. . . ."

Barley put a hand on his shoulder. "You might not come back," he admitted. "That's the truth. I wouldn't lie and tell you otherwise."

Lamech's lower lip quivered. "But no matter what happens, you shouldn't spend all your time chasing after one old farmer. You can't protect your folks by looking after me."

"I wasn't—"

"Most of them are just as homesick as you," Barley continued, nodding at the men lined up along the river. "Believe me."

"I know." Lamech sighed. "Guess I should get back to my squad." He bent down and began gathering up the refilled water-skins.

"One more thing," Barley said. He gestured at his axe, lying beside his pack where he'd dropped it. "See that?" He waited until Lamech nodded. "An axe is deadly because it's heavy, not because it's sharp. Understand?"

"Maybe."

Barley pointed at Lamech's pack. The sword his father had given him was lying beneath it, half out of its scabbard, the exposed section of blade speckled with dust. "That's not some old farm tool," Barley said. "It kills because it's sharp and quick, and because the soldier it belongs to cares for it like it was his own leg. Or his mother."

Lamech picked up the sword and carefully wiped the blade.

"Take care of your sword," Barley said, "and it might take care of you."

The sun was going down fast. Spears of red and orange arced across the sky, causing the dust that hung over the encampment to glow like gold. Somewhere, a soldier was blowing a dirge on a set of reed pipes. It wasn't a song Ander recognized, but he liked it all the same.

"Spread out," he commanded. "No more than two to a fire—and don't be afraid to add to the pot."

Ander watched as his troops moved through the camp, mixing with the other soldiers. At least the men from Ur would make them feel welcome, he thought. The others he wasn't so sure about.

When they were all gone, Ander began looking for a face he recognized. He hoped to find the thieves, or maybe Qadesh. Instead he found Barley, sitting alone beside a small fire. A cook-pot was balanced in the coals, steam rising from the top.

"Is that food?" Ander asked.

Barley picked up a stick and began to stir the pot. Some kind of meat, probably goat, floated to the top of the thick gray mush. "You plan to sit down or just stand there gawking?" he asked.

Ander sat down and pushed back his hood. "May I?" Barley nodded and Ander carefully fished out a long strip of meat with his thumb and index finger. It was tough and flavorless. "You're not much of a cook," he muttered.

"Try the mash," Barley said, offering him a long-handled spoon.

Seeing no way to refuse, Ander scooped a large dollop from the pot. He wished he hadn't. It felt like mud and tasted like paste. He bit into a lump of dry millet and cringed. Barley stared at him all the while, head turned so that his good eye was aimed directly at Ander's face.

"I thought you said you'd be back during the day," Barley said.

"We were supposed to be." Ander handed him the spoon. Even slave food was better than what the soldiers of Kan-Puram were eating. Ander didn't think he could choke down another bite. "I thought you'd get a lot farther," he said. "We had to come all the way back from the edge of the mountains to find you."

"See anything?"

Ander nodded. "Scouts. Pickets."

"When?"

"You mean, when did I see them last?" Ander shrugged. "There are pair of Niphilim right over there." He nodded at some boulders on the opposite side of the river. "They're watching us right now."

Barley turned to look. "I don't see anything," he said. "How do you know they're still there?"

"I've been following them all day."

Barley offered him another spoonful of 'stew,' but Ander refused.

"You're not making very good time," he said, changing the subject. "The army I mean. You'll have to march through your afternoon breaks if you hope to reach Akshur by the day after tomorrow."

"What's the hurry?"

"I need you to be fighting them on the third morning."

"How did you know about our breaks?" Barley asked.

"I keep my eyes open. Both of them."

Barley looked like he wanted to say something, but thought better of it. Instead he took a spoonful of mush from the pot and stuck it in his mouth. He didn't look much more pleased with the taste than Ander had been.

"I think I may have seen the black man the thieves have been looking for," Ander said. "He was wading through some tall grass, not far from where the Niphilim army split apart."

"You saw him?"

Ander nodded. "I thought he was a Niphilim at first. He's big enough."

"Sounds like him," Barley agreed.

"I tried to chase him down, but by the time I made it through the grass he'd disappeared. He must know what he's doing too, because I could find no sign of him anywhere. Not a mark."

"What about his dog?" Barley asked. "Did you see him?"

"No."

Barley thrust out his lower lip as he considered what he'd heard. "You say the Niphilim split apart?" he asked at last.

"Yesterday," Ander said. "A small force headed east toward Akshur. The rest continued northwest to Dagonor."

"How much farther do they have to go?"

"You can't catch them," Ander said. "The group that was headed for Akshur is there already. The rest will be in Dagonor by sundown tomorrow."

Barley frowned. He stared at the fire for a moment, and then turned to look at the boulders across the river. They sat, neither man saying a word, for nearly a quarter-hour. Ander was just about to give up—he still had to speak to Doran, and arrange some details with Isin—when he saw what looked like a few strands of blond hair whipping out from behind the nearest rock.

"I think I saw something," Barley said. His good eye was nearly as wide open as his bad one.

"They're out there," Ander assured him.

"What'll we do?"

"I'll be leaving again before sun-up." Ander waited to see if Barley might reply, but he just sat there. "I'm going to need more men though—including a few of yours."

"How many?" Barley asked.

"Fifteen or twenty."

"Who?"

"Men from Ur mostly," Ander said.

"Mostly?"

"I'd like a squad with battle experience. Preferably young. They'll have to march a long way, with almost no rations."

"What for?"

"Do you have a squad in mind?"

"Look there." Barley pointed at one of the closest fires. A group of young men sat around it, trying to decipher the images on their gaming tiles despite the waning light. One of them looked to be no more than about fourteen or fifteen. He had a Niphilim sword cradled in his lap.

"They'll do," Ander said. He got up and brushed the dirt from his cloak. "I'll tell them myself, as soon as I speak to Doran."

"What about Akshur?" Barley asked. "The Niphilim won't abandon it without a fight. Any ideas?"

Ander thought for a moment. He wondered what the Niphilim captain would say if she were in his place. No doubt something a good deal more insightful than anything he could ever come up with. "You'll be fighting uphill," he began. "Tell the men to stick together and conserve energy." As he spoke, Ander reached over his shoulder and pulled up his hood. He did it without thinking.

"Sun's gone down, you know," Barley said.

"My hood does more than just block the sun."

"Really? Like what?"

Ander just smiled.

CHAPTER 5

Lost in the Dark

*A*NDER STOOD AT THE TOP OF A LONG STEEP SLOPE, GAZING AT THE valley below. The gray and brown knobs of the Withered Hills extended ahead of him for as far as the eye could see, but Ander paid them no mind. He was focused on a lonely stand of dandy-willow, twisting out from amidst the scaly black rocks at the western edge of the valley.

"What do you see?" he asked.

Isin shrugged. "Our path." He gestured at the long swath of dark footprints that ran past the dandy-willow and over the hills beyond.

"Don't point," Ander snapped. "Just look—you see that brush?"

Isin wiped the sweat from his forehead with the back of his wrist.

"Now, can you see anything else?"

"Such as?"

"Anything."

Isin shook his head. "Just some dried up bushes and black stones." He turned to look behind them. "The men have almost cleared the next rise," he warned. "We should get moving—"

"Keep your eyes on the valley."

Less than two days had passed since Ander's encounter with Barley. Since then, his little band of scouts had been walking almost non-stop. They began each day before sun-up, and didn't stop until long after dark. They lit no fires, had no blankets or extra clothes, and dug no latrines. For food they had only dried goat and whatever greens they could gather along the path. Water was scarce. It had been a hard, grueling journey, over lands as unforgiving as any on earth. Soon, if they continued on their present course, they'd be skirting the edge of the great northern mountains. Ander wasn't sure if his men had enough energy left to carry out their mission, but he wasn't ready to give up yet. Not while there was even the slightest chance for success.

"I need you to catch up to the men," he said at last. "Fast as you can."

Isin looked behind them again. "I can't see them anymore," he muttered.

"They won't have gotten far."

"No, I suppose not."

"Force them to increase their pace," Ander said. "Be fierce if you have to."

"Where are we headed?" Isin asked.

"Up there." Ander turned and pointed over the hills.

"Into the mountains?" Isin sounded nervous. "I'm not sure if—"

"Listen to me," Ander cut him off. "That's Dagon's Mountain." He pointed northwest, toward one of the taller peaks in the range. If a man didn't stop to eat, and only rested when absolutely necessary, he might hike to it in a day and a half. "I don't need to tell you who lives in its shadow."

Isin winced. "The enemy."

"That's right." Ander moved his finger slowly eastward, picking out each major peak as he came to it. "That's The Watcher," he said. "Bad luck. Keep out of its sight as much as possible. Next is Mount Murat, then Mount Hit. And the one due north of us is Mount Van." There was a wide cleft next to Mount Van. Through it they could just make out the distant shapes of a half-dozen other peaks, floating over the pass like a pantheon of all-seeing, all-knowing spirits. "That's called Urmia's Gap," Ander said. "If you went through, you'd eventually come to the greatest mountain of all—look hard and you can see it, just a shade to the right of center."

Isin squinted. "What is it called?"

"Ararat. My stepfather used to call it the gatekeeper of the heavens."

"What's that one called?" Isin asked. He pointed to one of the smaller peaks in that section of the range, due east of Urmia's Gap.

"That's where you're headed," Ander replied. "The Bald Mountain."

"Bald Mountain," Isin repeated.

"Children in these hills used to call it Baldy."

"What's the white on top?"

"Rock or . . . I don't know."

"All the others are capped with black."

Ander shrugged.

"How far is it?" Isin asked.

"Don't worry, you won't reach it tonight," Ander assured him. "March hard and fast, until it's too dark to see. . . . I'll find you." He put a hand on Isin's shoulder. It was meant as a friendly gesture, but Isin didn't seem to have noticed. "Make sure the men rest as soon as you stop,"

Ander continued. "No gambling. No chatter. Tell them to keep their things packed, and to be ready to move out the moment I arrive."

"What are you going to do?" Isin asked.

"Nothing," Ander said. "Nothing at all."

Hours crept by.

Ander sat on his hilltop—water-skin in his lap and pack propped behind his back—watching the sun glide across the sky, sending shadows scurrying from one end of the valley to the other. A slight breeze picked up after noon, but it was barely enough to set the few blades of grass atop each hill to dancing.

As the time wound on, Ander found himself gaining new respect for the Niphilim guards. After less than a day spent watching a stand of dandy-willow, he knew how hard it could be. At least a dozen times he'd caught himself examining the sores on his toes—they still weren't accustomed to the sandals he'd been given—or gazing mindlessly at the horizon. Keeping your mind focused, your eyes trained on the target, was no simple task.

Then, partway through the sixth hour of his watch, Ander saw one of them.

He'd been just about to take another pull off his water-skin when a head of blond hair raised up over the brush, glanced around for a moment, and disappeared.

Ander's heart raced. The Niphilim were growing impatient, he guessed. Before long, they'd come after him. They didn't yet know that the other black-heads weren't camped in the next valley over, but they'd begun to suspect. There was no smoke, Ander realized. If his men were camped close by, there'd be smoke. And probably someone would have come to check on him, if not spell him at his post. The illusion he'd tried to create was unraveling.

A fire wasn't such a bad idea, Ander thought. If he built one, the Niphilim might assume that he planned to be there overnight. The only problem was, Ander didn't have anything to build a fire with. There was barely a fistful of untrammeled grass on his hill, and the only bushes he could see were in the valley below. He certainly wouldn't be going down there. Giving Isin time to outrun their pursuers was one thing, sacrificing himself to the Niphilim was quite another. Ander wouldn't do that for anything less than total victory—maybe not even then.

He was still looking around for something flammable when he saw the Niphilim again. There were two this time—both women. They peeked out from either side of the brush and took a good long look.

In a moment of inspiration, Ander leapt to his feet and threw back his hood. Instantly, both heads disappeared.

"I think I saw something," Ander screamed. He cupped a hand over his eyes, as though to block out the sun. "In that bush."

It was a good trick, but the effect wouldn't last. As soon as the Niphilim realized that no one was coming, they'd be out of their hiding place and up the hill. At most, he'd bought a quarter-hour. Maybe less. He just hoped that would be enough.

Quick as he could, Ander undid his belt and refastened it outside his cloak. The idea was to hold the material tight against his body, preventing its catching on thorns and thistles. Plus, his sword would be easier to reach should the need arise. Ander also tied his water-skin to his belt. He wouldn't stop again for the next few hours and wanted to be able to get at it quickly and easily. Finally, he put on his pack and cinched it tight.

Ander glanced down at the brush one last time. The Niphilim stared up at him from either side. He waved his arms and they disappeared, but not as fast as he'd have liked. Ander wasn't going to be able to hold them back for much longer. It was time to start the race.

He glanced at the sun. It wouldn't set for an hour at least. That gave him nearly two hours during which he could see the path clearly. He'd go as fast as he could in that time, only slowing down after the darkness had closed in utterly.

"I just hope Isin did his part," Ander whispered to himself.

Then he started to run.

Isin woke with a start. It was so dark that for a moment he had no idea where he was or what he was doing. Then he heard voices coming from the eastern perimeter.

"I swear it's a jewel," one of them said. "A ruby or—"

"It's not a ruby."

"Could be."

"There's not a ruby in the whole deck."

"I meant carnelian."

"It's not even red. Maybe it's a bronze—or a wood."

"Funny. It's a jewel tile, look at the—"

"Quiet," Isin growled. "You're supposed to be keeping watch."

For a moment, the camp was silent. Then, the man with the disputed tile whispered, "I told you to keep your voice down."

"He was talking to you."

Isin turned over, trying to find a comfortable position among the stones and clumps of dried grass that made up his bed. From all around him came the murmurs and sighs of snoring men. Isin was just as tired, but couldn't seem to get into a deep sleep. Every time he started to drop off, something woke him. Between the mosquitoes and the chattering of the guards, Isin was close to giving up.

"Maybe it's a pearl," the guard whispered.

Isin sat up. There was just enough starlight to make out the shapes of two men, huddled together a few paces from the camp.

"I can't tell," one of them whispered. Judging by the way his head moved, Isin guessed it was the one on the right.

"We should go down by the stream," his friend replied. "There'll be fewer shadows."

"Too bad we can't."

Isin reached for his pack. He picked his way between the sleeping bodies, careful to avoid the outstretched hands and feet. Neither guard noticed as he sneaked up behind them. "That's more than enough Bones' Luck for one night," he said.

Both men looked up, startled.

"We'll keep it down," the man sitting on the right said.

"Don't bother," Isin replied. "You go get some sleep. I'll take your post."

"Thank Kallah. I'm nearly asleep now."

"Thank Her indeed," Isin said. The guard gathered up his tiles and dumped them in his pack. Isin sat down in his place.

The other guard must have thought he was in trouble, because he didn't so much as glance in Isin's direction, let alone offer a greeting. He just sat there, staring at his hands.

"What's your name?" Isin asked him.

"Lamech."

"You're one of the young men Barley sent with us."

Lamech nodded. Isin had to squint to see it.

"I think the moon will rise soon." Isin pointed at the dark outline of a hill. There was a pale white glow along its upper edge.

"Where do you think Ander is?" Lamech asked.

"Not sure."

"We march as soon as he arrives?"

"That's right."

"You think maybe he just wants us to believe that? So we stay sharp?" There was a great weariness in the boy's voice.

"I doubt it," Isin replied. "Not this time."

Lamech nodded. "Me neither. You think he *would* lie to us, though." It wasn't a question.

Isin didn't respond. He didn't think he needed to.

"That's what makes him such a great leader," Lamech said. "He's driven. Barley is a good leader too, but he's nothing like Ander. . . . Barley cares about his men. Ander cares only about the Niphilim." He looked at Isin. "Don't you think?"

"He believes in his mission," Isin agreed.

"Of course he does. So do I."

"Do you?" Isin frowned. "Would you kill if he asked you to?"

"I will kill—*when* he asks me to. It's only a matter of time, isn't it? Wouldn't you kill the Niphilim if you had the chance?"

Isin had a hard time imagining himself a killer. He didn't even like seeing the temple butcher slaughter hogs. The idea of cutting up a man like that made his blood run cold. "Did you kill any of them?" he asked. "In the battle?"

"No."

"None?"

Lamech shook his head. "I may have killed a savage or two."

"May have?"

"When it started, I was toward the back. I saw killing. Lots of it. And I swung my mace when the time seemed right. I did my best, but. . . ." He shrugged. Listening to him made Isin uncomfortable. Though he was only in his middle teens, Lamech seemed old—older even than Isin himself. The battle had aged him in ways that had nothing to do with years.

"I saw a lot of dead men," Lamech continued. "My best friend in the world had his throat torn out by a savage." He had to stifle a yawn to get the words out.

"It must have been terrible," Isin said. It had occurred to him that, very soon, he'd be seeing the kinds of things this boy was describing. Would he ever yawn as he talked about them? Isin hoped not.

"If you need to lie down, go ahead," he said. "I'll keep watch."

"You sure?"

Isin nodded.

Without another word, Lamech lay back and let out a long sigh. A moment later, he was dead asleep.

Isin must have nodded off soon after, because the next thing he knew, Ander was crouched in front of him, whispering at him to wake up.

"Has the moon come up yet?" Isin asked, rubbing his eyes.

"Hours ago."

"We're ready." Isin yawned. "Just have to wake the men." He reached toward Lamech, but Ander stopped him.

"Let the boy sleep," he said.

"What about the others?"

"All sleeping."

"Should I get them up?"

"No." Ander pushed back his hood. "I need a drink of water." He scratched the top of his head. "And they need as much rest as they can get."

"You don't look good," Isin said.

Ander sighed. "Give me your water-skin."

Isin pulled it out of his pack and handed it to Ander. "Here."

"It's full."

"There's a stream on the other side of that thicket." Isin pointed to a patch of dense brambles.

Without a word, Ander stood up and tromped away. Isin glanced over his shoulder, wondering if the noise would disturb the men. But not one of them so much as stirred.

"Coming?" Ander asked.

Isin picked up his pack. "There are stinging nettles on the far bank," he warned.

By the time he'd emerged on the other side of the brush, Ander was at the stream's edge, his pack lying at his feet with his cloak and belt piled on top of it.

"Having a wash?" Isin asked.

Ander pulled his tunic off over his head.

Isin gasped. He couldn't help it. Ander's chest was even more color-less than his face. In the moonlight, his skin shone like ivory. His was either the most beautiful body Isin had ever seen or the most gruesome. At the moment, he had a difficult time deciding which.

"Your scars," Isin said. "Are they from the mines?"

"Some are."

"And the others?"

"Stepfather. Children in my village." Ander shrugged. "There was a time when I was glad to have them. Can you believe that?"

Isin shook his head.

"Scars are one of the few things that the Niphilim respect. Some of them have even more than I do."

"What for?"

"Scars make you tough," Ander said. "Once you've been shown the door to the underworld, you need never fear death again."

"I'm sorry," Isin whispered.

"They look worse than they are," Ander said. But Isin could hear the lie in his voice.

Ander knelt and began splashing his face and upper body. Isin watched, transfixed, as the water trickled over the muscles in his arms.

"Feel better?" he asked.

"Tired." Ander wiped his face. "More than I've ever been."

"Can I help?"

Ander shook his head. "I ran for three straight hours, fast as I could go." He took a deep breath. "But that's only the beginning." He looked at the stream. It appeared to Isin as though Ander was searching for his reflection. But the water was too stirred up to see anything clearly.

"You did well," Ander said at last. "Made it farther than I'd have guessed."

Isin nodded.

"I lost the Niphilim an hour or two back."

"Lost them?"

Ander yawned. "In the dark."

"You need to eat." Isin opened his pack and began searching for the little bits of jerked goat he had left. Ander needed the salt, if nothing else.

But he refused to take them. "I'm not hungry," Ander said. "Just need to catch my breath."

Isin looked at the piece of meat in his hand, not sure what he ought to do with it. Ander needed to eat, Isin was sure of that, but he had no way of convincing him. Finally, he put the meat in his mouth and began the slow process of chewing it up.

"We'll head southeast," Ander muttered.

"South?"

"All the way to Akshur."

"When?"

"Before sun-up."

Isin opened his mouth to protest, then stopped. Nothing could change Ander's mind once it was set. "Will we make it?" he asked instead. "Is there enough time?"

Ander smiled. "I hope you're ready for a run."

CHAPTER 6

Crossing the Tiger

*D*ORAN SHOULD HAVE BEEN WORN OUT. AFTER A FULL DAY'S MARCH, without so much as a stop to urinate, he should have been exhausted. But he wasn't. His legs were sore and his feet were blistered. The tendons in his right knee felt over-stretched, shooting pain up his leg with every step. The crotch of his breeches had worn against his inner thighs until they bled. But Doran still couldn't sleep. Before the war he'd been a good sleeper, capable of closing his eyes once and knowing nothing else 'til morning. No longer. Since the last council in Kan-Puram, when Isin gave away half his troops, Doran had spent whole nights staring at the ceiling of his tent.

Sleeplessness bored him. After the first few nights, Doran took to visiting the other leaders. He didn't like most of them, but they were better than solitude. He'd even spent a few miserable hours with Qadesh—a mistake he wouldn't soon repeat. Tonight he thought he'd try the common soldiers. He doubted he'd find anyone worth talking to, but wasn't willing to rule out the possibility. At least not yet.

For hours he ambled among the cook-fires, eventually finding himself among the followers of Moloch. He might have wandered past them as well, but happened upon a young man making sacrifice to his god. Spiritual devotion had become so rare in recent weeks that Doran couldn't resist pausing a moment to watch the ceremony.

The boy meticulously crumbled up a sprig of wild dandy-willow and scattering it over a strip of fat. He mumbled a few words, and was just about to set it in the fire, when he noticed Doran. The boy's hands shook as he held his offering over the flames.

"Proceed," Doran urged. "Don't let me stop you."

"Do you want to say something?" the boy asked. "Offer a blessing?"

Doran shook his head. "I liked yours." He searched through his pockets until he found the strip of jerky he'd saved from his evening meal. "Offer this for me."

267 / *Slaves of the Shinar*

The boy dropped both pieces of flesh into the fire. They sizzled for a moment, then turned black and fell apart.

"Can you tell me where Barley is?" Doran asked.

"That's his spot." The boy pointed at a pack and blanket, lying together beside the smoldering remains of a fire.

"Where did he go?"

The boy shrugged. "You can wait if you like."

Doran crossed to Barley's fire and sat down. The heat rising off it was considerable, though only coals remained.

A small pile of sagebrush, meticulously trimmed of leaves, lay within easy reach. Doran didn't know if Barley had already cooked his evening meal, but thought he'd add a bit of fuel to the fire just in case. Before long he'd built up a respectable blaze.

He was just about to add a few more sticks when he saw Barley trudging toward him, the last of the sun's afterglow shining off his scalp.

"I stoked your fire," Doran said. "Only coals were left. I thought you might like to do some cooking."

Barley looked at the fire and frowned. "Thanks," he grumbled.

"Where have you been?"

"Fetching water." Barley held up a full skin. "Then I went to the latrine."

"You always take your axe to the latrine?"

"I guess so. To be honest, I can't remember the last time I left it alone." Barley tossed his newly filled water-skin onto his pack and sat down. The axe he laid across his lap, its enormous square head resting on one of his thighs.

"Beautiful sunset this evening."

Barley shrugged.

"My mother used to say that a red sky at sunset meant dust-storms in the western desert. 'Red sky at night, farmers take fright,' she used to tell me—"

"It wasn't dust."

"No?"

Barley shook his head. "It was the smoke from our fires, drifting in front of the sun." He picked up his cook-pot and began wiping it clean with one corner of his blanket.

"You've stopped meeting with the other leaders," Doran said.

"Can't spend all my time clicking teeth and swinging tongue."

Doran laughed. "You've been missed," he said. Barley didn't respond, so Doran picked up another piece of sagebrush and dropped it on the fire. "As has your charm."

Barley glared at the stick as it burst into flame. He set his pot aside.

"Cook if you like," Doran urged. "I won't be offended."

"Not hungry."

"You must be," Doran argued. "You marched us for better than eight hours without rest. When we finally stopped, I was so hungry I ate a whole packet of jerky. Go ahead, cook your meal."

Barley sighed. "I can't cook until the flames burn down," he explained. "I have to wait 'til it's just coals."

Doran looked at the fire, then at the pile of sticks he'd been feeding it. Until that moment, he'd always considered himself better for not having to do menial tasks. "I didn't know," he stammered.

"Flames die," Barley said, waving off his apology. "Same as everything else."

They stared at each other through the smoke. Doran was careful to avoid looking too long at Barley's bad eye, or at the scar running across the top of his head. "Can I ask you something?" he asked finally.

"Go ahead."

"Did you know Isin was going to offer you a portion of the men from Ur?"

"Not 'til it happened."

"Thinking about that moment has kept me awake nights. Do you remember where you were standing?"

"Not far from Nippur. A shade closer to the tent wall."

Doran nodded. "Did you happen to look at Ander?" He waited until Barley shook his head, then continued. "I did. He had an expression of. . . ." Doran licked his lips nervously. "It wasn't happiness or pleasure. . . . Nothing so human. I think it was a look of triumph." Doran hid his face in his hands. "He terrifies me," he stammered. "I think he's trying to take over."

"Take over what?"

"Everything."

Barley scoffed. "He's strange, but—"

"I found it hard to imagine at first," Doran admitted. "After all, Isin has been travelling with him all this time, and he and I are like brothers.

Then it occurred to me. Ander's not trying to win over the priests. He's after the men—and he's succeeding. They're in awe of him. Even my own men, the ones I've worked with from the very beginning, have fallen under his spell. I just don't understand why."

"I think I do," Barley said.

"Then please, tell me."

"It's because he's a leader."

Doran was appalled. For a moment, he was so filled with venom that he could find no words. There were dozens of perfectly good leaders, he thought, but other than Ander, and to a lesser extent Barley himself, no one paid them any mind. But before he could say any of it, Barley continued.

"Your problem is," he said, "you're a commander, not a leader."

"What's the difference?"

"A leader decides on a course of action, and then shows his men how to follow it. A commander tells his men what to do, then watches as they struggle."

Doran thought for a moment. "That's why you always march at the head of the column, cook your own food, fetch your own water."

"I try." Barley took a stick from the pile and began stirring his fire. At first, the flames leapt up stronger than ever. But before long, Doran saw, they'd dissipate, leaving only coals. It would be just as though he'd never sat down.

"Will you do me a favor?" he asked.

Barley picked up his cook-pot and set it on the coals. "You want to lead the battle tomorrow," he said. "Don't you?"

"I can march at the head of the lines. My men will see that I'm with them."

"Experiencing the same dangers," Barley said, finishing his thought.

Doran smiled. "By noon tomorrow," he said. "I'll have you in Akshur."

The army of Kan-Puram crossed the Tiger River before sunrise, and swept into the Withered Hills beyond. They made their way up a wide valley, just as the Niphilim had a month before, and within an hour had reached the base of a long slope. Doran never even paused to catch his breath.

It was a strange army that climbed the hill that day. Every man, without exception, was wet to the top of his thighs, and muddy at least to his knees. But Doran didn't suppose they needed to be clean or dry to win a battle. According to Ander, they outnumbered the enemy at least a hundred to one. Doran was surprised that the Niphilim women—so far as he could determine, there were no men among the soldiers waiting at the top of the slope—hadn't already fled. They had no prospects for victory, and no hope of reinforcements. Fate was so clearly against them that day.

Then, as though they'd heard his thoughts, the Niphilim did just that. Without even drawing their swords, they turned and disappeared over the crest of the hill.

Doran was astonished. For a moment, he had no clear idea as to what he should do. He was in a state of blissful shock. Only sheer habit kept his feet moving at all, and even that threatened to stop at any moment.

Unfortunately, the men around him were not so easily staggered.

The moment the Niphilim women disappeared, the whole front portion of the column dashed after them. Better than a thousand men went racing up the slope, like dogs chasing a hare. Doran didn't try to stop them. In fact, once his bewilderment had passed, he was filled with a joy that bordered on rapture. With luck, he imagined, they'd be able to overtake the Niphilim and drive them to their graves. And even if they failed at that, they'd still be among the first to see Akshur. It sent chills up his spine.

But all hopes of glory faded as Doran came over the crest of the hill and found the Niphilim, lined up and ready.

Beyond them, the buildings and gardens that had once been the town of Akshur waited. For a brief moment, Doran had a clear picture of thatched roofs, mud walls, and the bent and splintered posts that had once outlined goat-pens. There were no people visible amidst the little houses and shops, but he could imagine them. Young men with pitchforks and shepherd's crooks, going to their work in the fields. Mothers with babies pressed to their bosoms. The old and frail sitting in their doorways, watching life do its magic. It was right there—just a few hundred strides across a field of sun-scorched grass. But Doran would never reach it. He, and the better part of his men, had raced into a trap.

Doran had seen a device like this once before, while on a mission to Ur with some of his brethren from the temple. The farmers that worked the lands south of Kan-Puram used a similar trap for hunting deer and antelope. Just over the top of the hill, where none of them could see it, the Niphilim had constructed a barrier. It consisted of nothing more than sharpened staves, driven into the earth at an angle designed to catch a man between his navel and upper thigh. Normally, this kind of fence would be erected along a path where herd animals were known to migrate. According to the farmers Doran had spoken with, getting the beasts to stampede into it was no more difficult than starting a few small fires—nothing that couldn't be extinguished when the time came—and letting the smoke drift with the breeze. As the soldiers of Kan-Puram were learning, the same thing could be done to people, and with similar results. The worst part was, even those who saw the barrier in time, like Doran himself, weren't able to stop. Their friends and comrades, still racing up the hill, blissfully unaware of the danger, shoved them onto the spikes.

There was only one gap in the barrier, right at the center, and that's where the Niphilim were positioned. The few individuals lucky enough to avoid the spikes were quickly forced onto their swords. Doran saw that he'd be one of them, and began shouting and waving his arms wildly. It did no good. No one could hear him over the screams of the wounded and dying.

Finally, in a last effort at saving his own life, Doran tried to plant his feet and shove backward through the crowd. Predictably, the effort was a failure.

The last thing Doran saw, just before he was lifted and flung at the Niphilim swords, was a dirty brown hood and cloak, drifting like so much smoke from behind the largest building in Akshur. And it wasn't alone.

Somehow, Ander had managed to outflank the Niphilim. He and his entire team of scouts were, at that very moment, racing in to save the army of Kan-Puram. Ander would be a hero.

And so, with a curse on his lips and a prayer of forgiveness in his heart, Doran, priest of Kallah, went to his death.

CHAPTER 7

Debts of the Flesh

*T*HE VULTURES WERE BACK. NOT THE HUNDREDS AND THOUSANDS they'd seen in Kan-Puram, but still more than any man liked. They took turns landing on the blood-soaked hill, inspecting it for some tiny bit of offal, and then lifting back into the pale blue sky. Thankfully, most went away hungry.

Barley sat by himself at the top of the long slope, a mere stone's throw from the spot where so many men had been slaughtered, and watched as the priests of Kallah made final preparations for lighting the pyre they'd constructed in the valley below. The Niphilim had burned or otherwise used up most of the loose wood in Akshur, so the followers of Kallah had torn down whole buildings—hauling away the straw-thatched roofs and chopping up the meager furniture—leaving nothing but smashed bricks and crumbling mortar. Anything and everything that could be burned was gathered together—even the staves from the Niphilim trap, still coated with the blood of its victims. By the time they were finished, a respectable pile of debris had been assembled—more than enough to cremate the fallen heroes.

The task of hauling the bodies down the hill and lifting them onto the pyre was somewhat easier, though not without its challenges. All too often, just as they'd begun to disentangle one of the corpses from the morass of clinging bodies, they discovered that it was, in fact, still alive. On at least a dozen occasions, Barley had watched as priests were called to staunch a nasty wound. They tried dozens of methods, from poultices and tourniquets to cauterizing with a hot blade. Always in vain. The spikes had been set up too well. In most cases, they'd pierced the lower abdomen right where the blood was pooled most densely. Once tapped, no force on earth could stop its flow. The search of the battlefield also uncovered Niphilim women who had been wounded and were suffering, but no one bothered to torture them with treatment. When a Niphilim was found to be breathing, she was quickly and unceremoniously put to the sword, her remains dragged down the hill and flung on the pyre with all the others.

It was late afternoon by the time the last body had been placed atop the waiting pile of wood and straw. Soon after, the entire army, regardless of religious affiliation, began filing into the valley to witness the ceremony. Barley was particularly surprised to see Qadesh and the other followers of Marduk, standing shoulder to shoulder with priests from every temple in Kan-Puram, heads bowed reverently. Before the war, the sects would never have dared to share in each other's ceremonies. Fear of godly reprisals went too deep. No longer. At least for now, brotherhood and fellowship were more important than caste and affiliation. Barley hoped that such noble sentiments would last long after the war, but wouldn't wager on it. A large contingent of Ander's men was conspicuously absent, but that was no surprise. They'd been gone so often that Barley no longer even thought of them as part of the army.

Watching the priests go about their duties—building a tinder pile and anointing a ceremonial torch with ash—Barley was reminded of his first funeral. There'd been vultures that day as well. In the Shinar, not so much as a mouse could die without having at least one of those ravenous gluttons swoop in to announce its passing.

A wave of black fever had swept over Kan-Puram, and Barley's grandfather was among the unfortunate dead. Barley was only six at the time, so he didn't recall much of what transpired. He didn't even remember the priest tossing the ceremonial torch into the pile, though that must have happened. Mostly he remembered the vultures sailing in their usual lazy arcs, and asking his mother why they'd come.

"Vultures are always invited to a funeral," she'd whispered. "They were the first beasts the Creator breathed into existence."

Barley remembered staring up at the enormous birds, puzzled that a god would take so much care and trouble over something so hideous. His mother must have seen the wonder in his eyes, because she told him about how "They were fashioned from the desert sands and set to watch over all the beasts of the earth, both the quick and the dead."

"Why do they go in circles?" Barley asked her.

"Because they recall the days when the whirlwinds would pick them up and spin them over the dunes."

The next thing Barley remembered was a pillar of black smoke and his grandfather's outstretched hand, the white hairs on his knuckles just beginning to smolder. Years later, it would occur to him that all life ends either in ashes or dust. At the time, he was more aware of the way the smoke twisted as it climbed into the sky, not unlike a dust devil. The similarity seemed to him fraught with significance. The Creator must be terribly interested in dead people, he'd thought.

"Mama," Barley had asked. "Will I be burned when I die?"

"No," she whispered.

"Why not?"

"Because you're a follower of Moloch."

"Doesn't he like us to be burned?"

"No, honeycomb. Moloch's followers burn in life. They rot in death."

Barley was still thinking about the gentle way his mother had of explaining death when he heard footsteps, closing on him from behind.

Ander sat down less than a stride away. There were spots of fresh blood on his cloak, as well as on the front of his tunic. His hood was pulled low over his head, blanketing his whole face in shadow.

"You missed the meeting in the granary," he said.

"I assigned myself guard duty."

"Why?"

"Has to be done."

Ander considered for a moment. "You could have gone down there, you know." He waved at the soldiers amassed in the valley. "I'd have sent one of my men to take your place."

Barley shook his head.

"You didn't want to go?"

"No," Barley replied. "Nothing lonelier than the company of men."

Ander nodded. If anyone could understand what he was feeling, Barley thought, it'd be Ander.

"We interrogated the prisoners," he said.

"Tortured," Barley corrected.

"Don't feel too bad for them. They've done much worse, I promise."

"It wasn't them I was concerned about."

Ander shrugged. "We also found some survivors." He gestured back toward the town with his thumb. "Akshurite women. Locked inside a shed behind the smokehouse, starving to death. I found five cases of dried venison just going to waste, but they hadn't had a morsel of food in two days."

"Will they live?"

"They should."

While they talked, a sort of makeshift orchestra had been forming in the valley below. It was nothing extensive, just a handful of fifes, a set of reed pipes, and a shofar. The last had been carved from one of the twisted horns of a mountain ibex. In Kan-Puram it was common practice for the dead to be serenaded into the next world.

"What will they play?" Ander asked.

Barley shrugged.

"My mother used to sing while she carted wool. She had a wonderful voice."

"I thought you had no parents," Barley said. For some reason, at that moment it delighted him to be cruel. Especially to Ander.

The response he got was instantaneous and clear. Ander gazed at his own hands, pale as summer grass, and frowned. There was something horribly accusatory in the way Ander glared at his skin. It reminded Barley of a jackal, one paw badly wounded or caught in a trap, ready to gnaw away its own flesh and bones for the sake of freedom.

"I'm sorry," Barley said. He'd never been able to hold on to spite. "I shouldn't have said that."

"No, you were right. I had neither mother nor father." Ander clenched his hands into fists, then drew them back into his cloak, hiding them from sight.

Barley was about to say that his own mother had passed away when he was just a boy, but Ander waved at him to be silent. "They're about to play," he whispered.

The high, almost bird-like sound of a lone fife reached up to them. Barley couldn't tell who was playing, nor did it matter. The others joined in soon enough. So far as he could determine, they weren't playing any kind of melody, much less a recognizable song. But their tone was clear, their notes well chosen and eerily calm.

"It's happier than I'd expected," Ander observed.

"They hope to cheer the spirits of the newly dead," Barley explained. "To remind them that their ancestors wait with open arms."

"Who is that?" Ander pointed to a man who was rapidly tearing off his clothes.

The person in question had his back turned, but Barley thought he saw something looped around his neck. "Doesn't Isin wear some kind of charm?" he asked.

Ander nodded. "An idol, his goddess."

When he'd finished stripping down, Isin looked like nothing so much as an old beggar. He didn't even pause to rearrange his loin cloth, which was thin and insufficient to its purpose. No sooner was he out of his breeches than one of the other priests handed him a clay jar. Isin made a show of drinking from it, then flinging the jar onto the pyre. Barley had heard that the priests of Kallah in Ur did something similar whenever they sacrificed a child, but he put no stock in such tales.

"Why are you really sitting up here?" Ander asked.

"I wanted to see it," Barley said.

"But why?"

"Because we killed him."

"Who?"

"Doran."

Ander's face was as devoid of color as ever, and yet somehow he managed to grow even more pale. "I never touched him," he said at last.

"Doran wanted his men to respect him—the way they respect you. That's why he was at the front of the column. And I gave him the idea."

"So now you feel guilty."

Barley didn't respond. He might have said that unlike the Niphilim, or Ander himself, he actually felt bad when his actions led to the death of a friend. But his earlier remark about Ander's parents had left him feeling more empty than vindicated, so he held his tongue.

"Isin is like you," Ander continued. "He feels responsible. He doesn't think he should have left Doran alone."

"Doran wasn't alone."

"No, he wasn't." Ander paused. "Do you want to know the real reason he died?"

Barley wasn't sure that he did, but nodded anyway.

"It's because he was a priest, and war calls for soldiers." As he spoke, a look of sadness flashed through Ander's eyes, almost as though he wished he were lying.

"I'm finished," Barley said. "Done."

"With what?"

"I'm not going to be a leader anymore."

"What about your men?"

"I don't care. Isin can lead them. Most are followers of Kallah anyway."

"Isin isn't in command," Ander said. "I am."

Barley flinched. He felt as though a knife had been shoved between his ribs. "Doran was right," he said at last. "You are taking over."

"Does that mean you've changed your mind?" Ander asked.

"No." Barley tore a handful of dry grass out of the dirt between his feet and tossed it in the air. "Do what you want. You will anyway."

Ander considered for a moment. "I'm going to do something against my better judgement," he said at last. "I'm going to give you a choice."

Barley said nothing.

"Either return to Kan-Puram with the wounded and the women, or. . . ." Ander stared into Barley's good eye. "Or you can lead the scouts."

"I told you—I won't lead."

"I wish you'd reconsider," Ander said. "Lead the scouts and you'll be free of interference. You won't have to see me again until the war is over."

Barley was about to say that he'd rather go back to Kan-Puram with the wounded. But just then, a voice called out behind them, shouting for Ander.

It was Lamech, trudging toward them across the field. He was a grisly sight. The cuffs of his breeches were muddy. Blood covered the sleeves of his tunic from wrist to elbow. But worst of all were his eyes. Instead of the brooding boyishness of youth, Lamech had a look reminiscent of Ander himself. Barley was stunned.

"Pops sent me to find you," Lamech said.

"Did you finish burying the rest of those bodies?" Ander asked him.

Lamech nodded. "We had to bury the prisoner you wanted kept alive, too."

"What happened?"

"Sneaker. . . . He wanted to ask her some questions. We couldn't convince him that she didn't understand a word he said."

"So he killed her." Ander shook his head. "What a waste."

"He kept asking her if the Niphilim had wagons. And when she wouldn't answer, he slit her throat. Pops tried to save her, but she bled to death." When he'd finished telling the story, Lamech glanced over at Barley and blushed.

"How are you, boy?" Barley asked him.

"Fine."

"You look tired."

"I had a long night."

"I'll bet you did."

"Tell Pops I'll be there shortly," Ander said, cutting them off.

"One other thing," Lamech said. "I don't know if it's important, but the women from the shed . . . a few of them are sick."

"What's wrong with them?" Ander asked.

"A rash, on their arms and chests." Lamech rubbed the skin that showed through the neck of his tunic. "They say it's sensitive to the touch."

"Body lice," Ander said. "Nothing to worry about. Tell Pops to find them some new clothes. Cut off their hair if you have to." He paused. "All their hair. Understand?"

"I'll tell him." Lamech was about to turn and head back to Akshur, but hesitated.

"What is it?" Barley asked him.

Lamech squinted down at the pyre. A narrow column of greasy smoke rose from one corner. "Why'd they build it down there?" he asked.

"The grass up here is dry," Barley explained. "Isin didn't want it accidentally catching fire."

Lamech stared down the hill a moment longer, apparently transfixed by the gathering smoke, then trotted away.

As soon as he was out of earshot, Ander turned to Barley. "I'll make sure the women are free of lice before you start back," he said.

"I've decided to lead the scouts," Barley replied.

Ander was surprised, but pleased. "Excellent," he said. "I should tell you, though—I don't really need you to scout."

"Then what?"

"If we're to win this war, we'll have to draw some of the enemy's attention away from the main battle."

"How?"

"Attack from the rear." Ander pointed west across the Withered Hills. "You'll march straight through, staying as close to the foot of the mountains as possible. . . . I'll draw you a map."

"When do we leave?" Barley asked.

"Before sun-up. Most of your travelling will have to be done at night, I'm afraid. With luck, they won't know you're coming until you're almost upon them. We'll take the easier plains road, just as soon as we've destroyed the rest of this town."

Barley glanced at the little buildings, sitting so peacefully on the edge of the field. "What for?" he asked.

"The Niphilim will never again use Akshur as a base for launching an attack on the south."

"How many men do I take with me?"

"A hundred. There are fifty left from my group. You can pick the other half. Take anyone you want."

"I've got just one demand," Barley said.

"What's that?"

"I don't care who else comes, but Lamech's with me."

"The last time we spoke, I'd have sworn you wanted to get rid of him."

"My mistake," Barley said. "The truth is, I don't want him around you anymore. He's a good boy."

Ander laughed. "So be it. From now on, Lamech is yours."

Book IV
COMES THE DARK

*F*OR FORTY CENTURIES THE SHINAR WAS THE ABODE OF MEN, WHILST nary a female creature existed upon the earth. Males of every species there lived. It was a land of manes and horns, antlers and beards. Only among the gods were there females. This was called the first age, and it was a legendary time.

Every sort of manly endeavor was practiced. Morning, noon and night, the men tussled with each other, both in good humor and in bad. They fought over the best land for farming, and the best streams for fishing. When they desired a rest from their toil, they wrestled or boxed. In the evenings they retired to their separate huts and slept alone.

But there was one man who, though possessed of a thick beard, was unhappy with life as the men lived it. His was the smallest farm, the tiniest portion of stream for fishing. Never did he best his fellows in wrestling or boxing. He was called Adamath.

It occurred to Adamath one day, whilst tending his plants, that he could conquer the others if only he had a helpmate. He had heard that the goddess most receptive to prayers was Baal—she of the rains, mistress of fertility.

Forty days and forty nights did Adamath wile away in prayer. At last, Baal heard. The goddess came, visiting Adamath in his hut.

What do you Adamath, most humble of men?

"O Baal, most beautiful of gods, I desire a helpmate," Adamath said. "So that I may defeat my enemies and my friends."

No helpmate need you. The plants of the field are yours. The fish of the river. The men of the earth. You have all that you require. Be fruitful. Be satisfied.

"I cannot," Adamath answered. "For I am weak. My farm yields sparse grain. My stream is all but empty. The other men defeat me in wrestling and boxing. Indeed, my life is loathsome to me. Without a helpmate, I should be forever miserable."

You are a fool, Adamath. What right have you to be miserable? Are you not a man? Have the gods not provided all that you shall ever need? Why should one such as I care for your hopes and dreams? But I shall grant you your heart's desire. Go to the mountains. There you will find a cave. Delve deeply into it. Inside you will find your helpmate, lying in a pool of milk.

Adamath thanked Baal, and went that day to the mountain. As the goddess had promised, he found a cave, and inside of the cave he found a pool of milk. Lying in the pool of milk was a baby. Adamath had never seen a baby before, but he was not afraid. He picked it up and carried it outside. Once in the sunlight, he saw that the child was like him in all ways but two. First, it lacked a beard. Second, the baby lacked a part inherent in all men, and over which they took great pride. Seeing that this part was missing, Adamath was sore afraid. He thought that he should take the babe back to the pool in the mountain, but could no longer find the cave. So he carried the baby back to his hut. Once there, he told the other men of his find. They wondered what he intended to do with this new thing, and what he should call it.

"I shall raise it to be strong," Adamath said to them. "When it is grown, it shall be my helpmate. Together we will have the largest farm in all of the Shinar. And the largest section of stream. When we sleep in my hut, we will sleep together. Never again shall I be defeated in wrestling or boxing, because my helpmate will stand with me. For this reason, I shall call her 'woman.' For woe will be the lot of any man who should dare to stand against us."

At this the other men went away. But they could see that what Adamath said was true. And so they desired helpmates of their own. But they could not find any. At last, one of the other men, whose name was Allum, conceived a plan. He went to Adamath, demanding that the woman be given over to him. Adamath refused, so Allum slew him with a spear.

This was the first death in the Shinar.

I Will Lift Up Mine Eyes
to the Mountains

U RUK WATCHED AS THE LAST TROOP OF MINERS STOWED THEIR GEAR —hammers in the storehouse, baskets stacked in neat towers beside the door—and then shuffled back to their barracks. The guard waited until the last man was safe inside, then slid a heavy crossbar into place, effectively sealing the door.

The other Niphilim, those who'd escorted the slaves out of the mine, wasted not a moment before tromping off to bed, leaving one lone guard to watch over the whole of Dagonor.

Being no more concerned with his duties than he had been on previous nights, the guard sat down on the slave barracks steps and leaned his back against the door. It'd be at least four hours before anyone came to relieve him, and he was settling in for a long boring night.

Uruk patted the dog on the shoulder. "Stay here," he said. "I will not be long."

The dog's ears perked in what looked like a mixture of confusion and annoyance. But he made no move to follow as Uruk slipped out of their hiding place and started down the mountain.

It was a steep climb, and difficult. One misplaced step and the loose stones that littered the mountainside were liable to go careening all the way to the bottom. Even a drowsy guard, expecting no more provocation than could be meted out by a few stinging flies, would be roused.

As he neared the base of the slope, and was about to make a last dash across the strip of open ground separating him from the storehouse, Uruk looked back over his path. He wasn't surprised to see the dog, sitting in a patch of dandy-willow just a few dozen strides behind, eyes glowing like a pair of infatuated lightning bugs. It might have been better if he'd stayed farther up the mountain, but so long as he remained hidden Uruk had no reason to complain. In fact, he was moved by the dog's loyalty. It felt good to know that there was at least one being in the world that didn't want to let him out of its sight.

Kishar flipped through the maps on his table, pausing when he came to one with a leaf-shaped symbol emblazoned in the upper-right-hand corner. It was a chart that Kishar himself had drawn, detailing the fields north of Kan-Puram, the grove that formed the field's border, and the position of their camp during the last campaign. The city itself was little more than an amorphous blank covering the lower third of the parchment. When he'd first begun work on the chart, Kishar was excited by the opportunity to explore the streets and alleys of the great metropolis. It would have taken weeks to get it all down, years to perfect it. But he'd have done it eventually. The challenge only intensified his desire to begin.

"Have you found the map of the eastern hills?" he asked.

"Not yet." Lagassar sat cross-legged beside the fireplace, Simha's pack open in her lap, rapidly sorting through its contents. "You're sure it's not with all the others?"

Kishar shuffled through the charts again. "It's not here."

Since moving into the captain's chambers, Kishar had only made a few minor changes. He'd replaced Simha's bedroll and personal gear with his own, and he'd had a wooden rack set up against the back wall. It stood chest high, and had formerly been used by the slaves for drying cloth. Kishar planned to hang his maps on it. Over the last few months he'd become concerned that the symbols, each so carefully plotted, were being destroyed by constant folding and stacking. Eager to put the rack to use, Kishar picked the maps up from his table and began hanging them over the rods. There wasn't space for them all, so he carefully folded each chart into thirds, markings out, before draping it over the rack.

He'd only just finished when Lagassar held up a piece of hide she had discovered wadded up at the bottom of Simha's pack. "It's got a mountain drawn on one corner," she said.

"That's it." Kishar took the map and spread it over the table.

He planted himself in the captain's chair, surprised once again at how hard and uncomfortable it was. "We need to have a sconce fixed to the wall," he muttered. "I can barely see in this gloom."

"Simha tried that," Lagassar reminded him. "The torch put out too much smoke. Antha-Kane made her get rid of it."

Kishar held up one corner of the map, trying to catch as much light as possible. "Come here," he said, waving at Lagassar to join him.

There was only the one chair, so Lagassar squatted at Kishar's side. Simha had always liked her lieutenants to stand. It gave her the opportunity to judge their readiness for battle. Kishar thought he'd have another chair or two brought in.

"I want to issue new orders for defending Dagonor," he said.

Lagassar squinted at the map.

"This is the main road through the hills." Kishar pointed at a narrow valley that wound south from the temple to the grasslands.

"That's where you think their attack will be launched?"

"Most likely."

"The enemy will march past the hills." Lagassar ran her finger over a myriad of tiny lines, meant to represent grass. "We can form our defense here."

"On the plains?"

Lagassar nodded.

"For the sake of argument, let's imagine that a portion of the attackers were to somehow force its way through our lines." Kishar slid his finger up the narrow valley. "Our forces would be cut off from Dagonor." He pressed his finger down on the box that represented the temple. "There'd be nothing to prevent their burning and looting the house of god."

"Purely hypothetical," Lagassar said. She meant that an army of black-heads had no hope whatever of breaking their lines. It was a prejudice that most Niphilim shared. Kishar had encountered it every day of his life. Even Simha had been guilty of it, and had paid the ultimate price for her arrogance. The Niphilim thought of themselves as a kind of natural force, not unlike a tornado or avalanche. Even their failures in the recent campaign were seen as a kind of victory in waiting, a sort of calm before the real storm.

"The possibility doesn't concern you?" Kishar asked.

Lagassar shrugged. "Our army will not break."

"What if they come over the hills?" Kishar pointed at the headwaters of the Tiger River, then drew a straight line to Dagonor. "There are no scouts or guards in this area. They could come on us by surprise."

Lagassar leaned over to examine the path Kishar suggested. "The

Hills will keep them out," she said. But she didn't sound so sure this time.

"I've been over those hills. They're not as rugged as we've always imagined. A fast runner might cover the whole distance in a single night."

"What do you suggest?"

"Sentries—posted at each of these points." Kishar picked out a plateau overlooking the Tiger River, followed by a number of largish hills, forming a line from the base of the Karun Mountains all the way to the grasslands of the Shinar.

Lagassar considered for a moment, then nodded. "I don't think they'll be necessary, but a handful of men will make little difference."

"They have to be fast runners."

"I'll send them at first light."

"Good." Kishar looked at Lagassar's hands. Scabs ran across the first two knuckles, reminders of the recent battle. Her nails were chewed to the quick. "There's a third possibility," he said. "They could split their force in two, sending half over the hills and half over the plains."

"Even black-heads aren't that stupid."

"What do you mean?"

"Divide their army?" Lagassar scoffed. "They wouldn't last an hour."

"No? Remember, our forces would be divided as well."

Lagassar frowned. She glared at the map as though expecting to see the imagined armies marching across the parchment, like so many ants scurrying over a piece of discarded bread.

"How would you stop them?" Kishar asked.

"I suppose I'd have to split our forces in two. . . . Attack from dual positions."

"Simultaneously?"

Lagassar nodded.

"They outnumber us," Kishar reminded her.

"What else can we do?"

"We must think of a way for a smaller army to effectively stop a larger."

"How?"

"Eliminate the advantage of numbers." Kishar pointed to a spot in the valley they'd been looking at earlier. Tall hills stood to either side, over-looking a place where the valley widened into a meadow, and then narrowed again as it neared Dagonor. The Niphilim often practiced unarmed combat in that meadow. They knew it well.

289 / Slaves of the Shinar

Lagassar peered at the map with what could only be described as grave doubt. "It's awfully close to the temple," she said.

Kishar agreed. "It possesses certain challenges," he admitted. "But there are also many advantages to the site."

"It's possible for a pair of smaller groups to loop around, here and here." Lagassar pointed at the northern contours of the surrounding hills. "With some careful planning we could attack the invaders from either side. If we're quick, and the black-heads don't see it coming, we might even split their column."

"Exactly." Kishar was pleasantly surprised at the speed with which Lagassar had made the discovery. He'd seldom known her to possess such vision. Lagassar was a soldier more in the vein of Simha herself—a fighter capable of nearly superhuman endurance and speed, but also one more likely to charge headlong into a battle than to find a strategic method for winning it.

"It could work," Lagassar admitted grudgingly. Likely she still wanted to meet the enemy on an open field, but could see the wisdom in the alternative.

"I'm glad you think so. You'll be in charge of making sure that it does."

"And what if that second troop comes over the hills?"

Kishar grinned. "By funneling them into this valley, we'll have enough men in reserve to meet all challenges."

Both were quiet for some time after that. Maps often spoke to Kishar during moments of quiet contemplation, but not this time. If there were any further mysteries to be culled from this chart, Kishar wasn't seeing them.

They were still studying the parchment when the door to Antha-Kane's inner sanctum creaked open and a young woman with long black hair stepped out. She had a tray balanced across her forearms and a slop bucket dangling from one wrist. She'd also been struck recently, and had red finger-marks across one cheek to prove it.

The girl said not a word as she went about her tasks, closing the door with her elbow and then peering into the slop bucket in the corner to see if it too needed emptying. Fortunately for her, Kishar preferred to do his business outside, as had Simha before him.

"Wait," Lagassar said.

The girl had been about to open the outside door, but stopped.

"Come here." Lagassar led her toward the fire. Kishar noticed that the girl's arms were shaking, but suspected that was more from nerves than whatever strain she felt from the weight of her load. She was unusually well constructed for a black-head, tall and lean.

"How did you hurt yourself?" Lagassar asked her.

She glanced at the door to the inner sanctum. "The great one is angry."

"How did you provoke him?"

"Provoke?"

"Anger. How did you anger him?"

"I was looking." The girl blushed so furiously that, for a moment at least, her left cheek reddened to match her right.

"What were you looking at?" Lagassar pressed on the girl's wounded cheek with her thumb. The girl winced but didn't try to get away. Kishar was beginning to like her very much.

"His. . . ." She hesitated, scouring her mind either for a word she couldn't quite remember, or for a way of presenting the facts so that her audience would be less likely to take offense. "His washing," she finished at last.

Kishar chuckled. The girl was at that age when most Niphilim youths began to sneak peeks at each other while bathing. There was no harm in it—unless you happened to be peeking at Antha-Kane.

Lagassar scowled. "She's been serving us for years, but still hasn't learned the superior tongue." She grabbed the girl by the hair. "Look at this. Black as soot. And her skin. . . ." Lagassar shuddered in disgust. "She's more animal than woman."

"Let her go," Kishar said.

Very reluctantly, Lagassar did as she was told.

The girl didn't move. She stared at Lagassar, then at Kishar, obviously unsure as to what she ought to do next.

"You heard the captain," Lagassar growled. "Go."

Kishar watched as the girl crossed to the door and, working the latch with her elbow, slipped through.

Once outside, the girl raced toward the storehouse, making a quick stop at the slag-heap to empty Antha-Kane's bucket. It was a dark night, but she could have walked that path blindfolded. She'd been over it at least five times a day, sometimes more, for better than two years. She didn't expect to leave it behind for good until she was dead, and even then she couldn't be sure. At night, when she was huddled in the darkness of the slave barracks, bodies pressed against her on every side, she had visions of her spirit carrying a never ending supply of slop-buckets, loaded with every imaginable noxious fluid, from one end of Dagonor to the other.

She was supposed to clean the bowls and utensils and wipe down her tray before going to bed, but decided to leave them until morning. As usual, she'd be among the first slaves rousted from the barracks. She'd do the cleaning then, just before taking Antha-Kane his morning bread and, once again, changing his bucket. Hers was a challenging job. If not for the naps she was able to sneak between washing Antha-Kane's sleeping clothes and preparing his midday meal, she might not have survived.

Her tray safely stowed out of sight, the girl hastened to the slave barracks. With luck, she'd be able to get a full four hours rest before the next shift of guards came to wake her.

"Finished?" the guard stationed at the door asked.

She nodded.

"You're early," he muttered, slowly rising from his seat on the steps.

He was about to lift the crossbar out of its slides. But just as he reached for it, an enormous, bestial shadow detached itself from the corner of the building.

It moved faster than anything the girl had ever seen. Only when his arm looped around the guard's neck did she realize that she was looking at a man, and not a lion or half-human savage that'd wandered in off the western hills.

She'd never seen a black man before, though she knew they existed. He looked nothing like she'd imagined. His face was broad, with deep-set eyes and full, expressive lips. He was so handsome that she didn't even think to scream or call for help. Not that she would have anyway—the Niphilim didn't look kindly on slaves that made a lot of noise.

The guard struggled, mouth open and sucking for breath. His attacker, by contrast, was the very picture of calm. Sweat ran down his face, and the muscles in his arms were taught, but no other sign of strain could be seen.

Finally, the guard's eyes rolled up in his skull and his legs went limp.

Uruk set the guard down on the steps, leaning him against the door so that he appeared to have fallen asleep while performing his duty.

The young woman watched his every move, wide-eyed and trembling.

"He will live," Uruk assured her. At first, he didn't think she'd understood. Her eyes remained as blank and overwhelmed as before. "Can you speak?" he asked.

She nodded.

"Good enough."

The girl squeaked as Uruk grabbed her by the upper arm and threw her over his shoulder. "Be quiet," he commanded. Her teeth clicked as she closed her mouth.

Uruk ran up the mountain at full speed, the girl bouncing on his shoulder with every step. He leapt over bushes and rocks, and sprinted up narrow banks of hardened clay. Eventually he found himself on a narrow ridge of stone.

Finally, as they plunged through a line of small trees, Uruk stopped. He set the girl on her feet and leaned over to catch his breath. The girl was trembling, but didn't say a word.

"Can you climb?" Uruk asked her.

She nodded vigorously.

"Good." Uruk pointed at a stand of brush farther up the mountain. "That way." He turned, and was just about to lead her up the hill when an idea struck him. "If you try to run away, I will give you back to the Niphilim," he threatened. He hoped he looked sufficiently ominous. There was no way this girl could outrun him, but he'd just as soon she didn't try.

It took another quarter-hour of hard trekking, up a path clogged with brush and trees, but finally Uruk ducked through what appeared to be a vast wall of thorn bushes and emerged into a grassy clearing. The dog was overjoyed to see him.

The slave-girl, who'd struggled mightily to keep up, crawled through the brush a moment later, breathing as though she'd been running for hours. The dog sniffed her over and then let out a deep growl, scaring her into almost complete immobility.

Uruk took one of her hands and led her onto the grass. "Sit down," he invited.

As usual, the girl did what she was told.

"Do not worry about Dog," Uruk assured her. "He hates women, but will not attack unless I tell him to."

She looked less than comforted.

"If you are to stay with us, you are going to have to learn to answer when I speak to you." Uruk went to the hole through which they'd just crawled and bent down. From there he could see all but the westernmost buildings of Dagonor. They had to be careful going in and out, especially during the day, but otherwise this little clearing provided everything necessary for scouting the enemy.

"I have to go back now," Uruk said. "Our trail will be obvious even to them. But first, tell me your name."

"Antha-Kane calls me 'black-head,' or 'girl.'"

"So that is your name?"

"Adah. My name is Adah."

"A fine name. I am Uruk. That is Dog. He will be in charge while I am away. If you try to leave, or make too much noise, he will make you sorry. Understand?"

Adah nodded.

"Do you understand?" Uruk asked again.

"Yes."

"Good." Uruk motioned to the dog. "Sit here," he said. "Do not let her leave."

The dog growled ominously.

"Don't worry," Adah whispered. "I'll be here when you get back."

Uruk smiled. "I know you will."

CHAPTER 2

Adah Speaks

*U*RUK DIDN'T RETURN UNTIL LATE MORNING.

The dog must have heard him coming, because all at once he was on his feet, tail wagging furiously. He was so excited that he began to pant, though he'd done nothing more strenuous than lick his nose in hours.

"Everyone still here, I see," Uruk said as he crawled through the hole in the brush, dragging a large basket behind him.

"Still here," Adah agreed. In fact, she hadn't moved so much as an inch since he'd left, more than six hours before. The dog was a tough guard. If she even took a deep breath, his fur bristled violently. Adah would have liked to stretch out on the short turf and close her eyes, but didn't dare. It wasn't so bad really. Once, not long after coming to Dagonor, she'd spilled one of Antha-Kane's buckets, and was made to spend an entire night standing with her back pressed against the stone wall of the temple. That was much more difficult. Sitting in this soft grass was a treat by comparison.

"Are you hungry?" Uruk asked.

"Thirsty."

Uruk reached into his satchel and brought out a pair of water-skins. He tossed the smaller one to Adah. "Drink all you want," he said. Then he grabbed the dog and, cupping one hand around his muzzle, funneled a tiny stream of water into his open mouth. "Dog spills," Uruk explained.

Adah took a long pull at the skin he'd given her. The water was warm and tasted like leather, but she swallowed it down without complaint.

While she sucked at the water-skin, Uruk casually stripped off his tunic and spread it over some bushes. It was made of a fabric Adah had never seen. Even soaked with sweat the tunic looked as soft as lamb's wool, and shone like polished leather. But Adah was more impressed with Uruk himself. His body was spectacularly muscled and glistened with sweat. He was even more handsome than he'd appeared the night before, though older as well. He had gray on his temples and the deep lines in his forehead. All in all, Adah thought him very distinguished.

"The air is wet," Uruk said. He wiped the perspiration from his ribs and then dried his hands on his breeches. "Wetter than I have seen it in this country."

Adah looked down at her own tunic. Dark circles had formed around both armpits and under each breast.

"Take it off if you want," Uruk said.

In years past, she might have done just that. Humidity was rare in the Shinar, but not unknown. Adah remembered days when her mother wore nothing but a loincloth. Her father could go whole seasons without once wearing his tunic. But things were different in Dagonor. The slaves were modest to the extreme. They had nothing to protect but their bodies, and so they hid them from sight with a single-mindedness that bordered on mania. The women didn't undress even in front of each other. Men were no different. Going topless in front of Uruk was unthinkable, no matter how good it might feel to get out of her sweaty clothes.

"You do not talk much, do you?" Uruk asked.

"Antha-Kane prefers silence," Adah mumbled.

"Hungry yet?"

She nodded.

"Good. So am I." He went to the nearest tree and pulled a bundle of heavy oilskin out of its branches. Adah had been watching it since first light, wondering what was inside. Very carefully, Uruk unfolded the bundle and brought out a small carcass. It wasn't even as big around as one of his forearms, and its flesh was riddled with black streaks from having been cooked over an open flame.

"What is that?" Adah asked.

"Rabbit." Uruk tore off one of the hind legs and tossed it to the dog. The other he gave to Adah.

"Dog killed it," Uruk explained. "So he gets the first taste." He pulled a long strip of meat off the ribs and held it out. The dog bolted down what was already in his mouth, and then licked the bit of flesh out from between Uruk's fingers.

Adah considered what she'd just seen, then did likewise. She carefully tore a bit of charred meat off one end of the leg and held it at arm's length. But the dog took no notice of her.

"Throw it to him," Uruk said.

"But he's not watching."

"No? Try it."

Reluctantly, Adah did as she was told. She half-expected to see her offering strike the dog on the top of the head, or stick to the fur on his back. But the meat had only just left her fingers when the dog leapt up and snapped it out of the air. It happened so fast Adah couldn't help flinching.

Uruk stared at her as she gnawed the rest of the meat from the rabbit leg, but didn't utter a word. Adah wondered why Uruk had stolen her. He wanted something. That much was clear. But what? Uruk was a fast eater, Adah noticed. The ribs and forelegs of the rabbit, which he had taken for himself, were already bare. A tiny bit of meat still clung to the spine, but that wouldn't last much longer.

"Want to know why I brought you here?" Uruk asked, flinging the last of the now clean bones into the bushes.

Adah shrugged. As a slave she'd learned not to let her desires show. Certain Niphilim—the women mostly—took great pleasure in dangling hope before their captives' eyes, only to snatch it away.

"Let me show you something." Uruk pointed to the hole in the brush, through which they'd climbed the night before. "Sit here."

Adah crawled over, one fist still closed around the remains of her breakfast, and was surprised to discover that she could see the entire valley, from the storehouse where she kept her brooms to the open field where the Niphilim did their exercises. She could even see the Withered Hills, extending south all the way to the horizon.

"What do you see?" Uruk asked her.

Adah squinted. "Buildings. Workers." When she was a girl, Adah's father used to herd his goats into the high mountains, searching for fresh grass. He'd promised to take her when she was old enough. *You're just an ant from up there,* he'd told her. Now, looking down this mountain, Adah saw that he'd been wrong. The people weren't like ants at all. Even as small as they were, ants still had distinct heads and abdomens. Their legs were readily identifiable. The people she saw were fuzzy, like fish seen through cloudy water. Adah couldn't distinguish men from women, or Niphilim from slaves. From this height they were all the same.

"Look at the forge," Uruk suggested.

She was surprised to see that there was no smoke coming from the chimneys. "The fires are out," she said. In all the time she'd been work-ing among the Niphilim, Adah had never known the fires to go out.

Uruk nodded.

"Why?"

"They are hauling everything into the mine," Uruk said. "Tools, food, even the slaves themselves. The army of Kan-Puram must be close."

Adah squinted at the hills again, half-expecting to see soldiers come pouring over them. But the hills were just as dry and empty as ever. The only thing moving was a pale blue wave, nearly transparent, hanging between earth and sky. It certainly didn't look like an army. Nor did it resemble the grasslands she knew to be on the other side of those hills. In fact, it looked like water. Adah gaped. She'd never seen the ocean, but she'd heard of it. *A river with only one bank.* That's how her father had described it when she was a little girl. Adah pointed. "Is it the sea?"

"No," Uruk said. "There is no water out there."

"My father told me that there's a great sea beyond the plains."

"He was right. I have been there. Not so long ago."

"You've seen the great water?"

"Many times." Uruk patted her on the shoulder. "But it is so far away now that I doubt I ever will again."

"If that's not the sea, then what is it?"

"Maybe the sky reflecting off sand, like a mountain reflecting off a still pond." Uruk shrugged. "When I crossed the desert, I saw it often. At first I hurried toward it, thinking it was water. It never was."

"You crossed the desert?"

Uruk nodded.

Adah wasn't sure whether to believe him. It was a lot to take in. If not for the quiet assurance with which he'd made his astonishing claims, Adah would have considered Uruk a liar. But this seemed like more than *big talk*, as her mother used to say. If anything, Adah sensed a kind of shame in Uruk. Because of that, she couldn't help believing everything he'd said—no matter how ridiculous it might sound.

"How long have you been a slave?" Uruk asked her.

"Since I was thirteen. Almost three years." Adah looked down at Dagonor, wondering who had been forced into taking her place in Anth-Kane's sanctum. A troop of slaves was marching past the temple. From that distance, the baskets they carried looked like enormous heads, balanced precariously atop comically undersized torsos. "They aren't even looking for me, are they?"

"Of course they are." Uruk pointed. "In the hills, south of the temple."

"Why there?"

"I changed the markings, made it look like you ran that way. If they thought you were up here, they might eventually find us."

"Why steal me at all?" Adah asked. "You still haven't told me."

Uruk looked at her.

Adah had never been so thoroughly sized up in her life. It made her feel like a little girl again. Her father used to look at her that way just before telling her to wipe her nose. She couldn't help wondering if Uruk had noticed the welt on her cheek, or the blemishes on her forehead.

"I am looking for someone," he said at last. "A man called Jared." Uruk scowled. "I have watched this valley for three days, even sneaking down at night to sift through the garbage. But there is no sign of him anywhere."

"I've never heard of him," Adah said.

"No matter. I already know where he is."

"You do?"

Uruk nodded. "He is in the mine. It is the only place I have not looked. And the only place I cannot scout before entering. I need information from someone who has been inside. That's why I took you."

"He's a prisoner?"

"Captured in Kan-Puram."

Adah thought for a moment. "Well, if your friend's alive. . . ."

"Jared is not my friend," Uruk snapped. "Dog and I owe him a life debt. Nothing more."

Instinctively, Adah put her hands up to protect her face. His voice had an edge she'd heard many times. "I'm sorry," she squeaked. "I didn't mean anything."

Uruk pulled her hands away. His fingers were calloused and rough, but also very gentle. "You have no reason to apologize," he said.

Adah didn't believe him, but nodded all the same.

"What were you about to say?" Uruk asked.

"Only that if Jared—" Adah paused to emphasize the name—"is among the new prisoners, he'll still be in the cell."

"Cell?"

Adah nodded. "Every new slave is kept there 'til the Niphilim think they're ready to work." She shuddered. "It's a horrible place."

"How long does that take?"

"A week or two." For Adah it had taken just four days. Her father never made it out at all. "Sometimes it takes a month or more. There are men from Akshur who still haven't come out."

"Could you find this cell?" Uruk asked.

"It's near the back of the mine. There's an iron door with—"

"Guarded?"

"Night and day, not that there's any difference down there."

"How many guards?"

"Four or five," Adah stammered. "Maybe more or less. I don't know."

"Is there another way in? Other than through the door?"

Adah shook her head emphatically, happy to have a question she could answer with authority. "The walls are solid stone."

Uruk wiped his mouth with the back of his arm. "Very difficult," he muttered.

"You want to go in?"

"Of course. I must." He glanced at the dog, still gnawing his bone. "We must."

"What about me?"

Uruk looked puzzled. "You?"

"What'll you do with me when you go in the mine?"

"I will have no use for you then."

Adah gasped. For an instant, she honestly thought he intended to send her back to Dagonor. Her chest went tight and her heart skipped. Being a slave, even to a good master, as Uruk seemed to be, was terrible, but it was better than death. If she went back, she had no hope. Her head would be mounted on a stake and planted in front of the temple. She was ready to get on her knees and beg him to reconsider. But then Adah realized something. Uruk couldn't take her back.

"You'll leave me here?" Adah asked hopefully.

"Not here," Uruk replied. "We have to get much closer to the mine entrance. But once Dog and I go inside, you can go wherever you want."

Every hair on Adah's body felt like it was standing on end. For years she'd imagined hearing those words. She had always wanted freedom, but had never really believed such a thing was possible. Even the Niphilim lived their lives under the weight of rules and orders. Antha-Kane was so trapped in his responsibilities that he couldn't even leave the temple. The ability to choose where to go, what to do, seemed like the vainest desire of a rogue god. No mere human could be worthy of such a gift. And now, here was a man unlike any she'd ever encountered, giving freedom to her as though it was as common as pebbles in a riverbed.

"What if you get caught?" she asked.

"They will kill me."

"Doesn't that scare you?"

Uruk shook his head. "I am more worried that I will fail."

Adah stared. She'd never heard anything so outlandish in all her life.

"Do you think you could draw me a map of the mine?" Uruk asked her.

"Maybe." Truthfully, Adah had grave doubts as to her ability to create anything even remotely usable, but didn't dare say so.

Uruk reached for his satchel. From it he took a small purse, not much larger than one of his fists. "Hold out your hands," he said. Adah did as he asked and Uruk carefully poured the contents of the purse into her palms. Three small pieces of silver and a pair of bright yellow stones tumbled out.

"What are they?" Adah asked.

"Amber."

She picked up the larger of the two and held it to the sun. The light shining through it was like a ribbon of gold. "So beautiful," she breathed. "What's it worth?"

"Almost nothing," Uruk said. "A rich woman might make it into a comb, or a merchant might trade it for a few goats. But try drinking it when you are thirsty, or eating it when you are hungry. See what defense it provides you when lions are on your trail."

"If I had so much wealth, I'd build a house," Adah said. "And have slaves to do all my work."

"Draw me a map and I will give them to you."

"Really?"

Uruk nodded. "If Dog and I make it out of this mountain, they are yours. And if Jared is with us, you can expect a good deal more."

"What if you don't make it out? Or what if I run away while you are in the mine? What if the Niphilim find me waiting?"

"There is a risk," Uruk agreed.

Adah considered a moment. "How will the dog get in unnoticed?" she asked.

Uruk pointed at the basket. "Inside that."

"And you?"

"Hopefully no one will pay attention to me." Uruk pointed at Dagonor. "There is a whole pile of provisions and equipment still to be hauled to the Niphilim army, and just one troop of slaves to carry it. They will not finish until long after dark. When they finally return to the mine, I plan to slip in with them."

"That's why we've got to get closer."

Uruk nodded.

"I won't wait forever," Adah warned.

"Of course not." Uruk plucked both stones, as well as the silver, out of her still-open palms and dropped them into his purse. "But you will wait?"

Adah nodded.

"Good. Then it is time to go." Uruk reached for his tunic. As he pulled it on over his head, Adah took one last bite of her breakfast. There was still a good deal of meat left on the bone, but for some reason it no longer tasted good to her. She tossed what remained to the dog, who snapped it up greedily.

"Can I carry anything?" Adah asked.

"Just that." Uruk pointed at the water-skin she'd left lying in the grass.

As she climbed to her feet, Adah noticed that something was wadded up in the bottom of Uruk's basket. It looked like a tunic, though made of rough brown canvas like the one she was wearing.

"What is that?" she asked.

"My disguise."

Adah looked at him doubtfully. No mere tunic was going to hide him from the Niphilim. And the basket he'd chosen was meant to be carried by two slaves, not one. Uruk was going to be caught the moment he stepped into the mine. It seemed a shame. She'd begun to like Uruk, to respect him even. That was something she hadn't felt in a long time. Not since her father had gone into the mine, never to come out again.

"I'm surprised you found a tunic that would fit," she said. "No slave I know is big enough."

Uruk smiled. "Can you sew?" he asked.

CHAPTER 3

Rites of Passage

"**W**AKE UP," URUK SAID, AND GAVE ADAH'S SHOULDER A FIRM SHAKE. She rolled onto her back, eyes still closed. Her mouth fell open. For some reason, she'd cut her hair short. In places she'd chopped it so close that Uruk could see her scalp. He looked around for the knife he'd loaned her and saw it sticking out of the front of her breeches. A few dark hairs still clung to the handle.

Uruk squeezed her hand. "Wake up," he said again. "It is time."

Adah's eyes fluttered. "Is it midnight?" she asked.

"Closer to morning. You fell asleep."

"I just laid down for a moment," she stammered, scrambling to her feet. "I was watching, just like you said, but I was so sleepy and. . . ." She stifled a yawn.

"Here." Uruk handed her a small loaf of black bread. He had split it in two and stuffed a large chunk of stew meat inside.

Adah looked at the food doubtfully. After peeling back the top of the loaf to inspect the meat, she tore off a piece and held it out to Uruk.

"Just eat it," he grumbled. "Dog and I have already had our share."

She took a bite. "Not bad," she said, clearly surprised. "Dry, but tasty."

The dog sat beside her, staring at the food. Adah gave him a piece of crust.

"The supplies have all been delivered and the slaves are on their way back," Uruk said. He stripped off his silk tunic, wadded it up and flung it in the nearest bush.

Adah reached into the basket and brought out the canvas tunic he'd taken from the storeroom that morning.

Uruk pulled it on. "Fits better," he said.

"I lengthened the sleeves." Adah turned one of them inside out so that he could see the stitches. She didn't have any thread, so she'd used the cord from Uruk's satchel. The work wasn't pretty, but it would hold.

"You can put your thumbs through these holes," she explained, "so the sleeves don't ride up. I'd have added a collar and taken out the sides as well, but ran out of material." Adah held out the mangled hem of her own tunic, now shorter by a considerable degree.

He stuck his thumbs through the holes she'd showed him and raised his arms over his head. The sleeves stayed down over his wrists. "You did a good job," Uruk said.

Adah grinned.

"Why did you cut your hair?"

"Does it look terrible?" She nervously tugged at the hair over her ears, as though she could somehow stretch it long again. "I tried to think of a way to make the clippings into a beard, but I couldn't get the hair to stick."

"A beard?"

"I didn't draw you a map," Adah admitted. "I tried, but I've only been in there a few times and. . . ." She frowned. "There's no picture in my mind."

Uruk didn't know what to say. He kicked the basket in frustration.

"So I'm coming with you." Adah paused, no doubt waiting for Uruk to talk her out of it. But he didn't. He wouldn't. "I think I can find the cell once we're inside," she explained. "And I can help you. I can speak the Niphilim language."

Uruk thought for a moment, then picked up a handful of dirt and wiped it over her chin and cheeks. "Now you look like a boy," he said. "Dirty." Then he touched one of her breasts with his index finger. She flinched. "How do you plan to hide those?"

"I'll cover them." Adah picked up the basket and set it on her shoulder, shading her breasts with her upper arm. "See?"

Uruk nodded. Her disguise was far from perfect. Anyone who looked at her would see a girl with dirt on her face trying to masquerade as a man. But Uruk's own disguise was even worse. "Are you sure you want to come?" he asked. "It will be dangerous."

"I don't want to be left alone," Adah said. Uruk was surprised to see her trembling. He didn't know whether she was scared or excited. Uruk couldn't imagine what was going through her mind. But whatever it was, he didn't have the heart to tell her 'no'—or the luxury. He could use her guidance.

"We are going to run straight down this ravine," he said. He was glad to see Adah smile, though her trembling actually increased. "When we get to the edge of the mountain, we climb."

"I'm ready," Adah said, "but. . . ."

"What is it?"

"I have friends. If there's any chance to rescue them. . . ."

Uruk shook his head. "We have to be careful."

"I know. But if there's a way."

"We shall see." He took the basket from Adah and started down the ravine. As usual, the dog raced ahead. "Stay close," Uruk called after him. Then he looked back at Adah. "Both of you."

Isin watched as Ander stirred the coals from their fire into a pile. His hood was thrown back and his cloak was loose on his shoulders. A cook-pot lay beside his outstretched legs, but Ander showed no interest in food. So far as Isin knew, he hadn't had a thing to eat in two days. Lots of water, bags and bags of it, but nothing else. Ander had lost so much weight that his eyes had begun to sink into his skull. The flesh around them was turning purple. When the embers were all piled together, he leaned over and blew on them, eventually managing to coax out a few tongues of yellow flame.

Theirs was the only fire in the camp still burning, but that was no great surprise. Ander's habit of sitting up had become the stuff of legend. The soldiers believed he could cast spells and read futures in the orange-glowing coals. Isin knew otherwise. Over the weeks, he'd learned to see the doubt and fear at Ander's core. If he didn't sleep, it was because he couldn't bear to be left alone in his own mind.

"If you'd quit stirring it, the fire would go out," Isin said.

Ander picked up a pair of sticks from the pile beside him. One was long and thin. The other short and thick. "Which do you think will burn up first?" he asked, and dropped both onto the coals.

"Have you even tried to sleep?"

Ander glared. His eyes were bloodshot. "Clouds are amassing," he said. "Wind's picking up. Probably sandstorms in the desert."

Isin pushed his blankets aside. "Summer's almost gone," he said. "Rain is coming. It's always that way in the Shinar."

"Agony and torment," Ander agreed. "Do you ever wonder if the gods hate us?"

"Hate us?" Isin shook his head. "I don't think they hate us. For the most part, I don't think they pay much attention to us." He gestured toward the mountains. "The gods created all that. They didn't begin creation with man. Nor has creation ceased. And yet we think that everything—" he picked up a fistful of dust and let it slowly sift between his fingers—"that all of this exists for our benefit."

"So you think the gods don't care?"

Isin smiled, like a kindly grandfather talking to a little boy. "The priests of Moloch have a song they're fond of reciting. In it, a boy on the verge of manhood demands to know what great purpose was served by his birth. The gods respond by asking him who gave birth to the lightning, winds, and flood? Who gave the falcon his wings? Or the fish his tail? Does grain ripen by man's wisdom, or dates by his tears? Can a man drag down a lion or outrun an ibex with the strength of his laughter?"

Ander stared at him.

"There's more to the song, but you get the idea."

"What does it mean?"

"Kilimon once told me that it was a kind of riddle. It reminds us that the whole world exists for the pleasure of the gods."

Ander picked up another stick and began to stir the coals. "So the gods don't care," he muttered. "But if that's true, why pray? Why offer sacrifices?"

"Simple," Isin said. "Because we *do* care. The gods may not be listening all the time, but that doesn't mean they're deaf."

Ander thought about that as he stared into the fire. "You should be praying right now," he said. "At the top of your lungs. Who knows when the gods might be listening?" He gestured at the hills. "We'll encounter Niphilim tomorrow. If the gods are to help us, it'll have to be soon."

"Do you ever pray?" Isin asked.

"I used to." Ander shook his head. "I prayed for vengeance with every stone I lifted, every basket I carried through the darkness. But the gods didn't listen."

"You don't know that." Isin reached for his sword. The metal was warm from lying beside the fire. "These weapons. The men from Ur. Certainly we've been fortunate."

Ander laughed. "Maybe next time the gods decide to forge iron, they should do the mining themselves. You forget, I know who made these swords, and they're not gods."

Isin winced. "The ways of gods are not the ways of men," he said.

"That's certainly true. Men work. Men suffer."

"Maybe it's our suffering that draws their gaze," Isin said.

Ander smiled wickedly. "If so, we're about to be watched over as never before."

"Here they come," Uruk whispered.

Adah craned her neck. "I can't see anything."

They hid behind a boulder, a mere stone's throw from the mouth of the mine. Anyone approaching from the east would have seen them, lying together in the shade of the mountain, a basket beside their heads and a dog crouched between their outstretched legs. But from the west, and Dagonor, they were invisible.

"Quiet." Uruk threw an arm around her waist, drawing her tight against his chest. "Listen."

The slaves were marching up the ramp.

There must have been a guard at the head of the line, because just as the sound of footsteps reached the top of the slope, a pool of orange light swept down the mountain, illuminating stones and loose soil no more than a hands-breadth from Adah's shoulder. If Uruk hadn't pulled her close, she might have been seen. Lying there, not even daring to breathe, Adah began to wonder if she'd made a mistake.

"What's this?" a man yelled in the Niphilim language.

"Last group," another replied. He was so close that Adah wondered if he could be leaning on the opposite side of their boulder.

"Late, aren't they?"

"You know these black-heads—too lazy to get any job done on time."

The first guard laughed. "Well, take them in."

A moment later, the light that had been streaming down the mountainside was gone. The slaves began moving once more.

When the sound of tromping feet was at its loudest, Uruk leaned in and whispered directly into Adah's ear. "What did they say?" His lips brushed the short hairs on the side of her head.

"He told them to go inside," Adah replied.

Eventually, the sounds of footsteps died away.

"Stay here," Uruk whispered. Adah didn't even have a chance to respond. Uruk rolled over her—she was amazed at how much he weighed—and was gone. He'd never said a word to the dog, but didn't need to. No sooner had Uruk started up the mountain than the dog was loping after him.

Adah heard them race across the top of the ramp and into the mine. It was all happening so fast. Uruk was gambling on his ability to catch the Niphilim guard unaware. There was just the one stationed here at the entrance, and Uruk figured he could probably kill him before the man had a chance to raise the alarm. Adah shuddered as she heard a man gasp, cough and then slump to the ground.

By the time Uruk came back, she was curled into a ball, head cradled in her arms.

"It is done," he said.

Adah looked up. "Is the guard dead?"

He nodded.

"I was afraid it might be you."

"Not yet." Uruk grabbed her around the shoulders and lifted her to her feet.

They climbed to the mouth of the mine, pausing only a moment before plunging inside. "Where's the body?" Adah asked.

Uruk pointed. "But you need not look at it."

An oblong of hazy gray light extended a short distance into the mountain, then faded to black. The dead guard was slumped against the wall just a few strides from where Adah stood, but only his feet could be seen clearly. The rest of him was almost entirely lost to shadow. Adah had seen bodies before, from the desiccated heads mounted outside the temple to her best friend, who'd drowned in the village stream when Adah was only ten years old. Compared to those, the dead guard seemed peaceful. He looked as though he might stand up any moment. His blood didn't even look red.

"Get in, Dog," Uruk said. Adah turned just in time to see the dog curl up atop Uruk's sword and belt, which had been carefully wedged into the bottom of the basket. There was no room left for Uruk's satchel, so he took it off and flung it down the mountain. Adah knew that he'd planned to leave it behind, but was still surprised, and a little saddened, to see it go.

"The amber?" she asked.

Uruk patted the front of his breeches. "In here." Then he lifted the basket to his shoulder. "We have to hurry," he said.

Adah nodded. "No, wait. Other side."

"What?"

"When we come out of the tunnel, the guards will be on our left. That should be my side."

Uruk quickly shifted the basket to his other shoulder and Adah moved into position.

They ran into the mine. In moments, they were utterly lost in the darkness, unable to see roof or walls. With his free hand, Uruk grabbed Adah's upper arm, holding her steady and close at his side.

"We should come to the first turn soon," she whispered.

"Which way?"

"I can't remember."

Uruk slowed almost to a stop. "The passage is getting tight," he said. "Barely enough room for both of us together."

"I don't think it gets any smaller."

"Good. Hold out your elbow. Let it scrape along the wall. Whenever you feel the tunnel begin to turn, whisper. Agreed?"

Adah nodded.

"Agreed?"

"Yes," she said. "Yes."

They went as fast as they could, hoping to catch the slaves. A couple of times they missed a turn and ran headlong into the wall. Once they hit so hard that the dog yelped and Adah was convinced she'd broken her nose. Still, for the most part they were able to traverse the path quickly.

"Toward me," Uruk whispered, steering Adah around a sharp corner. "And again."

Before long, Adah had lost all sense of direction. To her it felt like they were moving in circles. She began to wonder whether there might not be other tunnels in the mountain. Unused tunnels. Places the slaves never went. She imagined herself starving to death, lost in an endless tomb of dark, twisting rock.

She was so engrossed by her thoughts that she missed the last turn. Fortunately, Uruk was listening. The instant her elbow left the stone, he shoved her to the side, narrowly avoiding another painful meeting with the wall.

Adah was about to whisper an apology when she saw, directly ahead, an upright rectangle of hazy orange. She blinked. They'd only been in the passage a short time, but already the torchlight seemed fiercely bright.

"We made it," she whispered. "We're almost there."

"Relax," Uruk said. The moment she saw the end of the tunnel, Adah lurched ahead. Uruk had to grab her around the hips to keep her from running headlong down the passage.

Uruk was worried. How long had it been since the last slave emerged from this tunnel? And where did he go? If it had only been a moment or two, Uruk thought, he and Adah might get past the guards with little more than a glance. Much longer and one of them was sure to notice. According to Adah there would be at least three or four Niphilim stationed at the end of this tunnel. No way could he fight them all, especially now that his sword was out of reach.

"Stay quiet," he whispered as they neared the end. Adah didn't respond. That was for the best.

They stepped out of the passage and, amazingly, right into the back of the slaves they'd been following. It was as though they'd been part of the troop all along. They only had to shift sideways a tiny bit so that Uruk could hug the shadows. No one saw them. The slaves, especially those at the end of the line, might have heard or felt them, but they weren't talking.

Four Niphilim guards, all men, stood together at the head of the line. All four had swords and whips, same as the guard Uruk had killed. The shortest, a wiry man with a mole on the end of his nose, gestured toward a line of torches leading further into the cavern. He shouted in a peculiar, grating falsetto, growing ever more animated as he spoke, even taking on a staggering limp and slack-jawed expression. The other guards laughed uproariously.

'Jokes,' Uruk thought. Not one of the guards was paying even the most cursory attention to the slaves. Not one. They were utterly convinced that the slaves posed no danger, that they were defeated in body as well as spirit. Only hard, cruel men could be so sure of themselves.

The Niphilim kept talking, telling more jokes. Uruk wished he knew what they were saying. Something useful might slip out, even amidst so much inane chatter. Adah understood every word, but he didn't dare ask her. Uruk found it all extraordinarily frustrating. Given a few months, he could probably develop a working knowledge of the Niphilim language, but that didn't help him at the moment.

Beside him, Adah began to shudder. It was nerves, Uruk guessed. He gave her hand a quick squeeze. Her palm was sweaty, but she squeezed back. Hard. There was iron in that grip.

Eventually, the Niphilim grew more serious. Three of them ambled back toward the passage while the fourth, torch still in hand, led the slaves into the darkness. Uruk and Adah shuffled along just as though they'd been there the whole time. Uruk found it hard to imagine, but the Niphilim didn't appear to notice the two additional figures carrying the large basket at the back of the line. They failed to see the black feet on the figure to the right, or the broad hips on the slave to the left.

The trail through the mountain went farther than Uruk would have ever thought possible. He was amazed both at the complexity of the path and the ease with which they could follow it. So long as they went from one torch to the next, always moving in a straight line through the darkness, there was very little chance of tripping or falling in a crevasse. It was no wonder the miners could carry out such enormous baskets of rock without spilling. Their path through the mountain was one of the smoothest Uruk had ever seen, in the Shinar or anywhere else.

After what must have been at least a quarter-hour, they filed between a pair of boulders and started up a long, winding hill. Torches became more common as they climbed, signaling both turns and potential dangers. The path was rougher too, no longer so even or free of debris. The stone seemed to ripple and twist beneath their feet. The slaves knew this path well. They never hesitated. Uruk and Adah weren't so lucky.

"Should we run?" Adah whispered.

"No."

"But we're falling behind."

"I know," Uruk said. "Walk."

They walked for a quarter-hour more, making numerous turns, when suddenly the path broke in two. The line of torches they'd been following continued up the hill, while a secondary line twisted away to the left. From where they stood, four tiny points of fire were easily visible, and the light from a fifth could be seen shining on the wall of the cavern, far in the distance.

"Where does that go?" Uruk asked. The slaves were still on the first trail. He could hear their feet slapping on the rock.

"I have no idea," Adah whispered.

They moved on. Moments later, they came upon yet another line of torches, this time leading to the right.

"Maybe they lead to other tunnels," Adah ventured. "Other caverns."

"Hush." The sound of footsteps had suddenly stopped.

A man's voice boomed through the cavern, echoing off roof and walls.

When the footfalls started again, they sounded muffled, as though the slaves had finally reached the top of the hill and were now going down the opposite side.

"What did the guard say?" Uruk asked.

"They're going somewhere called Black Cavern," Adah said. "He told them to drop their baskets before entering the tunnel."

"Good." Uruk took Adah's hand and pulled her off the path.

It took a long time to move even a short distance, but at last they stumbled upon a fairly large mound of jagged rocks. Rubble left behind by an earlier generation of miners, Uruk guessed.

"This is a good enough place," he whispered, steering Adah around the pile. "Impossible to see. Difficult to reach. We will hide here."

"Why? Jared can't be far off now."

"Even the bravest hunter does not leap into the brush, hacking at whatever moves. He waits. Watches."

"For how long?"

"An hour, maybe two. I want to know who else uses that path." Uruk set the basket down. The dog leapt out, happy to be free. "Also, I want Dog to sniff around. If there are any guards hiding in the darkness, he will know."

"Can we stop?" Lamech begged. "I need to . . . you know."

"Is it getting worse?" Barley asked.

Lamech nodded. Both of his arms were gripped round his belly, as though he expected it to burst open any time. And he wasn't the only one. At least a dozen men were suffering from what Barley's mother used to call a 'quick stomach.' A few were complaining of rash as well, but so far that hadn't presented much of a problem. Barley saw them scratching their chests and underarms, but figured they'd caught lice from the women in Akshur. Nothing to slow them down. This stomach illness was a different matter all together.

"All right, everybody listen," he called. They'd just reached the end of a long dry gulch. There were dandy-willows along both sides of their path, as well as a few stunted trees. "We're breaking, but only for a quarter-hour."

Lamech threw down his pack and ran behind the nearest bush. A half-dozen men followed. Moments later, their groans were replaced by other, even more unmistakable sounds.

Barley sat down on a rock and untied his sandals. Stomach sickness and rash weren't the only infirmities in the ranks. He had blisters on his toes and heals, and his ankles were swollen. "Gods-damned river," he muttered.

Since crossing the Tiger the morning before last, things had been growing steadily worse. In addition to the sickness, which Barley attributed to contaminated water, ticks and biting flies had descended in force, vying with the mosquitoes for the chance to suck them dry. Barley was beginning to wonder whether the gods were protecting the Niphilim.

While he rubbed his feet, Barley studied the map Ander had drawn him. It was a hopeless conglomeration of hash marks and twisted lines. As far as Barley could tell, they'd skirted two peaks and one pass. At their present rate, he expected to reach Dagonor by noon. He was just measuring out the distance on the map with his thumbs when Lamech came stumbling back, breathing like he'd just run all the way to Kan-Puram.

"Feel better?" Barley asked him.

"Don't know." Lamech sat down on his pack. "Everything's churning. I'm thirsty but I can't keep the water in."

"It's the water making you sick. Everyone who filled their skins at the river has come down with it."

"What should we do? Pour it out?"

"I don't think so. You need water, even if it. . . ."

Lamech nodded.

"How are the others?" Barley asked.

"Most are worse off than me," Lamech whispered. "It's disgusting."

"I'd say we could try to find a spring, but I don't think there's much hope of that." Barley looked down at his map and frowned. "These hills are dry."

"We aren't making very good time, are we?"

Barley shook his head. "We need to stay out of ravines. They keep leading us off course."

Lamech opened his mouth to say something, but his stomach interrupted with a deep gurgle.

"You'll be all right," Barley assured him. He reached down and began working his feet back into his sandals.

"Do we have to go already?"

Barley nodded and Lamech shook his head miserably.

"Off your asses and on your feet," Barley called. His announcement was met with a loud chorus of groans.

As they crested the next hill, Barley noticed clouds gathering in the western sky. "Strange," he muttered to himself. "It's still so damned hot."

CHAPTER 4

Heard and Not Seen

*I*T STARTED TO RAIN JUST BEFORE SUN-UP. THE DROPS WERE THIN and weak, barely more than mist, but heavier showers were coming. Judging by the density and color of the clouds, the Shinar was in for a deluge.

Isin woke and quickly folded and stowed his blanket in the bottom of his pack. It wouldn't stay dry, but he did what he could. Sleeping under wet blankets was one of the many things he couldn't bear. Even as a boy, when his mother brought his bedclothes slightly damp so that he'd stay cooler during a hot night, Isin had dreaded the feel of all that soggy cloth.

When his blanket was packed and safe, Isin picked up his sword. 'I wonder if it needs to stay dry,' he thought, cradling it in his lap. Not that it made much difference. He had no way of keeping it dry. But maybe he should wipe it down, or put something on it. Isin had learned a lot during his time with Ander, but weapons were still a mystery. He'd never even drawn his sword from its scabbard. Not in anger anyway.

"Should I. . . ." Isin started to ask. Then he noticed that Ander was sound asleep, slumped over with his head between his knees. His hood was still thrown back and the rain had soaked his hair. Rivulets of muddy water ran down his face. He looked so calm. So peaceful. Even the muscles in his brow and jaw were relaxed. 'This is the man he might have been,' Isin thought. It seemed a shame to wake him up.

"What are we waiting for?" Adah shifted her weight for the thousandth time. She'd tried everything she could think of, from sitting on her hands to lying on her back, but there was no way to get comfortable. The rock was just too hard. "We've been sitting here for. . . ." She realized, even as she spoke, that she had no way of knowing how long they'd been waiting, only that it had been a long fearful time. "However long, it's been a waste. We haven't discovered a thing."

"It has been about two hours," Uruk said. "But you are mostly correct."

"Mostly?"

"We now know that this cavern is more or less deserted. Only one Niphilim soldier has passed, and that was just after we sat down."

"Someone passed?" Adah looked over her shoulder, toward where she imagined their path lay hidden in darkness. "You heard him?"

"Dog did. I listened after he began pawing the rocks."

"How do you know it was a guard?"

"Slaves have bare feet. Different sound."

Adah wiped her palms on the legs of her breeches. Just talking about guards made her sweat. "What should we do?" she whispered.

"You said you were ready to move. I think one of us should have a look."

'One of us,' Adah thought. 'Not we. Not I.' She bit her lip. 'He means me. Uruk wants me to go alone.' Adah knew why he wanted her to go. She could translate for him. But why would he want her to go alone? She hoped he had some kind of plan. "Can I take the dog with me?" she asked.

"No."

Adah waited, hoping he'd say more. But as usual, Uruk told her no more than what was absolutely necessary at that moment. This time, Adah wasn't going to give up.

"Why not?"

"If you get in trouble, Dog and I will come." Uruk put a hand on her knee. It was both heavy and comforting. "And you will be better off alone. Dog is seldom able to hide effectively. He pants."

"Fine." Adah squeezed his hand. "Then let's go."

"You will have to get extremely close," Uruk warned. "Extremely."

Adah tried to imagine what would happen if she were caught. Strangely, she couldn't. Uruk had changed everything. A small part of her actually hoped to get caught. How nice it would be to have Uruk race in to save her. But what if Uruk wasn't able to save her? Or even worse, what if he chose not to? She didn't really believe that Uruk would do such a thing. But if it'd get him any closer to freeing Jared, Adah knew he'd give it some serious thought.

"Let's go," she said at last. "I want to get this over with."

Adah heard Uruk buckling his belt. "Dog and I will accompany you to the top of this hill," he said. "After that—"

"I know."

By the time Ander opened his eyes, smoke was puffing out of cook-fires all through the camp. Most of the men had already eaten and were now strapping on their armor, preparing to march. Ander yawned and ran a finger over his teeth. "How long has it been raining?" he asked.

Isin put a steaming cup in his hand. "Take this," he said. "It'll make you feel better."

The cup was half full of clear liquid. "What is it?"

"Hot water. So you can wash."

Ander stared into the cup.

"Were you successful?" Isin asked. "Did you have visions of victory?"

"I don't understand."

"That's what the men thought you were doing—meditating on the coming battle." Isin waggled his fingers at Ander, mimicking the sorcerers and evil priests popular among storytellers of a certain class. "They think you were bending demons to your will, or some other such nonsense."

"Are they ready to march?" Ander asked.

"Almost. The thieves are slow in getting up, and some of Qadesh's men have been complaining of a rash. Under their arms and across their chests. Sweaty clothes rubbing on skin, no doubt."

"Any word from our scouts?"

Isin shook his head.

Ander yawned. "You know, I think I may have actually been in a trance this time," he said. "I haven't felt so drained in years. Maybe never."

"Wash your face. It always makes me feel better."

"Where did you get the cup?"

"I've had it in my pack since we left Kan-Puram the first time. I wasn't used to drinking out of a skin." Isin shrugged.

Ander sipped the water. Heat spread through his stomach. It felt good. He drank the rest of the water in a single gulp. "We should get moving," he muttered, handing the empty cup back to Isin. "Before the rain gets too heavy."

Isin nodded.

It occurred to Ander that this might be their last conversation. His plans called for the remaining leaders to be distributed throughout the ranks. Isin had been assigned to the middle, just behind Qadesh. What he'd do there,

Ander had no idea. He just hoped the priest wouldn't have to call a retreat or lead a counterattack—he didn't know how to do either. Ander was surprised to find that he was concerned about Isin. They'd been together almost non-stop for weeks. Against his better judgment, Ander had actually come to like him. 'After all,' he thought, 'without Isin there'd be no war. No justice.'

"You know they're watching us," Ander said. "Probably from those hills." He gestured toward a group of wide flat mounds. Unlike most of the Withered Hills, these were covered with thick patches of brown grass. "The Niphilim are waiting."

"I know."

"I've been looking forward to this moment all my life."

Isin smiled. Ander waited, hoping he'd say something insightful. But what, exactly? Congratulations? Good luck? Isin would say neither, he knew. To do so would be to admit that this whole war was being fought for the sake of one man's vengeance. Isin couldn't do that. Too much was at stake.

"I'm ready," Ander said at last. He pulled his hood up over his head. "I only hope I live long enough to see this through to the end."

"Look," Uruk whispered as they crested the subterranean mount.

Just ahead, the line of torches they'd been following split. One path—the brighter of the two—led straight down the opposite side of the hill. The other twisted away to their left, descending even more steeply into the darkness. Taken all together, the torches looked like a constellation reflected off the surface of a pond.

"Do you see where it leads?" Uruk asked.

"The Black Cavern?" Adah guessed.

"The other one. Do you see where the brighter line stops?"

Adah looked, but saw nothing unusual.

"The last three," Uruk whispered.

Adah squinted. Obviously there was something to see, but she had no idea what. The orange specks ran in a straight line down the hill, becoming ever smaller and closer together before finally disappearing into impenetrable night. "I can't. . . ." Adah began. And then, like the first rays of morning sun piercing the darkness, she understood. The last three torches weren't just closer together. They were also the same size, height and intensity. Almost exactly. "It's the end," Adah said. "That's the cell."

"At last."

"I guess I should go."

"Dog and I will stay close," Uruk promised. "But no matter what happens, do not look for me. Do not call out. If there is danger, we will come. You have to trust that. Can you?"

Adah nodded.

"Can you?"

"Yes."

"Good. I want you to give me back the knife."

"Why?" Reluctantly, Adah pulled the dagger out of the back of her breeches.

"In case you get caught."

"You won't let them take me away will you?"

"No. I promise."

"And do you promise, too?" Adah patted the dog on the neck. He licked her hand.

"Now go," Uruk said.

Adah crept down the slope as quickly and silently as she was able.

She was more than halfway down when she got her first view of the guards. At that distance they were little more than vague, shadowy outlines. And yet, Adah found it difficult to go on. Her heart was beating so powerfully that she could feel it throughout her whole body. Even her fingers and toes throbbed. She expected to pass out cold, or discover that she could no longer control her legs. But instead, she kept walking.

Adah stopped just ten strides from the Niphilim—close enough to see the blue in their eyes.

She was surprised to find that she recognized both men. Shagar sat on the right. He was the older of the two, with thinning hair and a thickening belly. Unlike most Niphilim, who viewed any contact with the slaves as a form of punishment, Shagar was assigned guard duty because he was good at it. He was seldom cruel, using his whip only when necessary, yet he still managed to glean a hard day's work from each slave.

The other man Adah would have known anywhere. His name was Zal. He was the very same guard who'd been at the barracks door the night Uruk stole her.

Both men sat, backs against the stone wall, elbows propped on their knees, staring into the darkness. They looked sleepy.

"Tell me again," Shagar muttered. "How'd that girl get away?"

"I told you. She didn't run away, she was stolen."

"By a giant."

"Yes. Well, he wasn't a giant, but he was huge."

"And he stole her for . . . ?"

"How should I know? I can't imagine why anyone would want that one."

Adah ground her teeth.

"I don't know about giants," Shagar said. "But these are evil days. I heard that two of our women are . . . big."

"No."

"That's what the chief told me. Lagassar's considering whether to send one of them into exile."

"I can't believe it. No one has had permission in ten years."

"It's worse than that. One of them may have been with a black-head."

Zal laughed. "Ridiculous," he said at last. "Unbelievable."

"Is it?" Shagar frowned. "Most of us have—"

"But you're talking about a woman."

"So?"

"Our women don't do those things."

"Right," Shagar said. "And neither do our men. But it still happens."

"Why would they want to?"

"Why would anyone?"

Zal nodded. "Once, one of our women—I won't say who—invited me to bathe with her. Alone. You know where that leads."

"Evil days," Shagar muttered, shaking his head.

Adah listened with rapt attention. She'd never heard the Niphilim talk like this. In the captain's quarters they discussed battle plans and training schedules, but they never just talked.

"When will Lagassar decide about the exile?" Zal asked.

"Chief thinks it'll be just after today's battle. If a lot of women are killed they'll probably let her stay. Assuming she's willing to get rid of the . . . embarasment."

"Of course."

Both men nodded together.

"Who are they?" Zal asked. "From which ranks?"

"One's fourth line," Shagar said.

Zal whistled. "Lagassar's own?"

"That's what I hear."

"And the other?"

Shagar shrugged. "Maybe Barash knows. He ought to be here any time."

"There he is now."

Both men stared into the darkness to Adah's left. Mysteriously, Adah couldn't see a thing. She had no doubt the guards saw something. Their eyes were intent on some object. But no matter how she craned her neck, or where she looked, there was nothing but darkness.

Suddenly, a torch appeared not a dozen paces away, and it was moving fast. He must have been in a tunnel or behind some big rocks. Adah wondered what else could be hidden in that mine. Maybe there were things even the Niphilim had never seen and knew nothing about. She glanced over her shoulder, and was surprised to discover that only a single line of torches was visible, leading straight back up the hill. The path to the Black Cavern was utterly lost. Must be lots of rocks, Adah reasoned, or a long ridge.

Both guards stood up as Barash drew near. He was short for a Niphilim, and his long hair was streaked with gray. The lines around his eyes and mouth were deep. He'd been a soldier for a long time.

"This is it for the day," Barash said, dropping a large sack at the other guards' feet. He had a second canvas bag, about the same size, still slung over his shoulder. "No more food or water 'til after the battle. Captain's orders."

"Why not?"

"Can't spare the manpower. The slaves are all shut away in the Black Cavern, and every available soldier is at the battle. We've got no one left to carry it in. Chief says that the black-heads have brought close to three-thousand men."

The other guards were stunned.

"Don't look so worried," Barash said. "Captain's got a plan. The black-heads will never reach Dagonor."

"Of course not." Shagar shook his head derisively. "We can't be defeated. Dagon is on our side."

Barash motioned to the bundle he'd brought. "Bread and water," he said. "You'll have to eat like a slave for one day. Can't be helped. All meat's being sent to the lines. Lagassar appropriated a huge portion for her women, just in case the black-heads are slow in coming."

Adah was getting tired of hearing that term—black-head. She'd been called that at least twenty times a day for as long as she'd lived among the

Niphilim, and never given it a moment's thought. But now the words grated.

"Chief says to keep them docile." Barash indicated the cell with a flick of his torch. "If any of them makes trouble, don't hesitate to get rid of him."

"Trouble? Them?" Shagar laughed. "They can't even piss without our say so."

"That's good, because after the battle the chief is going to want you to stick them in with the rest of the slaves. We're sure to need space in the cell. Lots more workers will be on the way."

Zal picked up the sack Barash had dropped and untied the top. Three good-sized water-skins were at the bottom. Zal carefully lifted them out, handing two to Shagar and taking the last for himself. They'd let the slaves drink only after every crumb of bread had been choked down. Adah remembered the days she'd spent in the cell. Always thirsty, wishing she could have just a single mouthful of water before the guards brought in all that dry, tasteless bread.

"Sorry I can't stay to help divvy it up," Barash said. "I've got to carry this other sack clear across the cavern. Those swords the slaves hauled in don't guard themselves." And with that, he turned and started up the path.

Adah froze. Barash was coming right at her.

It was still early morning, the battle not even started, when the first man collapsed on the trail and died.

They were skirting the southern reaches of Mount Murat. Four or five more hours of hard walking and they'd be in Dagonor. Even the rain couldn't hold them back for long. Many of the men still suffered from stomach ailments, but none fell behind. Lamech was proud to be a part of such a group. These men were tough, no mistaking it.

And then suddenly, with virtually no warning, one of the men coughed, rubbed his chest as though cold, and fell face-down in the mud.

By the time Barley reached him, all signs of life were gone. Only a carcass remained. The dead man's skin was already going cold.

"What happened?" Barley asked.

The troops stared at each other. No one seemed to know.

"Who was he?"

"I think his name was Jabal," someone said. It was the man they called Tubs.

"Jabal," Lamech agreed. "That's right. He played the pipes."

"Was he sick?" Barley asked.

"He'd been coughing . . . . It didn't sound good."

Barley stripped back the dead man's tunic. A rash covered his chest—turning purple, nearly black, in his underarms. Dozens of tiny lacerations were etched into his skin. "He's been scratching," Barley said. Lamech grimaced. The rash, or whatever caused it, had itched so badly that he'd drawn his own blood.

"Who else has this?" Barley asked.

A boy not much older than Lamech raised his hand. Like the dead man, he was thin and wiry.

"Let's see it," Barley said.

Slowly, the boy lifted his tunic. The same rash ran over his chest, though it had yet to turn purple in his underarms.

"You feel all right?"

"Well enough." The boy's face was pale, almost white, but Lamech attributed that more to fear than sickness.

"Who else?"

No one stirred.

Barley asked again, louder. "If you've got it, say so now."

Three men nervously put up their hands.

"Anyone else?"

Barley looked around. Another hand timidly stretched upward.

"Feel sick?"

All four men shook their heads. They looked miserable and scared, and they were muddy, cold and wet, but no more so than the rest. Barley didn't look terribly well himself, Lamech observed, and he always looked strong and healthy.

"Fine," Barley said. "Then we keep going."

The troops gaped. No one moved.

"What about Jabal?" Lamech asked.

"We can't do anything for him," Barley said. "We march. Now." He looked at the men who'd admitted having a rash. "You five, stick close to me."

The troops formed into their accustomed lines and trudged away. All but one.

Lamech stood over the dead man, watching as raindrops splashed off his swollen purple belly. The rain was beginning to come down hard. Big, heavy drops.

He was just about to turn and go after the others when it occurred to him—the dead man's name wasn't Jabal. It was Jubal. He had a new wife but no children. No one to carry on his love of music, Lamech thought. He wondered what his own father would want him to pass on to the next generation—assuming he lived. "Boats," he muttered to himself. "Before he lost his leg, father loved boats."

The other troops were getting a long way ahead. Lamech needed to get moving. But first, he reached into Jubal's pack and felt around for his pipes. It was a simple set. Just four hollow reeds lashed together with twine—hardly more than a whistle. Lamech blew a few notes, then put them into his own pack.

CHAPTER 5

Bloody but Unbowed

*B*ARASH STOPPED. HE WAS STILL A HALF-DOZEN STRIDES FROM ADAH, but with the torch in his hand that was close enough. She was caught.

Adah quaked with fear. What could she do? She might have run the instant the guard started toward her, but it was too late for that now. Calling out would do no good. And besides, that was the one thing Uruk had warned her against. For a moment, she considered attacking Barash, knocking the torch from his hand and making her escape.

"What is it?" Shagar asked.

"A boy." Barash sounded as though he could hardly believe it himself. "Standing right here."

"What's he doing?"

Barash ignored the question. Instead, he waved Adah forward. "Come here."

Adah didn't move. She was like a hare, mesmerized by a flash of lightning into utter immobility. Her muscles were as stiff and hard as iron.

"Step forward," Barash said. His voice was deep and husky. Commanding.

Adah blinked, trying to clear her mind. 'Nothing to do,' she thought. 'I'm trapped.' She took a deep breath and stepped toward the waiting guards.

"Who is he?" Zal asked, coming to stand beside Barash. Shagar maintained his position in front of the cell door.

"Who are you?" Barash asked.

Adah tried to think of a boy's name—anything that sounded masculine. Her mind was uncomfortably blank.

"Tell us," Zal said, and crossed his arms.

"Kadim," Adah mumbled. She cringed as the name left her mouth. How could she be so stupid? An escaped slave whose head, even now, was rotting on a stake in front of the temple? Why couldn't she think of any-

325 / Slaves of the Shinar

thing else? Even if the average Niphilim soldier didn't recognize that name, surely three guards would.

But none of them did.

"I've heard that name," Zal said at last. "I think he works in the cook-house."

Adah was amazed.

"What are you doing here, Kadim?" Barash asked her.

"I. . . ." Adah began. But she didn't know what she was doing. She hadn't prepared for this. No lies came to her—at least nothing plausible.

"Bring him into the light," Shagar called. "So we can get a better look at him."

Zal took Adah by the arm and pulled her forward. As they neared the torches, Adah hunched her shoulders and hung her head. Such bad posture would have been suspicious anywhere else, but not here. Among slaves, especially those that did heavy work, bent backs were as common as flies on a corpse.

"Now then," Barash asked again, "what are you doing?" He put down the sack he'd been carrying and reached for his whip.

"The captain. . . ." Adah stammered. "He sent me to find the chief."

"The captain sent you?" Shagar asked.

Adah glanced over her shoulder. She knew she shouldn't have—the guards would take it for a sign of guilt—but she couldn't help herself. Adah kept expecting Uruk to come flying out of the darkness, sword drawn and ready. Where was he?

Zal squeezed her upper arm. "Lies," he said. "Look at this." He pointed at the hem of her tunic. "It's been cut."

"What does the captain want?" Barash asked her.

"More troops," Adah said.

"How many more?"

"Twenty-five."

The guards looked at each other. Barash pursed his lips. Shagar furrowed his brow. Zal merely scoffed. They seemed almost to be conferring over the number Adah had given—deciding whether it was reasonable. Uruk would have known the right number to give them. He'd spent hours watching the guards as they made their way from the surface. But Uruk wasn't there.

"How many?" Shagar asked again.

"Twenty-five," Adah said, this time with more confidence.

"Twenty-five."

She nodded.

"It's a lie," Shagar said.

Zal nodded emphatically. "I say we whip the truth out of him."

"Maybe. . . ." There was a pause as Barash considered what to do. "Stand him against the wall," he said at last.

Shagar and Zal each took one of Adah's arms, turned her around and slammed her against the wall. She let out a yelp as the back of her head struck rock. Worse yet, Adah could no longer slouch—the guards had her pinned too tight—and her tunic was pulled snug across her chest.

"It's a girl," Barash said. "Look."

By that time, Adah had all but given up on Uruk. She glanced at the line of torches leading to the top of the hill, imagining him up there somewhere, back turned and running for safety. She wasn't surprised. After all, what could one man do against three Niphilim warriors?

"What should we do with her?" Zal asked, breaking the silence.

"We have to take her to the chief," Shagar said.

Barash nodded in agreement. "But search her first. She could have a weapon."

Adah shut her eyes as Shagar and Zal went to work. She'd been searched hundreds of times—it was one of the hazards of working in the temple—but had never gotten used to it. She flinched as the men's hands roamed over her body, both inside and outside her clothes, pausing on her breasts and crotch, then moving behind her and running over her legs, back and haunches.

"Nothing," Shagar confirmed, pinning her against the rock once more.

"Good." Barash held his torch up to Adah's face. "I don't recognize her," he said. "Shagar?"

"No."

"Zal?"

"Maybe if she weren't so dirty."

"We can wipe her off," Barash offered.

"No." Zal grabbed Adah's chin. The creases in his forehead deepened as he scrutinized her every feature. "You know who this is?" he said at last. "It's the escaped slave. My escaped slave."

"Can't be," Shagar said, looking her over again.

"It is. I'm sure it is."

"Then she knows her punishment," Barash said. He looked her up and down, his face set in an expression Adah might normally have mistaken for lust, but was actually much worse. "First law of the slaves. You remember it don't you?"

Adah nodded. "Escape is. . . ." She choked on the words. "Escape is . . . ." She was about to say 'death,' but was interrupted by the sound of footsteps.

Barash spun around and Adah craned her neck to see. Shagar and Zal gripped her even tighter. Days later, Adah would find bruises on her arms that exactly corresponded to each man's fingers, though at that moment she barely noticed.

Uruk walked toward them at a brisk pace. He carried the basket in front of him, hip high, squeezing the top together with both hands so that there was no sign of what might be inside.

"Stop," Barash commanded. He raised his whip.

But Uruk was too fast. In one swift motion, he opened the basket and flung its contents into Barash's face. The dog came out in a rage. Teeth and claws tore, slashing into the guard's neck, face and chest. Blood poured forth in sickening amounts.

The rest of the battle happened in a blur. Even years later, when her youngest son asked what she'd done in the war, Adah skipped over this fight. It was too much to tell.

All at once, both Shagar and Zal let her go, and Adah toppled forward. They'd been holding her so tight against the wall that neither she nor the guards realized that she hadn't actually been standing under her own power.

Instinctively, Adah reached out for anything that might slow her fall. By luck, she caught the arm of the closest guard, Shagar, and held on.

"Let go!" he screamed, and tried to wrench free. He hit her in the shoulders, back, top of the head and face. Jaw-rattling, ear-ringing blows. It was pain unlike anything she'd ever known. Her legs flopped on the floor and her head snapped around. But no matter how many times he struck her, Adah wouldn't release his arm. She closed her eyes, set her teeth, and clung for all she was worth.

Then suddenly, Shagar fell—and Adah was dragged down with him.

"Captain! Captain!"

Kishar turned and saw a youngish soldier, clearly a messenger, charging up the hill. Mud was slathered on his boots and breaches, and clung to his hair and tunic. One hand was cupped over his eyes to block out the rain.

"Just a moment," Kishar said, bending over his maps once more.

The messenger stopped where he was and stood at rigid attention.

Kishar sat on a campstool, leaning over a table the slaves had constructed the night before. The legs were rickety and the top was sopping wet, but it was also level and perfectly positioned so that Kishar could see every inch of the valley below. Halaf, Kishar's favorite drummer, crouched to one side, tightening the leather head on his drum and muttering curses under his breath. Halaf hated the rain.

The Niphilim were already set in their ranks, with the largest men in front, nearly two-dozen across at the widest point, and the quicker, fiercer men and women behind. Line after line of them stood, shoulder to shoulder, beginning about thirty paces into the valley and extending nearly a quarter of the way up the northern ravine toward the temple. Kishar had never seen so many Niphilim packed into such a small space.

Steep hills rose both east and west of the valley, preventing any sort of flanking maneuvers or strategic advance. Not that Kishar expected any complicated movements on the part of the enemy. No, the black-heads would march straight into battle, trying to swamp them with superior numbers. In their place he might have done the same. A superior attacking force should never hesitate to overwhelm a smaller army. By breaking enemy combatants into smaller groups, the larger army can bring more soldiers to the fight, usually resulting in victory. *Usually*. Skill, training, and bravery could often turn even that rule into a lie.

Kishar ran a finger over his map, tracing the outline of the valley below. The parchment was wet and limp, but the lines were still crisp and clear. He'd been nervous about bringing his charts out in the rain. The irreplaceable ones he'd left in his quarters.

The map wasn't entirely accurate—a fact he'd noticed and puzzled over a dozen times before. It showed the gully leading from the southern edge of the valley as making a slight bend to the east, and then quickly straightening and heading south once more. In fact, the ravine made a radical curve, bending until it was headed almost back in the direction from which it had come, before shifting and running straight onto the plains.

329 / Slaves of the Shinar

Kishar had been musing over that strange twist in the hills for hours, wondering how he could take advantage. He'd considered having a group of Niphilim stationed on the surrounding hilltops, ready to throw rocks or javelins down on the black-heads as they marched past. It was an idea he'd quickly abandoned. To a Niphilim soldier, throwing rocks or sharpened pieces of wood was a great dishonor, worse even than defeat. Kishar had also played with the idea of starting the battle at the point where the ravine first emptied into the valley. Using the twists between the hills as a kind of blind, so that the enemy would be surprised when they rounded the corner and stumbled into the jaws of his waiting legions. But in the end, Kishar had decided to leave things as they were. Many a great leader had crafted defeat out of victory by meddling too much, exactly as a potter will destroy a vase by sticking his fingers too far into the clay. Besides, Lagassar was going to supply all the surprise they'd need.

Finally, Kishar turned to the waiting messenger. "What do you want?" he asked.

The young soldier sighed as though he'd been holding his breath. "The black-heads are in the Withered Hills," he said.

"How long 'til they reach this position?"

"Within the hour."

Kishar nodded. "Do they have scouts?"

"They did. Five. All have been dealt with."

"So they know nothing of Lagassar's troops?"

"No, Captain." The messenger shook his head for emphasis.

Kishar smirked. The war was all but won. "Tell Kamran that I want the other drummers in position," he ordered. "After that, go to the rear of the lines, all the way to the back, and tell them to be ready."

"You can let go," Uruk whispered. "He is dead."

Adah moaned. Her whole face was throbbing. Blood and mucus ran from her nose and mouth. She tried to open her eyes but couldn't. It was as though, in the space of a few breaths, the hinges on which her eyelids swung had rusted shut.

"You are all right," Uruk said. "You have a few bruises, and your nose is broken, but you will live." Adah felt his big hands slide under her head, lift it, and cradle it in his lap. The dog's nose touched lightly on her ear and sniffed over her face.

"Can you open your eyes?" Uruk asked.

Adah shook her head.

"Blink hard and fast."

She did as he said and, after a few moments, her left eye cracked open. The whole world was blurry and seemed to be spinning. Adah thought she was going to be sick.

"Breathe deep. Focus on one thing," Uruk said. He and the dog were both looking down at her. One of the dog's ears was cut and bleeding.

"Dog's hurt?" Adah croaked.

"He has seen worse."

"Do I look awful?" Her hands trembled as she felt her cheeks and nose. She was lumpy all over. Tears welled up but she quickly wiped them away. She didn't want Uruk to see her cry.

"No one who hunts lions can expect to live without scars." Uruk touched Adah's still unopened eye and she flinched. "You can not open it?" he asked.

Adah shook her head. "No."

"I can fix your eye, but it will hurt a little."

"What are you going to do?"

"There is a lot of blood above the lid. I have to get it out."

Uruk took out the dagger Adah had used to cut the bottom off her tunic. "Hold still," he said. Adah squeezed both eyes shut and waited for the cold sting of the blade. She felt a tiny bit of pressure, but the searing pain she'd expected never came.

"It is done," Uruk said. He wiped the blood off her face with his sleeve. "Blink hard and then open your eyes."

Adah did as she was told and this time both sets of lids parted. She still couldn't see clearly, but at least she could see.

"I can fix your nose too," Uruk said. "But not now. Can you stand?"

"Yes."

"Good." Uruk lifted her by the shoulders and set her on her feet. She teetered forward and back, and had to hold his hand for balance, but didn't fall. Eventually she began to feel steadier. Stronger. Able to stand without help.

"What happened?" Adah asked. A pair of dead bodies lay at her feet. Shagar and Zal. The basket lay to one side, near a torch that had all but gone out, leaving nothing more than a few red sparks and a pillar of smoke rising up to join the overwhelming darkness. Barash was nowhere to be seen.

"I killed him," Uruk pointed at Zal, "while you held that one."

"And the third?"

"Ran away during the fight. Limped actually. Dog hurt him badly." Uruk patted Adah on the back. "You did very well. Holding that man's sword arm was brave. It gave us just enough time."

"But he'll be back with more soldiers."

Uruk nodded. "Eventually. But he has a long way to go. Uphill and losing blood with every step."

"Why didn't you kill him?"

"I had to make a choice," Uruk said. "Many more blows and I am not sure you would be standing."

Adah's face throbbed as blood coursed into it. Despite the bruising and swelling, she blushed.

"But you are right." Uruk picked up one of the water-skins Zal had dropped and tied it to his belt. "They will come," he said. "We must hurry."

Uruk turned toward the cell and Adah stumbled after him.

The door was wood, overlaid with strips of iron and set into the wall on enormous iron hinges. The workmanship was simple and clean. Powerful. The rock into which it was hung would give way before the door did.

Uruk slid the bolt back and pulled. Heavy as it was, the door swung open silently. Behind it, all was black.

"Dark," Adah muttered.

Uruk took a torch from one of the sconces beside the door and thrust it into the passage, illuminating the first few strides of a long tunnel. If they followed it, Adah knew, they'd eventually come to a dangerously steep flight of stairs at the bottom of which was a long narrow chamber. If Jared were still alive, he'd be there.

"Smell that?" Uruk asked.

Adah leaned through the door and sniffed. The odor that met her was like a punch in the face, causing her eyes to water. "What is it?" she asked, fighting not to gag.

Uruk shook his head. "Smells like a slaughterhouse."

"Play," Kishar commanded.

Halaf responded with two hard strikes to his drum. *Boom-Boom.* He paused for a moment before striking twice more. This time, the sound was echoed by three other drummers, scattered across the surrounding hills. The cadence was almost exactly the same as the one they'd used during the battle in Akshur—a rhythm meant to mimic the sound of the human heart. Simha had considered it at once the most compelling and terrifying sound in the world. Kishar tended to agree.

The black-head army was just beginning to pour into the field and form into lines. Kishar was impressed. These weren't the same scared men he'd seen on the fields of Kan-Puram, where they were driven almost to collapse by a host of naked savages. No. These men were hardened. They formed up and strode forward without hesitation. Kishar was almost proud of them. After all, it was he and his brethren who'd taught them war. It was the Niphilim who'd taught them to be brave.

As the enemy approached, Kishar began looking for leaders among their ranks. As yet he could find none. Usually a leader was easy to spot. The men around him were crisper, more disciplined. Even among the Niphilim that was true. Wherever a Lieutenant marched, there the line was at its strongest and best. But no matter how long he searched, Kishar couldn't find a single leader among the enemy. The monstrous horde seemed to move without direction. They were less like an army than a river, rushing here and there to fill its banks, the entire mass following the will of the earth.

As they came closer, Kishar was able to see their weapons. Many of them had the same heavy wood and copper maces they'd used in the battle for Kan-Puram. The rest carried swords. Iron swords. Kishar shook his head. He'd known they were coming, and yet the sight of all that blue-black metal was still terrifying to behold. 'The black-heads would have been fools to bring anything else,' he told himself. Lagassar had been concerned about javelins and pikes, remembering the damage those weapons had done during their first battle. But Kishar knew better. The javelin is a worthless offensive weapon. As your army advances, the throwers, who have to be stationed toward the back for their own protection, are as likely to throw their barbs into their own men as into the enemy. Likewise, a pike requires planted feet. It can't be wielded effectively by an advancing soldier.

"Play the flourish," Kishar said to Halaf. He had to shout to be heard over the thunder of trudging feet.

Halaf pounded out a rapid succession of beats before returning to his original cadence. The other drummers echoed him.

The Niphilim drew their swords.

Even Kishar reached for his weapon, just as he had since he was a boy, learning under his quartermaster's whip. Energy raced through his arm as he squeezed the hilt. It was as though his blade were imbued with godlike power.

Kishar thrust his sword up over his head, twisting it as Simha used to do. Rain pelted the blade and ran down his arm. No matter. The power of that image, like a thorn piercing the sky, was enough to raise the hearts of his army. A chill ran up Kishar's spine as the Niphilim cheered. They were ready for battle.

The black-heads never faltered.

At last, the two great armies came together and the roar was unlike anything mortals had ever known. Kishar imagined the sound as being like an entire forest of trees falling at the same moment, branches scraping, roots groaning as they're torn up—and then, the overwhelming explosion of uncountable trunks slamming against the earth.

Blood spurted into the air as the first line of black-heads went down, almost to a man, and was trampled under by the next. The second line did better and the third quite well. Soon, the two armies were pushing and shoving, so close that not even light could ferret its way into the cracks between the straining bodies. In places, dead and wounded soldiers remained pressed among the crowd, like driftwood floating on the tide.

For a long time, longer even than Kishar would have thought possible, the Niphilim army held its ground. If one man fell, two more leapt into his place—each of them shoving with every ounce of force he could muster. But the sheer weight of the enemy couldn't be denied. Wave after wave of black-heads hurled themselves at the lines. Some didn't even bother to swing their weapons. They just smashed into the Niphilim warriors with their chests and shoulders, forcing them back toward the northern ravine. It may take hours, and thousands of deaths on both sides, but eventually they would reach Dagonor. Something had to be done.

Kishar sat down on his campstool and looked at the eastern sky. It was difficult to estimate the time without seeing the sun, but he guessed it was almost noon. An hour since the black-heads first appeared. "Get ready to change the cadence," he shouted.

Halaf nodded without breaking rhythm.

Kishar watched as the Niphilim lines slowly receded, coming ever closer to the hill on which he stood. It was a slow, dangerous and agonizing process, but getting faster all the time.

Finally, when he couldn't stand to see his troops fall back any farther, Kishar called to Halaf. "Now," he screamed. "Change it now!"

Instantly, Halaf broke out of the original cadence—two beats followed by silence—and into a faster rhythm. No silence at all. Just a frantic *boom-boom-boom-boom-boom*.

The whole field seemed to take a deep breath. Enemy soldiers, who'd been pushing and shoving each other for the chance to get into the battle, paused. Some even looked over their shoulders, puzzling over the change, wondering what it could mean—feeling in their hearts that something terrible was about to commence.

Suddenly, a formation of two hundred Niphilim women came screaming over the western hills, Lagassar at their head, and slashed deep into the enemy flank. Corpses were scattered in their wake.

A moment later, yet another squadron of women came pouring over the hills to the east. Despite slightly superior numbers, this group wasn't quite as successful. They drove into the enemy's unprotected side, just as Lagassar's group had, but not as far or as fast. Still, the damage was done. The enemy advance had stalled and the main force of the Niphilim army was mounting a counterattack. The soldiers of Kan-Puram were milling in disarray.

Victory was within reach. There was very little chance that the enemy could regain their momentum. Their seemingly unstoppable onslaught had failed miserably. The time of their slaughter had begun.

Kishar glanced at the eastern sky again. "I have to go," he shouted to Halaf. "Kamran will be in command until I return. You'll have to follow his drummer."

Halaf nodded. He resented having to change his cadence to match another drummer, but he'd do it. At heart, Halaf was a soldier, and that meant following orders. Something he'd been doing all his life.

Kishar folded his maps and stuffed them in an oilskin bag. He took one last look at the battlefield, and then he was gone, racing down the hill.

The same young messenger he'd spoken to earlier found him just as he reached the bottom.

"Captain!" The messenger was breathing hard. "Scouts just arrived from the east," he said. "The smaller army is approaching."

"How far?"

"An hour. Maybe more. They are moving slowly."

"Find Kamran. Tell him that Lagassar's attack was successful, that she all but cut them in two." He handed the oilskin bag to the messenger. "Then take these to my quarters and hang them on the rack. Build a fire. I want them dry as dust when I get there tonight."

CHAPTER 6

Nor Iron Bars a Cage

"WHICH ONE IS HE?" ADAH ASKED. SHE CUPPED A HAND OVER HER nose, but the miasma of filth and decaying flesh could not be warded off.

There were forty men in that chamber, nearly all of them in an advanced state of emaciation. Most still lived, but if they were in possession of their souls Uruk could see no evidence of it. Even those few who looked up, eyes drawn to the flickering light, were as blank as the desert sands. The dog had resisted coming into the cell, and now Uruk knew why. The smell they'd discovered was not merely that of a slaughter-house. This was something much worse. These men were being butchered alive. The Niphilim had devised a way of scooping them out. The lungs still filled and emptied, the hearts still beat, but the men who'd once possessed them were gone.

"You survived this?" Uruk asked.

Adah nodded. "And remember every moment. The Niphilim think we don't, but they're wrong. We never forget."

Uruk moved through the room, inspecting each face in turn. He saw spittle running off chins, bile and stomach acid vomited onto the fronts of tunics, and eyes rolled back to reveal off-white ovals speckled with blood.

After looking at no fewer than a dozen mindless, half-dead bodies, Uruk had to stop and regroup. He'd have fled all the way back to the stairs, but just as he was backing away from the corpse of a recently deceased man, spider0000000000000000000000000000000000000000webs woven over his face and between his fingers, Uruk noticed the dog. He was sitting next to a pair of muscular legs, halfway down the left-hand wall.

Uruk bent over the naked figure and was shocked to see that it was, in fact, Jared. His hair was no longer the ebony mane dusted with silver that Uruk remembered. It was dirty, lifeless gray. His beard had grown out as well, and was specked with clumps of dried blood. Gone were the twinkling eyes and rakish smile that had lent him such an air of carefree superiority. The man Uruk saw had little in common with the one who'd gone bounding down the tower of Moloch just a few short weeks before. He had the same structure, bones and blood, but nothing else. The King of Thieves was effectively dead.

"What is wrong with him?" Uruk asked.

"Too much darkness," Adah muttered, peering into Jared's eyes. "Not enough food or sleep."

Uruk stared at her.

"I know, it seems like they have nothing to do *but* sleep." Adah shook her head. "Lack of sunlight twists their minds. Some prisoners will go days without rest and never even know it."

Uruk pointed to the blood on Jared's face, and at the bruises on his chest and thighs. "He has been beaten."

"He tried to escape," Adah said. "Probably while they were bringing him here. That's why they took his clothes."

"What can we do?"

Adah shrugged. "He's only been down here a few days. Given an hour or two, we might—"

"An hour or two?"

"It usually takes days. Longer than that and they never find their way out, though that's rare."

"Maybe he is not so deep," Uruk said.

Adah waved a hand in front of Jared's face. "Hard to tell," she said. "When they do come back, it's sudden. Like a flash from a lightning bug. One moment, darkness. Then—" she clapped her hands.

"We have to bring him out now," Uruk said. "We may need him."

Adah considered for a moment. "Give me the dagger." Uruk pulled it from the waistband of his breeches and pressed it into her palm. She cut the cords around Jared's ankles, then reached behind him and cut the ones binding his wrists. Jared did not move either to help or to hinder her.

"Now give him some water," she said.

Uruk untied the skin from his belt and put it in Jared's hands. He had to hold it in place or it would have rolled off his lap and spilled on the floor. "Drink it," he urged.

Amazingly, Jared did as he was told. He lifted the skin to his lips and began to greedily suck at the liquid inside. The water came out so fast that he couldn't swallow it all. Soon his beard and chest-hair were soaked with the overflow from his mouth.

When the skin was empty, Jared let it drop. His hands went limp and his jaw dropped open. A string of slobber slid off his tongue.

"Can you speak?" Uruk asked him.

Adah shook her head. "They're like puppets. They can follow simple instructions, but—"

A glimmer of recognition flashed through Jared's eyes. Recognition and hatred. Adah must have seen it as well, because she stopped talking and stared.

Uruk picked up one of Jared's hands and squeezed. "Look at me," he commanded. He held the torch up so that it illuminated his face. "I am no jailer." Jared stared at him, but didn't move or even blink. The glimmer they'd seen a moment before showed no signs of returning.

Then Uruk had an idea. He held the torch over the dog. "Look at him."

Jared's eyes swiveled toward the dog. They were like the eyes of some insect or lizard, moving to follow its prey. He stared for what seemed a long time. Then, very slowly, he closed his mouth.

It happened exactly like Adah said it would. All at once, the gleam returned to Jared's eyes. He wiped the slobber from his chin with the back of his hand. "I told them someone would come," he croaked. "They didn't believe me."

"We owed you," Uruk said.

Jared nodded. "The window." He patted the dog on the head. "Good thing I caught him."

"Let's stand him up," Adah suggested.

She took one of Jared's hands and Uruk took the other. But before they could haul him to his feet, Jared turned toward Adah and said, "Who are you?"

"Her name is Adah," Uruk replied. "She helped me find you."

Jared pondered that for a moment. "What happened to your face?" he asked.

"What happened to yours?" she snapped back.

Jared smiled. "Are you going to help me up or not?"

They did. Jared held fast to Adah's arm for a few mincing steps, then let go and took a few more on his own. "The Niphilim make them exercise," Adah explained. "Walk. Bend and stretch. That sort of thing."

"Worst torture I ever experienced," Jared agreed.

"What now?" Adah asked. She watched as Jared ambled toward the stairs, still trying to coax the strength back into his legs.

"Head for the surface," Uruk said. "Fast as we can."

"What about them?" Adah waved at the other prisoners.

Uruk thought for a moment, trying to estimate how much time had passed since they'd first entered the cell. The wounded guard must have reached the opposite end of the mine by now. He could have passed out somewhere on the hill, from shock or loss of blood, but Uruk didn't dare hope so.

"We take them with us," he said at last.

For a split second, Adah looked like she might reach up and kiss him. Instead, she turned and raced to the other side of the room. "I'll start over here," she said, pulling her dagger from its sheath and bending over the man closest to the stairs. It took her only a moment to cut his bonds.

"What should I do?" Jared asked.

Uruk handed him the torch. "Find clothes," he said. "There are a few dead bodies over by that wall."

Jared looked like he'd just as soon stay naked, but he went toward the corpses anyway. In the meantime, Uruk drew his sword and began slicing the bonds from the bodies on his side of the chamber. He found more corpses as he went, but didn't say anything. Adah didn't need to know.

"If they are unable to walk, we leave them behind," Uruk said as he sawed the leather bands from a last pair of bony wrists. "Agreed?"

"Fine," Adah said. She'd just finished with her side of the room, and was crossing toward a body that lay slumped in the shadows at the far corner. She was about to cut the bonds from its feet, but as she reached out with her dagger, the legs kicked defensively. Adah screamed.

"What is it?" Uruk asked, racing toward her.

"Look."

It was a savage—an old female with long thin teats and stripes of white hair that ran across the top of her head and down her chest. She growled as Uruk approached, displaying a full set of sharp yellow teeth. Everything else about her might have grown weak, but not those. Uruk guessed that she'd like nothing more than to sink them into his neck or bite his fingers clean off.

"What should we do with it?"

Uruk thought about his first encounter with the dog, along the banks of the Ibex River outside Ur. The dog had growled at him too, Uruk remembered. Even when he'd done nothing more dangerous than hold out a piece of meat—more than the dog had eaten in a fortnight, judging by the way his ribs stuck out—the dog was suspicious. "We will let her free herself," Uruk said. "No animal deserves to die in this hole. Not even this one."

"She'll attack," Adah warned.

But Uruk wasn't listening. He grabbed the savage by the feet and yanked her away from the wall. She twisted and flopped like a landed fish as he turned her onto her belly, but Uruk didn't let go. "Let me have the dagger," he said.

Reluctantly, Adah handed it over. "What are you going to do?"

"Just a small cut," Uruk said, and began to saw back and forth on the leather straps around the savage's wrists. When he'd cut a groove no deeper than a fingernail paring, he handed the dagger back.

"You've destroyed them," Adah said, clearly alarmed. "She'll break those cords now for sure."

Uruk nodded. "But it will take time. More than enough for us to escape."

"Speaking of which," Jared said. He was standing in the middle of the room, pulling a threadbare tunic down over his torso. The breeches he'd found hugged his body like paint. The result was obscene. Rather than hiding his masculinity, his clothes actually emphasized every curve. Adah blushed and looked at the ground. "How," Jared continued, "are we going to move these mindless ghouls up all those stairs?"

"That's simple," Adah said, still staring at her feet. "Like I said before, they're puppets. All it takes is the right tone."

Uruk and Jared looked at each other and shrugged.

Adah smiled. "I'll show you." She took a deep breath. "Line up. I want every one of you black-heads ready to march," she shouted. And after she'd given the orders in the common language of the Shinar, she gave them again in the Niphilim tongue. Uruk didn't understand a word of that, but he recognized the sound. It wasn't a language he liked. Hearing it come from Adah's mouth was like biting into grit.

The effect, however, was miraculous—if a bit frightening. The slaves literally bounced to their feet and raced to the center of the room. Even Jared gave a little jolt.

Watching the prisoners press into single file, Uruk was reminded of something he'd seen many years before. The Aegyp warlord Thoth had a trick he liked to do for special guests. He'd line up his servants, then go to each in turn, whispering in their ears. Once he'd spoken to them all, he'd clap his hands and every one of them would collapse into a deep trance. After that, he could tell them that the river had turned to blood, or that his staff was a cobra, and for a while at least, they'd believe it. He could also make them do things—shameful things. Once, Uruk had seen a grown woman take off all her clothes and act like she was bathing. Another time, one of Thoth's male servants crawled about on the floor, legs beating back and forth, imagining he was a crocodile lazily swimming though the reeds. These prisoners were just like that man, Uruk thought. Their muscles functioned and their eyes were open, but the mind that controlled it all was somewhere else. Uruk wondered what they were seeing. Not crocodiles, he knew, and not reeds. But maybe something much, much worse.

By the time Adah had finished, no fewer than twenty-two men were on their feet. One or two others had struggled to stand, but failed. They were beyond help. If he'd had more time, Uruk would have put each and every one of them to death. As things stood, he doubted they'd suffer much longer anyway.

"Take them up," Uruk ordered.

Moments later, Adah had the whole line climbing the stairs. The dog was in the lead, followed by Uruk—sword drawn just in case—and then Adah. Jared brought up the rear.

As with every journey, no matter how short, the path in seemed a good deal longer than the one coming out. In no time, they were passing the iron-bound door and into the main chamber. They still weren't outside—that was a good hour's hike away—but at least they were out of the cell. And the smell was almost sweet.

The dead guards were right where they'd left them, as were the bag of bread and both remaining water-skins. Even the torches beside the door were burning exactly as they had earlier.

The only thing that had changed at all was the path leading over the hill. And that had changed completely.

Adah noticed it first and gasped. Where before the hilltop had been marked by a single torch, now there were at least two dozen. They had no way of guessing how many Niphilim were arrayed beneath those flickering lights, but the fact that guards were preparing to come after them was painfully clear.

"What now?" Jared asked.

Uruk looked at Adah. "Can you make them fight?" He gestured at the prisoners, still lined up and ready.

"Maybe," she said. "But what's the point? They'll just be killed."

"At least this way their deaths will have meaning."

"Really? What?"

"If they fight," Jared said, "a few of us might go free. That's something."

"We have to hurry," Uruk said. "No telling how long the Niphilim will stay on that hill."

He and Jared went to the bodies of the dead guards and quickly removed their swords. Jared strapped one over his shoulder, Niphilim fashion. Uruk brought the other to Adah. "Let me tie this around your waist," he said.

"I don't want it," Adah pouted.

Uruk ignored her. He looped the straps high on her hips. "Just in case," he said.

Adah started to argue, but fell silent. She looked into the darkness, as though seeing something for the first time. "What if there's another way?" she asked.

"What other way?" Uruk never stopped moving as he listened to her.

"When I was watching the guards earlier, I saw one of them come out of a passage." She pointed. "It was directly opposite the cell. I remember thinking how strange it was that I couldn't see him from the path."

"Do you know where it leads?" Uruk asked.

Adah shook her head. "Not exactly."

"It's worth trying," Jared said.

Uruk frowned. His instinct was to head to daylight by the shortest possible route. He wanted out of this cavern as quickly as possible. But that would also mean fighting, during which the majority of these prisoners would likely die—and maybe Adah or Jared as well.

"Could it possibly be worse?" Jared asked, pointing up the hill. A few of the torches had begun to break off from the herd and were slowly coming down the slope. If they were going to try Adah's alternate path, they had to do it now.

"You both want to do this?" Uruk asked.

Adah nodded.

"I'm always up for a gamble," Jared said.

Uruk looked at the dog. "Fine." He picked up the water-skins and tied them to his belt. The bag of bread he handed to Jared. "Dog and I will be in front," he said. He took the two remaining torches from the wall. "You bring up the rear."

"Always at the back," Jared grumbled. He glanced up the hill. The torches were coming closer by the moment. "Of course, if there's to be any fun on this little journey, it's likely to come at us from behind."

Uruk handed one of the torches to Adah. "Show us your path," he said.

A moment later, they were threading their way through a pair of natural stone pillars and into a narrow corridor. Uruk had a feeling that they were headed nowhere good. If he'd been a praying man, he might have offered up a word or two to Mana. As it was, he set his teeth and strode on.

"We leave our packs here," Barley called. "Drink your water and eat whatever you've got left. From now on we carry nothing but weapons."

He watched as they shrugged out of their packs and lifted their water-skins to their mouths. Lamech pulled out a last strip of jerky, inspected it, and then tossed it in the mud. Over the last few hours, he'd overcome most of his bout of stomach sickness, but still had no appetite. Barley could understand that. He hadn't felt so much as a gurgle, but he wasn't hungry either.

When the men had squeezed the last drops of water from their skins and taken a moment to rest their feet, Barley called for them to move on. There were no groans this time. Too many were suffering to waste their breath on meaningless, useless noise. It was work enough just to stand and walk.

Over the last hour, no less than twenty-three men had come to Barley complaining of welts and rashes. A handful of the cases looked like nothing more sinister than chafed skin—the result of rain, sweat and a long march—but the others were much more serious. Some of the men were already wheezing and coughing, furiously wiping their mouths and scratching their chests. If he dared to look close enough, Barley guessed he'd see flesh under some of their fingernails.

He'd considered giving up. At least a dozen times, Barley had been on the verge of raising his hands and saying—'Enough. We're too sick. The rest of the army will have to find a way to win without us.' The temptation had become almost more than he could bear. In fact, there was only one thing that kept him going, and that was a sincere belief in his men. Somewhere deep down, beneath the sickness and despair, they wanted to fulfill their mission. Barley was sure of it. If they quit, just laid down their swords and walked away, they'd always look back on that moment with shame. How could a man live, knowing he'd chosen comfort over justice, his own life over the lives of his comrades and the future of his city? A few of the men were still moving for no reason other than because they were too proud to fall. Well, if those men could stay on their feet, Barley could lead them. He wasn't sure that they'd be able to do much of anything when they reached Dagonor, but they'd do their best. In all likelihood, not one of them would live to see another sunrise—maybe not another sunset—but that was hardly relevant. The gods wanted a sacrifice, and these men had the guts to make it.

They stumbled along for another half-hour, eventually finding a ravine that would lead them to the foot of Dagon's Mountain. As they started down it, Barley glanced to the side and saw the remains of some dark blue silk, clinging to a stand of dandy-willow. He stared. Seeing such beautiful cloth this far into the wilderness was as startling as seeing a savage walk through the middle of Kan-Puram. He reached out to touch it. But just as he did, one of his men stumbled, slumped to his knees and then collapsed. His sword, which he had drawn for some reason—possibly sensing that they were in danger—plopped into the mud in front of him.

Barley hurried to turn the man over. If nothing else, Barley didn't want to see him drown, face down in the dirt.

"Damn," Barley cursed. He searched for a pulse but found nothing. Pink bubbles expanded from the dead man's mouth. His cheeks were speckled with blood. Barley pulled back the man's tunic to reveal a chest gouged by fingernails and spotted with disease. The rest of their little troop gathered around them. For a moment, no one said a word. Then, one of the men in the circle moaned.

"What is it?" Barley asked. He half-expected to see another man collapse in the mud. When he saw what it actually was, he moaned too.

The Niphilim had arrived.

At least six dozen blond warriors had emerged from the top of the neighboring hill. The weary, diseased soldiers of Kan-Puram gaped. Less than half even bothered to draw their swords. Most stood dumbfounded, or dropped to their knees in despair. The battle had been lost before even a single blow fell.

Barley screamed at his men, begging them to defend themselves. But it was no use. As the Niphilim swept down the hill, his troops clumped together like goats facing off a pack of wolves. And with similar results.

Out of almost a hundred men, only one fought back—Barley himself. He even managed to kill a pair of Niphilim. The first one's head he split wide open, all the way from crown to chin. The second he caught in the chest. Both were dead before they even hit the ground. But the head of Barley's axe got stuck between the second man's ribs. And no matter how he pulled, Barley couldn't seem to work it free.

He was still struggling over it when a third Niphilim, approaching from his blind side, tackled him to the ground. Barley kicked and punched, even bit at the arms of the men who rushed in to help pin him down. It did no good. After a few moments, he found that he could not so much as turn his head.

The last thing Barley saw was a Niphilim man—a leader of some kind, judging by the look of contempt on his face—casually peering down at him. Barley cursed and spat, but the man just grinned. 'At least we drew a few of them away,' Barley thought. 'We did that much, by Moloch.'

Standing over him, Kishar was stunned speechless by the man's scars. His face, what remained of it, was a work of art. No Niphilim had ever possessed so magnificent a trophy. This man's whole visage was ruined, the scar running from the top of his bald head, through one garishly destroyed eye, and on down through his cheek. One of Kishar's men wanted to kill the struggling black-head, before he caused any more trouble. But Kishar couldn't allow it. Antha-Kane would want to see this one, he thought.

"Hold him still," Kishar said. He kicked the scar-faced man in the side of the head, knocking him senseless. "Bind him well. I want him ready to march."

"March where?" one of his men asked, still kneeling over the unconscious man.

"To the mine, of course." Kishar looked at the rest of the black-heads, huddled together just a few strides away. "Take them all."

"Some are diseased," another Niphilim said. "Look." He pointed at the corpse over which the black-heads had been standing. The dead man's chest was purple.

"Fine." Kishar turned toward Dagonor. "Kill the diseased ones and send the rest to the mine. I am returning to the *real* battle."

"What is this place?" Jared asked.

The corridor they'd been following had come to an abrupt end, emptying into a rectangular chamber large enough for all the prisoners to be lined up shoulder to shoulder against the walls. Out of the chamber led four passages, cut through the center of each wall. Judging by the patterns that had been tread through the dust on the floor, Uruk guessed that this room saw a lot of use, as did three of the portals leading out from it. Only the doorway directly opposite the one they'd come through had any dust at all, and it was positively filthy.

"Some kind of crossroads," Adah replied.

Uruk agreed. "I suspect that passage," he pointed to the doorway on his left, one of those leading perpendicular to the path they'd been following, "would eventually lead back to the main chamber. So that one—" he gestured to his right "—probably leads to the Black Cavern. And that—" he pointed at the doorway filled with dust "—I have no thoughts about. Adah?"

She shook her head. "I've never been here."

"Do you think they'll follow us?" Jared asked. He peered into the tunnel from which they'd just emerged.

"No. If they come after us, it will be through one of these other passages." Uruk gestured at the way they'd come and shook his head. "That way is too narrow."

"What now?" Jared asked.

"One of us should see what the Niphilim are doing," Adah said. "Make sure they aren't about to launch an attack."

Uruk nodded. Adah was learning fast. She'd be a hunter in no time.

"I can do that," Jared offered.

"Also, we should investigate each of these passages," Adah continued. "There may be some way to slip past the guards."

"I will check that one." Uruk gestured at the tunnel to the Black Cavern.

"Then I'll go that way." Adah pointed down the last of the four tunnels. Her hands were trembling, Uruk noticed. She was probably thinking about the last time she'd gone off alone. The bruises on her face may soon fade, but Uruk doubted her memory ever would.

"No," Uruk said. "You stay here—with them."

"But I'll just. . . ."

"We will scout that passage together when I get back."

"Shouldn't I do anything?" Adah asked.

"Talk to them, wake them up." He gestured at the sack of bread, and the water-skins lying in the center of the floor. "Feed them."

"Fine." Adah crossed her arms. "But I won't wait forever."

"Dog, stay with Adah," Uruk said.

Reluctantly, the dog sat down beside her. Adah patted him on the head. "That's all right," she said. "We'll drink all the water before they come back. That'll show him."

"If you have trouble, send Dog to find me." Uruk pressed his torch into the hand of one of the prisoners. The man's eyes were as wide and vacant as ever, but his grip was surprisingly strong.

"Just make sure you stay out of sight," Adah warned. "Dog and I don't want to have to rescue you."

CHAPTER 7

Not Without a Fight

*B*Y THE TIME URUK RETURNED, ADAH AND JARED WERE HUDDLED together at the center of the crossroads. One of Jared's arms was looped around Adah's waist. They might have been father and daughter, conferring over something as benign as a winter wedding. Even the tilt of their heads was remarkably similar. Seeing them like that, Uruk felt a twinge of jealousy tht he couldn't quite place.

The moment Uruk stepped out of the passage, Dog went to welcome him. Uruk scratched behind his ears and roughed up the hair along his back.

"You have something on your face," Jared said.

Uruk scrubbed both cheeks with his sleeve. "Smoke." Jared waited, clearly expecting some kind of explanation. Uruk gave none. "What did you find?" he asked.

"They're waiting for us," Jared said.

"How many?"

"Thirty-five at least. Possibly more."

"Preparing to attack?"

Jared shook his head. "Not yet."

"They know we've got no food," Adah said. "Or not much anyway. They can just sit on their hilltop and wait for the war to end."

"In other words, they've got us," Jared said. For the first time since Uruk had met him, Jared seemed in no mood for levity. He actually appeared concerned. Uruk wondered how much of that was as a result of their being trapped, and how much was the lingering effect of the cell.

"We should still look down that other passage," he said. "Maybe there is—"

"Don't bother," Adah said. "It's only about four hundred paces long, and at the end's a pool of cold water." She rubbed her arms for emphasis. "I only stepped into it—" she snapped her fingers "—that long. And my whole foot felt like it was on fire."

"I asked you to wait," Uruk said.

Adah shrugged. "I took the dog with me. If there were anything dangerous, we'd have come back. Besides," she waved at the prisoners, still lined up against the walls exactly as Uruk had left them, "I already gave them the bread. They were fine."

Uruk scowled. "How big is this pool?"

"I threw some stones, but never managed to hit anything solid. And there's no way around. I looked."

While Adah described her investigation of what sounded like a subterranean lake, Uruk took a quick survey of the prisoners. Most had breadcrumbs sprinkled through their beards, he noticed. Little else had changed. A few stared at the torches, mesmerized by the flickering light. But far more were peering up at the ceiling, just as they had in the cell. One of the men appeared to be watching Adah. Uruk hoped that was a good sign. "Were you able to work with them at all?" he asked her.

"Sort of."

"What does that mean?" Uruk looked at Jared, who shrugged.

Adah pointed to a pair of prisoners. The one on the left had a long string of drool clinging to his lower lip and teeth the color of lichen. His neighbor looked to be about ten years younger, with a beard of wiry black curls that blended perfectly with the hair tufting from the open neck of his tunic. The front of his breeches was soaking wet. "See those two?" Adah asked.

Uruk nodded.

She waved her hands in front of their faces. Neither so much as blinked. "Still lost," she observed. "But I think we can use them."

"How?" Jared asked, just beating Uruk to the same question.

"Watch." Adah stood in front of the older man—the one with the mossy teeth. "Look at me," she said. Uruk noticed that she hadn't given the command in the Niphilim language, but that it didn't seem to make much difference. The man's eyes rolled down until he was staring more or less right at her. Adah held his gaze for a moment, then pointed at the other prisoner. "Hit him," she said.

Without a second's hesitation, the man spun around, long string of drool breaking from his lip, and struck his neighbor full in the chest. Until that moment, he'd looked no more energetic than wet canvas. No longer. Even as he sunk back into his place against the wall, Uruk saw the viciousness that bubbled beneath his skin. These men were like sling-shots, he thought, just waiting for the right hand to lay stones in their pockets.

Jared was less enamored of Adah's experiment. He grabbed the victim around the upper arm and lifted him to his feet. "Breathe deep," he whispered, patting the man on the shoulder. "Relax and let the air come back."

"You wanted to know if they'd fight," Adah said. "Now we know."

"How many times have you done that?" Jared asked.

Adah ignored him. "You haven't told us what you found yet," she said to Uruk.

"The Black Cavern."

"And the slaves?" she asked hopefully.

He nodded. "Sitting in rows toward the back."

"Guards?"

"Half-a-dozen."

"I don't guess we can get out that way."

"No. The cavern is closed on all sides." He pointed down the tunnel. "That is the only way in or out."

"Are there any weapons?" Jared asked.

Uruk shook his head. "Just what the Niphilim are carrying."

"Can we beat them?"

Uruk had been mulling over that very question, but still had no answer. "They are watching their end of the tunnel very closely," he said finally. "They may know we are here."

"We still have to try," Adah said.

Uruk looked at her. "We have only three swords," he reminded her.

"We can make *them* fight." Adah indicated the prisoners with a wave.

"They could be killed," Uruk said. "Earlier, you were afraid that—"

"But they'll have a chance this time," she argued.

"They always had a chance."

Adah thought for a moment. "I want to do it," she said at last. "I want to set the other slaves free."

"So do I," Jared agreed. "With them to help us, we might have a real chance against the Niphilim on that hilltop. Imagine how surprised the yellow-haired devils will be when we come at them with a hundred men." He grinned. "I can't wait to see it."

Uruk nodded. He didn't share in Jared's giddiness, but did recognize that freeing the slaves was their best chance for escape. There was strength in numbers.

"What if the guards attack while we're gone?" Adah asked. "They could prevent us from getting back here."

"They could," Uruk agreed. "But we would be no worse off."

"What'll we do?" Jared asked. "Sneak in and—"

Uruk shook his head. "I have an idea. It will be risky, but—"

"Say no more. I can already tell it's the plan for us."

"You will follow Jared," Adah said, then repeated it in the Niphilim language just to be sure. She didn't want to leave anything to chance.

The prisoners were lined up two-abreast, facing into the passage. Jared was at the front, a torch in one fist and his sword in the other. His mouth was split into a toothy grin. Adah couldn't tell whether Jared was anxious for some kind of revenge, or if he just liked the adventure. She guessed it was some of both.

"Remember," Uruk cautioned. "Give the order as soon as you see light, then get out of the way."

"But I want to fight," Adah argued.

"Not this time." Uruk glared at her. "This is no game. You have to do exactly as I tell you. If you cannot do that, say so now."

"No—I can do it."

"Good."

"Are we ready yet?" Jared asked.

Uruk hesitated. "Are you sure you are strong enough to stand at the front?" he asked. "If Adah does not manage to fool them, there could be fighting."

"What?" Jared reacted as though struck. "I was doing battle while you were still holding your mother's spear. Besides, my hair may be gray instead of blond, but I still look a heck of a lot more like a Niphilim than you do."

"Fine," Uruk said. "Be in front."

"Good. Now, if we're all ready." Jared waved at Adah to take her place at the head of the line. As soon as she was in front of him, he patted her on the hip with the flat of his sword. She gave him a dirty look, but Jared just smiled.

"Do you want Dog to come with you?" Uruk asked them.

Jared scowled. "For the last time—no."

Uruk nodded morosely and shuffled back to his place at the end of the line. Adah tried to catch his eye, but he wasn't paying any attention to her.

If Uruk's plan worked, being at the rear wouldn't matter. Their whole group would be out of the tunnel and into the Black Cavern before the guards realized that they were anything more than an ordinary line of slaves being moved from one cell to another. Of course, if things went wrong Uruk would be stuck at the rear, unable to do anything to help. That's what really bothered him, Adah knew. Uruk wasn't a man used to letting others fight for him.

"Stay right with Jared," Adah shouted to the prisoners one last time.

She was about to give the order again, in the Niphilim language, but Jared stopped her. "Enough," he said. "They'll do it. Go."

Adah peered into the tunnel. The light from Jared's torch illuminated no more than a half-dozen strides, but that was enough for her to make out the first sharp turn. Uruk had told her that the passage was full of twists and bends. Adah was surprised to see them start so soon though.

She rounded the first few corners very slowly, not wanting to lose the men behind her. It also gave her time to think. Adah was concerned about her part in Uruk's plan. She'd been told that she was stupid at least five times a day, every day, for as long as she'd been in Dagonor. Even simple things, like cleaning floors or washing clothes, brought her nothing but complaints and misery. She got blamed when the fires were too low, and then again when they were too high. But by far the most common source of criticism was for her use of the Niphilim language. Somehow, it never sounded quite right coming from her mouth. No matter how much she practiced, she couldn't seem to master the nuances. Contractions were beyond her, as were most of the idioms that the native speakers bandied about so easily. And now, it was her ability with the Niphilim language that could decide the outcome of this plot. Adah was nervous.

As she walked, she tried to imagine what the old captain might have said if she were there. The sounds were the important part, Adah decided. The emphasis.

Another quarter-hour to practice and she might have gotten it. But just as she'd decided on what to say, and how to say it, Adah made a final turn and saw the end of the tunnel. Instantly, the words she'd so carefully chosen were gone. Her mind was blank.

She glanced over her shoulder. Jared was just a few strides behind. There was no time left for her to think. Adah took a deep breath and called, in the loudest voice she could muster, "Step aside. Right now. We are bringing many prisoners. Step aside for all of the prisoners."

Her lower lip twisted into a frown. She'd failed and she knew it.

Instead of stepping out of the way, allowing Jared and the prisoners to come through unmolested, the Niphilim moved to cut them off. Adah considered drawing her sword and attacking them, but thought better of it. She remembered the look on Uruk's face when she'd told him she wanted to fight. After all he'd done for her, she wouldn't betray him now.

Adah raced ahead, searching the right-hand wall for the alcove Uruk had described. After giving the order to the Niphilim guards, she was supposed to hide out, staying clear of the battle. She found a slight hollow, not more than ten strides from the end of the tunnel, and pressed herself inside. There she crouched, within spitting distance of the guards, as Jared marched past her, followed by a blur of dark, empty faces. Adah wanted to scream, to tell them she'd failed. But before she got a single word out, Uruk was standing in front of her. It was so dark that she could just barely see the glittering blade of his sword, and the whites of his eyes. He reached into the alcove and grabbed her by the front of her tunic.

"It didn't work," Adah squealed as he dragged her back into the tunnel.

"Draw your sword," Uruk said. "Be ready to—" The sound of clattering metal drowned out the rest of his reply.

It was deafening. The echoes seemed to increase in intensity as they blasted up the tunnel. Adah felt sure the ceiling was about to collapse, crushing them beneath uncountable tons of rock, or trapping them forever at the heart of the mountain.

"What should we do?" she screamed.

But Uruk had already gone.

Adah reached out, searching blindly for him. Feeling nothing but bare rock, she pressed her cheek against the passage wall, hoping to be able to see past the line of prisoners. Her heart skipped as she caught sight of him, shoving his way down the left side of the line. The dog was nowhere to be seen, but Adah felt fairly sure that he was there as well, clawing past legs and over feet.

"Help them," she shouted at the prisoners. She shouldered the man ahead of her, trying to shove him forward. But it did no good. Not one of them moved.

Adah reached for the sword Uruk had given her, but couldn't manage to pull it free of its scabbard. It was simply too long. Or her arms were too short. She'd have had to grab the sword by the blade in order to slide it all the way out. Finally, after struggling with it for what seemed a long time, Adah gave up. She thrust the sword back into its scabbard and reached for her knife.

"Help them," she called again. She gripped the handle of her dagger so tightly that her forearm threatened to cramp. Still none of the prisoners moved. She'd been so sure they would fight. Given instructions, they should do anything. But now, when the time came, they seemed content to stand stock still while Uruk and Jared were slaughtered. It was infuriating. Finally, Adah tried something different.

"Kill the Niphilim," she screamed.

This time, the prisoners in front of her began to shove forward.

"Tear them to bits," Adah urged.

A moment later, they were moving through the tunnel like water sucked through a hollow reed. The Niphilim were in trouble, Adah thought. She was glad she'd be there to see it.

The war wasn't going well. Even Isin, mired at the center of a rapidly losing army, soldiers milling hopelessly all around him, could see that. The women who'd slammed into them from either side were threatening to cut their entire column in two. Qadesh's men were entirely lost to sight, most probably dead. The rain was coming down harder than ever, and the field was slick with mud. Worst of all, Isin had lost his sword. That might have been excusable if he'd somehow let it get stuck in the ribs of an enemy soldier, he supposed. But that's not what happened—not nearly. Isin had been marching along, waiting for his chance to get into the fight, when the women attacked. Somehow, in the rush to get out of their way, his sword had gotten caught and twisted out of his hand. Isin didn't even bother looking for it. The whole army was moving by that time. Trying to swim against the current would have been madness.

The battle reminded Isin of a bread riot he'd seen years before, not long after he'd first joined the temple. Rains were sparse that year, floods almost nonexistent. There was just enough water to wash away the topsoil, not enough to replace it. What little grain there was had been snapped up by the rich. The poor had nothing to eat and no way to feed their livestock. Kan-Puram stunk of misery and death. Isin remembered waking up that morning to screams and curses, bounding to his window and seeing the street choked with beggars. The temple guards fought to seal off the kitchen doors, but the people were desperate. They beat their way inside, destroying ovens and overturning more than a dozen barrels of flour. Not one of the beggars appeared to have gotten so much as a mouthful. The rioters were more interested in destroying what the priests had than in taking anything for themselves. "That's their whole problem," the old priest he'd roomed with in those days said. "They never think about how to prosper. It's all mere survival."

"Mere survival," Isin muttered to himself. Over the last few hours, Isin had developed a new appreciation for exactly how foolish that old priest's sentiments really were. Survival's not always so easy, he thought, especially when you can barely stand upright without having someone knock you down or tear you apart.

Isin cupped both hands over his eyes, blocking the rain just enough to see what was going on. The women attacking from the west were getting uncomfortably close. And Isin still didn't have a weapon.

He looked at the mud around his feet. Nothing presented itself, but Isin didn't give up. He couldn't have been the only one to lose a weapon. There must be hundreds of them somewhere. Maybe thousands. He just had to find *one*. A sword would be preferable, but a mace would do. Even a dagger.

Unfortunately, Isin was still well away from most of the fighting. There were a few bodies scattered about, but most of them had been trampled. He saw an arm and two feet sticking out of the mire, not three strides to his left, but no weapon. Whatever the dead man had been carrying, it must have already sunk beneath the mud. Before long, the body would be gone as well.

Isin kept searching, but had begun to lose hope. In places, the mud was close to knee-deep. Anything heavier than a loaf of bread would be swallowed up in seconds. In desperation, Isin began kicking through the morass. He didn't want to be killed empty-handed.

Finally, after nearly a quarter-hour of searching, Isin saw what he'd been looking for. A mace was standing handle-up in the mud not two strides away. He reached over and yanked it free.

The mace was much heavier than his sword had been, but Isin didn't care. 'A hungry man doesn't complain about spice,' as his mother used to say. He was still congratulating himself on his find when he heard a scream, coming from behind him.

Isin turned, fearing another sneak attack, wondering if it was his turn to die. His breath caught as he saw a wedge of soldiers closing on him from the back of the lines. But unlike the previous two, which had so destroyed their army, this one was composed entirely of men with black hair—and it was aimed at the Niphilim women.

They were coming on fast. Other soldiers seemed to be leaping out of their way, scattering like grasshoppers before a fast-moving wagon. Isin marveled. The wedge was almost on top of him before he saw how they were doing it.

The men at the front of the wedge had maces—just like the one he'd found—and they were using them to knock their fellow soldiers out of the way. Killing most, Isin guessed. Crippling the rest.

As they came closer, Isin recognized a few of the faces. They were thieves, mostly. Sneaker was at the point. Seeing him, Isin couldn't help remembering that night in Kan-Puram, when they'd sat together at a campfire discussing how best to convince the other leaders to support the war. Now here he was again, killing his own countrymen in his desire to get at the Niphilim—and their treasure. Isin was almost ashamed.

Then he saw Ander, striding at the center of the wedge. His hood had been thrown back and his face was as stony and unreadable as ever. Over is head he held an iron sword, twisting it back and forth just as Isin had seen the Niphilim commanders doing.

As they reached the Niphilim women, the thieves seemed almost to explode. They chopped through them like an axe through a dry log, splitting their lines right down the middle. Women were cut down mid-stride. Thieves were caught on the ends of swords and eviscerated. Blood and screams filled the air, for a moment even eclipsing the grating hiss of metal striking metal. The dead on both sides piled up, rivaling even those heaps that had marked the battlefield in Kan-Pram, and still the thieves' counterattack pressed forward. For the moment, at least, it was unstoppable.

The army of Kan-Puram flowed into the hole the thieves had opened up, bursting through in a single mad torrent—a flood of flesh, blood and destruction. The line of Niphilim women, who had so efficiently cut through the army of Kan-Puram, was itself being shattered.

Isin glanced at the mace clutched in his fist and knew what he had to do.

This was no time for moralizing. In the hours to come, should they be victorious, Isin would have plenty of time to consider the ethics of what had just occurred. But not now.

Fast as he could, Isin made his way toward the breach in the Niphilim ranks. Warriors, their faces and chests coated in gore, rose up before him, but Isin didn't care. His heart was beating and his body tingled. The mace felt almost hot in his hands. Isin felt more virile than he had in a score of years. Death could be waiting for him. If it was, he was happy to go meet it.

All around him, men were smiling and laughing. They had it, too—the ecstasy of blood. Never mind their friends, fathers and brothers, who'd been beaten down, sliced to pieces and trampled under. Never mind the children who'd never again be held by their fathers, or the wives who'd never again snuggle against the chests of their husbands. This was a time for killing.

Ander had awakened something in the army of Kan-Puram. It was no longer a force of men, driven by fear or feelings of duty. This was an army of zealots, worshipping at the altar of blood. Nothing less than total domination would suffice.

The army of Kan-Puram was on the march once more.

CHAPTER 8

Sow Your Seeds in Double Rows—
One to Rot, One to Grow

Adah STOOD NOT TEN STRIDES FROM THE MOUTH OF THE TUNNEL, bandaging the last in what had seemed a nearly endless parade of dirty and oozing wounds. Across from her, sitting against the wall, were the slaves the Niphilim had fought so hard to keep, and which Adah had come to the Black Cavern to set free. She glanced at them as she worked, wondering at the way the vast majority of them stuck to the spots in which the Niphilim had placed them. At her feet, close enough to touch, lay the bodies of the dead. When she was done, Adah wiped her brow with the back of her wrist. Sweat was running down her chest and underarms as well, but she had no adequate way of dealing with that just now.

"Finished," she said.

Uruk examined her work. "How does it feel?"

Jared opened and closed his hand, making sure the tattered canvas she'd used to bind the gouge in his forearm wouldn't bunch or slide off, then pronounced it "good as ever."

"That dressing is already starting to spot," Uruk observed. "It will have to be changed soon."

Jared rolled his eyes.

The battle was long over. Truth be told, the small part of it that Adah had witnessed wasn't much of a battle. By the time she'd reached the Black Cavern, five of the six guards were already dead, and the last was bleeding profusely. It took much longer to sort through the bodies, determining which were dead, which were mortally wounded and in need of a merciful end, and which just required bandaging. Most fights were like that, Jared had explained as she wrapped his bleeding arm. The winner was obvious from the start. "Imagine the two of us fighting with knives," he'd said to her. "Someone would get cut in no time. Now, imagine we're fighting with swords."

It hadn't started out so easy. The Niphilim, despite being outnumbered better than two to one, had them pinned inside the tunnel, with little hope of escape. Adah thought it was her instructions to the prisoners that had turned the tide—the way she'd told them to *kill the Niphilim*. In fact, it was a small group of slaves, just nine men in all—a mere handful of the multitude that sat rigidly against the rear wall of the cavern—who had left their assigned spots and sneaked up behind the guards. They had no weapons, not even loose stones, so they'd grabbed the guards by whatever part of the body they could and held on. The vastly stronger Niphilim were soon able to shake them off. But not before Jared made good his escape, followed closely by Uruk and the dog. The rest went according to plan. Seven of the twenty-two prisoners that they'd brought out of the cell were killed, but that was better than Uruk had expected. The fighting had done the survivors little good, unfortunately. Far from being shocked into consciousness by the experience, the prisoners appeared to have regressed even deeper into the cages of their minds. They looked like a gang of forgotten scarecrows, standing guard over an already harvested field. Adah was beginning to wonder if they'd ever wake up.

"What now?" she asked.

Uruk pointed at the small band of slaves who had attacked the Niphilim from behind. "Do you know those men?" he asked.

Adah looked closer. One pair of slaves hung back, clearly wanting nothing to do with the prisoners, either alive or dead. She recognized both of them. But the rest were a mystery. For some reason, these other men were examining the bodies of the dead prisoners, even wiping the blood and spittle from their faces. What they hoped to find, Adah couldn't guess. Her attention was drawn to one young man, not much older than she was, bent over one of the corpses, tears running down his cheeks. She'd certainly never seen *him* before. "I recognize those two," she said at last, pointing to the pair of slaves she'd looked at first. "That's Tubal. He works in the forge. The man beside him is Irad. A cook."

"What about him?" Uruk gestured at an older man. He had white hair and knuckles swollen by years. Age spots dotted his cheeks and forehead. But his eyes were the cold gray of a predatory bird. He was standing face to face with one of the prisoners, snapping his fingers in front of the man's eyes. Predictably, he got no response.

Adah shook her head. "I have never seen him before."

"We should introduce ourselves," Jared said.

They made their way across the cavern, sidestepping the bodies. The dog was ahead of them, sniffing at a smoke mark on the wall. The whole chamber was riddled with them, each more or less the same. They looked like cat's eyes. Adah guessed that the marks probably predated the Niphilim, who had no time for decorative flourishes as a rule. It must have taken months, if not years, to produce them all. There were even marks on the ceiling. After inspecting the symbol closely, the dog proved unimpressed. He lifted his leg and urinated on the mark, then hurried to join Uruk at the center of the room.

The old man was still working with the same prisoner as they sidled up. He'd left off snapping though. Now he was gently shaking the man's shoulder and whispering in his ear.

"He'll find his way out in time," Adah said.

"I hope you're right."

"Do you know him?"

"We were friends once." The old man smiled at her. He gestured at the slaves who had joined him in fighting the Niphilim, and then at the prisoners from the cell. "These are my people. We are all that's left of Akshur."

"Who are you?" Uruk asked.

"My name is Rahmat, though for as long as I can remember, friends have called me Falcon."

"I'm the King of Thieves," Jared said. "That's Uruk, and this is Adah."

The Falcon gave the dog a friendly pat on the head. He suffered it graciously.

"We need to get the rest of the slaves up and moving," Uruk said, pointing to the men and women that still sat against the rear wall. "There are guards in the main chamber. We may be able to fight through, but we have to hurry."

The Falcon looked at the slaves, then shook his head. "I don't think they'll come."

"Not come?" Jared asked. "But why?"

"They're afraid."

"I can't believe that." Jared pointed at Tubal and Irad. "What about those two?" He elbowed Adah in the shoulder. "You said you knew them."

"They are the only ones that would help us," the Falcon said. "I'm sorry."

Tubal and Irad must have heard them talking, because they chose that moment to join the conversation. Adah gave each a short wave, but neither responded.

"We need to get the rest of the slaves ready to march," Uruk said to them.

"Where's Ander?" Tubal asked.

"Ander?" Adah was surprised to hear that name. "Ander's dead."

"No he's not."

"Of course he is. Ander and Kadim both. . . . Kadim's head is mounted in front of the temple."

"I know nothing of this Kadim," the Falcon interjected. "But the last I saw of Ander, he was running south toward Kan-Puram. Something could have happened to him on the road, I suppose, but—"

"No, he made it to Kan-Puram," Jared assured them. "Never met him myself, but I heard about him. Last I knew he was headed to Ur."

"Ur?" Tubal looked sick, as though someone had just reached down his throat and given his guts a good hard squeeze. "But he promised me he'd come back. I gave him that hammer and he promised." Irad patted his friend on the shoulder.

"Maybe he has," Uruk said.

"What do you mean?" Tubal asked.

"An army is attacking Dagonor even as we speak."

"An army?" the Falcon gasped. "Then we must help them."

"Have to get out of this pit first," Jared reminded him.

"We can fight." The Falcon waved at his men. "We want to fight." Tubal nodded anxiously. Irad didn't look so sure.

"We will fight," Uruk assured them. "But first, we need more men."

The Falcon glared at the slaves. "They won't even try to escape."

No sooner had the words left his mouth than the slaves let out a low murmur. It was the first time any of them had so much as sneezed. Even Adah, who knew each and every one of those faces as well as her own—better in fact—had begun to think of them as a kind of living formation of stone.

Their muttering lasted only a moment before the whole group lapsed back into silence. Uruk looked at Adah. "What did they say?" he asked.

She didn't know. With so many voices speaking together, picking out individual words was exceedingly difficult, to say nothing of whole sentences. Adah glanced at Tubal and Irad. Judging by the looks on their faces, they knew exactly what the slaves had said. Adah was about to ask them, then stopped. "Escape," she said.

Just as before, the slaves began to murmur. This time, Adah didn't need to pick out words to know what they were saying. She did manage to catch one word though. The last in the sentence. *Ereshkigal.* It was the first bit of Niphilim language she'd mastered, all those years ago. It literally meant 'to put an end to.' But in this case it was a threat. Adah looked at the Falcon, then at Tubal and Irad. "*Escape is death,*" she said.

All three nodded. "It's one of the only phrases I know," the Falcon admitted. "But I know it well."

"Escape," Adah said again, shifting back to the common language of the Shinar.

The slaves responded just as before. No mistaking it now.

"*Escape is death.*"

Adah was about to translate for Jared and Uruk, but saw it wouldn't be necessary. Jared had a look of pained disbelief etched over his usually carefree facade. Uruk winced as though struck. They may not have understood the words, but they both understood what the words meant. The slaves wouldn't fight.

"You can go back to your villages," Jared offered. "Back to your lives."

Only a handful of the slaves dared look at him, and they were openly hostile. "*Escape is death,*" they replied again. The Niphilim had trained them well.

"They are not so far from the cell as we had hoped," Uruk muttered. For the first time, Adah thought he looked tired.

"We still have to try," the Falcon urged. "There are only a few of us, but. . . ."

Uruk turned to Irad and Tubal. "Choose weapons." He gestured at the dead guards, swords lying at their sides or still gripped in their lifeless hands. Then he looked at the Falcon. "Take one for yourself," he said. "Give the other three to the men you think can best use them. Not the weakest. Not the men who need them most. The three best."

The Falcon called to his men, telling them to assemble in front of the tunnel. Irad and Tubal followed.

Jared was still fixated on the slaves. "Last chance," he said. When no one responded, he turned on his heel and stomped away. He didn't even bother trying to avoid the bodies this time, but just tromped right through, as though they were nothing more troublesome than a few fallen logs—their blood mere puddles of rain. "Let's get these men lined up and ready," he said, emphasizing the word 'men.' "We should see what the Niphilim are doing anyway."

Reluctantly, Uruk trudged after him, as did the dog.

Before Adah followed, she took one last look at the slaves. They filled her with shame. "I was *free*," she said, more to herself than to them. "I came back for *you*."

She was headed for the passage out when one of the slaves finally spoke. It was only a single word, but it was enough to bring her back.

"Adah?"

The voice was deep and masculine. She searched the faces closest to her, but saw no likely source. "It's me," she said. "It's Adah."

Then she noticed Enoch. He'd been there, she remembered, the night Kadim and Ander tried to escape. His troop had been working the hammers. For some reason, Enoch had been accused of complicity by the Niphilim guards. Adah wondered if the whip marks on his back had healed.

As usual, Enoch was surrounded by the other miners. A hint of smile flickered over his lips. But what really gave him away were the men seated at his elbows. They stared at him with contempt.

"Enoch?" His name felt like a prayer in her mouth.

"What happened to you?" he asked.

Adah ran her fingers through what was left of her hair. She blushed, and the wounds in her face throbbed. "A guard—" she began, then paused. In the past, if a slave had asked her about a bruise or cut, Adah would have said that a guard had beaten her. But that didn't seem right this time. Adah had earned these wounds.

She glanced over her shoulder, hoping that Jared and Uruk were still waiting, and discovered, much to her surprise and delight, that they were standing not two strides behind her. The dog had come back as well. Adah reached down and stroked the soft fur behind his ears.

"Go on," Uruk said. "Tell them."

Adah turned back to the slaves. "I fought him," she said at last.

"You escaped?" Enoch asked.

The slaves repeated their hopeless mantra, but Adah didn't listen. "We killed them," she said.

Enoch stared. The whole chamber was eerily silent. Even the Falcon's men, who had been whispering excitedly throughout the whole exchange, paused to watch. Adah thought she could hear water running in some far off part of the mine.

At last, Enoch climbed to his feet. "I'll go with you," he said.

Adah grinned. It was just one more man, she knew. And they didn't even have a weapon for him. But she still felt as though some wall had been broken down. For the rest of her life, no accomplishment would ever seem so monumental as convincing that one lone miner to stand up.

She waved him forward. "We have no weapon for you," she apologized.

"That's all right," Enoch said. "I know where there are lots of swords."

That broke the silence. Both Uruk and Jared charged forward until they were standing shoulder to shoulder with Adah. "Where?" Uruk demanded.

"It's a long walk, but—"

"We can get them?"

Enoch shook his head. "We can't—but Adah can."

"There are guards all over the main chamber," Jared warned.

"That's all right," Enoch said. "Better actually."

"Where are these swords?" Uruk asked again.

"I'll have to show you," Enoch said. "All we need are a couple of strong men to help us carry them back." He looked at the slaves who'd been sitting to either side of him. Both hung their heads, utterly refusing to respond.

But Enoch didn't give up. "Who'll come?" he shouted.

He didn't have to ask again. Two other miners, Javan and Tiras, climbed to their feet. They were friends of Enoch's, Adah recalled. And like him they worked with the hammers. Enoch had asked for strong men, and these were two of the strongest.

Adah was about to wave the men forward, just as she had Enoch, when something wholly unexpected occurred. Without another word

365 / Slaves of the Shinar

said, a dozen more slaves stood up. And not all were miners. In fact, four of them were women—Adah's friends. Zillah, one of the women she'd liked to do laundry with, waved. Adah grinned and waved back.

Before long, thirty-one slaves had left their seats. Not the whole group. Not even half. But for the first time, Adah began to feel they had a chance. If Enoch was right, and they could find swords for all of these hands, they might actually defeat the Niphilim. Or at least fight their way to freedom, which was the same thing really.

Every time another slave got up, Jared laughed. More than once he elbowed Adah in the ribs and said she'd saved them all.

Even Uruk seemed happy. He grabbed Javan and Tiras out of the growing ranks of volunteers and dragged them over to where Adah and the dog were waiting. "Now," he said to Enoch, "take us to these swords."

"What about me?" Jared asked.

"Take the others back to the crossroads. And make sure the Niphilim stay on their hill until we return."

"How will I do that?"

"Just be sure you do."

"All right," Jared groused. "But there'd better be plenty of swords. I can swing one with each hand, you know . . . and a third with my teeth."

Adah laughed.

They threaded their way across the cavern, passing the Falcon and his men, and were about to plunge into the tunnel when Tiras first noticed the dog. "It's not coming with us, is it?" he asked.

"Always," Uruk said.

CHAPTER 9

Through Fire and Water and Stone

ENOCH LED THEM BACK TO THE CROSSROADS, TURNED RIGHT without pausing, and started up another tunnel. "Careful," he called back. "There's water ahead."

"I found the pool," Adah said, "but could find no way around it." She was right behind Enoch, followed by the dog and Uruk. Javan and Tiras brought up the rear.

"There's no way around," Enoch agreed. "We have to go through."

Uruk was amazed at how smoothly Enoch was able to move through these passages. He had a way of sidestepping at corners and pushing off walls that was almost insect-like. Similar to the way Uruk imagined ants and termites must crawl through their nests. Enoch had only slowed down a handful of times, and always to warn Uruk and Adah of a nasty crack or low-hanging rock. If he'd wanted to, Uruk felt sure, Enoch could have outrun them and disappeared in the darkness.

"Here we are," Enoch said, stopping abruptly.

"I can't see anything," Adah replied.

Enoch held out their torch, illuminating a seemingly endless sheet of still water.

"How far does it go?" Uruk asked.

"Two hundred and twelve steps."

Something splashed in the distance. The water rippled over the stones at their feet.

"What was that?" Adah hissed.

"A fish maybe," Enoch said. "Or an eel. They're all blind. The eels don't even have eyes. They come to the surface whenever there's noise, no doubt hunting for insects that fall into the water. Don't worry, they won't bite."

"Is it a lake?" Uruk asked.

"River, I think."

"You don't know?"

"I've only been about two hundred paces up and down." Enoch swept the torch back and forth. "But there's a second stretch of water on the other side of the main chamber. I think it connects with this one."

"No one has explored it?" Uruk asked. "There could be a way out."

Enoch shook his head. "Slaves only come down here when Antha-Kane gets a craving for eel. They're pretty tasty, but full of bones. I only discovered that you could get out on the other side a few months ago. Touch it. You'll see why."

Uruk bent and stuck his fingers into the river. He gasped. The water was so cold it hurt between his knuckles—as though sewing needles were being passed back and forth between his bones. He'd never dreamed that such cold was possible.

"We have to cross fast," Enoch said. "Stay in too long and you won't be able to feel your legs. After that the cold becomes dangerous."

Uruk nodded.

Enoch was about to step into the water, but Adah grabbed his arm. "How deep is it?" she asked.

"Up to my waist at one spot, but that only lasts a moment." He smiled. "We'll go first. That way you can see how far it is."

Javan and Tiras shuffled past Uruk. From the look in their eyes and the set of their jaws, Uruk guessed they'd been in this river before.

Enoch strode in, followed closely by the other two men. They walked fast, churning the water around their knees to foam. In no time, they were little more than a single point of orange fire surrounded by an uncanny trinity of dark shapes.

"Our turn," Uruk said.

The dog dipped a paw into the water then sat down with a whimper.

"What's wrong with him?" Adah asked.

"He does not like to swim." Uruk picked the dog up by the scruff of the neck and threw him over his shoulder.

"Straight across," Enoch called. His voice echoed off the surrounding rock.

Uruk took a cautious first step, groaning as his foot sunk to the ankle. Two more steps and the water was over his knees.

He walked as fast as he could, his eyes trained on the light from

Enoch's torch. Even though he knew he'd be able to see it all the way across, Uruk didn't dare turn his head, or even blink. The water was so cold. Getting lost, even for an instant, would be intolerable.

Uruk had gone a little more than a hundred paces when he heard Adah step into the river and let out a squeal. "Fast as you can," he called back to her. The water was just an inch or two below his crotch now and still rising.

"Keep coming," Enoch said. Uruk was close enough to see him waving from the opposite bank. "You're almost there."

Uruk redoubled his efforts. The pain in his heels was intense. His toes, no longer able to flex, kept stubbing against the bottom. For the first time in his life, Uruk actually wished he was wearing boots.

Finally, Tiras grabbed him by the elbow and helped him step out onto the far bank. "Better?" he asked.

Uruk grimaced. "I will be."

As soon as Uruk set him down, the dog trotted over to the river's edge and began calmly lapping up the water. His two front paws were submerged in the numbing flow, but the dog didn't seem to have noticed.

Adah was still only about two-thirds of the way across. Just far enough so that they could barely see her, slowly making her way step by agonizing step.

"Faster," Enoch urged. "You'll feel warmer if you pick up your pace."

She responded with a long shuddering moan.

Adah took a few more steps, until the water had risen above her waist, and stopped. Her arms were wrapped around her chest and she was convulsing wildly. She needed to get out of the river fast.

"I'll get her," Javan said. He waded out, picked her up and carried her to shore.

"Put her down over here," Enoch said.

Javan gently lowered her to the floor. Enoch pushed her breeches up until the better part of both thighs was exposed, then took off his tunic and hugged Adah's feet and legs to his chest. Tiras stood over them with the torch.

"How is she?" Uruk asked.

"She'll be fine," Tiras said. "She's smaller, so the cold affects her more."

Adah nodded. Her shivering was already beginning to subside. "I'm fine," she managed, despite viciously chattering teeth. Her lips had turned a deep blue.

"One time, we were down here catching eels and Tiras fell," Javan muttered. "He got so turned around that he couldn't find his way out of the water."

"Nearly killed me," Tiras admitted.

Enoch reached for his tunic. Even in the half-light, Uruk could see that his chest had turned a pale pink. Adah was still shivering, but her lips had regained some of their normal rosy color. Javan helped her to her feet.

"How do you feel?" Uruk asked.

"Better," Adah said. "I'll make it on my own next time."

"You'll have to," Tiras reminded her. "Our hands will be too full to come after you."

Enoch led them away from the water. The passage they followed was wider than the one on the opposite side of the river, but they still went single file.

They'd only gone a short distance when Uruk noticed a large hole punched through the stone on their right. "Is that another tunnel?" he asked.

"Probably," Enoch said. "Most lead to water, or nothing. But a few go on and on. A man could get lost in one and never find his way out."

"How far have you gone?"

"Not far. Most of these are just empty holes, like I said. But there's one—"

"You shouldn't talk about that," Tiras piped in. "Not here."

"Why not?" Adah asked.

"He's afraid of the dead," Javan said. Uruk could hear the smile in his voice.

"Tiras hasn't even seen it, but he still hates the thought," Enoch said.

"The thought of what?" Adah asked.

"There's a passage, not far from here, that leads to a good-sized cavern. Nothing like the main chamber, but—" he shrugged. "This room's full of pillars and the kind of rocks that seem to drip from the ceiling." He made stretching motions with his hands. They reminded Uruk of a baker pulling dough. "Toward the back is a pile of old pots. Hundreds of them. All beautifully made. Perfectly round, with thin sides and delicate handles. And every single one is broken. Some are smashed to pieces. Others have a single hole, no bigger around than my little finger, drilled through the bottom. But behind the pots. . . ." He paused to look around, as though no longer entirely sure of where they were going. Uruk wasn't fooled. He'd heard five thousand stories recounted by ten thousand tellers—from the banks of the Black River, deep in his own jungle, to the dunes of Timbuktu—and every one of them paused just as the tale got most interesting.

"What did you find?" Adah asked.

Enoch looked at her and grinned. "Skeletons."

"Human skeletons?"

"Among others. Dogs. Birds. That sort of thing. But most are human. Some have been there a long time. One is so crusted over with limestone that it's become part of the floor. All that's left to cover are the front teeth."

Uruk grunted derisively. He'd seen such things before, many times, and always considered it a waste. In his experience, the gods cared little for human sacrifice, or sacrifice of any kind. When the gods wanted blood, they took it. And no amount of bribes or bartering would turn them away.

"You shouldn't tell about those things," Tiras hissed. "The Kenanites never meant for those bodies to be found."

Enoch shrugged. "They didn't mean to be wiped out either."

They followed that same tunnel for at least a quarter-hour more, never turning. For some reason, Uruk felt like they were headed back toward the entrance to the mine. He wasn't sure where the feeling came from—all sense of direction had fallen away a thousand turns and a half-dozen hours before. Or was it days? He knew that couldn't be, and yet he felt as though he'd been stuck in that pit of endless, appalling night almost forever. No stars. No sun. Nothing but the strange, uneven puffs of sub-terranean wind to remind you of the wider world. Now that Jared had been set free, Uruk's one hope was to somehow find his way out of these tunnels. Even if he were to die on the side of the mountain, a single step from the mouth of the mine, it would be worth it. Just so long as he got to see open sky again.

Enoch slowed as they approached the end of the passage. A pair of tunnels led to either side, but neither was as large as the one they'd been following.

"Which way?" Uruk asked him.

Enoch glanced down the passage to their left. "There's water down here," he said. "Must be the other way."

"Are you certain?" Uruk asked.

"Fairly. I don't remember passing through any more water."

While they talked, the dog trotted up the tunnel to the left. Uruk heard him splash through the puddle and scramble onto dry rock beyond.

"Where's he going?" Adah asked.

"Let me look," Uruk said.

He held his breath as he made his way into the passage, expecting the water to be cold. But it wasn't. In fact, it was pleasantly warm. Uruk ran his hands along the walls and found them dripping wet. For some reason, water was flowing into this passage from above.

The dog was waiting for him as he clambered out of the pool on the opposite side.

"What is it?" Uruk asked him.

The dog turned and ran further down the tunnel.

Uruk had only followed him a short distance before he began to smell smoke. He splashed back through the pool and found the others waiting. "This way," he said. "Dog has found something."

They trudged up the passage until everyone could smell the smoke.

"This is definitely the way," Enoch affirmed.

Moments later, they made their way around a last corner and were greeted by two spots of flickering light. The dog sat between them, waiting patiently.

"Stop here," Enoch whispered.

The dog trotted back and sat down at Uruk's side.

"What are we doing?" Adah asked.

"The weapons are on the other side of that wall," Enoch explained. "The chamber has a low ceiling. Those holes pull the smoke from their torches out of the room."

Uruk crept to the end of the tunnel and peered through one of the holes. At first, he couldn't see a thing. The smoke coming from the hole wasn't thick, but it was enough to make his eyes water. He had to wipe them repeatedly, and lower his chin all the way to the floor before he was finally able to see. Even then, the view wasn't great.

Tools and bags of flour were stacked on a series of shelves hung along the opposite wall. Cooking utensils and woodworking implements, even an assortment of leather punches and knives, were all piled in heaps. Baskets loaded with thread, scraps of wool, leather and linen were stacked neatly at the top. Uruk even saw a roll of silk. But no weapons. Not even a decent butcher's cleaver.

He lifted his head, hoping to see more, but it was no use. The moment his chin left the stone, his eyes began to water uncontrollably. Eventually he gave up.

"I could see no weapons," he whispered as he crept back to the group.

"They're there," Enoch assured him. "We carried them in ourselves."

"What about guards?" Javan whispered.

"No guards either," Uruk said.

"Most of them are probably in the main chamber," Enoch said. "It isn't far. The rest will probably be leaning against the other side of this wall, where you can't see them. That's the way they usually do."

"I thought you said we could get the swords," Adah whispered.

Enoch shook his head. "I said *you* could. And you can, soon as we figure a way to get rid of the guards and shove you through one of those holes."

"Can I fit?" Adah asked, looking doubtfully at the circles of light.

"I think so," Uruk said. "Though it will be tight."

"But the guards. . . ."

Enoch pointed at Uruk. "I'd hoped he'd be able to do something about them."

Uruk scowled. He wasn't prepared for this. If they'd told him the situation before, he might have devised some special tool, or at least done some serious thinking. Jared might have had ideas as well. After all, he was the more experienced thief.

"I know," Javan whispered. "We can shove the dog through."

"No," Uruk said. Even if they managed to get the dog through the hole without making too much noise, he'd still have to drop all the way to the floor and then single-handedly fight off any number of guards, armed with as many swords as they could lay their hands on. It would be certain death.

"Too bad we don't know how many guards are in there," Adah whispered.

Uruk nodded. It was impossible to devise a plan without some idea of the numbers set against them.

"What if we throw a stone through the hole?" Tiras said. "Then, when the guards start looking around, wondering where the noise came from, we can count them."

Enoch shook his head. "It won't take them long to figure out where the stone came from. Then there'll be no way to get her through safely."

"Unless there's just one guard," Adah said.

"What do you mean?" Uruk asked her.

"Well, if there's more than one I won't be able to go through anyway. They can just stand there waiting. Or go for reinforcements. Either way it's too dangerous. But—"

"How far would they have to go for reinforcements?" Uruk asked, cutting her off.

"Not far," Enoch replied. "That room is just a short dash from the passage out. And there are always guards stationed at that tunnel. Always."

"As I was saying," Adah continued, "if there's just one guard, we can lure him over. Then you," she pointed at Uruk, "can stab him through the smoke-hole."

"It's a good plan," Enoch said. "Certainly worth a try."

Uruk nodded. "A very good plan. And we have no time to think of another anyway. Jared must be ready by now."

"So let's do it," Javan said

"Dog and I will take care of the whole thing," Uruk said. "The rest of you stay back until I say."

"I want to come," Adah said. "It was my plan."

"Fine. But when I wave, you get out of sight."

The three of them crept back down to the holes. Uruk looked through the one on the left again, the larger of the two, but could see nothing different. Adah looked through the hole on the right.

"Ready?" he mouthed.

Adah nodded.

Uruk pulled his sword from its scabbard, careful not to make a sound. Then he put his mouth against the dog's ear. "Bark," he whispered.

The dog looked at him.

He tried again. "Bark. Make noise."

The dog pawed the ground nervously. Finally, he let out a sort of high-pitched moan.

"Yes. More," Uruk whispered, and stroked him behind the ears. The moan turned to a howl, loud enough to reverberate off the surrounding rock.

Someone in the room beyond cried out.

Uruk thrust the point of his sword into the hole. The instant a face appeared, he'd strike, aiming for the eye or throat, or whatever other target might present itself. Thus far, he hadn't seen a thing.

"It's a girl," Adah hissed.

"What?" Her voice was barely audible over the dog's continued howls.

"A girl."

Then Uruk saw her. A Niphilim girl, not much over fifteen, walked across the room directly in front him. Her blonde hair was cut short and spiky.

The girl went to one of the shelves, selected a large wooden box, and turned the contents out on the floor. The box would be just tall enough for her to stand on and look through one of the smoke-holes.

She thinks some animal has gotten lost in the tunnels, Uruk imagined. It was exactly what he'd been hoping for. Uruk ground his teeth. They needed those swords, but he didn't feel right about killing this girl.

"Here she comes." Adah scrambled back from the hole where she'd been looking.

Uruk did the only thing he could think of. He turned his sword around so that he was holding the blade. On the other side of the wall, the girl was just setting the box down with a clatter.

The moment her face appeared, Uruk thrust forward with all the strength in his arm. He aimed for her forehead, just below her hairline, but his sword's hand-guard glanced off the surrounding rock and the pommel struck her between the eyebrows. Instantly, the Niphilim girl crumpled from view.

"Enough, Dog," Uruk said, and patted him on the neck. "No more howling."

"Is she dead?" Adah asked.

Uruk shrugged. "I do not know."

"Can I go through?"

"I think so. Remember, we need extra torches and a roll of heavy cord in addition to the weapons."

Adah nodded, then went to get the others.

Uruk heard her telling them all about the Niphilim girl, but didn't listen. He was busy inspecting the cut on his palm. It started just below his index finger and ran all the way through the heel of his hand. Uruk wiped the blood on the front of his tunic. The dog leaned in and licked his cheek.

"Let's get her through," Enoch said, sidling up behind them.

Uruk lifted his sword out of the hole where he'd dropped it, wiped the blade on his breeches, and slipped it into his scabbard. "Better take off your sword," he said to Adah. "It is sure to get caught."

She untied it from her waist and handed it to him.

"Go feet-first," Enoch said. "Keep your legs together and push with your hands."

Adah did as instructed, managing to squirm into the hole almost to her waist.

"Now put your arms over your head. I'll push you the rest of the way." Enoch placed his hands on her shoulders and began to shove.

"My tunic's riding up," Adah complained. "My chest is getting scratched."

"Is there anything we can do?"

"Hurry."

Enoch gave her another hard shove. Soon, only her head was visible.

"I think I can make it now," Adah said. It took a few more seconds of hard wriggling, but she was finally able to squeeze the rest of the way through. Uruk listened as she dropped to the floor on the other side.

"Are you hurt?" he asked.

"Do you see the swords?" Enoch called. "They should be stacked on shelves to your left."

"I see them."

"Start handing them through."

"Wait." Uruk moved to the other hole. He could see Adah, an armload of weapons already cradled against her chest. "Look at the girl," he said. "Is she alive?"

Adah nodded. "Just unconscious. I can see her breathing."

"Good. Watch her. If she moves—"

"Don't worry. If she so much as takes a deep breath, I'll kill her."

CHAPTER 10

Greater Love Hath No Man

SOMEHOW ANDER HAD LOST TRACK OF WHERE HE WAS. THERE WAS a hill in front of him, and a Niphilim drummer standing atop it, but he didn't know whether he was still facing north or had somehow got turned around. A Niphilim man lost his footing in the mud and Ander cut a gouge in his neck large enough to pass a hand through.

Another shape rose up on his side and he lashed out, hooking it in the belly with the point of his sword. As the man's guts spilled over the mud, Ander saw that he'd mistakenly killed one of his own men. He wasn't sorry. Other than as an extra sword-arm, the man's existence bore no meaning for Ander. He had killed black-heads before, some on purpose and some by accident, and would gladly kill a hundred more if it would get him one step closer to Dagonor. Before he died, Ander wanted to set eyes upon that temple one last time.

He wanted to see it burn.

Adah tapped her foot in mock impatience. Icy water dripped from the cuffs of her breeches and ran down her ankles, which were pimpled with cold.

"Gods-damned twine," Jared cursed. He tugged and twisted, trying to work his fingers into the knot. It didn't work. Uruk had made these bundles himself. Unless they were untied properly, the cord would continue to cinch ever tighter—a fact Jared had only just discovered. "Whoever bound these accursed faggots wanted them to last 'til the creator himself—" At last he found the correct loop and pulled. Swords skittered across the floor.

Adah gathered up as many as she could comfortably carry and hurried off. Uruk watched as she made her way through the crossroads, handing a sword to each slave she passed. One of the women hesitated to take the offered blade, but Adah pressed it on her. Most of the slaves were overjoyed with their weapons. They practiced swinging and thrusting as though born soldiers. Uruk was amazed at how quickly they'd changed.

He was still watching them, and wondering if their newfound courage could survive an encounter with the Niphilim, when Javan strode over and began to gather up the swords Adah had left behind. Only two bundles remained. Uruk bent and untied the closest one.

"We will not have enough for everyone," he whispered.

"I know." Jared glanced at the tunnel to the main chamber. They'd sent Tiras to find the Falcon nearly a quarter-hour before, but he still hadn't returned.

"What else needs doing?" Uruk asked.

"We still have to deliver torches to the men from Akshur, and the rest of the slaves need to be separated into groups, but—"

"Split them up?"

Jared nodded.

"Why?"

"Falcon has a plan."

"What plan?"

Jared grinned. "According to one of the miners, there are two routes to the top of that hill." He paused as Enoch crossed toward them and began picking up the swords Uruk had just untied. Pitifully few remained.

"Enoch, do you know anything about another path over the hill?" Uruk asked.

He considered for a moment. "There's an old trail," he said at last. "It goes up and across the ridge. We haven't used it for maybe three years."

"That's the one," Jared said.

"But you don't want to go that way," Enoch said. "The path up is steep, and there are loose stones everywhere. Besides, it won't take us around the guards. The trail ends at the top of the hill, same as the new one."

"All part of the plan," Jared said.

"Maybe you could tell us more about this plan," Uruk suggested. "Before the Falcon arrives."

Jared thought it over, then nodded. "Adah should hear this too. We're sure to need her help." He frowned. "I just hope I can make her see reason."

"You think she might refuse?" Uruk asked.

"She should. A girl her age ought to know the evil of old men when she hears it."

The Falcon guided Adah into the tunnel. "It's not far," he said. She must have looked nervous, because he patted her on the shoulder. "Don't worry."

"I just want this to be over," Adah grumbled. Her voice echoed down the corridor.

"Do you know which group you'll be in?"

"The third."

"Enoch's?"

Adah shook her head. "We're short one miner, so the dog's leading a group. It'll just be Uruk and me, and one or two others. Uruk figures he can sniff his way along."

"You're comfortable with that?"

Adah shrugged. "Uruk is, and I trust him."

The Falcon didn't respond. Adah was glad of that. She was nervous enough already. Things had been decided. Dwelling on the potential dangers wouldn't help anyone.

"We'll be right behind Enoch," Adah explained. "That way the dog will know at least one person from the group ahead. Someone whose scent he recognizes."

"Sounds well considered."

Adah nodded. "Uruk thinks of everything."

It took a full quarter-hour to reach the main chamber. Adah was in no hurry and the Falcon didn't rush her. He was a hard man not to like.

The first thing she noticed as they stepped out of the tunnel was the sheer magnitude of the cavern. After being so long in a maze of tunnels and small rooms, where walls and roof seemed perpetually close enough to touch, the main chamber felt like open air. On the hilltop, the Niphilim torches looked like the lights of a small city.

"So many," Adah whispered.

"Forty-two," the Falcon replied. "Though my count could be off."

Adah didn't say it, but she guessed that the Falcon was seldom 'off.' There was something in his eyes, or the set of his jaw. He didn't seem like the kind of man who was accustomed to making idle guesses.

At the moment, his attention was centered on a group of men slowly marching from one side of the path to the other, not even a dozen strides away. All four were from Akshur, Adah saw. One waved.

"What are they doing?" she asked.

"Those are our sentries," the Falcon replied, and waved back.

Adah wasn't sure she understood that, but nodded anyway.

The prisoners from the cell, whom she'd been brought to see, were lined up along the wall to their left. They looked as ragged and skinny as ever. Their bandages, which she'd so carefully tied into place only an hour or two before, were now grubby. A few were so soaked with blood that they'd begun to seep and run.

"Why aren't their torches lit?" Adah asked. Each prisoner had been issued a pair of torches, which they gripped with an almost savage intensity.

"They will be," the Falcon assured her.

"When?"

"As soon as you're all gone."

Adah looked at the prisoners again. Suddenly, she was struck with a realization. Each man was carrying two torches. Two. One for each hand.

"They don't have swords," she said.

The Falcon shook his head sorrowfully. "There weren't enough."

"But they should have been armed first." Adah felt her voice rising beyond what was safe or reasonable, but couldn't help it. "These men will have to fight." She gestured at the tunnel. "Most of *them* will probably steal away without so much as a scratch."

"We knew that," the Falcon agreed. "But we also knew there'd be more fighting outside—fighting that matters at least as much as this."

Adah started to argue, but there was little she could say. Jared had already explained the situation to her in detail. Their plan was a good one—even Adah had to admit that. The Falcon would somehow goad the Niphilim down off the hill, while the rest of them went around via the other path. It gave the vast majority of them at least a possibility of reaching the exit. No matter what they did, a certain number of slaves were bound to die. Hard as it was, Adah had already made peace with that fact. She just couldn't help thinking that everyone should have an equal chance. An equal chance to live and an equal chance to die. Maybe that was foolish, but it was how she felt.

"What do you want me to do?" she asked.

The Falcon looked at her. For the first time, Adah understood how he'd come to be called 'Falcon.' His eyes focused on hers with an intensity unlike any she'd ever encountered. She couldn't help shivering.

"Help me," he said, and gestured at the prisoners. "Help me with them."

"I'll try." Adah searched her mind, hoping to find something profound lurking in the recesses of her memory. But it was no use. Adah didn't have that kind of wisdom. "Do whatever he tells you," she commanded, first in the Niphilim language and then in the common tongue of the Shinar. "The Falcon is a good man. He's your leader from now on." Adah felt a tear roll down her cheek, but quickly wiped it away.

"Is that enough?" she asked.

"I don't know," the Falcon replied. "Is it?"

Adah thought for a moment. "One more thing," she said. "No one has to stay. Do you all understand that? Anyone who wants to leave—I'll stay in your place." She paused. But as usual, the prisoners were wholly unresponsive. "I just wish one of you would say something."

One of the prisoners cleared his throat. For an instant, Adah thought it might have been the Falcon. But he looked just as surprised as she was.

"Who was that?" Adah demanded.

"I. . . ." one of the men whispered. His voice cracked and died, but that one syllable had been hideously clear.

Adah grabbed him by the wrist. "Go on," she urged. "Do you want to leave?"

He shook his head. "A sword," he croaked.

Adah untied the sword from around her waist. Her fingers shook so that she could barely work the knot. "Draw it when the Falcon tells you," she instructed, fastening it low and snug around his hips. "And use it bravely."

But the prisoner had already lapsed back into silence. His eyes rolled up until not even a sliver of brown could be seen.

"What's your name?" Adah asked. But whatever spark of life had flashed through the darkness of his mind was gone.

"I didn't save them," she muttered.

"Neither did I," the Falcon said.

Adah looked at him. The Falcon's eyes were the same cold gray they'd always been—only now, instead of a hard glare, Adah saw grief. His eyes twinkled with all the tears a man could never shed.

"It's almost time," he said.

The first of the small groups had just emerged from the tunnel. Tiras was in the lead, followed by Jared. Both waved as they filed around a pile of jagged rocks and disappeared in the darkness.

"Go with them," Adah said. "Take my place."

The Falcon smiled. "No. I should have been buried two battles ago—but this hole will serve."

"What about them?" Adah gestured at his men, still shuffling back and forth as though searching for something amid the rubble to either side of the path.

"I've begged them to leave," the Falcon whispered. "I'd have gotten on my knees and wept, but I'm afraid it would have done little more than strengthen their resolve. They're fools of the worst sort—too stubborn to leave an old man to his destiny—and I'm tired of trying to convince them. Each man must make his own decisions—that way he can go to his grave satisfied."

As he spoke, a second group began filing out of the tunnel. Enoch was at the front. He glanced over at them but didn't wave. In a moment, he too had disappeared into the ever-present black.

"It's not fair," Adah whispered. "You don't deserve this."

"No one *deserves* anything. We play with the tiles the gods have dealt us, that's all. Whenever possible, we can try to be good neighbors and friends—good fathers and mothers. Of all things, these are the most important. And as for fairness—" The Falcon chuckled. "Nothing in this world is fair. Too much is beyond our control. And so long as it is, words like 'fair' and 'deserve' will have no place. You waste your breath by saying them. Instead, set your mind on goodness. There are only one or two occasions in most lifetimes when what's good shows itself with absolute clarity, begging us to take action. Watch for those times. Don't let them get by you."

He'd only just finished speaking when the dog came nosing his way out of the tunnel, followed closely by Uruk, Tubal and Zillah. They stopped and Uruk waved at Adah to hurry.

"I always thought I'd be a good mother," Adah whispered. It wasn't what she'd intended to say, or how she'd meant to say it, but the Falcon seemed pleased.

"You shall be the mother of kings," he said. Then he turned away.

Adah ran to her place in the line, directly behind Uruk.

"Hold on to this," he whispered, and pressed a length of cord into her hand.

"What is it?"

"The only thing that will keep us following Dog, so hold tight."

And then they were off. Adah couldn't see where they were going, or what might await them, but she could hear the dog snuffling over the rock floor, and feel him tugging at the loop of cord fastened around his neck.

In no time, they'd reached the base of a steep incline and began slowly inching their way up. A single wrong step and any one of them might have gone tumbling to the bottom. Still, Adah couldn't resist a quick glance over her shoulder at the men they were leaving behind. At that distance they were little more than blurry shapes, vaguely outlined by the dusky red light from their torches. The prisoners weren't even that. Only the Falcon was distinct. His silver hair glowed like the morning star in an ocean of night.

The ramp was rapidly coming to an end. Very soon, it would make a sharp left turn and begin its descent into the mountain. Where the trail would lead after that, Lamech couldn't even guess. It would be dark though. Of that he was certain.

The guards had made it amply clear, through a series of hand gestures and beatings, that the new prisoners were to keep their eyes focused on the man in front of them, and nothing else. But Lamech couldn't help stealing a final look at the Withered Hills. After days of forced marches—first under Ander, and then under Barley—through an endless string of valleys laced with nettles and over ridges where nothing but dandy-willow could grow, Lamech knew he shouldn't think them beautiful, but he did. The rain had turned the hills a rich brown that Lamech had rarely, if ever, seen. Even in the spring, when the farmers were tilling their fields, preparing them for seed, Kan-Puram never looked like this. Never even close.

But it wasn't just the beauty that kept him staring out over the mounds, arrayed at their feet like so much wool waiting to be carted. Lamech had another reason. He was looking for the rest of their men.

Before marching them away, the Niphilim had split their tiny army into two groups. The first, the one Lamech had been stuck in, was smaller. He hadn't been able to count, but Lamech guessed that there might be as many as thirty-five of them lined up single file. Barley was at the front.

Of the second, larger group, there had as yet been no sign.

Lamech was still peering over the edge of the ramp when something struck him across the shoulder. For a moment, he couldn't think what it might be. If felt like lighting, or a hot bronze spike driven through the meat of his upper arm. Lamech squealed as it struck again and again, the last time swiping across his cheek and neck.

By the time it was over, the skin on his upper back felt scorched. Barley had been whippen at least five times—most recently for trying to get a peek into the old satchel the Niphilim had discovered lying amid the rocks at the base of the mountain—but he hadn't screamed once. Lamech couldn't even imagine the self-control that must have required.

He was still thinking about Barley as they passed through the natural stone arch that marked the start of the mine, and Lamech found himself blinking into a pit of what he imagined must be total darkness. It wasn't of course. The truly dark places, deep at the heart of the mountain, were yet to come.

Lamech's eyes were so unused to the dim that he failed to notice the Niphilim soldiers, three of them, huddled together just inside the mine, looks of horror etched over their usually smug faces. Nor did he observe the body that had been covered—all but its booted feet—with a strip of dusty canvas. The only thing Lamech saw was a deep black hole, like the throat of some mythical leviathan, waiting to swallow them up.

CHAPTER 11

The Watches of the Night

"STOP." URUK GAVE THE CORD A SHARP TUG AND THE DOG SAT DOWN.

They waited, not daring but to breathe. Finally, Adah heard a succession of dull clicks. "Sounds like pitch in a fire," she said.

"No," Uruk said. "Not quite."

"Where's it coming from?" Tubal's breath puffed against Adah's ear.

"The Falcon," Uruk replied.

"What do you think they're doing?" Adah asked.

"Hard to say. The simplest things are usually the best."

They listened a moment longer.

"Sounds like they're throwing rocks," Zillah said.

"Maybe," Uruk said. "If so, their battle is about to begin."

Adah's chest constricted. Her heart rose into her throat. "But we're not ready," she said. "What should we do?"

Uruk gave the cord a shake. "Take us the rest of the way, Dog."

"Stay out of the light." Jared motioned for Adah to come around to the other side of the hilltop. "Keep that path open." He grabbed Tubal by the front of the tunic and propelled him after her.

The torch marking the crest of the hill still burned, casting a warm glow over the lazy half-circle of slaves milling to one side of it. No one seemed entirely sure of what to do next. Just getting here had seemed so improbable a chore.

Enoch stood at the edge of the light, absentmindedly fiddling with a length of cord. Down the hill behind him, Adah saw a second torch, and beyond that, well below where they were standing, a third. These were the first in a long chain of points marking the trail out.

"No guards?" Uruk asked.

"We arrived just in time to see them march down the hill," Jared said. "They left behind a nasty looking boy with a patchy beard."

"Just the one?"

Jared nodded. "I thought I'd have to kill him. But he only hung back a moment, then left." He gestured down the path toward the surface. "Probably reporting to the others."

"Probably," Uruk agreed. He patted his thigh and the dog trotted toward him.

While Uruk untied the cord from the dog's neck, Adah took a look around.

The Niphilim were nearing the base of the hill, perilously close to the Falcon's men. All torches were lit now, Adah was glad to see, though the prisoners holding them were spread far apart, leaving large areas swaddled in darkness. From a distance, Adah might have thought them a real army. She wondered what the Niphilim would make of their strange formation—whether they'd assume that there were more combatants hiding in the shadows, or guess that the rebelling slaves were trying to exaggerate their numbers. Either was fine, she thought. So long as they paid no attention to what was happening on the hill behind them.

Thus far, the Niphilim had done little more than make a few half-hearted feints. Trying to draw the Falcon into an attack, Adah guessed. Every so often, a voice would echo off the surrounding rock, but what was being said, or even whether they were speaking in the Niphilim language or the common tongue of the Shinar, Adah couldn't tell. More rocks were being launched at the attacking guards as well. She could hear the unmistakable crack as they struck the stone floor. She couldn't tell whether any of the rocks were actually striking their intended targets, but doubted it. After all, the Falcon wasn't trying to enrage the Niphilim, just distract them.

"We can sheak down behind them and attack, just as soon as the others arrive," Jared whispered.

"That is not our plan," Uruk said. The dog, newly loosed from his bonds, lay on the floor at Uruk's feet, scratching his neck with his hind foot.

Jared started to answer, but Adah cut him off. "Look," she said.

Suddenly, the Niphilim surged through the darkness. Torches flew from either side. Screams filled the chamber.

The Falcon's men closed ranks, but not quickly enough. Those at front were overrun or forced back. Many disappeared entirely as their torches were snuffed out, or fell to the ground and left to gutter in the dust.

In a matter of seconds, Adah was unable to determine where the Niphilim ranks ended and the Falcon's began. All that was left was a mass of flaming specks, racing across the darkness like a late summer wildfire flying before the wind.

"To hell with our plan," Jared announced, and reached for his sword.

"It is already too late," Uruk said.

"What? Why?"

"Look." The combatants from both sides were rapidly funneling into a line and disappearing. "The Falcon is leading them into the tunnels. Nothing we do can save them. They are already gone."

"We have to try," Jared growled.

"No. We have to move the battle outside. The rest of this cavern should be more or less unguarded. If we attack now, the Niphilim will realize that they were outflanked and turn back, probably before the last of our people can get here."

Jared slammed the point of his sword into the rock at his feet. "And I'm supposed to do nothing?"

"You, Dog, and I will guard this spot until the last group comes—"

"I'm staying with you," Adah said.

"Not this time."

"But—"

"You have to lead them out." He nodded at the slaves. Judging by the looks on their faces, Adah knew that flight was the wiser choice—at least for now. "It will not be difficult," Uruk continued. "We will send each group after you as soon as it appears."

"How will we get past the—"

"You will know what to do when the time comes. Just keep moving."

"He's right," Jared admitted. "Get going." He pointed down the hill, toward where the Niphilim were lining up to storm the tunnels. "They won't be gone forever. Soon as they discover what we've done they'll be back—looking for blood."

Adah considered arguing, but could see no point. "I'll do my best," she muttered. She reached for her dagger. The bronze blade shone red in the torchlight. "Show us the way, Enoch."

He didn't have to be asked twice. "Stay close together," Enoch commanded. Like Adah, he held up his sword as though it were a beacon. The other slaves fell in line behind him.

Adah was just about to join Enoch at the front when Uruk grabbed her shoulder. "Be safe," he whispered. His lips brushed the short hair on the side of her head. Then he gave her a gentle push and she was gone.

"Give the signal to fall back," Kishar shouted.

Over the last few hours, the battlefield had undergone a number of changes. That sense of ordered madness—of men and women united to destroy a common enemy—had been replaced by a stinking pit of bodies, filth and brutality. Kishar could no longer even tell who was winning.

"What happened?" He had to scream to be heard over the drums.

Kamran shrugged. "Lagassar's troops had all but split the field. The black-heads were cut in two. Then suddenly. . . ." He grimaced. "A small band counterattacked. Our women on the eastern flank fell apart."

"Fell apart?" Kishar was stunned. "How does a full squad of our best fighters fall apart?"

Kamran shook his head.

Kishar surveyed the soldiers he had left, still lined up in the ravine. Instead of pushing to get at the enemy, they were slowly retreating. Their sneers had been wiped out, replaced by a heavy dose of rain, mud and consternation. Once again, just as at the battle for Kan-Puram, their captain was asking them to fall back—and they hated it. Kishar loved them for that.

Very soon, he would go to join them. Kishar would stand shoulder to shoulder with his troops, spilling black-head blood. Simha had long considered him a weak fighter. Kishar always found ways to exceed her expectations, but could never seem to change her opinion of him. Now she was dead and Kishar was captain. He gripped the handle of her sword, now his, and hoped that Dagon would let her see his victory.

"How far will we let them go?" Kamran asked.

"There's another small meadow, about three-quarters of the way back. If we can get the black-heads into this ravine," Kishar waved at the valley below, "we should be able to compress them down to a more manageable size." He licked his lips. "We, on the other hand, can spread out. When they try to break into the open, we'll slaughter them."

"I know the meadow you're talking about," Kamran said. "It's only a stone's throw from Dagonor."

"Don't worry, I've considered this possibility from the outset. By the time they get near the temple, we'll have them whittled down to nothing." Kishar smiled. "It takes time to cut down a whole forest, but it can be done."

"We have another problem," Kamran said. "Antha-Kane must have heard the change in the drums. He'll want to know why."

Kishar felt the blood rush from his face. "I'll send a messenger."

"Don't send anyone too valuable—or too proud. None of the women."

"I'll send one of the older men," Kishar said. "But first I have to move Halaf. The drummers won't be safe for much longer."

"Just don't wait too long. Antha-Kane will be waiting."

Barley let out a deep, racking cough. Lamech, who'd been placed at his immediate left, felt him shudder as he fought to bring up whatever fluid had collected in his lungs. The effort left him gasping for breath. "Damn," he wheezed, and spat on the rock floor. There was blood in his spittle.

The Niphilim were standing just a few long strides away. But if they'd heard Barley's muttering, they didn't show it. In fact, after checking the bindings on their wrists and forcing them to their knees with a swift kick to the back of the legs, the Niphilim had paid little if any attention to their new prisoners.

They'd been kneeling for the better part of a half-hour, long enough for Lamech's legs to first tingle and then go numb, when another guard suddenly appeared out of the darkness.

He said something to the other Niphilim, then pointed back the way he'd come.

Whatever he said, the other guards were taking it very seriously.

"Something's wrong," Barley whispered. His words were barely recognizable. As a boy, Lamech and his friends had often teased a neighbor girl who'd been born spastic, and whose words, when they came out at all, sounded a lot like Barley did now. They'd thrown rocks at the girl and threatened to make her eat goat droppings, but mostly they just called her names. Idiot, frog-face, whore-child, and the like. That went on for weeks. Until one day, Lamech's father caught them. He whipped each of the boys. And then, after sending the others home, he'd marched Lamech to the girl's door and forced him to apologize. Lamech would never forget that little girl, naked and hiding behind her mother's legs. She'd had a black eye and her bottom lip was split open. Lamech explained that he'd had nothing to do with her wounds, but his father wouldn't listen. "You shame me by passing blame," he'd growled. The girl tried to say something, but the words wouldn't come. Finally, she'd just given up. Tears of frustration rolled down her cheeks. The sight of them burned into Lamech's soul.

"Look at the torches," Barley said.

Lamech didn't want to respond, but could see no way around it. If he ignored him, Barley was likely to go on talking. Eventually, the Niphilim were sure to notice. Lamech turned his head just enough to see the torches, mounted around the passage through which they'd been marched. He could see nothing unusual about them and shook his head, hoping that would satisfy Barley and keep him silent.

"No," Barley hissed. "Out there. In the mine."

Lamech looked past the Niphilim soldiers, into the darkness beyond. He'd first noticed the tiny pricks of light just after they'd been forced to their knees. They appeared to mark a path. Lamech had seen that done before. After planting, farmers set up torches marking the roads into the city. They didn't want wagons hauled over their seedlings.

He was still staring at the darkness, and thinking about the coming seasons, when Lamech noticed a strange flicker pass through one of the torches. It was as though something had crossed in front of it.

Lamech looked at Barley, eyes wide in amazement.

Barley grinned. One of his teeth was cracked, and the top of his head was netted with tiny lacerations, but he looked happy.

"Something's happening," he whispered.

CHAPTER 12

Cracks of Dawn

"HOW MANY ARE LEFT?" URUK ASKED. THE MOST RECENT GROUP of slaves had only just disappeared over the hill, but he was already feeling anxious.

Jared counted on his fingers. "Just one."

Uruk nodded. He gave the dog a quick pat on the head.

"Think Adah made it out yet?" Jared asked.

"She should have." At the moment, Uruk was more concerned about the Niphilim. They'd been gone a long time. Too long. The only explanation he could think of was that they'd split up and were searching the tunnels. He smiled as he imagined them wading across that bone-chilling river.

"You're always so quiet," Jared said. "At first, I thought you were just nervous. That was back at The Horn. You remember."

"I speak," Uruk said.

"But you never talk—no boasts, no stories. You didn't even tell me you were going after Kilimon—though I guessed it when I saw you sneak out."

"I keep to myself," Uruk agreed.

Jared waited for him to continue. He didn't. "See? This is exactly what I'm talking about. After all we've been through together, you've still got nothing to say. It's mighty peculiar, if I'm any judge."

"I suppose."

"Suppose no longer. It's peculiar." Jared paused a moment. "I think of you as a friend—a damned good one—and I don't know the first thing about you."

Uruk frowned. Jared's use of that term, 'friend,' brought him up short. Despite all his best efforts, Uruk had somehow managed to collect a whole band of devoted companions. "Friends," he muttered, and shook his head.

"That's right," Jared said. "I consider you my friend. No one else came to rescue me."

"You know why I came," Uruk said.

"I know. The dog and the window. But let's not say it again. I'd rather think you couldn't live without me."

"What do you want to know?" Uruk asked.

Jared thought for a moment. "Where are you from?"

"My land has no name."

"Somewhere south east of the Coastal Cities though, right? Don't look so surprised. You're not the first black-skinned man I've come across."

Uruk smiled.

"So why'd you leave?"

"Foolishness," Uruk said. "Boyish vanity."

"I'll bet a woman was involved." Jared's teeth shone orange in the torchlight.

"Two—if you can call Mana a woman."

"Mana." Jared rolled the word off his tongue. "A fine name. Makes me feel strong to say it . . . Like the old blood's still pumping."

"Mana," Uruk repeated.

"Women." Jared smacked his lips. "They do create problems for a young man, don't they?"

Uruk shrugged. He didn't know what Jared had in mind exactly, nor did he want to guess. His own thoughts were of Numa. He remembered the way she used to lean against him, the muscles in her back melding perfectly with his chest.

"I wouldn't have made it out of there," Jared said.

Uruk looked at him.

"Out of that cell, I mean." Jared shook his head. "I tried to escape. Twice. I would have tried again, but they tossed me in that hole. I'd have died in there."

"You seem fine now."

"I'm trying." He smiled. "I don't know about you, but I'll be glad to get out of all this dark. Endless night makes me feel old."

"Not night," Uruk corrected him. "There are no stars."

Jared started to respond, but instead pointed down the hill. "Trouble," he whispered. The Niphilim torches had begun reemerging from the darkness.

"Where is that last group?"

The Niphilim fanned out, forming a line of defense around the passage to the surface. They had to hurry. The sounds of running feet echoed off ceiling and walls, growing in intensity with every passing second.

"What is that?" Lamech asked.

Barley's good eye squinted to little more than a dark slit. "Help me up," he whispered.

"What?"

Barley responded by shoving against him. It was so forceful and sudden that Lamech nearly toppled over. But it worked. A moment later, Barley was standing.

"What are you doing?" Lamech expected one of the guards to come racing, but none did. Their attention was focused on the approaching footsteps.

"Come on. Get up," Barley said.

In the years to come, whenever his children asked him how he'd found the courage to climb to his feet, arms bound behind him, Lamech usually said something like "I must have been crazy." The truth was, not another man in all the Shinar could have convinced him to do it. Not his father or his priest. Not even Moloch himself. No one. There was just something in that fat old farmer—the way his belly heaved up and down as he breathed, and his whole forehead wrinkled when he smiled—that brought out the best and bravest in all who knew him.

Quick as he was able, Lamech scrambled to his feet. His legs felt wooden, and he came close to falling, but so long as Barley wanted him standing, Lamech wouldn't give in. With more time, Barley probably would have gone down the line, getting as many men up as he could. But just as Lamech gained his feet, the runners hit.

The battle, such as it was, could have gone either way. The attackers fought passionately, and they outnumbered the guards at least two to one. But the Niphilim were trained soldiers, with experience and discipline. Their defense was simply too good.

Lamech watched the fighting for a moment, then turned toward Barley. He was surprised to see him inching past the other men in their group, headed toward the tunnel out. Lamech hurried after him.

They were halfway to the passage, and might easily have slipped through, when suddenly, Barley lowered his shoulders and, like a goat ramming a fence post, charged.

Lamech watched in stunned amazement as the crown of Barley's head slammed into the back of a Niphilim warrior, lifting and driving him forward. The guard screamed as he plunged onto the swords of the attacking slaves.

For an instant, the whole battle stopped. Both sides paused to consider the blond warrior, now slumped facedown on the stone floor. No one seemed to understand what had just occurred—least of all the other Niphilim.

The only one who didn't stop fighting was Barley himself. Somehow, he'd managed to avoid falling, and while everyone else was staring at the downed guard, he pressed his attack. In one fluid motion, he turned and slammed his forehead into the jaw of the man on his right. The sound was like a hammer driving a stake into a clay floor.

Lamech didn't wait a moment longer. He lowered his head, just as Barley had done, and ran. Unfortunately, his aim wasn't as good. He managed little more than a glancing blow before tripping over his own feet and falling onto his chest.

But the damage was already done. The slaves exploited the hole Barley had created, separating the Niphilim and driving them against the wall. By the time Lamech flopped onto his side and sucked the air back into his lungs, the battle was over.

The guards were dead. All that remained was a ragged bunch of dirty men and women, with shaggy black hair and identical canvas tunics and breeches.

Lamech watched in astonishment as a young boy—his face full of dirt, cuts and bruises, but without a single whisker—took control.

"Make sure the Niphilim are dead," he commanded. His voice was strangely shrill. "Then cut these others free. They can take swords from the corpses."

He'd only just finished giving orders when another half-dozen tattered human shapes came wandering out of the darkness.

The boy looked the new-arrivals up and down, then gave them the same instructions he'd given the others. "And let's get this done fast," he said. "I want to see the sun."

"Don't leave us!" It was a woman's voice. She sounded close. "Please wait!"

"We won't leave you!" Jared called. Then he looked at Uruk. "What are the guards doing?"

"Coming," Uruk acknowledged.

The Niphilim torches were streaming up the hill. They'd reach the top in, at most, a quarter-hour. Fortunately, it was the slaves who arrived first.

Their leader was a buck-toothed miner with bizarrely close-set eyes. Behind him, struggling to carry a second, unconscious man, were four women. Two of them lifted the injured man's knees, while the other two supported his shoulders. All but the leader were smeared with blood.

"What happened?" Jared asked.

"He slipped," the buck-toothed man replied. "Back on the slope. I wanted to leave him, but they wouldn't do it."

"We couldn't," one of the women said. The others nodded in agreement.

"We have no time for this," Uruk grumbled. "You six, get moving." He pointed down the path to the surface. "Jared, put out the torches as you go—"

"I won't let you stay alone," Jared said.

"I am not staying." Uruk bent and lifted the injured man to his shoulder.

"You can't carry him all that way," Jared said. "And without light?"

Uruk turned and started down the hill, headed for the surface. The dog trotted ahead of him.

They were well into the switchbacks by the time the slaves ran past. Uruk tried to keep up, but the extra weight slowed him down. In no time, they had outdistanced him entirely.

Jared caught him a moment later. "They're right behind you," he said.

"Put out the torches, that will slow them down." Uruk was already starting to breathe hard. Talking was no help.

"It'll hold you up, too."

"Dog is with me. We will make it."

"But if they catch you—"

"This is the best chance for everyone."

All at once, Jared stopped. Uruk wondered if something had happened, and was about to look back when he heard a loud chop. Then he saw a torch fly end over end off the path.

Jared dashed by him a moment later. "I'll look for you at the surface," he said.

Uruk reached the next torch just before Jared cut the leather straps binding it to the stake and flung it away. He was only about three-quarters of the way to the one after that, and by the fourth he was only a quarter. A short time later, Uruk saw a torch go flying and discovered that he was in total darkness. Fortunately, he was already near the bottom of the hill. If memory served, he just needed to get past a pair of boulders, and then it was a long straight shot to the other end of the cavern.

"Dog," he called. "Where are you?"

The dog barked, ahead and to his left.

Uruk stumbled toward the sound. "Show me the way out," he said.

Jared reached the base of the ramp and started across the field. His normally gray hair and beard had turned brown—the dust from the mine mixing with the rain to form mud. The bandage on his forearm had partially unraveled, leaving it to flop miserably against his wrist. Watching him approach, Adah was reminded of the hill-savages the old men of her village used to describe—waiting for naughty children who roamed too far from their mothers.

"They're getting close," Jared said. He pointed at his ears.

Adah nodded. The Niphilim war-drums sounded like they were just over the nearest hill. She could even hear metal clashing together. But neither of those facts interested her at the moment. "Where's Uruk?" she asked.

"Carrying a wounded man. I raced ahead to douse the torches."

"How's he going to find his way out?"

"Dog's with him. I heard barking as I started up that last passage. Don't worry, they'll make it."

"What are we supposed to do 'til then?"

Jared looked past her, at the tiny force amassed in front of the temple. Adah could guess what he was thinking. These were the unlikeliest of warriors—messy, unkempt, malnourished and wet to the bone. "What are we doing now?" he asked.

"I sent the men without swords to the storehouse. There may be an axe handle or meat skewer or. . . ." Adah shrugged.

"And them?" A handful of women were pushing mud into a pair of shallow holes, using their swords as shovels.

"Burying the remains of some escaped slaves," Adah said.

Just then, Barley strode over to where Adah and Jared were standing. A boy not much older than Adah came with him. "We must attack," he said. "Now."

"Who's this?" Jared asked Adah. He stared at the scar running over Barley's face, and at his bulging off-yellow eye.

"A farmer from Kan-Puram," Adah said. From the moment they'd come out of the mine, Barley had been telling her what to do, demanding that she abandon Uruk and go to war against the entire Niphilim army. "He and his men were captured earlier," Adah continued. "They were being held at the edge of the main chamber, right in front of the passage out."

"I wondered what'd happened," Jared said. He looked Barley over again, then frowned. "But he's right. We need to call our troops together."

"Without Uruk?"

"We can't wait any longer. Don't worry, he'll find us."

Adah looked up the ramp, but there was still no sign of him. She hung her head.

Zillah, one of Adah's closest friends, was among the first to assemble. "Do we all get to fight?" she asked. The rain running off her hair, and dripping off the end of her nose, looked a little bit like tears.

Jared put an arm around Adah's shoulders. "I've learned a thing or two about the strength of women," he said. "Let no one say this old man can't learn to suck eggs."

Zillah grinned.

"Keep going," Uruk shouted.

The dog barked and Uruk corrected his path accordingly. His feet were sore and his back ached. The man he was carrying grew heavier with every step. Uruk needed to stop, to catch his breath, and would have if not for the guard at his heels. So far there was only one of them, but that was enough.

The guard would have caught Uruk already, if not for the torch Jared had left burning. When he first saw it, Uruk was annoyed. 'Jared thinks I can't find the tunnel,' he'd thought. But as the footsteps of his pursuer began to close in, Uruk learned to love that tiny twinkle of light. The dog's barking still helped immeasurably, but it was the torch that guided him now.

Uruk looked over his shoulder. The guard was right behind him, close enough for Uruk to discern the length of his nose by the light from his torch. Worse yet, a second guard had appeared. He was well behind the first, still no more than a speck of light in the darkness, but not out of range. If Uruk tripped, or was otherwise made to slow down, they'd catch him.

In a fair fight, Uruk felt certain he could kill the lead guard, or at least immobilize him. But he'd have to put down the man he was carrying, and that would give the second guard time to catch up. Uruk could probably fight him too, if forced, but eventually the whole garrison would be upon him. He couldn't very well fight them all.

Uruk knew what he had to do. Turn and strike. His one chance was to wound his pursuer and run on. Not even put down the man he was carrying. Quick and simple.

He took a deep breath to settle his nerves, then spun around, whipping his sword from its scabbard. The guard was close enough for Uruk to see the beads of sweat on his cheeks. Unfortunately, he saw Uruk too, and remained safely out of reach.

Uruk waved his sword, hoping to goad the guard into attacking. It didn't work. This man knew his job. He didn't have to kill Uruk, just slow him down enough for the rest of his squad to catch up.

The second guard was closing in now as well. Uruk ground his teeth in frustration. He'd have to fight. "Dog," he called, and felt a furry body rub past his legs. He was about to drop the wounded man, when suddenly the guard came under attack.

It was a savage. Stripes of white fur ran over her head and chest. She leapt onto the guard, teeth sinking into his cheek, fingers clawing the soft flesh of his neck. One leg wrapped around his waist while the other hooked his ankle. The guard screamed and tried to get away, but managed only to send them both cart-wheeling off the path.

Uruk didn't wait to see what happened next. He turned and ran, yelling at the dog to find the exit.

They reached the end of the cavern, and Uruk saw why Jared had left a torch burning. Getting to the passage in the dark would have been no easy trick. Doing it without tripping over a corpse may have been impossible.

"Do you smell Adah?" he asked.

The dog sniffed his way to the tunnel, paying no particular attention to the bodies.

That was all the assurance Uruk needed. He might have missed Adah in all that carnage, but he knew the dog wouldn't. Uruk cut the last torch down with a single hack of his sword.

As they made their way up the passage, Uruk thought about the savage. She'd saved him, he knew. Whether she'd done it to repay him for loosening her bonds, he couldn't guess. But he hoped that was it. So long as he was collecting friends, he may as well add a savage to the list.

Uruk was still pondering this most unusual turn of events when he felt the wall fall away from his right elbow. He made a sharp turn and saw, at the far end of the tunnel, a bleary gray half-circle of rain-streaked sky.

It was the finest bit of weather he'd ever seen.

Book V
A DOG'S LIFE

Let no more be said of me than this—That I had a friend, whom I loved with all my heart. And when he succumbed at last, and had gone out of this world forever, and I saw then that I too should one day perish, it was the hope of a reunion with him, more even than a reunion with god, that sweetened my passage toward death.

—King Aggaseir I

CHAPTER 1

The Hunt

*U*RUK KICKED THE CROSSBAR OUT OF ITS SLIDES AND SHOVED THE door open with his hip. Just like the rest of Dagonor, the slave barracks was deserted.

An almost supernatural stench blasted into him as he stood in the doorway, surveying the long empty room beyond. The odor of dirty bodies, sickness and decay, was so strong that Uruk had to open his mouth to breathe.

"I will just set him down," Uruk said to the dog, referring to the injured man. "Then we can go after the others."

Normally, that kind of putrid filth would have warned him away. Uruk's nose was unusually sensitive for a human, and he was well aware of the link between refuse and disease. No amount of gold would have been worth subjecting himself to such an unlivable environment. But these were no normal circumstances. Uruk was desperate to get away from Dagonor. When he'd finally emerged from the mine and discovered that his friends were gone, he came as close to weeping as ever he had. After years of fleeing from happiness, Uruk wanted to join, to be a part of something. He wanted to stand beside true friends—to believe in something bigger and nobler than his own destiny.

There were five small pallets arrayed in a circle around a support beam at the center of the barracks. Uruk's feet would have stuck off the end of the largest, and he couldn't have turned over without rolling off, but he thought the injured man would probably be more comfortable on a small pallet than on the floor.

Very gently, Uruk lifted the wounded man from his shoulder and laid him down. After taking a moment to stretch, Uruk looked around for something he could use to prop up the man's head. He grabbed a handful of greasy rags from a pile in the corner and began tying them into a makeshift pillow. As he worked, Uruk thought about Adah. He wondered where she usually slept—if she'd had a spot, or just curled up anywhere there was room. He imagined the slaves, lying on every available inch of floor, pressed against each other, sweating through the night.

When he was done tying the rags together, Uruk slipped them under the injured man's head. As he did, the man's eyes popped open.

For a moment, Uruk thought he'd woken up. "You should be safe here," he began, then stopped. The man's eyes were too flat. His gaze lacked focus. Uruk waved a hand over his face and got no reaction. He leaned over and put his ear against the man's lips. No breath.

Uruk shook his head miserably. He knew he should be sorry for the man's death, but he couldn't help wondering when it had happened. If he'd known, he'd have left the body in the cavern. Over the years, Uruk had passed by innumerable tribes and villages that took great pains over their dead—anointing the corpses, or going through elaborate ceremonies for cremating or burying them. Uruk wouldn't waste his time. Dead bodies were like sticks of wood or old clothes, he thought. They should be burned or buried as quickly and easily as possible. The gods would care for the dead. Let the living care for the living. Even after spending so much time struggling to save Numa, Uruk had done little more than make sure that she was wearing her best mask when they laid her on the pyre. He'd loved *her*, not her corpse.

"We need to get going," Uruk said, striding back toward the door. He was anxious. Every passing second made finding Adah and Jared less likely. He wasn't sure if he could stand coming all this way just to see a friend reduced to rotting flesh.

But the dog wasn't waiting for him at the door. Nor was he sitting outside, or hunting for mice in the field. The dog was nowhere to be seen.

"Dog?" Uruk called. He listened for a bark, but heard only the boom of the war drums and the pitter of rain. "Dog!"

Tracks ran south, past the forge. Uruk couldn't imagine why the dog would have gone that way, but it made little difference. Adah would have to wait. He just prayed that it wouldn't be long.

As he left the shelter of the slave barracks, Uruk saw something moving on the mountain, not far from the top of the ramp. The first guards had finally emerged. More would be close behind. Uruk didn't know whether they'd chase after the fleeing slaves or stay at their post. They could even split up and do both. Adah might have been willing to hazard a guess, but Uruk couldn't ask her until after he'd located the dog. 'Typical,' he thought. 'Nothing comes easy.'

Antha-Kane heard the door to the captain's quarters creak open. He'd only just finished stuffing the broken and mutilated body of the messenger Kishar had sent him into the tiny room where he normally kept his bucket. If this was yet another old soldier, come to explain to him the changing cadence of the war-drums, Antha-Kane would find a place for him as well.

On cat feet he slipped through the hazy half-light of his inner sanctum, passing into the hallway that led to the outside world. A smell, not unlike roasting flesh, wafted under the door. Something was cooking in the captain's chamber.

He grabbed the latch, and was about to turn it when he heard a clattering in the room beyond. Quietly as he was able, Antha-Kane pulled open the door.

There was a beast in the captain's quarters. It must have smelled Kishar's maps, drying in front of the fire, and come to investigate. The animal had overturned the rack on which the maps had been so carefully hung, and dragged the largest of them under the table. There it lay, gnawing the parchment into bits.

Antha-Kane's hands shook. He had not been through this door in years. But he wanted that animal. He had to have it.

Carefully, he slid from the shadows. His fingers stretched toward the beast's tail.

Isin looked around him. He could no longer distinguish friend from enemy. The ordered lines of the battlefield, so crisp and even when they'd begun, all those lifetimes ago, were now gone, leaving nothing but a mass of hacking, chopping figures, all of them wet and covered in mud. The faces of the survivors were blood-smeared, as were the faces of the dismemebered, and the dead. Isin lifted his mace, bringing it down on the outstretched arm of what looked to be a woman, feeling it break bone. His stomach lurched as the mouth of his victim opened wide, and out of it spilled the lowest-pitch howl of pain and outrage Isin had ever heard. Then a sword caught the man under the chin, all but severing his head from his shoulders, and down he went, sinking into the morass.

* * *

A black-head, mortally wounded and slipping beneath the mud, reached toward Ander. His mouth was working, but no words came out. Ander planted his foot on the man's back and leapt into a knot of Niphilim women beyond. The domed top of Dagon's temple was just visible over the next hill.

Barley bulled his way into the rear of the Niphilim rank-and-file, scattering them like so much straw. He had a sword, taken from one of the dead guards in the mine, but it never even occurred to him to use it. Barley ripped through as many blond soldiers as he could reach, kicking, biting, and choking them to death with his bare hands. It wasn't enough to kill them. Barley wanted to feel the life go out of their bodies

A blade whistled past Jared's face. The woman who wielded it had intended to catch him in the neck, but Jared sidestepped and the sword waved harmlessly by.

His attacker was not so quick. She tried to get away, but Jared slid the point of his sword between her ribs. It wasn't a deep wound, but it would do. The woman collapsed at Jared's feet, coughing up blood.

Kishar sprang upon the nearest black-head. He was older than most, and remarkably awkward. As Kishar raised his sword, the man held up a mace, trying desperately to ward off the blow. Kishar ran his blade down the shaft, sheering the man's fingers off at the root. The black-head toppled backward, his hand clutched to his chest. Kishar peered down at him for a moment, and then raced on. His eyes scanned the battlefield for prey.

Adah hid beneath the body of a Niphilim soldier. She'd lost her dagger the first time she tried to use it, leaving her weaponless on the field. At first she'd tried to run. But everywhere she looked, soldiers from both armies were hacking away at everything that moved. Nowhere was safe. So, in desperation, she played dead. It wasn't easy. The weight of the corpse threatened to sink her beneath the morass. Adah had to kick out with her legs at least half-a-dozen times just to keep her nose and mouth above the mud. Booted feet splashed all around her. Adah prayed for darkness.

Uruk slipped through the temple door.

The room he entered was a surprise. It had none of the magical clutter that usually characterized such places. No decorations. Nothing that appeared particularly useful for communicating with or showing fealty to the gods. It seemed to him more like the back room of a merchant's shop than a place of worship. Of course, most of the temple could be very different, Uruk reasoned. He glanced at the closed door leading to the heart of the sanctuary. The crack at the base was dark.

The dog's muddy prints ran around the table, right to the edge of the fire. Uruk looked at the wooden rack, lying on its side in front of the hearth, even touching the tip of one of the maps and feeling it crinkle between his fingers. He bent close and sniffed, understanding at last what had attracted the dog. They'd gone too long without food. The smell of those hide, drying in front of the fire, was just too good to pass up.

Uruk looked under the table and saw the remains of a map, partially chewed and surrounded by more pawprints. Then he noticed the marks where the dog had been dragged away—like spears thrusting at the door to the inner sanctum.

He crossed to it and silently lifted the latch. The door only swung back a few inches before striking something. Uruk pushed, but the door wouldn't budge. It was wedged from behind.

Thus far, Uruk had been able to avoid making noise. No longer. The dog was on the other side of that door and Uruk's time and patience were running short. He reared back and kicked, sending both the door and whatever lay behind it crashing inwards.

The hallway beyond was dark, and had a strong smell of urine. A bit of dim light emanated from the opposite end, but very little could be seen in the interim. Uruk had only gone a half-dozen or so steps when his foot sunk into a pool of warm liquid. He set his jaw and went on.

At the end of the hall he found a wooden bucket lined with clay. The same warm fluid was trickling out of it. 'A chamber pot,' Uruk recognized. It had been set behind the door so that he'd be unable to enter quietly. 'No matter,' he thought. 'I can always clean my feet.' Still, he was disgusted by the idea of someone willfully contaminating his own space, to say nothing of the house of his god. By the time Uruk was old enough to talk, he'd known to relieve himself well away from the camp. The idea of doing it indoors always struck him to the core.

Two passages split from the end of the hall. The one on his left was utterly dark. The one to his right was dimly lit by a series of cracks cut through the wall, allowing a few gossamer strands of natural light to filter in.

Uruk followed the corridor to the right. He had no particular reason to think the dog was that way, but the light seemed a good sign.

He hadn't gone far when the passage came to an abrupt end, emptying on a large, stuffy chamber. It was lit much as the hallway he'd been following, with dozens of tiny cracks cut between the stones in the walls, creating a mottled series of shimmering streaks on the floor. But Uruk barely noticed the room.

The dog was lying on his belly against the far wall. Blood ran from his nostrils. His front paws clawed at the floor while his back feet hung limp.

And he wasn't alone. Crouched over him, his back to Uruk, was a man. He wore a long woolen robe, so that only his head and hands were visible. He was gross, both in size and complexion. His skin was the color of ivory and, from what little Uruk could see, utterly hairless. The fingers of one hand combed through the soft fur on the dog's neck. The other was spread across the top of his own head, steadily kneading his scalp. To Uruk, it looked like a pale, bloated spider trying to sink its fangs through the shell of an egg. 'Antha-Kane,' Uruk thought, remembering the name from one of his conversations with Adah.

As he made his way across the room, Uruk noticed that Antha-Kane was muttering to himself in a low voice. At first, though it seemed familiar, Uruk didn't recognize the language. It wasn't Niphilim, nor the common tongue of the Shinar. It was too full of long vowels to be either. But it was something he'd heard before. Uruk was sure of that. Finally, he heard a word he knew—*olo'koudon.* Shock ran through him like serpent venom. Antha-Kane was speaking a dialect from the mountains southeast of the headwaters of the Nile. Uruk could only speak a few words, but he was sure that was it.

He was only a few strides away when Antha-Kane suddenly went quiet.

Uruk stopped. He knew better than to get too close. "Dog?" he said.

The dog's eyes rolled forward and he let out a short yelp. His forepaws began to scrape with ever more urgency.

"I will get you out of here," Uruk promised.

"No." Antha-Kane shook his head. "It goes nowhere." He stood up straight, his arms and legs seeming to unfold and stretch like bat wings. Even compared to Uruk he was tall. As he turned around, Uruk couldn't help lifting his sword defensively.

Antha-Kane had neither eyebrows nor eyelashes, nor any sign of a beard, but Uruk barely noticed. He couldn't look at anything but his eyes. They were the same sick white as his skin. No irises. Not a single speck of color. Just two pallid orbs pierced with a dot of ebony.

Uruk wondered if Antha-Kane could be blind. But as he stepped forward, raising his sword and pointing it at Antha-Kane's face, there could be no doubt. Those eyes, strange as they were, tracked his every movement.

"The beast goes nowhere," Antha-Kane said again. He crossed his arms. His hands disappeared up his sleeves.

"I will not leave without him," Uruk said.

Antha-Kane smiled, displaying two rows of perfect white teeth. Not even his tongue was red. "You will not leave."

Uruk had no illusions about his opponent's speed or strength. The mere act of breathing, his chest slowly pulsing in and out, told Uruk what kind of body was hidden beneath those robes. Nor did he think he could threaten Antha-Kane. But he wouldn't back down either.

"Why have you come?" Antha-Kane asked. He spoke in the language of the Aegyps.

Even knowing that language as well as he did, it took a moment for Uruk to process what he was hearing. "For him," he replied. He used the common tongue of the Shinar. Uruk had already decided that he'd speak nothing else.

"Is it really such a valuable creature?" Antha-Kane looked down at the dog. "It seems . . . inconsequential." He smiled. "It was easy enough to catch." His hand flashed out, as though snatching an insect from the air. "Easy."

Uruk said nothing.

"I have long wondered whether animals have a language," Antha-

Kane continued, still using the tongue of the Aegyps. "I have decided that they don't. Once, I had a savage tied up in these very rooms. I wanted to learn the system of grunts and gestures they use to communicate. I failed." He grimaced. "The savage would not respond to me. Torture was useless, as was kindness. Every skill I had mastered, from a whole lifetime of study . . . all a waste." He shrugged. "That's how I knew that the savages could not be truly dominated. Enslaving them would not further the glory of Dagon. So they were rounded up and used . . . as I saw fit."

"Why?"

Antha-Kane shifted into the common language of the Shinar. "It is the god's will that we free the earth from its ignorance . . . embrace it with truth." His voice was hard. "I learn the language of the heathen, using it to understand the infidel mind and develop a plan of conquest . . . and my *teacher* learns the language of the god. The trade is painful but necessary. We are all slaves to Dagon after all. . . . Whether we know it or not." He smiled. "Just as this creature is a slave to you."

Uruk shook his head. "I do not own the dog."

Antha-Kane's eyes widened. "Strange," he mused. "You should be its master. Its lord. You might have compelled it as Dagon does the earth." He rubbed his chin thoughtfully. "I wonder if you are a man at all," he said at last, looking Uruk up and down. "Were you created in the image of god?" He spoke again before Uruk could respond. "No. I can see that you are a man . . . though clearly of a lesser shade."

Uruk took a step forward, the point of his sword trained on Antha-Kane's chest. He wasn't in striking distance yet, but soon would be.

"Dagon told me you would come," Antha-Kane said. He didn't appear to have noticed Uruk inching toward him, or the weapon leveled at his heart. "When I heard this beast moving through my outer chamber, defiling the house of god, I knew you'd be close behind." As he spoke, he reached into his robe and pulled out a bronze dagger. It was strikingly similar to the one Uruk had given Adah. "I thought the god had sent you to teach me a new language. But something tells me that you would die before you'd submit. . . . So be it. You shall stand as a symbol of that other world, soon to fall away." He licked his lips. "Do not fear. Your death will be remembered. Dagon has foreseen it."

"Destiny," Uruk said. His voice was little more than a whisper.

Antha-Kane nodded.

Uruk shook his head. "No. I am taking the dog. We will escape your destinies, or Mana's, or anyone else's."

Antha-Kane laughed. "Escape is death."

Uruk attacked, swinging his sword as hard as he could. He hoped Antha-Kane would try to deflect the blow with his dagger. Uruk had little doubt that the bronze blade would be sheared in two.

But Antha-Kane didn't raise his dagger. Instead, he caught Uruk's wrist in one hand, as quickly and easily as a child might catch a ball. No effort. No struggle. With a squeeze of his powerful fingers, he snapped the bones in Uruk's arm, forcing his hand open and letting his sword clatter to the floor. Then, with a smile, Antha-Kane shoved his dagger into Uruk's stomach.

Uruk gasped as the blade sunk to the hilt. It wasn't the pain—at most, the dagger felt like a cold blast of wind waking him from a deep sleep— he just couldn't seem to get any air.

"So the world falls before the might of Dagon," Antha-Kane said.

Uruk collapsed to his knees. He could feel his heart racing, pumping blood to the injured tissue, speeding up his death. His eyes were already filming over. Soon he'd slump to the floor, probably onto his face, and let out his last breath.

"Dog," Uruk coughed.

Antha-Kane looked down at him. "Still concerned about your little beast?" He crossed the floor in a handful of strides, grabbed the dog by the scruff of his neck and flung him toward Uruk. The dog landed just out of Uruk's reach, his head bouncing once and then coming to rest on his paws. Normally, it would have taken Uruk less than a second to cover that distance. Now, he wasn't sure he could get there at all, even if he crawled.

"Dog?" Uruk wheezed again.

The dog's eyes slowly peeled open. They focused on him one last time, then closed. A tremor ran the length of his body.

When his eyelids parted again a moment later, Antha-Kane grinned. "Empty," he said. "You see? They did not roll forward this time." He shoved the dog with his foot. "I believe the beast has finally died."

While Antha-Kane studied the dog, Uruk carefully placed both hands on the dagger. Just touching it took his breath away. It took every bit of strength he had not to moan in agony.

"He is dead?" Uruk asked. Tears rolled down his cheeks.

"Very." Antha-Kane leaned over and put a hand against the dog's nose. "No breath." His eyes were focused entirely on the dog. So much so that he didn't notice Uruk struggling over the handle of the dagger, or the blade beginning to slide free. "I suppose you'd like to touch him. . . ." Antha-Kane said. He ran his fingers through the fur on the dog's back. "Though I can't see why."

A wave of blood poured out of Uruk's stomach, splashing on the floor. Antha-Kane turned toward him, but it was already too late. Uruk lunged and drove the dagger into his side, just above the hip.

Antha-Kane roared. He reached for the dagger, but could only get one hand on it. His eyes squeezed shut. He seemed to want to say something, but couldn't. With a single thrust, all of his languages—a whole life of collecting—were wiped clean. Only gibberish remained. Not even his own tongue was left to him.

Uruk had intended to drive the blade into his back or chest, but it made very little difference. Antha-Kane was mortally wounded. He threw up violently, then staggered toward the passage out. Uruk, lying on his belly at the center of the chamber, watched him go. He wondered how far he would get.

When Antha-Kane was gone, Uruk reached toward the dog. He shook his head, trying to fight off the swirls of black that swam before his eyes, but the darkness wouldn't go away. With the tips of his fingers, he brushed the whiskers on the dog's snout. Then he took a deep breath and. . . .

Uruk ran.

He recognized the grass. There were no hills. No valleys. Just grass. All of it the same—the color of dust.

'I'm going the wrong way,' he thought. He turned around, and there was the stream he'd seen so many times before. The fish were still swimming by, just under the surface. Trees and vines rose from the opposite bank as thick as hair.

Uruk crossed his arms and waited. Moments later, the jungle parted and the woman stepped out.

She was as beautiful as ever. Clean, smooth, radiant. Naked as the sun. Just as she had every other time, the woman set her spear down on the sand and bent to drink from the river, lapping up the water with her tongue. The points of her teeth glittered in the starlight.

When she'd finished, she stood up and looked at him.

"I can't get across," Uruk said.

She winked.

"Do you have a boat?"

The woman motioned him forward.

"It's too cold," Uruk said. "I can't. . . ."

She laughed, picked up her spear and playfully thrust it at him.

Uruk dipped the toes of one foot into the water. It was burning cold, but for some reason the temperature didn't bother him. He put his whole foot into the stream, and it felt as though a fire deep inside his flesh suddenly went out. His whole leg felt better. More alive.

When he was half way across, Uruk cupped a handful of water and carefully raised it to his lips. As he swallowed, he realized that he'd never in his whole life felt quite right. He was always too hot or sweaty. His muscles hurt. His stomach was upset. Something. But one sip of that water made it all go away.

Uruk stepped onto the opposite shore and took a deep breath. The smells of the jungle filled him with life.

"I've been waiting," the woman said.

Uruk looked her up and down. "You're naked," he replied, then grinned. That wasn't what he'd wanted to say.

She smiled. "Would I be improved by clothes?"

Uruk shook his head vigorously. "Should I take mine off?"

"Would you be better without them?"

Not sure what to make of that question, Uruk decided just to take off his tunic. He slipped it over his head and flung it in the stream. It quickly sank out of sight and was gone, as though it had never been.

"Better?" the woman asked.

Uruk nodded. For some reason, he very much desired to take off his breeches as well, but decided not to. "Who are you?" he asked.

The woman giggled. Her laugh was so perfectly good. So girlish. Uruk had never known an adult to make such a wonderful sound.

"How did I get here?" he asked.

"It was your destiny."

Uruk sighed.

412 / J U S T I N A L L E N

"Not every person has a destiny," she continued. "Most exist as mere obstacles to be overcome."

"I wish my destiny had been different," Uruk said.

"You have seen more of the world than anyone alive."

"I would've liked to know more of my fellow men . . . and women."

She giggled again. "That was not chosen for you."

"I should have listened to Numa. She told me to accept my fate."

"That was not chosen for you either."

Uruk stared at her. "What now?" he asked.

"What would you choose?"

Uruk took a moment to consider. "A hunt," he said at last. "You and I together."

"What shall we hunt?" She put a hand on his shoulder. Her touch was almost too much to bear. "One of the great lizards of old? Behemoth . . . or maybe leviathan itself?"

Uruk shook his head. "No. I can think of only one animal."

"Which?"

"The lion."

She smiled. "Prepare yourself," she said. "For the three of us shall hunt the lion over every land through which he roams."

"Three?" Uruk asked.

"You could not leave your best friend behind?"

Uruk frowned. "My best friend?"

She pointed.

The dog came racing over the plains. He leapt into the stream without pausing, drinking it up as he swam.

Uruk jumped on the dog and together they went rolling through the sand, laughing and barking and clawing at each other joyously.

The woman leaned over them. "The hunt," she said.

Both man and dog rolled to their feet. "And after?" Uruk asked. "What then?"

With the point of her spear she gestured at the stars.

Uruk nodded. He could just make out the shape of Numa's face outlined in the tiny points of light.

CHAPTER 2

He Who Wills the Means

T HE MORNING SUN ROSE OVER THE EASTERN HILLS, PAINTING SKY and earth in rich hues of purple and gold.

Ander sat on a campstool at the top of a short rise, looking over the remnants of the battlefield. To his right lay a crude table, its legs broken and scattered through the mud. At his feet was a pair of Niphilim boots.

"What are you doing up here?" Isin asked, still huffing and puffing from the climb. His left forearm was bandaged and bound to his chest. Isin had lost all four fingers on his left hand and most of his thumb. Jared thought that by elevating and immobilizing the wound, they could stop the bleeding. The technique proved sound—though Isin's strength had yet to return.

"Watching the dead," Ander replied.

Isin tried to follow his gaze, but could see nothing special about this spot. Bodies were lined up all the way to Dagonor. There were plenty of dead and dying to be seen without making a special trek.

"Look at that one," Ander said. "Almost looks alive, doesn't she?"

"Her chest is split open."

"But look at her eyes."

Isin turned away. He didn't need to see eyes like that ever again. Over the last few hours he'd had more than his fill. And it wasn't just eyes. There were smiling mouths, and mouths frozen in screams. Dead hands gripping swords. Men and women with hair blowing in the breeze, so that at a distance their heads seemed to nod in satisfaction.

"Where did you get the boots?" Isin asked.

Ander pointed at the valley.

"From a body?" Judging by the size, Isin guessed that they'd belonged to a Niphilim woman. "What for?"

"I may need them. Who knows what conditions prevail over the northern mountains?" Ander picked up one of the boots and ran his fingers over the leather. "According to the Niphilim, there are places where the clouds turn cold and fall from the sky."

"And cover the ground?" Isin scoffed. "I've heard those tales. Pure nonsense."

Ander shrugged. He pulled the boot onto his foot.

"You should come back to Kan-Puram," Isin said.

"No."

"You'd be a hero."

Ander shook his head.

"People would write songs."

"Look at those bodies," Ander said. "They all belong to someone."

"It was worth it, though," Isin said. "Wasn't it?"

"Maybe." Ander reached for the other boot. "But not to them. Not to a lot of people."

"What will you do?"

"There are tracks leading into the savage lands. At least twenty-five Niphilim got away. My guess is that they'll head west until they reach the Ibex River, then turn north."

"But we've won."

"I haven't won. I'm winning, but I haven't won."

Isin looked at his own feet—at the brown skin peeking out from between the leather bindings of his sandals. He wasn't sure what to say.

"I'll be gone by midnight," Ander said. He stood up, glanced at the Niphilim woman lying at the base of the hill one last time, and started toward Dagonor.

"Wait," Isin said.

Ander stopped.

"I almost forgot. We've found no sign of the treasure." He paused, but Ander didn't respond. "The slaves don't know where it is. Most claim there isn't one."

"So?"

"Where should we look?"

"Try the mine," Ander said. "On the other side of the underground river. I once saw a pair of Niphilim men carrying a box that way."

"The thieves have looked. They say the tunnels are endless."

Ander shrugged.

"They're right, aren't they? There's no treasure."

"Keep looking." Ander smiled. "Look forever if the treasure's so important. Who knows what you might find?" He paused. "But when you've finished, do me a favor."

"What?"

"Seal it off."

"The mine? Why?"

"Nothing good ever came out of that mountain."

Lamech opened his eyes and saw a stand of dandy-willow, just coming into bloom. The small white buds were only partially formed, and surrounded by gray leaves. He blinked, and when his eyes opened again the plant was gone.

He was moving—Lamech realized that now—being dragged over some pretty rough ground. Pebbles tumbled beneath his shoulders and hips. He blinked once more and saw a corpse, slumped facedown in the mud, glide past on his right.

Lamech rolled his head back, trying to get a look at who or what was dragging him, but only managed to see a pair of hands, knuckles turned white with effort.

The next thing he knew, the sun had gone down and his journey was over. Stars flamed across the sky.

"Who . . . ?" he croaked.

The only response was the crackling of a fire somewhere close by.

"Anyone. . . ." he whispered. "Barley?"

"Quiet," someone answered.

Lamech groaned. "Water. . . ."

"Can you sit up?"

"I think so." Lamech struggled to get his elbows under him. Waves of pain surged from a spot on the back of his skull.

"Don't be stupid. Let me help you."

An arm slid under his shoulders, lifting him onto what felt like someone's thigh. Lamech was surprised to see the boy from the mine. His face was as bruised as ever.

"Drink this," the boy said.

Lamech sucked water from a wood bowl at his lips. When he'd had enough, the boy lifted Lamech by the shoulders again, removed his thigh and gently lowered him to the ground.

"My head's killing me," Lamech whined.

"Go to sleep."

Lamech turned his head, hoping to find a more comfortable position. He tried to roll over but couldn't. "Is there food?" he asked.

"No."

"Nothing?"

Lamech heard shuffling, and then the boy was leaning over him again. "Here." He handed Lamech a piece of bread no bigger than his index finger. "Chew it well. If you throw up, you'll sleep in it."

"Where's Barley?" Lamech asked, still chewing. The last thing he remembered clearly was coming around a bend in the ravine and seeing the Niphilim army. Barley was in the lead, as usual. Lamech tried to keep up, but quickly fell behind. His memories grew strange after that. He vaguely recalled seeing a man with a sword standing over him, rain dripping from his golden hair. But that might have been a dream.

"He's asleep," the boy said. "You'll see him tomorrow."

"But he's alive?"

"And ugly as ever."

Lamech thought for a moment. "Why aren't we in one of the buildings?"

"What buildings? Your army burned them up—along with almost everything else. All that's left is the temple. It wouldn't burn, and was too hard to pull down. But I won't go in there."

Lamech shut his eyes for a moment, hoping the pain in his head would go away. His stomach felt queasy, but he didn't dare say anything. He was fairly sure he wouldn't throw up. "Where are the others?"

The boy bent over him again—almost nose to nose. His eyes were pink, Lamech saw, as though he'd been crying. "Be quiet," the boy hissed. Spit rained off his lips, landing on Lamech's nose and mouth. "Nearly everyone died. And of the few that lived, most are severely injured. Lost arms and legs, belly wounds. A lot of good people have died screaming, and even more won't make it through the night. Still others are burning with disease." He grabbed Lamech by the ears and squeezed. "There are men and women here with bigger problems than a little bump on the head. So keep quiet."

Lamech flinched. He thought the boy was about to strike him, and brought his hands up to protect his face. As he did, his fingers brushed what felt like a woman's breast. It was round, firm and terrifying.

"You're a girl?" he squeaked.

She shook her head. "I just wish the Niphilim were as stupid as you." A tear rolled down her cheek, but she quickly wiped it away. Her lips pursed as she fought to stop crying.

"What's your name?" Lamech asked her.

"Adah." She sat down next to him and took a deep breath. Her hands shook as she crossed her arms.

She was worn out, Lamech guessed. Probably hadn't slept in days. "Do they have rashes on their chests?" he asked.

Adah squinted down at him. "Who?"

"The ones with the disease."

She nodded.

"Some of my friends died of it," Lamech said.

"You think that makes you special?"

"I just meant that—"

"Well don't. Don't say anything."

Lamech closed his eyes. He hoped to sleep, but doubted he would. The pain in his skull wasn't easily ignored. "Thanks for finding me," he whispered.

"It was luck," Adah said. "You coughed as I walked by, and no one else wanted to bother. They figured you were dead anyway."

"Well . . . thanks."

"Tomorrow I'll help you get up to the mine with the others."

"I think I'd rather stay out here."

Adah laughed. "Me too."

"Can you carry this?" Adah handed Lamech a large bundle, tied at both ends.

Lamech took off his pack and undid the top. "What is it?"

"Meat. Wrapped in bread."

"Together?" Lamech turned up his nose. "Why ruin both?"

"Uruk taught me," Adah said. "You'll like it. I promise."

While Lamech secured the food in his pack, Adah pawed through the rest of their gear. There was a pile of metal cookware, some iron spits, and a whole box of wood dishes. Over the last three days, Lamech had argued almost non-stop for her to leave it all behind. She'd agreed—for the most part. The one thing she insisted on bringing was an enormous water-skin. It was only about three-quarters full, but incredibly heavy. Lamech intended to drink the water as fast as she'd let him. The Tiger River was not that far away, and the weight was sure to slow them down.

"What are you looking for now?" Lamech asked. He watched as Adah shuffled through a stack of old hides. "I thought we agreed—"

"Found it." Adah held up a sword. It was the finest Lamech had ever seen. The blade was little more than half as thick as the one he'd lost—the handle simple but elegant. Adah fastened it around her waist. "Uruk's," she said.

"I thought it was buried with him."

"That's what we told everyone. But Uruk wouldn't have wanted that. He wasn't sentimental. To him it was just a tool. Burying it would have been a waste."

"Are we ready now?"

"You're sure you feel well enough?"

Lamech looked at the temple. The walls were covered over with the bodies of Niphilim soldiers. Swords had been stuck through their hands and feet, and into the cracks between the stones. Lamech hadn't seen it done, but he could imagine the screams. One of the bodies was burned from the middle of the abdomen up. Thieves had slit open his belly, lit his intestines on fire and then shoved them back in. "I think we should get away from here as soon as possible. Leave this place to the vultures."

Adah nodded. "We'll go slow." She glanced up the mountain, at the men sitting on the edge of the ramp. "Jared will lead the survivors out tomorrow."

"How many are left?"

Adah shook her head. "I'm not sure. A couple hundred?"

"Including prisoners?"

"Maybe more." Adah twisted the straps of her pack, trying to find a way to make them more comfortable. The water-skin was already weighing on her. "The passage into the mountain is just about sealed up."

"Good," Lamech said. "Let's go."

Adah stirred the remains of their fire. The sun wasn't up yet, but soon would be.

"What are you waiting for?" Lamech asked. "We're almost home."

They'd made good time over the last few days. It had taken the better part of an afternoon, hiking over the hills, just to reach the open plains of the Shinar. Then another day to the Tiger River, where Adah had thrown away the large water-skin, disgusted with herself for having lugged it all the way from Dagonor. Barley and Jared caught up with them the day after that, and by the fifth had pulled away.

Lamech was getting stronger with every step. And more excited. By the time Adah got her pack on, and Uruk's sword tied around her waist, he was almost dancing with impatience.

"Today you'll see the trees I told you about," Lamech said. "With any luck, they'll be starting to turn. It ought to be beautiful this year, what with all the rain. There's sure to be women in the grove, gathering the last green leaves to make wreaths." He stopped. His eyes were as round as the moon. "Maybe my mother."

"You're sure she won't mind my coming home with you?"

"Like a stray dog?" Lamech asked, still grinning.

"Exactly."

"I'm sure. She always wanted a daughter. You'll be like a gift—her son goes off to war and brings home a sister."

They walked through the day, only stopping once for rest and water. By dusk they could see the lights of the city. Adah searched for any sign of Lamech's grove, but could only make out a few small trees, their branches twisted and broken as though by a recent storm. She wasn't impressed. There were larger, healthier trees on the mountains overlooking Dagonor.

Lamech didn't say anything, but his face was drawn and pinched.

When they reached the little stand of trees, Adah saw that there really had been a grove, but that it'd been chopped down. All that remained was a field of fresh stumps and sawdust.

Beyond the stumps were a series of flat mounds, each about as tall as a large dog. A horrendous stench hung over the whole area. Something was rotten.

"What are these?" Adah asked.

Lamech didn't respond.

A few moments later, they happened upon Barley. He was sitting all by himself, staring at one of the largest mounds. At first, Adah didn't think the old farmer recognized them. Then Barley smiled. "You made it," he said.

"What happened?" Lamech asked him. "Where are the trees?"

"Cut down. All but those few frail things you see out there."

"Why?"

"For the pyres. And they buried the remains in these . . . hillocks."

Adah put a hand on his shoulder. "Why don't you go home?" she asked.

"This was my farm. Right here." Barley pointed at the mound closest to them. "I don't guess it is anymore. This land won't be any good for . . . probably longer than I'll be alive."

"Come with us," Lamech urged. "My family would be honored."

"Thanks, but Jared's letting me stay with him. He's got a beautiful home."

"We'll walk you," Adah said.

"No. I'd like to stay out here a while. The air's fresher."

"Can't be," Lamech said.

"The disease is here, too. The women from Akshur brought it. So did we." Barley looked from Adah to Lamech. "You'll see."

They hurried up the long, deserted streets. Adah gaped at the sheer enormousness of everything. Houses were stacked on top of each other. Towers, some as many as four stories tall, peeked over the roofs of tanneries and weavers, slaughterhouses and granaries. It was amazing.

"The city doesn't usually smell like this," Lamech assured her.

They passed an open door. Inside, they could see a woman crying over a pair of corpses. One was an old man, his whole body mottled with welts. The other was a child. Their faces were blue from lack of air.

By the time they'd reached Lamech's house—on the second floor of an abandoned tavern—they'd seen dozens of grieving families. Often as not, it was the little children who were left to do the weeping, naked and alone.

They climbed the stairs—Adah hated the way they shook beneath her feet—and Lamech opened the door. Inside were a table, a clay washbasin, and a pair of ratty sleeping mats. Overturned boxes served as chairs. An old man with one leg was sitting on one of the boxes. On the table in front of him sat a pitcher of warm beer, but no cups.

"Papa?" Lamech asked, still standing in the doorway. Adah had to look over his shoulder to see.

The old man reached for his crutch. "I knew you'd come," he said. "Knew it. I told Tova, the lard-wife. You remember her. Thin woman with a mustache? Anyway," he climbed to his foot and stumped round the table toward them. "She said you'd never make it. Not when we saw how few—"

"Papa," Lamech said, taking his father's arm. "What happened? Where's Mama?"

The old man shook his head. "Haven't kept up the old room have I? Your mother got sick and I just couldn't seem to—"

"Where is she?"

"Priests took her last week."

Lamech hung his head.

The old man patted his son on the shoulder. Then he noticed Adah, still waiting on the stairs outside. "Who's this?" he asked, gently pushing Lamech aside and reaching for her hand.

"I'm Adah."

He led her to one of the boxes and motioned for her to sit down. "Someone's hit you," he said, squinting at the bruises on her face.

"You should have seen me last week." Adah glanced at Lamech, hoping she was doing the right thing, and saw tears coursing down his cheeks. "I was a terrible sight."

"Oh well." The old man chuckled. "You'll be beautiful again in no time."

It was the first time since her father's death that anyone had called Adah beautiful. She squeezed his hand.

"But we should celebrate. Why don't you run and get us a loaf of bread?" Lamech's father pulled a tiny piece of copper from his pocket. He winked at Adah as he tossed it to his son. "Give us a chance to get acquainted."

Lamech backed through the door and was gone. He never even took off his pack.

"How far does he have to go?" Adah asked.

The old man smiled. "He'll never find anything. Not at this hour. I just thought he could use a moment to himself. Moloch knows I needed one after … you know." He handed her the pitcher. "Now Adah, my boy thinks highly of you—anyone could see that—so why don't you tell me about yourself?"

"We're just friends," she said.

"Just friends? Then you must have someone else."

"No." Adah took a sip from the pitcher. It was the first time she'd tasted beer. She wasn't impressed. "There was a man, but he was more of a. . . ." The old man waited patiently as she searched for the right words. Finally, Adah just shrugged.

"I see," Lamech's father said. "Well, since you're just friends, and you've been traveling together all this time, I guess you can share that sleeping mat." He pointed at the larger of the two. "That's if you don't mind, of course. And just 'til we find you one of your own."

Adah blushed. "No hurry," she said.

Ander crouched at the edge of the river, inspecting a boot-print.

It was large and deep, especially where the toe had sunk into the mud. A half-dozen blades of dry grass were mashed into the bottom.

He followed the prints upstream. The Ibex River, once so enormous, was now only about twice as wide as a man was tall. Soon, Ander expected to be able to jump over it. After that he wasn't sure. No map he'd ever seen covered the area beyond the head of the river. He wondered if he really could go so far that he'd see clouds fall from the sky. The weather had already turned colder, and the air was thinner. He hoped he'd make it. After so many years stuck in the mine, he wanted to know the world.

Around noon he came to a sandbar and the remains of a camp. Latrine, cook-fire and all. The coals were cold and the latrine was dry, but he was getting close.

He'd just bent over to drink from the stream when he noticed another footprint. It was comparatively small, and a fair distance from all the others, but what really set it apart was that the foot that made it had been naked.

Initially, Ander guessed that a Niphilim woman had bathed in the river. But the toes were too splayed out. This foot hadn't spent a lifetime cramped into boots.

He searched through the grass further up the bank and discovered more naked prints. Dozens of them. In one he found a long white hair. Certainly not a Niphilim hair. It was too thick to have come out of one of their golden heads. In fact, it looked to him more like a strand of body hair. Or an animal hair. Ander puzzled over it for quite a while before finally coming up with an answer. It was from a savage, he decided. An old one, judging by the color.

Ander moved very slowly after that, searching for every track he could find. He was no expert, and the work was slow, but by sundown he was relatively sure of one thing. He wasn't the only one hunting the Niphilim.

It was cold that night, so Ander rolled up in his cloak to sleep. As he drowsed, he thought over all the stories he'd heard about the savages. According to one tale, the Niphilim had a female that they kept locked at the heart of the mountain. She was bound, hands and feet, because she couldn't be tamed. Not even Antha-Kane had been able to break her spirit. She was a pack-leader, some said—queen of the savage lands.

Ander didn't know whether the stories were true, or just the fanciful dreams of slaves. He imagined an enormous beast, teats hung low from all the young she'd borne, teeth dripping foam, fingernails hooked like claws.

'I just hope she leaves me one or two,' he thought. 'Just one or two.'

Epilogue

*A*NOTHER SUMMER WAS RAPIDLY BURNING ITSELF OUT.

It had been one of the most severe in recent memory. Blankets of dust hung over the streets. Heat radiated from the sandstone walls. Weeds turned brown and died. Even the canals were reduced to little more than trickling bogs.

Fortunately, relief was on the way. The high puffs of white cloud, usually no more than dots in an otherwise azure sky, had begun to descend and thicken. Kan-Puram was swamped with humid air. Even the birds, for months exiled to the coast, sensed that the season was coming to an end. As they made their way into a narrow back-alley, passing between high walls of rose-colored stone, Adah glanced at the sky and saw a heron flying east toward the river.

"Did you see that?" she asked.

Eva, balanced precariously on her mother's hip, stared upward. "No."

"What was it?" Lamech asked. Their son, Aggaseir, walked beside him, reluctantly holding onto his father's outstretched hand.

"A heron," Adah replied.

"It's about time." Lamech's tunic was soaked with sweat.

They reached the door at the end of the alley and Aggaseir knocked. The door was stout, constructed of cedar planks bound with bronze. His fist made barely a whisper, though he beat upon it with all his might.

"I wonder what Jared has planned," Adah said. She set Eva down beside her brother, and then hastily smoothed out the wrinkles on her tunic. Adah had gained some weight over the last few weeks, but hoped it wouldn't show.

"Gambling," Lamech guessed. "Same as always."

Just then, the door swung open and Melesh peered out. "You're here," he muttered. Adah couldn't tell whether he was surprised.

"Are we early?" Lamech asked. The corridor behind the thief was dark.

"Not you." Melesh smiled at the children, then turned and led the way inside.

They followed him through a maze of rooms, each hung with elaborate tapestries and glowing with bronze- and copper-inlaid furniture. Passages twisted away in every direction. Stairways rose towards sunny upstairs apartments and descended into cellars smelling of spice and beer. Finally, at the center of the house, they came to the grand hall. Jared had designed it as a place where thieves could come together and talk, but it was seldom used. The Snail's Horn was just too inviting.

Of all the rooms in his house, this was at once the simplest and most ornate. There were no tapestries—no decorations of any kind—and the only furniture were row upon row of chairs, arrayed in a half-circle facing the rear wall, and a banquet table heaped with fine foods. There was roast poultry, pork and goat, breads, cheeses and yogurts, bowls of dates, pitchers of beer and trays of sweets. But what really gave the room its splendor were the smoke-holes. Most of the other rooms in the house were similarly equipped, but unlike those more utilitarian openings, meant to draw out fumes from the torches, these had a second function. They were also skylights. No matter the time or season, there was always at least one hole spilling natural sunlight into the room.

They'd only just stepped into the hall when they found Jared. He was standing with a band of thieves, each consuming food as though he'd spent the last week trudging across the desert and was famished near to death.

"You've arrived," Jared said. He roughed up Aggaseir's hair. Eva squealed as he tickled her ribs. "And all well?"

"Momma won't let us see the Anders," Aggaseir grumbled.

"No?"

Adah shook her head in disgust.

"It's just a bit of straw and some old clothes," Jared said. "You saw worse when you were their age."

"There's already been far too much killing and burning."

"It's not right," Lamech agreed. "Ander wasn't so bad."

"What's an Ander?" Eva asked.

"Idiot," Aggaseir scoffed. "It's a straw man. They burn him to scare away bad spirits. Right Jared?"

"Right. And I happen to know that the biggest pyre in all of Kan-Puram will be in the square at the end of my street."

"Can't we see it?" Aggaseir pleaded.

"Please?" Eva whined. "Please?"

The children stared up at their parents like dogs begging for table-scraps. Finally, Lamech relented. "As long as you don't get too close."

"What?" Adah glared at her husband.

"We can explain it to them when they're older," Lamech said.

"Can we see them build the fire?" Aggaseir asked.

"I know just the place." Jared pointed across the room. "See that door? Go through it and you'll find some stairs. Climb two flights. You'll have the best view in Kan-Puram. . . . Melesh will take you."

Aggaseir and Eva raced across the room, followed by their enormous sitter.

"How old is Aggaseir now?" Jared asked, watching them go. "Six?"

"You know as well as I do," Adah said. "You ask every time I see you."

"He doesn't know he's my heir does he?"

Adah shook her head.

"Good. Nothing ruins a boy like growing up rich. The thrill of life is in the struggle."

"It wasn't the thrill of my life," Lamech grumbled.

"Of course it was," Jared said. "Your parents worked hard. That's nothing to be ashamed of. Your father was a hand on trading barges wasn't he? Before his accident?"

Lamech nodded.

"And your mother delivered cheese to estates all over the city."

"So?"

"Were they unhappy?"

Lamech smiled. "When I was a little boy, I loved going with my mother to trade for milk. I thought we were rich."

"You see?" Jared clapped Lamech on the back. "It was hard work that made you the man you are."

"I didn't think you knew my parents."

"Know them?" Jared shook his head. "I didn't. But when Adah told me you were to be married. . . . Let's just say that I did some investigating." Lamech was obviously surprised. "I had to watch out for my girl, didn't I?" Jared gave Adah a fatherly pat on the belly, then drew back. "Are you . . . ?"

"Don't say it," Adah hissed. "It's bad luck."

"How long?" Jared asked.

"A few months." She smiled. "I think it's a boy. He's been kicking already, just like Aggaseir did."

"I want to name him Utnapishtim," Lamech said, "after my father. But Adah insists on calling him Noah."

"Noah," Jared mused. "A fine name."

"We haven't decided," Lamech muttered. Adah squeezed his hand. Jared had a habit of ignoring Lamech. He'd never complained, but Adah could tell he hated it.

"Why don't you two eat?" Jared suggested. "Before these brigands get it all." He winked. "Actually, there's plenty more in the kitchen. If you ever invite thieves to a feast, remember to get a bit extra for them to take home in their pockets. They can't help themselves."

"Thanks, we will," Lamech said, and led Adah to the table. The thieves stepped aside as she approached.

As the afternoon wore on, and the spots of sun streaming through the smoke-holes began making their way up the eastern wall, the meeting hall filled up. Most were thieves or prostitutes, but there was also a generous sprinkling of the rich and influential from throughout the city. Adah only saw a few faces she knew. None were close friends.

Barley and Isin were there, as was Nippur and the new High Father of the temple of Moloch. 'Is his name Shamash?' Adah wondered. She'd heard that name somewhere. Even the old priests from the temple of the Creator had come. Adah was surprised to see them. They looked uncomfortable outside the walls of their sanctuary.

Lamech had joined the younger men. They were talking about the way Kan-Puram used to be—before the war. Adah quickly grew bored, so she sat down with Barley. He didn't have much to say, which suited her just fine.

She was beginning to feel tired, and wondered how much longer they'd stay, when Jared slipped an arm around her shoulders. "Having fun?" he asked.

"Of course," Adah said.

Barley just nodded.

"Liars." Jared laughed. "Remember the first time I put my arm around you?"

"Just before the battle." Adah glanced at Barley. "I'm afraid I didn't like you much at the time."

"That's all right," Barley assured her. He'd begun to look old. The lines around his good eye had deepened. His muscles, while still large by any standard, had lost some of their solidity. Only the scar running over his face was unchanged. The ragged pink flesh still looked as tender and young as ever.

"I have to make a speech," Jared said to Adah. "I'd like you to be with me."

"What for?"

"It'll be just like old times." He pointed at a pair of chairs that had been set up on a raised platform. "You don't think Lamech will mind?"

"He will," Adah said. "But I'll do it anyway."

"Good girl."

Jared led her through the crowd and sat her down on the smaller of the two chairs. A cushion lay on the floor beside her. Adah wasn't sure whether she was meant to rest her feet on it or kick it out of the way. She decided to behave as though it wasn't there.

The chatter died noticeably as Jared took his seat. "If you'd all sit," he said. "I have one or two things to say." He gestured at the chairs. "I'm sorry there aren't more, but I have only so much room. If you're young enough, please stand in the back."

It took a while for everyone to get situated, but Jared was patient. When at last the room was quiet, he began—"I know you came here expecting to gamble, and gods know I won't disappoint you. Soon as I've said my piece, the tables will come out. Beer will flow." He pointed at an old man with a red nose. "Nikal's providing the brew, so you'll be sure to feel it in the morning." The thieves in the back cheered.

Jared was about to continue, but was interrupted by the sounds of a commotion coming from behind a door on the other side of the room. Adah looked at him, wondering what it could possibly be. But Jared just smiled.

The door burst open and in stomped Melesh. Eva sat on one of his shoulders, and Aggaseir on the other. Both children laughed uproariously.

"Mama!" Eva called. Melesh set the children down and they came running. "We had so much fun!"

"Melesh showed us the fire. It's just a pile of sticks right now, but it's huge." Aggaseir's eyes rolled. "Melesh says there are twenty Anders, and that they've been covered with grease so they'll sizzle."

"Did you know that Jared has a whole room full of toys?" Eva asked. "Dolls, wagons—he has everything."

"I'm glad," Adah whispered. She glanced at Jared and saw that he was listening intently to everything the children said. Lamech, who'd found a chair near the front, was just as amused. In fact, the only one who didn't appear happy with the talk of toys and burning Anders was Isin. He looked as though his chair was made of stinging nettle.

With no little effort, Adah managed to quiet the children down. Finally, and reluctantly, they sat on the cushion beside her feet. Eva immediately pulled her tunic up over her head and began humming to herself. Aggaseir looked out at the crowd and waved. A few of the thieves waved back.

"I'm sorry," Adah said. "Please continue."

Jared patted Aggaseir on the head, then turned back toward the assembled faces. His smile was gone. "I'm leaving Kan-Puram," he said. "And I won't be coming back."

Murmurs and shouts of disbelief boiled from the crowd. Jared waited until the worst had passed, then called for quiet.

"This morning," he explained, "just as on every Ander's Day since the end of the war, the three remaining Niphilim prisoners were taken from their cells and tortured. I won't say what all happened to them. I wasn't there, and most of you know anyway. No doubt many of you believe they deserved it—and maybe they did—but I can't stand the thought." He took Adah's hand. "There are a few of us here who've experienced torture, and know exactly what it means. Some might want revenge. I for one want nothing to do with it."

He paused. Other than Eva's humming, the room was deathly quiet.

"I'm going to start a new city," Jared continued. "It won't be far away. We'll be building it along the banks of the Ibex River, not far from Ur."

"We?" Isin asked. "Who else is going?"

"Thirteen families have elected to join me. Poor folk mostly. People who want a new life away from Kan-Puram. I'll be King, but every man and woman who comes with me will have the chance to govern his or her own destiny. I'll just be there to safeguard their lives and property, and to settle disputes." Jared paused, letting the idea sink in. "To join us, all you'll need is a sincere belief in goodness, and a willingness to work. And you have to accept that no one is poor because the gods hate them, or rich because the gods love them. Some are lucky. Some aren't. That's all."

"What about Kan-Puram?" one of the thieves asked. "What about us?"

"Barley will be taking my place," Jared said. The old farmer, now turned King of Thieves, blushed. "Melesh will help him—whenever discipline is in order."

"And what will you call this new city?" Adah asked.

"I've thought a lot about that, and I believe I've come up with a name. Uruk."

"What?"

"Mama," Aggaseir asked. "What's an Uruk?"

"He was a man," she said. "A friend. He helped us once—Jared and me—when we were in trouble."

Aggaseir looked as though he might ask something further, then nodded and went back to staring at the faces.

"I'll tell you all about him when you're older," Adah promised.

"You'd better," Jared said.

"Why Uruk?" Adah asked. The name felt strange in her mouth. She couldn't say it without thinking of the man.

"He'd have hated it," Jared admitted. "But I still think it's right. When we ask ourselves how we want our city to be, we can say, 'Let it be like Uruk.' He'll be the model for our future. I only hope we can live up to it."

"Uruk," Adah said. It did have a certain appeal. "Uruk."

KING GILGAMESH STOOD ON HIS CITY WALL, OVERLOOKING THE southern fields. To his right he could just make out a bend of the Euphrates, glittering blue in the morning sun. A farmer took a moment out from his planting to stare up at the great man. Gilgamesh waved. The farmer smiled and waved back.

Tales of a black man, nearly as large as the great king himself, had been filtering into the city for months. The country folk called him Enkidu. Some said he was a hunter, capable of running down antelope and wrestling wolves with his bare hands. Others claimed he was a common thief, stealing from their herds and sneaking into their huts to pilfer stores. Gilgamesh had even heard tales of a vicious dog, following Enkidu everywhere he went, fighting at his side and guarding over him as he slept.

The stories reminded him of some his city's oldest myths—of Jared and Aggaseir, and the war with the Nephilim—tales he hadn't heard since childhood. There was a connection between those myths and the ones about the great boat-builder Utnapishtim—also called Noah—who devised a barge massive enough to carry his entire family and flock. But what that connection was, Gilgamesh couldn't remember.

He didn't believe half of what he'd been told about this Enkidu, but thought he'd better investigate. It wasn't every day a black man made the trip across the desert. Not even Egyptians made that journey much anymore.

Besides, according to all reports Enkidu was strong, possibly a match for the king himself. 'Maybe we can hunt together,' Gilgamesh thought. There was a lion, a man-eater, terrorizing woodcutters in a village east of Assur. They called the beast Humbaba. Some claimed it was a creation of the wind-god himself—a worthy challenge for the King of Kings. If Enkidu were half the man the farmers claimed, he'd make an excellent partner—maybe even a friend.

As he made his way down from the walls, Gilgamesh called for his advisor. "Find the most beautiful woman in the city," he ordered. "Provide her with gifts of lapis and carnelian. Tell her to find this Enkidu and bring him to me. She may use any means at her disposal. . . . Any means."

Acknowledgments

*I*T IS POPULAR TO IMAGINE WRITING AS A SOLITARY, LONELY ACTIVITY, and writers as bookworms obsessed with the minutiae of their own imaginary worlds. But for me, the composition of this book was nothing of the kind. An entire army of friends, family, and well-wishers of every stripe stood at my side during the whole process. I was supported on a daily, and sometimes hourly, basis by no less a bundle of energy than my wife, Day Mitchell, with whom all my thanks rightfully begins and ends. My mother, Karleane, and my father, Gayle, listened for hours on end as I waxed poetic about my heroes and villains, both those in the novel and those in the real world. My friends, Jason Gatliff, Matt Lister, and Kennon Irons, read various incarnations of the tales between these covers, and answered such arcane questions as, 'What do you feel like the color of the narrative is?' Other friends, including the magnificent Gloria Loomis, sat with me time and again to discuss both business and art, to listen to my complaints and offer nothing but loving support. Nicole Aragi not only read my manuscript, but left it 'lying around' so that certain big-shots of the writing world could 'find it.' My agent, and one of my very best friends, Katherine Fausset, stood by Uruk and Ander (and Justin) pushing and prodding and cajoling, and designing flanking maneuvers worthy of a four-star general until she got the manuscript into the right hands. My editor, David Shoemaker, illuminated possibilities within the original text that I would never have seen, and brought from it a novel with a depth and richness that could not otherwise have existed. To all of these people and more, SLAVES OF THE SHINAR, and its writer, owe a debt of gratitude.

But one other deeply felt thanks is owed. To my reader, in whose hands this book now sits. Thank you for reading through to the end. Thank you for using the powers of your mind to give form and life to Uruk. Thank you for making the dog the loyal companion I so desire him to be. Thank you for understanding Ander. Thank you for whatever love you have to spare for Adah, Barley, Jared, and Lamech. Thank you for being such a font of vivid imaginings. Without you, these are merely sheets of paper ruined by ink. All the successes in this book exist because *you* made them. The failures are due entirely to me.

Lastly, another word of thanks goes to my wife, Day. I said that all thanks would begin and end with her, and I meant it. Let it be known that she read every word of this novel, beginning to end, no fewer than ten times. She read it aloud to me twice. She gave me notes on how to make it better, cried when I cried, laughed when I laughed, and sometimes laughed when I cried. These are not small contributions. It is her book as much as it is mine.